Carousel Dreams

4 Historical Stories

Susanne Dietze
Patty Smith Hall
Cynthia Hickey
Teresa Ives Lilly

BARBOUR BOOKS
An Imprint of Barbour Publishing, Inc.

Sophia's Hope ©2020 by Cynthia Hickey
The Art of Romance ©2020 by Patty Smith Hall
Carousel of Love ©2020 by Teresa Ives Lilly
The Carousel Wedding ©2020 by Susanne Dietze

Print ISBN 978-1-64352-470-2

eBook Editions:
Adobe Digital Edition (.epub) 978-1-64352-472-6
Kindle and MobiPocket Edition (.prc) 978-1-64352-471-9

All scripture quotations, unless otherwise noted, are taken from the King James Version of the Bible.

Scripture quotations marked esv are from The Holy Bible, English Standard Version®, copyright © 2001 by Crossway Bibles, a publishing ministry of Good News Publishers. Used by permission. All rights reserved.

This book is a work of fiction. Names, characters, places, and incidents are either products of the author's imagination or used fictitiously. Any similarity to actual people, organizations, and/or events is purely coincidental.

Cover Image: Irene Lamprakou / Trevillion Images

Published by Barbour Books, an imprint of Barbour Publishing, Inc., 1810 Barbour Drive, Uhrichsville, Ohio 44683, www.barbourbooks.com

Our mission is to inspire the world with the life-changing message of the Bible.

 Member of the
Evangelical Christian
Publishers Association

Printed in Canada.

Sophia's Hope

by Cynthia Hickey

And why are you anxious about clothing? Consider the lilies of the field, how they grow: they neither toil nor spin, yet I tell you, even Solomon in all his glory was not arrayed like one of these. But if God so clothes the grass of the field, which today is alive and tomorrow is thrown into the oven, will he not much more clothe you, O you of little faith?

MATTHEW 6:28–30 ESV

Chapter 1

Cottage City, Martha's Vineyard
Early summer 1889

Sophia Blackwell gripped the hand of her five-year-old charge and stepped on the ferry headed for Cottage City. The child tugged against her, straining to look over the railing.

"Settle down, Abigail. You would not want to fall over. It's quite a ways to the water." Sophia sighed. She'd been nanny to both Abigail and the girl's older brother for the majority of the winter. Now Sophia was headed to where the summer vacationers might remember her, ask questions, and express false pity for her family's fall from wealth. There was no help for it. She'd needed employment and had no skills other than watching over children. Her fate had been chosen through no choice of her own.

"We've rented the cutest little cottage for the summer," Mrs. Wesley said, gripping the railing with gloved hands. "I'm afraid you'll have to share a room with Abigail. I'm sure you won't mind."

"No, Mrs. Wesley." Sophia closed her eyes against the thought.

"There's a carousel and beautiful beaches. Please make sure the children enjoy plenty of hours outside. Mr. Wesley and I have a full social schedule."

"I will." Sophia stifled a sigh. She was all too aware of how full a summer roster could be. Tears threatened despite her resolve to find some way in which to enjoy herself, even if only a little bit. "I assure you the children will have a good summer."

Sophia glanced around for Rupert, the nine-year-old scalawag and heir to the Wesleys' fortune. Seeing him playing marbles with some other boys, she relaxed and once again stared across the water. The closer they got, the more excited those on the ferry became. Summer at Martha's Vineyard was the highlight of the summer for many. Sophia lifted her chin against the pitying stares of some of the people her family had once socialized with and stepped away from the railing, taking Abigail with her.

Finding a rather secluded spot on a bench near the piled luggage of the visitors, she folded her hands in her lap and waited to dock. She lifted her face to the midday sun, closed her eyes, and breathed deeply of sunshine and water. Yes, she would enjoy her summer with the Wesleys. *Count your blessings, Sophia. At least you're where you've spent so many summers before.*

By the time the ferry reached their destination, she'd composed herself and strolled down the ramp behind the Wesleys with determination. Two horse-drawn carriages awaited to take them to their summer cottages, and Sophia climbed into the second one with Abigail and Rupert.

"I'm going boating on Lake Anthony the minute we're unpacked," Rupert announced. "That's how the men spend their time here. You silly girls will attend the Methodist meetings, I assume."

Too snotty for his age, that one. Sophia blew air roughly out of her nose. "Since I have my evenings and Sundays free, I do plan to attend as often as I can. Also, I sincerely doubt your father will approve of you boating at your age."

He lifted his chin. "Then I shall ride the carousel and capture the ring in order to get a free ride."

"I'm sure you will." Sophia smiled and stared out the window. Already the beach was filled with people of all races and walks of life. One of the many things she loved about the area was its diversity.

"I'm going to ride the carousel too," Abigail announced. "Over and over and over. Miss Blackwell will ride with me, won't you?"

The child's question seemed more like a demand, but Sophia tugged one of her blond curls. "Of course I will. We'll go as soon as possible."

When the carriages stopped, it became apparent to Sophia that she wouldn't only be sharing with Abigail, but with Rupert as well. The adjoining cottages were much too small to house them all. She ran her hand over the bright blue gingerbread trim and led the children into the cottage.

Two hours later, she escorted Abigail and Rupert to the carousel. The two could barely contain their excitement. Sophia didn't blame them. A new attraction was always welcome to any summer vacation spot.

She purchased three tickets and entered the ride. "Look, children, the manes and tails are real horsehair." She ran her fingers through the dark mane of one of the carved horses then over the brightly painted body. Tinny music played nearby. After helping Abigail onto one of the smaller horses, she climbed on the back of the larger one next to it.

Seconds later, the ride moved slowly in a circle. Abigail shrieked and clutched the leather reins.

Sophia laughed and turned to see which horse Rupert had chosen. Of course the boy had chosen the largest. As the ride turned, he stretched to grasp the ring. Another laugh escaped Sophia as she clapped to cheer him on.

Drake Moreland checked the steam level on the carousel, turning at the musical sound of a woman's laughter. A dark-haired woman rode one of the horses, a small girl by her side. A few mounts back, a young boy reached for the ring.

He slipped.

The woman's laughter changed to a cry and she slipped from the back of her horse, rushing to the boy's side.

Drake turned off the ride and leaped over the railing, joining her and running his hands over the boy's arms and legs. "See to the girl, ma'am. I've got this one." He stared into eyes as dark as a summer night.

She nodded and hurried to help a now hysterical little girl. "*Shhh*, Abigail. Your brother is fine. He removed his safety strap like a naughty boy."

"I almost had it too." Rupert brushed off the seat of his pants. "I'm going to try again."

"I think we've had enough for one day." The woman glanced at Drake. "Thank you."

Struck by her beauty, all he could do was nod. She raised one finely arched eyebrow, a smile teasing her lips. "Have a good day, sir."

He nodded again and watched as she strolled away with the

children. *Idiot.* He sighed and shook his head.

"Smooth talker." Jim Downs pushed away from the side of the building.

"Stow it." Drake stepped aside as more riders entered the carousel.

"That lovely young lady that left you speechless is none other than Sophia Blackwell of the Boston Blackwells," Jim said. "A bit out of our league, I think."

Drake frowned. "I heard they were all but bankrupt."

"Still, blue blood is blue blood, and it appears they aren't too impoverished if they're spending their summer here. Don't despair. There will be plenty of lovely ladies within your grasp." He clapped Drake on the shoulder and marched away, whistling.

His friend was right. It was best Drake focus on his job manning the carousel, taking out the occasional tourist on his sailboat, working as a server at the restaurant, and preaching at the Methodist meetings. His summers were too full for romance with a woman who'd leave at the end of the season. He needed a hefty bank account, not a broken heart.

When the man who ran the ride during the afternoon arrived to take over, Drake couldn't have been happier to leave and make his way to where he docked his boat. He checked his schedule, saw that his afternoon booking hadn't canceled, then readied the sailboat to receive guests.

A man in a white suit and the same boy who had fallen from the carousel marched down the dock. "Look, father, this is the man who helped me."

"Lawrence Wesley." The man thrust out his hand. "My son seems to have taken quite a liking to the carousel and sees the ring as a challenge."

Drake laughed, returning the shake. "Many young boys do."

"His fall gave our nanny quite a fright."

Nanny? Perhaps Jim was wrong as to which branch of the Blackwells the pretty woman belonged to. "I found her to be brave. She jumped from the ride and rushed to your son's aid as if the horse wasn't several feet off the ground."

"Come on. Let's get on the water. I told Miss Blackwell I intended to go sailing, and she said you wouldn't allow it." The boy tugged at his father's hand.

"She's right, Rupert. You may only go when I accompany you." The man gave his son an indulgent smile. "We'll go when the captain says we're ready."

"Step aboard." Drake moved aside. Once the two were seated and their life preservers in place, he pushed away from the pier and sailed them deeper on the lake.

Despite the lad's bravado, Rupert clutched the side of the boat and held tight as a stiff wind set them skipping across the lake's surface.

"I don't recall seeing you here last summer," Drake said. Having grown up on the island, he knew just about everyone, summer resident or full-time.

"We've only arrived from England a few months ago," Mr. Wesley said. "My wife is from London, and we spent the last few years there. It's good to be back on American soil." He put his arm around his son's shoulder. "Relax, Son. This man won't let anything happen to you. Pretend you're flying."

The boy looked a little green to Drake's experienced eye. He wouldn't be the first person to experience sea sickness.

He wanted to learn more about Miss Blackwell but couldn't very well bring up the subject. As nanny to a prominent family, she still stood outside of his reach. Showing too much interest might cause her employers to refuse her bringing the children back to the carousel. He squelched his curiosity. Why did he find himself so intrigued by her? She wasn't the first pretty face to grace the island.

"I think we should head back, Captain." Mr. Wesley peered at his son's face. "Rupert here isn't the sailor he thought."

Drake turned them around and sailed back toward the pier. When they arrived, he said, "Here you go, lad," as he helped the unsteady boy from the rocking boat to the more solid footing of the wooden pier. "Maybe you ought to keep to playing on the beach rather than across the water." He ruffled the boy's hair.

As father and son marched away, Rupert complained about his disappointing day. First the carousel and then the sailboat. His loud demand that they return home caused nearby seagulls to take flight.

Drake shook his head. There were plenty of other things to occupy a young child on the island, and the next time Rupert rode the carousel, Drake would make sure the safety strap was firmly around his waist and strongly caution him to leave it fastened.

With the trip cut short, he had time to work on readying his boat for the upcoming race, one of the highlights of the summer season. He intended to win this year.

He glanced over as a woman's hat blew past, landing where the lake kissed the sand. He rushed to retrieve the floppy object before the wind blew it out of his reach. Shaking the water from the straw, he headed up the hill and found himself face-to-face with the very woman who had occupied his thoughts.

Chapter 2

"Thank you. This wind is something else." Sophia smiled into the sparkling hazel eyes of the silent carousel operator. "I've heard my young charge lacks sea legs."

"Uh, yes. Perhaps you'd like a ride someday?" He paled as if surprised to have spoken to her.

"Maybe." She tilted her head. "Do I make you nervous, or are you this tongue-tied around all women?" She slapped the hat on her head, laughed, and strolled to where Abigail played in the sand. Heavens, the man was as handsome as he was silent.

She sat in the sand next to Abigail, her gaze settling on the water. A few seconds later, a shadow fell across her. Keeping one hand on her hat, she glanced up.

"You're the only one who makes me nervous, Miss Blackwell."

"I'm at a disadvantage, sir, seeing as you know my name and I do not know yours."

"Drake Moreland. May I sit?"

She nodded. "You may call me Sophia. No need for formalities here." She smiled.

High spots of color appeared in his cheeks. "Call me Drake." He wrapped his arms around his bent knees.

His unwavering gaze on her face started to unnerve her. She swiped at her nose, wondering whether she had a smudge of dirt or ice cream from the treat she'd purchased for Abigail and herself. After a few minutes, she narrowed her eyes. "Now you're the one making me nervous, sir."

"My apologies. I've. . .it's just that, well, you're the prettiest thing I've ever seen." He jumped to his feet and rushed away.

Sophia's eyes widened as a giggle escaped her. "I don't believe I've ever met anyone quite like that man."

Abigail dumped sand from a bucket. "He's nice."

"Yes he is." Sophia pulled her gaze from Drake's retreating back and got to her feet. "Come. It's time to dress for dinner."

A few hours later, Sophia followed the Wesleys into the dining room of the hotel. She paused in the doorway, taking in the starched white tablecloths, flickering lanterns, and gaily colored gowns. She smoothed her hand down the aubergine-colored dress she wore, thankful her clothes from last year weren't so outdated as to attract attention. Head high, she took her seat between Abigail and Rupert, spreading napkins over each of their laps before picking up the menu.

While she perused, she half listened to Mr. and Mrs. Wesley talk of their day. Most of Mrs. Wesley's conversation was about the invitations to social events that had poured in. It wasn't until Mr. Wesley spoke of their boating excursion that Sophia's ears perked up.

"The man was quite professional," Mr. Wesley said. "He put us at ease right away, not making a fuss when Rupert didn't take to the water."

"He's a native to the island?" Mrs. Wesley set down her menu.

"You wouldn't know it by the way he carries himself."

Sophia smiled behind her menu. Obviously Drake only became tongue-tied around her. She set down her menu and came eye to eye with the very man who filled her thoughts. "Hello."

"Ma'am." He swallowed hard, his face reddening. "May I take your orders?"

"You, Mr. Moreland, are a jack-of-all-trades," Mr. Wesley said. "I admire a man who isn't afraid of hard work."

"I've some goals only money can meet." Drake turned his attention away from Sophia.

"The wife and I will have the roast beef, the children will have soup, and Miss Blackwell. . ."

"I'll take the fish." Sophia smiled up at Drake. "Is it fresh?"

He nodded, swallowing hard. "Yes, ma'am."

"Mr. Moreland and I met earlier today, both at the carousel and again on the beach when he gallantly rescued my hat." Sophia's gaze locked with his hazel one.

"Then we are indebted to you on more than one count," Mr. Wesley said, grinning. "I hope my family and our nanny do not occupy too much of your time this summer."

"My pleasure." Drake turned and rushed toward a set of swinging doors at the far end of the room.

"Quiet young man," Mrs. Wesley remarked before scanning the room. "Oh look. There's the Boatwrights. I heard they've fallen a bit financially but are staying strong. Did you know them, Sophia?"

"Only by name." She glanced up and met the snide gaze of a young man seated at the Boatwrights' table. For a time, her parents had entertained the idea of arranging a marriage between Sophia and the son. Thank goodness that had fallen through when he'd become engaged to another.

"Well, I heard through the grapevine that Theodore Boatwright's engagement fell through." Mrs. Wesley leaned across the table and lowered her voice. "Seems the lady wanted a man a bit richer."

"We mustn't gossip, dear." Mr. Wesley put his hand over his wife's.

Sophia's eyes widened. Theodore Boatwright smiled and winked in her direction. The nerve! She turned away and occupied herself with Abigail's napkin. Theodore Boatwright's reputation as a playboy would keep her as far from the man as possible.

She much preferred the gentle nature of Drake. She smiled. Although his intense gaze unnerved her on occasion, it was more honest than Theodore's blatant stares. His made her skin crawl.

"After dinner you may have the rest of the evening off, Sophia," Mrs. Wesley said. "We're taking the children with us as we stroll around the town."

"Thank you." A solitary stroll on the beach was all she needed to ensure a good night's sleep.

Why had Drake been surprised to see Sophia at dinner? There weren't that many places on the island to eat, and they were bound to see each other again. His mouth had dried up at the sight of her in the dress the color of a dark purple iris.

He bent and picked up a piece of driftwood, dropping it into his pocket. The damp sand cooled his bare feet as he searched for more items to adorn the picture frames he made and sold to a local gift shop. If things went well for him this summer, he'd have the funds needed to achieve his goal of purchasing a yacht big enough to take more than one or two people out on the water. Why, he could do fishing expeditions. Host parties. Years of hard work from sunup to sundown would finally be worth it.

He slowed, spotting a woman in a dark skirt and white blouse moving toward him. A breeze blew her hair from its bun. Too dark to see her features, he didn't need any light other than from the moon to know it was Sophia.

"Good evening, Drake." She stopped and smiled up at him, her teeth flashing. "A beautiful night, isn't it?"

"Yes." He glanced around them. "Are you alone?"

She laughed. "Not anymore."

"It isn't safe for a young woman to be alone at night. Most of the people here in Cottage City are respectable, but there are others who would take advantage."

She tucked a strand of hair behind her ear. "That's the most you've said to me all day. I wondered whether you could string together more than one sentence."

He stiffened. "I—"

"I'm only toying with you." She tapped his arm. "Since you feel I might be in danger, perhaps you should walk with me."

He turned and matched stride with her. "Will you be attending the Methodist meetings next week?"

"I fully intend to. Mrs. Wesley said once I had the children settled, I could do as I please."

"Like tonight?"

"Yes. Hold my arm." She took hold of him and bent to slip

her feet free of stockings and shoes. "Pardon me if you think this improper, but since it's dark outside and I've been longing to feel the sand on my toes, I thought I'd risk it." She let her shoes drop and hefted her skirts to run toward the water.

Drake had never met anyone like her. Beautiful, daring, a bit of a tease, yet every inch a lady when the circumstance warranted. Perhaps after he owned his yacht, he'd ask to court her. Maybe Sophia didn't stand upon the proprieties others did. They were closing in on the twentieth century after all. Times were changing. Cottage City most definitely didn't look upon people the same as other parts of the country.

"Don't just stand there like a guard at Buckingham Palace," Sophia called. "Get your feet wet."

She didn't have to ask twice. Drake ran to the water's edge only to be splashed by Sophia.

When he returned the gesture, she shrieked and darted away. Her skirts tangled, and she fell. Rather than cry as he'd expected, she laughed and held up her hand.

"Some assistance, please."

"I'm sorry." He gripped her hand in his and pulled her to her feet. "Are you all right?"

"Very much so. A little water never hurt anyone, although I am a bit chilled. I suppose I should collect my shoes and head back to the cottage. You have no reason to apologize, Drake. I started the splashing. The water was colder than I expected when it hit my face." Her eyes sparkled as she peered up at him. "Thank you for letting me forget how very proper a nanny should act."

"My pleasure," he said hoarsely. "Will you be at the carousel tomorrow?"

She smiled. "Most definitely. Rupert will want to ride

constantly until he's retrieved the brass ring." She bent and picked up her shoes then darted up the beach toward the cottages, tossing a "good night" over her shoulder.

"Good night," he whispered, already looking forward to the next day. Whistling, he set off for home, a small house set away from the more touristy part of the island. Home was a place he could relax, work on his frames, and dream of the future God had in store for him.

He spent the next hour gluing seashells to wooden frames and mirrors. They'd be dry enough for him to drop off in the morning. Nothing too fancy, but visitors to the island were always eager to take back a souvenir or two. The gift shop had an onsite photographer. Most often tourists purchased a frame to go with their photo.

He held up his latest creation and envisioned Sophia's smiling face peering back at him in black and white. He smiled and blew out the lantern. The sooner he went to sleep, the sooner he'd see her again.

Stretching out on his bed, he folded his arms behind his head and stared through the night at the ceiling, selfishly hoping Sophia managed to show up at the carousel each day and attend every night of the meetings.

Chapter 3

For the next three days, Abigail ran a fever, thus preventing Sophia from taking the children anywhere other than the tiny front porch of their cottage. She whiled away her time caring for the sick little girl, reading, and painting watercolors of the bright-colored cottages.

Every time someone came near their summer residence, she glanced up in hopes it was Drake. Rather silly, actually. She'd most likely made a fool of herself with her wayward behavior at the beach and sent what could have been a wonderful friendship to the bottom of the lake.

"I'm bored," Rupert complained. "Everyone else is at the beach. Can't we at least go berry picking?"

"Not until your sister is better. Maybe tomorrow."

He gave a dramatic sigh. "Mother and Father are having all the fun."

Sophia couldn't agree more. With their endless round of picnics and parties, and Abigail ill, she and the children had very little to do. She set down her book. Perhaps a short excursion into the woods wouldn't hurt. Some fresh air might do Abigail good. "Very well. Change into your play clothes. We're going for a hike."

"Yippee!" Rupert barged into the house.

Sophia followed at a more sedate pace and went to check on Abigail. Her fever had broken. "Do you feel up to a small hike?"

She nodded. "I'm bored."

"That makes three of us. You must promise to let me know when you start to tire, all right?"

"I will." Abigail hopped from her bed.

Sophia wrote a note letting the children's parents know where they were headed, pinned a straw hat to her head, and grabbed a basket in case they located berries. Their walk took them past the carousel. There was no sign of Drake, not surprising since it was well into the afternoon and he worked mornings. Still, her heart dropped a bit. She missed his handsome face and awkwardness when around her. She found it refreshing and endearing.

"That man is staring." Rupert pointed to where Theodore leaned against the wall of an ice-cream shop.

"Don't point. It's rude." Sophia lifted her chin and sailed the children past the insolent man and down the path behind the cottages.

The sun dappled the ground through trees thick with leaves. Birds serenaded as they passed. Sophia breathed deeply of flora and fauna. "Keep an eye out for blackberries. I have it on good authority there are bushes close by." In fact, the cook at the restaurant had mentioned it when Sophia had commented on how delicious her slice of pie had been.

Her mouth watered as she remembered the sweetness of the berries. "There's some!" she exclaimed as she spotted a clump of bushes. Let's see how many we can pick. They'll be delicious with cream."

The children set to picking in earnest while Sophia kept a watchful eye out for predators. Were there dangerous animals on Martha's Vineyard, or did she only need to look out for two-legged nuisances? She frowned at the sight of Theodore approaching.

"Good afternoon, Miss Blackwell." He tipped his boater hat.

"Good afternoon, Mr. Boatwright."

He chuckled. "I get the impression you don't like me."

"I don't know you." She stopped Abigail from tossing yet another berry into her mouth. "You'll spoil your dinner."

"I'd like to remedy that."

"Why?" She tilted her head.

"Because your parents have approached my parents about a possible union between the two of us. I must admit that I'm not averse to such a thing after seeing your loveliness. You're too good to be a nanny."

She pressed her lips together to keep from saying something she shouldn't. A conversation with her parents became imperative. She'd send a letter right away, letting them know she was not agreeable to such a union. "Time to go, children."

Despite their grumblings, she took their hands and hurried past Theodore. A union? Not likely. She didn't need to know the man to realize she couldn't care a whit about him.

Back at the cottage she located stationery and a pen. While the children played quietly in front of the cottage, she sat in a nearby lounge chair and composed a letter to her parents, asking for clarification. She chewed the end of her pen, trying to write her thoughts in a clear and concise way that allowed no argument.

"Good afternoon."

She smiled up at Drake. "Hello. Please forgive us for not visiting the carousel recently. Abigail has been ill. Today is the first day we've ventured outside."

He glanced at the little girl. "I'm glad to see she's feeling better."

"We went berry picking," Abigail stated.

"I can see that. You've juice on your dress." He smiled.

What a difference from the man he'd been when Sophia first met him. He spoke with ease, as if they'd known each other a long time.

"A man bothered Miss Blackwell," Rupert said, not looking up from his marbles. "So we had to leave."

Drake cast a curious glance at Sophia. "Did someone frighten you?"

She shook her head. "Just a friend of my parents who happened upon us. Nothing to worry about." The thought he cared warmed her heart. "We're about to have berries and cream. Will you join us? The cream should be delivered any moment."

"I'd be delighted." He sat on the porch step. "I can't stay long. I'll need to be at the restaurant in time for the dinner crowd."

"What are you working toward, Drake?" She didn't know anyone who worked as hard as he did.

"I'm going to own a yacht." He looked over his shoulder. "I'll have enough by next summer and will charter fishing expeditions and such."

"Would you leave this island during the winter once you've made your money?"

He shook his head. "This is my home."

One more reason he shouldn't get too attached to Sophia. She didn't strike him as a person who would enjoy year-round living on the island. She oozed city living, something she wouldn't get in this idyllic town. There would be few chances of her wearing fine gowns here.

"It is quite lovely." She stood as a delivery boy arrived with a bottle of cream. "If you wouldn't mind watching the children for just a moment, I'll prepare our berries and cream."

"I don't mind at all." He watched her disappear into the cottage. Then he turned and smiled down into two pairs of blue eyes. Would he have children of his own someday? He sighed heavily and showed Rupert a trick shot with his marbles. A family of his own wasn't very promising. He'd worked too hard for too many years to make many friends, much less a romantic involvement.

"Here you go." Sophia stepped out the door, carrying a polished silver tray laden with four bowls of blackberries floating in thick cream. "A treat to tide us over until dinner, which will be simple since your parents have an engagement."

Shoving aside cowardice, Drake blurted out an invitation before he could change his mind. "Would the three of you care to join me for hot dogs? I know a street vendor who makes a very good one."

A smile teased her lips. "I would like that very much. Children?"

"Yes!" Rupert jumped to his feet. "Can we go now?"

"Later," Sophia told him. "Eat your treat."

Drake laughed at the look on the child's face. The boy was used to getting his own way, no doubt, yet his nanny had a firm but kind way of steering him in the right direction. Drake dug into his own treat, very much looking forward to a hot dog with the prettiest girl on the island.

When they'd finished, Sophia collected the dishes and took them into the cottage, returning with her and the children's hats. "Let's walk off our treat so we're good and hungry for that hot dog."

Drake got as eagerly to his feet as the two children. He couldn't remember a more pleasant day off. Usually he combed the beach for artistic treasures or stayed at home working on them. Spending time with others was much preferable.

They passed Jim, the other man who worked the carousel. He raised a brow, glancing from Drake to Sophia then back to Drake and shook his head.

Drake shoved his hands into his pockets. He knew the thoughts running through the other man's head. He had the same ones tormenting him. Spending time with Sophia would only lead to heartache. He glared at Jim and continued. His heart was no one's business but his own.

"What's wrong?" Sophia stopped, peering up at him, one hand on her hat to hold it in place. "You've gone silent again."

"Nothing. I'm enjoying the day is all." He forced a smile.

She tilted her head. "I quite enjoy it when you talk. I like the sound of your voice. It's very soothing." She continued walking as if she hadn't caused his heart to skip a beat at her words. Could he hope she enjoyed his company as much as he enjoyed hers?

Drake stopped them in front of a white picket fence. "See the steel building there? That's the tabernacle, built in 1879. All the bright cottages replaced the tents families used to stay in."

"It's all quite modern, isn't it?" Sophia peered through the boards of the fence. "Why is this fence so tall?"

He shrugged. "I heard it was to keep out peddlers. It isn't very effective. They'll line up on this side of the fence and peddle their wares as attendees enter. Some of them make quite a lot of money."

She pressed her lips together. "It's been awhile since I've been to the island. So much has changed."

He wanted to tell her how sorry he was for her family's trouble, but the pain and sadness on her face kept him quiet. He crooked his arm. "Shall we continue?"

"Yes, let's." She slipped her hand through the bend of his elbow. "There's no sense dwelling on things that cannot be changed."

They continued their stroll around town until hunger drew them to the food vendors. Despite Sophia's objections, Drake purchased their simple meal and led them to a wooden table under a tree.

"When will the children's parents return?" He handed Rupert a napkin.

"Not until quite late, I'm afraid." Sophia took a bite of her food. "Yummy."

"Ah." Disappointment slumped his shoulders.

"Why do you ask?"

"I hoped we could enjoy another stroll on the beach." His gaze clashed with her dark one.

"I feared I'd made quite a fool of myself," she said softly.

He daringly put a hand over hers. "That is something you could never do in my eyes."

Her cheeks pinkened. "I do believe I like this side of Drake Moreland."

"Which side?" He grinned.

"The side not afraid to say what he's thinking."

"To do so would have me missing so many wonderful things." His gaze stayed focused on her face.

She pulled her hand free and put it at the base of her throat. "You unnerve me, sir. I feel as if you can see right through me."

"All I see is beauty. Tomorrow is Sunday. Will you spend the afternoon with me?" Hope leaped in his chest when she nodded.

Chapter 4

On Sunday afternoon, Sophia waited outside the cottage for Drake. How could she have been so silly as to think a summer of no fun and all work had lain before her? Rides on the carousel, strolls along the beach, simple food with a kind man—what more could a woman want? She smiled as Drake approached.

"You look pretty today." He propped one foot on the bottom step and grinned up at her.

Yes, she most definitely liked the talkative Drake over the shy one. "Thank you." She curtsied. "What are the plans for today?"

He straightened and offered her his arm. "The gate is open to the Methodist grounds, and later there is a game of croquet among some of the island residents. Would you enjoy that, or would you like something more. . .upscale?"

She narrowed her eyes. "Why would you think I would prefer that?"

"Well, you're a Blackwell."

"So?" She crossed her arms. "Please don't tell me you suffer from the same prejudices as so many others on this island." Tears burned the back of her throat. For too long she'd felt stuck between two worlds, but finally, with Drake's attention, she thought she'd found her place. Not so. Obviously she was nothing more than someone to pass the time with during the summer. "I must plead a headache." She turned to go.

"No, please." He put a hand on her arm to stop her. "I apologize. I meant no offense."

She took a deep breath and turned. "I am no longer a Blackwell in that sense. Do not put me in a class I no longer belong in."

"I won't." He put a hand over his heart. "I promise. I will look upon you as nothing more than a mere working-class gal."

Her anger dissipated into laughter. "You are a silly man." She linked her arm with his. "Lead on, kind sir. This princess demands a fun-filled afternoon."

They weren't the only ones flocking to the Methodist grounds. Excitement over the upcoming meetings filled the air.

"Hey, Pastor," a man called out to Drake. "Can't wait to hear you teach."

Drake waved. "Two times this year."

Sophia glanced up in surprise. "You're a pastor?"

"On occasion." He grinned. "Each summer anyway, for a time or two."

"Why not full-time?"

"Too many other things on my plate."

Ah yes. His quest for money. "Sometimes there are things more important than the almighty dollar," she said. "Finances can disappear in an instant, whereas your faith will endure."

"Well said. Perhaps you should step up to the pulpit." A flash in his eyes belied the casual tone of his words.

She sighed. The afternoon hadn't started on very good footing. Instead, they seemed to offend each other at every turn. She had so few friends left and didn't want to lose one as wonderful as Drake. "Let's start over." She stepped away. "Good afternoon."

He smiled. "Good afternoon. Shall we?" He crooked his arm.

"Yes, please."

They entered the grounds and stopped. People flocked around a water pump, filling jugs. The atmosphere closely resembled an outdoor party as people talked and laughed with each other. "Oh look." Sophia pointed. "The tent is up. It's very large."

"It seems to get bigger every year. I often wonder how long until no more can fit. Have you ever been here on Illumination Night? It's something to behold as everyone tries to outdo each other with their lanterns."

"No, it's been a long time since I've had the pleasure of being here." She studied those milling around. There didn't seem to be any distinction between islanders and vacationers. Everyone smiled and waved. This was how things should be, people of different races and walks of life gathering for a common purpose. "Is the island always like this, where everyone gets along?"

"Mostly. Martha's Vineyard is definitely in a league of its own." He led her past a souvenir shop.

"This must be why they don't want peddlers here. They don't want the competition." She ran her hand over a frame decorated with different colored glass. "This is pretty."

Drake picked it up. "It's one of my creations. You may have it."

"Oh no. I insist on buying it." She clutched it to her chest and made her way to where a young woman stood behind a counter. A few minutes later she was the proud owner of a very lovely picture frame. All she needed now was a photo to put inside.

"I could have made you a special one," Drake insisted.

"This one is special because you made it. What's next?"

"Ice cream?" He led her to where a man turned a crank on an ice cream tub. "What flavor are you making today, Henry?"

"Vanilla with fresh blackberries mixed in."

"We'll take two." He handed the man the necessary funds.

"I can pay my own way, Drake." Sophia reached into her reticule.

"Today is my treat. I may be an islander, but I can afford to take a pretty girl out for the day." High spots of color appeared on his cheeks.

"Let's not do this again." She withdrew her hand. Men could be such prickly creatures. "I thought we were spending the day as friends, which would mean paying our own way. Since you insist on being a gentleman, I'll step back and allow it." She smiled.

His features relaxed into a grin. "You can be exasperating, Miss Blackwell."

"No more so than you, Mr. Moreland."

He laughed and handed her the ice cream. "I signed us up for a croquet tournament before asking if you play."

"I do, and I'm quite good." She spooned in some of the ice cream and closed her eyes in ecstasy. "This is wonderful."

"You've some right here." Using his thumb, he gently wiped away a drop of cream from the corner of her lip.

Her breath caught as she opened her eyes to see his face mere inches from hers. His hazel eyes warmed, his lip curled, but he pulled away, leaving her disappointed. *Silly fool.* He couldn't very well kiss her in public. What if word got back to the Wesleys? She could lose her job if her reputation became tarnished. But oh how she had wanted him to kiss her.

Drake had almost stepped over the boundary of proper decorum. Being that close to Sophia had his thoughts running in directions best left unexplored. He continually had to remind himself she'd leave at the end of the summer season. Which left him wondering why he seemed so intent on spending time with her.

Because he liked her. It was as simple as that. He'd deal with her leaving when it happened.

Ice cream finished and the bowls returned to Henry, Drake led Sophia off the grounds and to the meadow where the croquet tournament would be played. They checked in at a table with a list of names, who they'd play against, and when. Then they retrieved their balls and mallets. Sophia chose yellow, while Drake picked blue.

"How in the world will we tell our balls from the others?" Sophia held up her ball. "Mine isn't the only yellow one here."

"You'll have to keep an eye on it." He grinned and led the way to where they'd play their first round. The couple they'd play against, Ida and Lincoln Brown, owned several of the rental cottages.

"A worthy opponent." Lincoln's teeth flashed against his dark skin. "I hope your lovely friend isn't a poor loser."

"You might worry more about your wife," Drake said. "This is Sophia Blackwell. Sophia, Ida and Lincoln Brown. You'll have to do your best if we're to beat them, but win we will."

"I suggest we stop talking and get to winning then." She grinned, bouncing her ball in the palm of her hand.

Good-natured ribbing, a few lost balls, and by the end of the tournament Drake and Sophia came in second. He clapped her on the back like he would any chap. "You weren't kidding. You're good."

She planted her hands on her hips. "If you hadn't bumped me, my ball wouldn't have gone out of bounds and we would have won."

"Maybe." He grinned and put an arm around her shoulders. "Hungry?"

"Famished."

"I know just the place." They returned their croquet equipment, and Drake led her to his favorite little-known seafood place on the other side of the lake. "It was quite a walk, but it will be worth it, I promise."

"It's very quaint." She glanced around the rough wood walls and sat at an outside table.

"Do you mind if I order?"

She shook her head. "You're familiar with the fare. I trust you."

Warmth crept up his neck at her sincere comment. He ordered a plate of sliced potatoes to share and two dishes of shrimp wrapped in bread, adding a bowl of the cook's famous sauce.

He returned and sat across from her and stared until she frowned. He chuckled, enjoying how nervous she got when his gaze didn't waver.

"Stop it." She smiled. "You know I don't like it when you do that."

"Yes you do." He reached across the table and took her hand, rubbing his thumb across her soft skin. "Do you miss it, Sophia?"

"Miss what?" Her voice barely rose above a whisper. Her hand trembled in his.

"The lifestyle you once had."

A shadow crossed her dark eyes. "Once, but I've not strayed that far from it. Being a nanny to a wealthy family lets me live in a fine house, eat at topnotch restaurants, and go on vacations."

"But you are at someone else's beck and call."

"So are you. You don't own the carousel or the boat you take fishermen out on." She pulled her hand away.

"I'm this close to quitting both of those jobs." He held his thumb and forefinger a hairbreadth's away.

"You're saying I have no other options available to me." Her eyes flashed. "You're right. I'm either a nanny, a shop girl, or a wife."

"Which do you want to be?"

"Why all the questions, Drake?"

Because he wanted to ask her to stay but was too much of a coward. All he needed was the slightest encouragement. He wasn't ready for a wife. A boat came before any thoughts of settling down. He'd written a list of goals, and wife came after establishing himself as a yacht owner. "I'm just curious, never having been in your situation."

"That's an untruth." She quieted until their food was placed in front of them. "Keep your secrets. I'm quite happy with my lot in life, surprisingly. In fact, we're headed to Europe at the end of the summer season. See?" She took a bite of her shrimp sandwich. "What more could a girl whose family had fallen from social graces ask? Oh, this is good."

He gave a sad smile. It would be a very long time before he could offer a woman a trip to anywhere. "I'm glad you like it."

This time she put her hand on his. "Don't revert back to the silent Drake because we don't agree on some things. You have grand plans for your life. I happen to go where the waves take me."

It pained him to think she had so few options. Again, he wanted to ask her to stay, but there weren't any jobs for a woman like her on the island. Not unless she worked in one of the gift shops or hotels. He sighed and finished his simple meal.

Having studied the Bible and been taught on its principles, he knew life wasn't fair. He'd been born to a poor man and woman, Sophia to wealthy ones. Now here they sat, circumstances very similar, but still miles apart. *You're a fool, Drake Moreland.* He should stop seeing her, stop the walks along the shore.

Instead of doing what he knew to be the wise choice, he stood and offered her his hand. "Care for a stroll on the beach?"

Chapter 5

Sophia woke with eyes gritty from lack of sleep. The stroll on the beach with Drake the night before had been silent, conversation stilted. Oh, he'd been kind enough, but something weighed heavily on his mind. She refused to believe it was because he thought her above him. She splashed water on her face from a nearby basin.

The children wanted to visit the carousel yet again, which meant seeing Drake. Not that she minded, but he seemed to go back and forth as to whether he wanted to see her. Unfortunate since Cottage City wasn't big enough for them not to run into each other. She'd make a point of seeking him out so as to convince him she thought them socially equal even if the islanders didn't.

With children in tow, she set off at a brisk pace for the carousel and got in line. Summer season often meant long waits for entertainment, but they had all morning. That afternoon she had a picnic on the beach planned.

Catching Drake's eye, she smiled and waved. He returned with a hesitant smile of his own before turning to listen to a talkative mother insist on standing next to the horse her daughter would be riding.

Drake kept his face impassive then nodded, saying she could stand there if she promised to keep one hand safely on the bar and not move while the carousel was in motion. He actually seemed relieved when Sophia stepped up and handed over payment.

"Difficult morning?" she asked.

"A bit." He handed her two tickets. "You aren't riding today?"

"I think the children have experienced the ride enough to not need me hovering over them. I can stand here and keep you company."

"All right." He turned to the next customer, making Sophia regret her suggestion.

She bit her lip. After several minutes, she wondered whether he intended to ignore her during the ride. The ride ended, and Rupert and Abigail got back in line. It was going to be a very long morning if Drake wouldn't enter into a conversation with her.

"The meetings start on Monday, correct?"

He nodded, handing a young boy a ticket.

"What night will you be speaking?"

"Wednesday."

"I'll be sure to attend that night. I'm hoping to be there every night the Wesleys don't need me."

"That's nice."

She exhaled heavily through her nose. "Have I offended you in some way?"

"No." His gaze flicked her way then back to the customers. "I'm working."

"Your tongue obviously isn't." She crossed her arms and watched as her charges climbed onto the backs of their favorite horses for the second time. "We're having a picnic on the beach later. You're welcome to join us." She glared at him. "Bring your voice with you, please." Chin up, she marched to a bench and sat next to an older nanny. Rupert had informed her earlier that he intended to keep riding until he caught the brass ring. She couldn't help but admire his tenacity.

She snuck a glance at Drake and heaved another sigh. He could be most exasperating.

"He is a handsome fellow," the other nanny said. "I'm Alice."

"Sophia. Yes he is, but he seems to think that because my surname is Blackwell I'm too good for him."

"Men can harbor strange ideas about their walk in life." Alice patted her hand. "Only time will show him any different."

"It's difficult when he's stopped speaking to me." Sophia fought to keep from glancing Drake's way. "We were getting along famously, and then he withdrew."

"What was the last conversation you had together?"

Sophia scrunched her lips and thought. "We spoke about the few options a woman has in life. Then I told him I didn't mind being a nanny because I still got to enjoy the finer things in life like vacations and fine restaurants."

"Things an islander might not be able to give you."

Sophia stiffened. "Are you thinking that Drake had intentions toward me? I really think we were only friends."

Alice laughed. "If you're only friends, he wouldn't care whether he thought himself below you. No, my dear, he seems to have feelings toward you and is pulling away to keep from getting his heart broken."

Sophia gasped and put a hand over her mouth. Could Alice be right? If so, what would Sophia do about it? "I've invited him to a picnic."

Alice's laugh drew Drake's attention. He stared for a moment then returned his attention to his job.

"In my opinion, you also think of him as more than a friend. It isn't wise to spend too much time with a young man when you'll be returning to your real life. No summer dalliance turns out pain-free." She stood and smoothed her skirt. "It was nice to meet you, Sophia." She called to three young boys to come then smiled at Drake as she strolled past him.

He cast a quick look at Sophia then away, a confused look on his face. Had Alice said something to him? She wouldn't!

Sophia's face flamed. How did she get herself into such fixes? She did like Drake, very much in fact, but the man had goals for his life that didn't include her. Would she stay on the island if he asked her? She didn't have an honest answer.

Ever since her family's financial ruin, her hope had been to be self-sufficient. Her job as a nanny gave her that opportunity. Good pay and a great lifestyle. She didn't mind watching over Abigail and Rupert. But was that all she wanted from life, or did she one day want a family of her own?

She took her bottom lip between her teeth and gazed at Drake. For the right man, she quite possibly would drop everything, but God would have to make it very clear who that man was.

༄

No other word for it. Drake had been rude to Sophia that

morning, and he had a strong inkling that she'd been talking about his behavior with the nanny she'd sat next to. The last thing he needed was for a customer to complain to the owner about his attitude.

Now he stood on a rise and watched as Sophia spread a quilt on the sand in preparation for a picnic. She removed her hat and placed it next to a wicker basket. She felt her pockets then searched inside the basket. Not finding what she sought, she placed her hands on her hips and glanced around.

Drake ran his gaze around the area in search of what she might be looking for. A gust of wind lifted her hat and sent it sailing toward him, drawing her attention to where he stood. He darted to the side and retrieved the hat. Now he had no choice but to return it.

As he headed her way, he did his best to come up with a good excuse to reject the invitation he knew she'd offer again. *Fool.* If he didn't want to join her and the children, he would have avoided the beach.

"Your hat." He held it out to her.

"Thank you." She set it inside the basket. "Since you seem to be the rescuer of my things on a regular basis, I've lost a letter."

"I'll keep an eye out for it."

"Please, have a seat." She waved a hand at the quilt. "I've brought plenty."

"I've a boating guest this afternoon."

"That's this afternoon. I'm sure you have time to eat." She sat and arranged her dark skirt around her legs. With the breeze blowing her hair from its bun, the sun sparkling in her dark eyes, she was a magnet he couldn't resist.

He sat next to her, legs outstretched, and leaned back on his arms to watch the children play barefoot at the water's edge. He smiled, remembering the time Sophia had played the same way. Today she was the epitome of a proper nanny.

"I see you still haven't found your tongue."

He chuckled. "I don't believe every moment needs to be filled with chatter."

"No worry about that with you, is there?" A smile teased at her mouth.

He laughed, scaring a flock of seagulls into the air. "I'm sorry for my behavior this morning."

"I shouldn't have bothered you at work." Her smile faded.

"That is no excuse for rudeness." He leaped to his feet as Abigail fell in the water. Within seconds, he'd plucked her from the lake and carried her, dripping and crying to Sophia.

"Again, you come to the rescue. Thank you. *Shhh*, Abigail. You're all right." Sophia wiped the little girl's face with a towel. "The sun will dry you in no time. Let's eat, shall we?" She called Rupert to join them.

"I didn't fall," the boy said with a scowl.

"Time to eat, pal." Drake ruffled his hair. "The lake isn't going anywhere."

"I've brought a kite for you to fly while your food settles." Sophia pulled it from her basket.

"You must have everything in there," Drake said. "Food?"

"Of course." She set several wrapped sandwiches in front of them then added four apples and a pitcher of lemonade. "Did I forget anything? Oh, napkins." She handed them each a linen napkin.

"Can't think of a thing." He grinned and unwrapped a ham and cheese sandwich. He could do this. A grown man could be friends with a beautiful girl, enjoy her company, and say goodbye when the time came to go their separate ways. Sure. If he said it to himself enough times, he might actually come to believe his words.

They ate, tossed pieces of bread to seagulls darting overhead, and spoke of nothing more serious than the next day's plans of renting bicycles for a jaunt around the island. Sophia definitely kept the children occupied during the long summer days.

When they'd finished, Drake put the kite together and led the others to an open section of the beach not crowded with people. He showed Rupert how to hold the string. "Now run so the wind can lift the kite."

By the boy's third try, the kite soared high above them. Sophia clapped. "Well done."

Drake's heart skipped a beat at the joy on her face. "Would you like to try?"

"I might when Rupert is finished."

As customary with children, the boy grew bored quickly and rushed back to the water, his little sister on his heels. Drake handed the string to Sophia, keeping his hands on hers to show her how to hold the kite. "I'm afraid you'll have to run. It might be improper." He winked.

"Don't be silly." She raced away as the wind lifted the kite. By now, her hair fell in a dark waterfall down her back, any trace of a bun lost.

He stepped back and watched her as she lifted her face to the sky, pulling and tugging on the string to make the kite dip and soar. "You've flown one before."

"Many times." She grinned. "You assumed I hadn't."

"My mistake." Dear Lord, his heart was in deep trouble. He

pulled a watch from his pocket. He was in serious risk of being late for his boating client. "I've got to go. Thank you for the sandwich."

"Anytime." She kept her gaze on the kite.

Drake raced up the bank. A scrap of white caught in a bush drew his attention. He snatched it as he ran by and tucked it into his pocket to throw away later. No matter how the islanders tried to keep things clean, some people couldn't resist throwing aside their garbage.

Half an hour later, he sailed two middle-aged men past the beach in time to see Sophia and the children packing up their things. They looked windblown, sun-kissed, tired, and happy. He would have liked to have spent the rest of the afternoon with them. But a paying customer meant money in the bank.

He'd almost forgotten the paper in his pocket until he removed his pants that evening and heard it crackle. He unfolded the paper and read:

Dear Sophia,
Of course you must marry Theodore. A chance like this
may not come your way again.

He stopped reading and plopped into a chair. Sophia was to marry another.

Chapter 6

Sophia sat knitting on the small porch outside the cottage the next morning while the children played at her feet. As her needles clicked, her mind went over her mother's letter, which, strangely enough, had been on the doormat that morning.

Not normally one to go against the wishes of her parents, Sophia wasn't sure they were right this time. Marry Theodore? She didn't like the man, not even a little bit. She sighed and set her knitting in her lap, her gaze falling on the children. Life was much simpler when one was young.

"What are we doing today?" Rupert glanced up from his marbles. "I want to go to the carousel."

"We're renting bicycles, remember?" Abigail would stay with her mother for a while because Mrs. Wesley didn't think the girl was old enough to ride one of those contraptions, as she called it, not even given the newer model was considered much safer.

"You'll have lessons first then a ride."

She stood as Mrs. Wesley approached with a young man carrying several packages. "I'm sorry to be late," she said, "but I'm not one to miss a sale on the latest fashions. Come, Abigail. Be safe, Rupert." She placed a kiss on his cheek.

"I'll take good care of him, Mrs. Wesley." Sophia set her knitting inside the door.

"I'm confident you will." She smiled and led her daughter into the cottage next door.

"Have you ridden before?" Rupert practically danced around her.

"Many times, although not this new version. The one I rode had a large front wheel and a tiny back one. This one is much safer, I've heard."

"I'm not scared."

Although she wasn't a novice, Sophia rode the bike around the yard a few times before feeling comfortable enough to hit the road. Rupert, being the adventurous sort, learned rather quickly, and an hour later they rode off, the young boy starting out shaky but getting smoother as they went.

Not wanting to lose her hat again, Sophia had chosen not to wear one and lifted her face to the afternoon sun. What a glorious day.

They heard the tinny music of the carousel before they reached it and waved at Drake as they rode past. He glanced up, not smiling, and turned back to a customer.

Sophia sighed and steered toward the boardwalk. She'd never met a moodier man in her life. It was a good thing she'd decided a visit to the carousel wasn't on the day's agenda. Maybe Drake would actually miss her.

Their ride circled back around past the carousel again. This time Sophia kept her gaze forward and stopped the bike in front of an ice cream parlor. "I do believe it's time for a break."

Rupert's knees buckled as he jumped from the bike, but the smile on his face said he agreed. Sophia reached out to steady him. Eating the treat wasn't as sweet as when she'd done so with Drake. Rupert's steady chatter helped pass the time, even bringing a smile to her face a time or two. The simple island life had erased some of his arrogance, making him quite likable.

"Father." He pointed to where Mr. Wesley sat with Theodore Boatwright. From the not-so-subtle glances sent her way, she had a strong suspicion she might be the object of their conversation.

"Let's resume our ride." She quickly gathered their things and ushered Rupert back to the bicycles.

Her parents had connections everywhere, despite their financial loss. In fact, being a Blackwell had helped Sophia with her employment. Her mother wouldn't stoop so low as to involve the Wesleys in matchmaking, would she? The thought churned her stomach. Some of the day's enjoyment vanished.

She helped Rupert onto his bike then climbed onto hers, grateful for the split skirt she wore. How did women manage before? She sighed. Thinking of clothing did not erase her trepidation over seeing Theodore.

"I want to go back on the boat," Rupert announced. "Maybe I won't get sick this time."

"What brought that up?"

He motioned his head toward the water. "That's Mr. Moreland's boat."

She laughed, almost wishing she could be as easily distracted. "Perhaps your father will take you again. You only need to ask."

"He's too busy." Rupert's face fell. "That's what he told me.

You'll have to take me."

Heavens, no. Having had a childhood friend fall from a boat and drown, she hated the very thought. She didn't mind wading, but being offshore sent shivers down her spine. "I can't swim."

"You'll be on a boat." He frowned. "Not in the water."

"That's enough, Rupert. We'll find some other way to keep you occupied."

"I'm telling Father." His chin quivered.

Sophia shook her head and led her charge to the bike rental. "Let's head home and rest for dinner, shall we? Your foul mood is evidence of your fatigue."

He pouted but did lie down, giving Sophia a break as well. By the time the dinner hour rolled around, she felt better able to face Drake, since he still worked at the restaurant. Maybe his mood would be better.

She stepped into the restaurant behind the Wesleys and froze at the sight of Theodore standing next to their customary table. *Please no, Lord.* She couldn't bear his company over dinner.

"There he is." Mr. Wesley beamed. "I've invited Theodore to join us tonight." He gestured to Drake, who stood waiting to offer his service. "Another chair, please."

The sight of a muscle ticking in Drake's set jaw was evidence enough his attitude had not improved. Sophia sighed and sat in the chair Theodore pulled out for her.

So it was true. Sophia now spent time in the company of her betrothed. If anything could convince Drake that a relationship with her was impossible, this would. He placed another chair at their table and handed them each a menu. "I'll be back to take your order in a few minutes." He left without meeting Sophia's gaze.

The time would come when he would ask for an explanation of her invitations to lunch and her readiness to stroll the beach with him, but the pain was too raw for him to ask at that moment. Not to mention the fact she ate with the man her parents wanted her to marry.

He entered the kitchen and leaned against the wall. Why did it bother him? He'd told himself time and time again he wasn't ready to settle down. Not until he established himself as more than a hired hand. His mind knew the truth, but his heart refused to accept the fact.

Taking a deep breath to compose himself, he approached the Wesleys' table and took everyone's dinner order. He couldn't avoid looking at Sophia this time. "Ma'am?"

Her eyebrows rose and her cheeks turned a bright pink. "I'll have the clam chowder, *sir*." Her eyes flashed as she handed back the menu.

"Make that two, chap," Theodore said. "And a bottle of your finest champagne."

"Celebrating?" Drake kept his gaze locked with Sophia's.

"Perhaps."

Sophia gave a subtle shake of her head. "We're only having dinner. Nothing special."

"Nonsense," Mr. Wesley boomed. "We're working toward a new future with these two young people. Bring the champagne."

"I don't drink, sir." Sophia shook her head again. "Water for me."

Drake nodded, pleased she wasn't one to imbibe. "Right away."

Sophia seemed more despondent as the evening wore on. Could Drake have been wrong all along? Were her parents setting her up with a match she didn't desire? Was God trying to tell him something through all this?

"Mr. Wesley has been telling me of your hard work," Theodore said when Drake arrived to retrieve the chowder bowls. "Heard you're looking for a yacht."

"Yes, sir."

"I've one for sale, if you'd like to take a look. It's moored in the marina. We could discuss terms tomorrow afternoon."

"Steam or sail?"

"Sail, of course. Who wants to spend time with coal when you could be zipping along the water. Am I right?" Theodore toasted Drake with his flute of champagne. "This is the golden age of yachting, my man."

"May I ask why you're selling?"

"I've purchased another. No need to have two." He set down his glass. "I realize many people procure items to excess, but I'm not one of them."

"Thank you. I will be by at two, if that is suitable."

"See you then." Theodore grinned then turned his attention to Sophia. "I can't wait to take you out on the water."

She paled and reached for her water glass, knocking it over. "Oh."

"I'll get it." Drake pulled a towel from his apron and sopped the water from the tablecloth. "Let me replace this."

"No, we're finished." Mr. Wesley stood and led his family from the table.

Sophia glanced over her shoulder with an apologetic look. "Thank you."

Drake nodded and began to clear the table. He'd never seen Sophia so despondent. It was none of his business. Her future was hers to determine. A man who wanted to remain on the island had no business interfering.

After work, hands thrust deep into his pockets, he strolled the beach, looking for odds and ends for his crafts. The moonlight often caught the glint of something interesting far better than the brilliance of the sun.

What would Sophia put in the frame she'd purchased? Most likely a wedding photograph or perhaps a postcard of the island. It didn't concern him. He brushed the hair from his eyes and turned to stare at the lake.

His troubled mind and pained heart kept him from enjoying the beauty. He might as well head home and prepare for speaking at the Methodist meeting the next night. The Wesleys had kept Sophia too busy to attend. Now he wasn't sure he cared whether she came to hear him or not. *Liar.* He cared very much.

"Hello."

He turned to see Sophia outlined by the moonlight. "Hello."

"You seem deep in thought," she said, stepping beside him. "You didn't hear me coming."

"Thinking about my message at the meetings tomorrow."

"I really hope to attend. I've asked the Wesleys to get a temporary sitter."

He cut a sideways glance at her. "That would be nice."

"I'd like to hear a sermon on deciphering God's will for one's life." She met his gaze. "It seems we both have tough decisions to make."

"What's mine?" He frowned. "I have my future mapped out."

"That's the problem, isn't it? You've got it all planned to the smallest detail, putting money before all else."

"How will I reach my goal otherwise?"

"Have you stopped to ask God if that is the goal He wants for you?" Her eyes shimmered. "What if you let something wonderful pass by because you fill every moment with work?"

"I'm not working now." He regretted the curt tone to his voice, but who was this woman to tell him about God's will? "I'm ready to purchase my yacht now and can quit all the other jobs and focus on the one I really want."

"Then what? Surely you've planned the next step."

"Same as you, I suppose. Congratulations are in order, I hear."

"Not quite yet. I've a lot to think and pray about. Just as you, I must be certain not to let a good thing get away. But I need to figure out what that good thing is." She turned to go, stopping a few feet away. "My hope is for you to experience all the happiness life has to offer, Drake."

That sounded horribly like a goodbye to him.

Chapter 7

Sophia did make it to the meeting to hear Drake speak on the very topic they'd spoken about. His quiet way of spreading the Word had everyone in attendance enthralled. "Slow down and listen," he'd said. "God would not disappoint but would instead make His will clear if only we'd wait." He'd gone on to speak on worry, quoting Matthew 6:25–34. Sophia had fallen asleep with a prayer on her lips and woke the next morning with a new resolve. She'd wait, listen, and continue to hope she'd get her heart's desire.

It had come to her in a dream. She had a husband and children. She couldn't see the husband's face but felt in her heart that he was out there waiting for her. All she needed to do was find him, so she'd decided to spend some time with Theodore to see whether he might be the one.

Now she sat at a writing desk, penning a letter to her mother to tell her she would allow Theodore to escort her to a few events during the time that remained of the summer, but if love did not settle in her heart for him, she would not marry the man. Satisfied she had stated her case as fairly as possible, she slipped out of the cottage to mail the letter before the children awoke.

Cottage City lay quiet in the early morning hour, and Sophia made it to the postbox and back before the children awoke. As she laid out their clothes for the day, Mrs. Wesley entered the cottage.

"I'll take the children with me today," she said. "I've an endless round of tea and lunch, but they will be fun. Mr. Wesley has informed me that Mr. Boatwright will be arriving to spend the day with you." The woman did not look pleased at the fact she wouldn't have the day to herself. Her gaze roamed over Sophia. "Perhaps you should wear the striped skirt and white shirtwaist. It's by far the best of your day costumes. He will come for you at 9:00 a.m." She left, leaving Sophia with her mouth hanging open.

She snapped it closed. Did she have no say in her plans for the day or the clothes she would wear? She would have to let Theodore know from the beginning she wasn't a meek woman to do as he said without expressing her opinion. She chose a plain navy skirt but did wear the white shirtwaist. A small act of rebellion that brought a smile to her face.

It was almost ten by the time she spotted Theodore strolling toward the cottage. Being late did not improve her opinion of him. She pasted on a smile and stood from the chair she'd been seated in.

"Good morning," he said. "Perhaps you should change into a split skirt? I'd planned on renting bicycles."

"Of course." That tidbit of news would have come in handy

when she got dressed. She quickly changed and rejoined him outside.

He crooked his arm, inviting her to place her hand there. A spicy aftershave wafted past her, causing her nose to itch. She sniffed and turned her head slightly away. She couldn't help but think of how she preferred Drake's scent of sun and water.

"I must say I was surprised and pleased when Mr. Wesley said you had agreed to allow me to court you." Theodore squared his shoulders. "Our fathers have been friends for quite a while, and even though I'm the youngest son, I can give you a life of luxury. You are a very lucky woman, Sophia."

She bit her tongue to hold back a sharp retort. Lucky because he paid her attention? The arrogance!

The man did not have the same tendency for quiet as Drake. In fact, he babbled on like a stream after a hard rain.

"I've arranged a dress fitting for you tomorrow morning, as I expect you to attend a party with me tomorrow night. I prefer my bride-to-be to wear custom gowns, but since you hesitated in accepting my attention, there's no time."

She halted, slipping her hand free of his arm. "Sir, you presume a lot. There's been no mention of a betrothal." She hiked her chin.

"Of course there has. Your mother informed me she wrote to you." He frowned, puzzled. "Did you not receive her letter?"

She sighed. "Yes, I received it, but in this modern age a woman has the right to speak and to make up her own mind."

His eyes flashed. "I see we have some boundaries to set."

"I agree." She crossed her arms.

After a moment, he burst into laughter. "You are quite the spitfire. I might enjoy sparring with you. Life will not be boring."

He offered his arm again.

She reluctantly took it, and they resumed their walk, stopping at the bike-rental shop. She waited outside while he made the arrangements. Glancing toward the carousel, she remembered that Drake would be looking over Theodore's yacht that afternoon. Could today be his last day operating the Flying Horses? Once he began spending the majority of his day on the water, she'd rarely lay eyes on him.

Theodore joined her, the bike vendor unlocking two bicycles. "Were you wanting to ride the carousel?"

She shook her head. "Just listening to the music."

He held the bike while she got on. "It is lively."

Minutes later, with Theodore leading the way, they rode along the boardwalk. Sophia was glad for the chance not to hear Theodore's outdated opinions. Not so. Theodore could talk over the wind whipping past as they rode.

"I'd like you to come with me when I show the boat this afternoon. Then we can indulge in an early dinner as I have another engagement this evening."

Wonderful. He had no intention of inviting her to his engagement. She needed to take Theodore in small doses, at least in the beginning. She hadn't tired of Drake when they'd spent time together. She also needed to stop comparing the two men. They were as different as night and day.

Drake paced the marina dock, waiting for Theodore. He'd already studied every bit of the hull he could see and couldn't abide people being late. Time was too valuable to be wasted.

He shouldn't have been surprised to see Sophia accompany

the man to the marina, but he was. Apparently she'd decided to give the man a chance to win her affections. He thrust out his hand. "Thank you for this opportunity."

Theodore returned his handshake. "My pleasure. Shall we go aboard?"

"I'll wait here." Sophia stepped back, eyes wide in a pale face.

"Nonsense." Theodore reached for her hand. "You mustn't be afraid of the water. Boatwrights like boats."

Drake wanted to go to her aid. Instead, he boarded the yacht and waited for what was none of his business to play out.

Sophia stepped farther away, coming dangerously close to the other side of the dock. "I cannot."

Theodore's eyes narrowed. "This is not the place for argument. Come with me before you fall in." He wiggled his fingers.

Sophia glanced down and gasped, rushing forward and up the ladder. "Don't let me drown," she told Drake.

He smiled. "I wouldn't dare. You'll be perfectly safe."

"Of course she will." Theodore climbed up after her. "First thing, Sophia, you must learn to swim."

She looked ill and sat on a cushioned bench that went all the way around the area they stood in. "I'll stay right here."

Theodore looked ready to argue. He sighed and gave Drake the tour. "We've used the finest materials in the building of this yacht. It's well worth the price."

Drake ran his hand over the polished wood in the cabin, which was bigger than the cottage he lived in. If he were to buy the boat, he could live onboard and save the rent. "I'll take it."

"Wonderful. I'll meet you back here in the morning to finalize the details. You'll have the funds necessary?"

"I will." Excitement rippled through him. In one day, he'd have fulfilled the dream he'd worked so hard for.

The two men stepped back on deck. Sophia seemed to have relaxed a bit until Theodore suggested Drake take the yacht out to see how she handled. "Must I?"

Drake handed her a life preserver. "Stay seated and you'll be fine."

Her dark gaze met his. "I suppose you'll stop working all your jobs now."

"Not until next summer. I need to save money to live on while I get established."

"Money isn't everything, Drake." Her sharp tone pierced his heart.

"Of course it is," Theodore stated, glancing from her to Drake. "Any man needs a healthy bank account. Women tend to have the strangest ideas."

Sophia's face darkened. "May we please get this over with? You did promise me an early dinner."

She remained quiet as they sailed across the lake. The yacht handled like a dream. Drake expected to feel fulfilled, but Sophia's remark about there being more important things than money rankled. One more year of saving and he would be able to think about settling down. Not until then would he be able to provide a woman and family with a secure lifestyle. Why couldn't Sophia see that? Besides, her future looked settled. His future remained his concern.

"This girl is simply wonderful," he told Boatwright.

"As my first, she is special," Theodore said, his gaze roaming the hull. "But as in everything in life, it's time to move on to something new."

"I will enjoy every moment of my ownership." Drake turned

the sails to the marina.

"Thank You, God." Sophia leaped to her feet and scampered down the ladder the moment they docked.

"I've some work to do with her," Theodore said.

"She's perfect just the way she is," Drake muttered.

"Pardon?" He cocked his head.

"Nothing. It will be difficult to get her over her fear of the water."

"Have you done so before?"

"A time or two." Drake smiled to where Sophia marched down the dock to solid ground.

"Wonderful. I would like to hire you to be her swimming instructor and to get her over this silly fear. I cannot marry a woman who won't set foot on the water. I'll bring her to you day after tomorrow." Without waiting for a yes or no, he climbed the ladder and with long strides full of purpose, joined Sophia on the bank.

Drake met her gaze then watched as she took Theodore's arm and strolled back to the bicycles. Sighing, he climbed down the ladder and headed for his afternoon job at the restaurant. As he donned his apron, he glanced up to see a pretty new waitress giving him a wide-eyed look. She smiled and turned away, ducking her blond head.

Maybe there were other women to catch his attention when Sophia returned to the mainland. All he had to do was continue working, keep his head down, and get through the summer. Something that would not be easy if he was going to teach Sophia to swim.

Chapter 8

Sophia stared at herself in the mirror, running her hands over the deep blue gown. At least Theodore hadn't escorted her to the shop and chosen what she'd wear to the party. The color accented her dark hair and pale skin. She gave a slight twirl, feeling very pretty indeed.

"Mr. Boatwright is here." Mrs. Wesley entered the cottage. "You look lovely. No one will know it's a store-bought dress." She clasped her hands under her chin. "Your escort will be smitten."

Sophia smiled. "I'm ready." She didn't feel much like a nanny at that moment. For the evening, she'd again be one of the elite.

Theodore's smile showed his approval of her attire. "Stunning, my dear."

Flushing, she slipped her arm through his and let him lead her to a waiting carriage. She held the hem of her gown a few inches from the ground as he helped her inside.

"I know we could easily walk, but wouldn't you rather arrive in style?"

She nodded, and the carriage moved. In the distance, a crowd of people left the Methodist grounds. Circumstances had kept her from going again. She'd looked forward to the meetings upon her arrival. Her heart hitched with disappointment.

"Why so glum?" Theodore asked. "You aren't one of those Holy Rollers, are you?"

She gave him a sharp glance. "I guess I am. Aren't you a spiritual man?"

"I've never seen the use of religion. My family made our money with no help from some entity." He brushed a speck from his jacket. "It's fine for women and children, I suppose."

"We aren't talking about fairy tales, Theodore." She turned her attention away from him.

"Don't sulk, darling." He patted her gloved hand. "I won't ask that you give up your faith."

"Isn't that courteous of you," she muttered.

He laughed. "I often forget the sharpness of your tongue."

The carriage stopped in front of the island's largest hotel. Theodore jumped down and helped Sophia to the ground.

The music of an orchestra led them to the ballroom, where finely dressed men and women in gowns of every color mingled. A few danced to a waltz. Many cast curious glances at Sophia, no doubt wondering why someone of her social status hung on the arm of a Boatwright. She hitched her chin. Let them speculate.

Less than an hour into the evening, she realized she hadn't missed the snide looks or gossiping disguised as concern one iota. When Theodore entered into a deep conversation with another man about the benefits of big boats and houses, she slipped out the french doors onto a garden patio for a breath of fresh air.

She grasped the railing and closed her eyes, lifting her face to the breeze blowing off the lake. She breathed deeply of water and sand.

"Sophia?"

She opened her eyes to the concerned face of Drake. He stood a few feet away wearing the white jacket of a servant. Of course he'd be working. That's all the man did. "Good evening."

"Are you all right?"

"Yes, just. . ."

"Too much of the party?" He stepped closer.

"You could say that. I'd forgotten how these people are when they think someone beneath them."

He tilted his head to peer into her face. "Was someone cruel to you?"

"Not openly." The looks and sickly sweet tone in their voices told her all she needed to know.

"It will change once you're married."

"Hmm." The more time she spent in Theodore's company, the less thrilled she was about marrying him. She didn't seem to know what she wanted, did she? Yes she did. She wanted a husband and children. She just wasn't sure she wanted those things with Theodore. She wanted a husband who would want to attend church meetings with her and let her speak her own mind without acting as if she were a child. "I'd best return before I'm missed."

He nodded. "You don't want to be caught hobnobbing with the hired help."

"I am hired help too." She sighed and hurried back inside.

Theodore was still deep in conversation, obviously not having noticed she'd slipped away. She sighed and retrieved a cracker and pâté from the tray of a passing waiter.

"Why, it is you. Sophia Blackwell."

Sophia grimaced then turned to face the woman who had once been her best childhood friend. "Lucinda Carter." They air kissed each cheek of the other.

"I must admit to my surprise at seeing you here." Lucinda patted her pale blond hair, her blue eyes cold. "After, well. . ." She waved her hand dismissively. "I suppose you'll rise socially when you're a Boatwright."

"I assume I would, if that sort of thing was important to me."

Lucinda's eyes widened. "It isn't?"

"Not particularly. I enjoy the life I have now. It has purpose rather than the shallowness of these sort of gatherings."

"I do believe my betrothed is feeling out of sorts." Theodore turned and took her arm. "Please excuse us while I find her a place to sit and rest." He dragged her along after him until finding a vacant settee. "Are you mad? Were you purposely trying to offend Lucinda Carter? Do you know who she is?"

"Of course I do. We were friends before her family rejected mine. Please do not manhandle me in that way."

"Then don't act in a way that makes it necessary. I use these functions to conduct important business. If you cannot behave yourself, then stay here until I come for you." He marched away, his heels clacking on the tiled floor.

Sophia laughed then clapped her hand over her mouth. She now knew how Rupert felt when she chastised him. Standing, she waved over a servant. "Please inform Mr. Boatwright that I've gone home." With that, she stepped into the garden and strolled along the walkway to the front of the hotel.

"Leaving?" Drake pushed away from where he'd leaned against the wall.

"Yes, I've had enough."

"You shouldn't walk the streets at night alone. Let me escort you."

She shrugged. "As you wish, but aren't you afraid your payment will be less?"

His eyes narrowed. "Obviously one party has turned you into a snob like those inside."

She exhaled heavily through her nose. "My apologies. I'm out of sorts, as Theodore said." She marched down the sidewalk.

Drake caught up with her. "What's wrong? You seem as if you're in the midst of a stormy sea."

Tears pricked her eyes. "I suppose I am." She stopped and faced him. "You seem to have everything figured out. I may not agree with your goals since they focus so strongly on money, but how did you determine what, exactly, you wanted out of life? I've had so many things out of my control." The tears escaped and trailed down her cheeks.

"Please, don't cry." Drake pulled her into his arms and behind a hydrangea bush, out of sight of any prying eyes.

He dried her tears with the hem of his jacket then cradled her head against his chest, closing his eyes against the pain of holding her. "I don't have it all figured out." He once had thought he had, but the arrival of a dark-haired, dark-eyed beauty muddled things. "Let's get you home."

"By way of the beach, please."

"You'll soil your gown."

She stepped back. "I don't care."

They walked in silence, stopping far enough from the water so as not to get their feet wet. Drake removed his jacket and spread it on the sand for Sophia to sit on. She might regret ruining her gown when she saw it in the morning if she dampened it with sand.

She bent her knees and wrapped her arms around them. "It appears you've been missing the meetings too."

"I sometimes go in between jobs." He sat next to her.

She sighed. "A benefit of being your own boss will be that you can do what you want when you want."

"Yes." The shimmer in her eyes gave him pause. *Please don't cry again.* He didn't know what to do with crying women other than hold them—something he didn't want to do with this woman who would leave him. "You'll have that when you wed."

"Not if I marry Theodore. I shouldn't be telling you all this."

"What are friends for?" he said softly.

"Right. Friends." She pushed to her feet. "I'd best get home if you're going to teach me how to swim tomorrow. I hope you aren't expecting an eager pupil."

He chuckled. "Not at all." All he expected was a difficult hour or two with Sophia in his arms as he held her up.

"Thank you, Drake. You're an easy person to talk to, and I've no one else."

He put a hand playfully over his heart. "You talk to me only because you have no one else?"

She giggled. "Of course not, silly. Now that you know how to speak, I find it quite enjoyable."

Pleased that her mood had improved, he offered her his arm and helped her up the bank to the boardwalk. Not quite ready to give up her company yet, he led her the long way home. "You'll have to find a way to make it to the Illumination on the last night of the meetings. You'll regret missing it. In fact, I'll purchase you several lanterns. Then you'll have to come or leave me with far too many. People will think me presumptuous."

"We can't have that, can we?" She squeezed his arm, sending his heart soaring like the gulls.

Much too soon they reached her cottage. "Are you all right now?"

She nodded. "Thank you for escorting me home."

"Miss Blackwell." Mr. Wesley stood from the chair on the porch of the cottage next door. "Who is that with you? Where's Boatwright?"

Drake stepped forward. "It's me, sir. Miss Blackwell wasn't feeling well, and since my work shift had ended, I escorted her home."

"Are you ill?"

"A headache. Nothing to be concerned about. It will pass by morning. Mr. Boatwright has insisted I have swimming lessons and will come for me at ten."

Mr. Wesley chuckled. "I don't believe my wife realized how often she would have the children with her when she encouraged this courtship. We may have to hire a part-time sitter."

"See you in the morning, Miss Blackwell. Sir." Drake shoved his hands into his pockets and turned to leave.

"Hold on a moment, please." Mr. Wesley stepped off the porch.

Drake turned as Sophia stepped into her cottage, closing the door against their conversation. "Yes, sir?"

"I hear you are now the owner of a fine yacht."

"I am." Drake's chest swelled with pride.

"I'd like to book an evening for the family. We'll include Mr. Boatwright of course. I'll be your first customer." He clapped Drake on the shoulder. "I'll be by tomorrow afternoon to finalize the arrangements. Well done. You'll make something of yourself yet."

"Thank you." He watched as the other man entered his cottage. Having his first booking put a bounce in his step and a whistle on his lips. He had time to take the yacht out a time or two before the summer season ended. Well done indeed.

At home he glanced around the room he'd already started to pack up. His needs were small. The cabin of his boat would be all he needed for a home, it being more than enough for one person.

He toed off his boots and removed his servant's uniform. He'd have little need of it soon and would be returning it, along with the key to the carousel. Jobs were few and far between in the off-season, but he took what he could.

He did worry too much about money. The purchase of the yacht had virtually cleaned out his bank account. Booking a few tours would help get him through the winter months. He pulled a sheet of paper from his desk and made a quick advertisement, which he'd drop off at the print shop first thing in the morning. If he was lucky, he would have several bookings a day and no worries over the winter.

Finished, he stretched out on his bed and stared at the ceiling. He again had a solid goal. He grinned. One Sophia would not approve of, most likely. At least he had goals rather than not knowing what he wanted from life. He reached over and blew out the lantern.

The last thought he had before falling asleep was why he thought so much of what Sophia thought of him.

Chapter 9

Sophia tied the white ribbon on her navy-blue swim clothes. Swimming had never been on her list of things to learn. Darn that Theodore. The man was quickly becoming a nuisance with his demands. Things would only get worse if she were to wed him.

Mrs. Wesley peered into the cottage. "Theodore is here. You mustn't keep him waiting. Do you know how long you'll be gone? I have an afternoon tea and really don't want to take the children with me."

"I'm quite sure we'll be back by the noon meal." She sure hoped so anyway. She tugged at the heavy top to her suit, grabbed a satchel with dry clothes, and marched out the door.

Theodore's gaze roamed over her appreciatively. "I am very pleased that you are a modest woman."

She fought the urge to roll her eyes. "Shall we get this over with?"

He took the bag from her in one hand and crooked his free arm. "I regret to inform you that I will have to leave you in the capable hands of Drake, as I have an important appointment."

"That would be quite improper." Her eyes widened. An unmarried man teach an unmarried woman how to swim without a chaperone? Drake would have to hold her in his arms. She put a hand to her chest. Her heart threatened to burst free at the thought.

"Are you all right?" Theodore frowned. "You look flushed. The day is quite pleasant, Sophia."

"It is trepidation over what lies ahead."

He chuckled. "What a ninny you are. You'll be perfectly safe."

She wanted to embed the heel of her boot into the top of his foot. "I'm sure I will be."

"I will find you a chaperone, if that is what is bothering you."

She glanced into his amused face. "It is."

"I will stay for a while then send one of the maids from the hotel."

"How kind of you." She bit her lip to keep further retort from escaping. The man acted as if he was doing her a great favor by saving her reputation.

They strode the rest of the way in silence. When they reached the beach, Drake, dressed in a green-and-white swimsuit, waited near the water's edge. The concerned look in his eyes told her he pitied her being forced into this.

Theodore set her bag on the sand and stepped back. "I will sit over here until time for me to leave." He sat on a nearby bench and studied his nails.

Drake held out his hand. "Are you ready?"

"No, but we might as well get on with it." She removed her

shoes then slipped her hand into his and let him lead her into the water.

"It will be much easier to learn to swim in a lake as opposed to the ocean."

"Oh goody." The water lapped around her ankles.

His laugh held no scorn, and she found herself smiling despite her reluctance. "I won't let you drown. Do you trust me?"

"Yes. What do I do now?"

"We move out until the water is midchest deep."

Her breath came in short, fast gasps the deeper they got. "I can't."

"You can. I'll hold you. Turn around. Lean against my arm."

She stiffened like one of the planks on the boardwalk, her feet staying as firmly on the bottom of the lake as possible.

"Relax, Sophia. Raise your legs in front of you. I won't submerge you." His eyes twinkled.

Her gaze clashed with his. "I don't think this is swimming."

"No, but we need to get you over some of your fear of the water. Keep your eyes on me."

"You'll never learn at this rate," Theodore said from the bank. "Kick up your legs."

She'd forgotten all about him. Taking a deep breath, she lifted her legs, grabbing for Drake's shoulders when the back of her head touched water.

"Let go, Sophia." Drake grinned. "Lay on my arm. Put your arms and feet out."

"You don't ask much, do you?" She did as instructed, her eyes widening. "I'm doing it. What, exactly, am I doing?"

"Floating."

"Bravo." Theodore clapped. "I've asked that woman with the

children to chaperone you. I must be going."

"It's the nanny you spoke to at the carousel," Drake told her. "She appears to find this entire lesson amusing."

"Hmm. May I stand now?" If she spent one more minute staring into his hazel eyes, she'd do something very foolish. Like kiss him.

"If I were Theodore," Drake lowered his voice to a husky whisper as he set her on her feet, "I'd not let another man hold you for any reason."

"Apparently Theodore thinks me so desperate as to not be enticed." She glanced at the bank where Alice stood, a knowing smile on her face. Sophia didn't know where to look. If she looked at Drake, emotions rose that had no business rising. If she looked at Alice, she'd see reflected on the woman's face what began to grow in Sophia's heart. She was doomed.

"Sophia?"

"Hmm?"

"Are you ready to move on to the next step?"

She nodded. "I suppose."

"Put your face in the water."

"What?" She locked her gaze on his. "You cannot be serious."

"Oh, but I am. Put your face in the water and blow bubbles. Your feet don't have to leave the bottom."

"Of all the ridiculous. . ." She took a deep breath and dipped her nose into the lake. A gentle push from Drake submerged her face. He let go and allowed her to straighten.

"See? You didn't drown."

She cupped water in her hands and threw it in his face. "How do you like it?"

"I love the water." He shook his hair out of his face. "Let's learn some basic strokes."

"Why bother?" She shoved wet strings of hair away from her eyes. "I'll never look on swimming as a favorable pastime."

"But you'll know enough to possibly save your life if you find yourself in over your head." He moved a strand of her hair she'd missed out of her face.

She was most definitely in over her head.

When Sophia had leaned over his arm, it had taken every ounce of Drake's willpower not to kiss her. The only thing that had stopped him was the sight of Theodore watching from the bank. Now a very amused nanny spent part of her time supervising children and the other watching him and Sophia.

"Rather than lean back over my arm," he told Sophia, "You'll lean forward this time."

Her eyes widened. "I cannot! What will people think?"

"That you are learning to swim." His mouth crooked.

She started to say something again but clamped her mouth closed instead. She turned around and flopped over his arm like a fish. Her face submerged, and she came up sputtering.

"A little slower this time and hold your face up." He laughed. "Look." He floated belly down in the water then moved his arms and legs to swim a few feet away.

"Your face is in the water."

"Because I'm a strong swimmer. You can't start off that way." He wiggled his fingers. "Come on."

With a dramatic sigh, she slowly leaned over his arm, taking his breath away with the softness of her curves. Why couldn't he be teaching the older woman on the bank instead? He wouldn't be tempted to do anything improper with her.

"Time to move out over your head," he told Sophia. Best for both of them. She'd have to learn to hold herself up.

The sun sat high in the sky by the time he felt confident she could at least tread water enough not to drown until someone could jump in and help her. He took her hand and led her from the water. "You're a hard worker, Sophia Blackwell."

"You're a slave driver, Drake Moreland." The smile on her lips belied her words. "Actually, you are a very patient teacher. Thank you. I know I have a long way to go, and I promise to at least try and practice."

"Liar."

She gave a full-blown, head back, mouth open laugh. Her hair streamed over her shoulders. She looked as young as a child sitting there in swimsuit, legs outstretched, joy radiating from her. "Oh Drake, if only Theodore could—" She clamped a hand over her mouth. "Never mind." She motioned her head toward the older nanny who headed toward them.

"Thank you for chaperoning my lesson, Alice," Sophia said.

"It was quite entertaining," she said, cutting Drake a quick glance. "Perhaps I should learn myself with such a handsome instructor." She tossed them a wink then led her charges away. Cheeky woman. It was as if she could see right to the heart of him.

"I need to get back. Mrs. Wesley has a function this afternoon. I fear I'm already late." Sophia got to her feet and grabbed her bag. "Wait for me outside the beach tent?"

"I'll be right next door and wait outside when I'm finished." He grabbed his own change of clothes and hurried to a vacant tent.

It didn't take him long. When he emerged, he spotted Mrs. Wesley and her two children scanning the beach. He gave a whistle then waved them over. "Miss Blackwell is changing."

"I really needed her back sooner." The woman frowned. "May I leave these two with you until she is ready?"

"Of course." He ruffled Rupert's hair. "How about a free ride on the carousel? Today might be your lucky day."

"You are heaven-sent, Mr. Moreland." Mrs. Wesley kissed each of her children's cheeks then bustled toward the hotel, calling back that he must inform Sophia to feed the children that evening.

Sophia exited the tent. "Another meeting I have to miss."

"Why not take the children? There will be many of the upper-society people there. Not everyone spends every minute with parties and teas," Drake suggested. "I can help you watch them."

Her smile lit up. "That's a splendid idea. Let's grab an early meal and find a good spot under the tent."

"You promised me a carousel ride," Rupert said with a scowl.

"So I did, and so you shall receive. How about hot dogs again? Then you'll have time for a ride or two before we head to the Methodist grounds."

Rupert seemed to think for a moment then nodded. "I think that will be fine."

Drake met Sophia's amused glance over the children's heads. He offered Sophia his arm. "A fine meal awaits."

"Let's eat." She rubbed her stomach. "Swimming makes one quite ravenous, doesn't it?"

"Yes it does."

After a simple meal full of good fare and a lot of laughter

as Abigail did her best to imitate her mother at a society event, they strolled toward the carousel. Drake couldn't help realizing how much like a family they seemed or how at ease Sophia was with simpler things. Perhaps he'd been wrong about her. He definitely needed to do some serious thinking about whether he wanted. . .this. A wife and family. He didn't want to wait too long and become a lonely old man with nothing but a boat to keep him company.

Rupert failed again and again to grasp the brass ring. The boy's arms were too short. After much encouragement from Drake and Sophia about trying again tomorrow, they merged with the crowd of people heading for the meeting.

Drake procured places to sit not too far away from the podium, not an easy task with tens of thousands roaming the grounds. "You'll like this speaker," he told Sophia. "He's a man after God's own heart and speaks on how we can apply God's Word to our lives. Last night he spoke about listening for that still, small voice in order to know the next step to take in our lives."

She tilted her head, a soft smile on her lips. "And were you listening?"

"Excuse me?" He glowered.

"You heard me. Is God telling you something?"

"Like what?" He crossed his arms.

"That money isn't everything."

"You're a fine one to talk."

Sophia opened her mouth, closed it, then made a sound in her throat before asking, "What do you mean?"

"Aren't you marrying for security?" He raised an eyebrow. "How is that any different than my working for a secure financial future?"

"Many do," she mumbled. He was right. Her plans were no different than his. Maybe worse was the fact she would settle on a marriage to a man she didn't love in order to please her parents and get the family of her own she wanted. Drake didn't seem inclined to base any decisions on anything but what he actually wanted. She sighed and directed her attention to the podium.

The service nearly over, Rupert began to fidget, and Abigail laid her head in Sophia's lap. Gently raising the child back to a sitting position, Sophia stood. "It's too late of an evening for these two. Thank you for bringing us, Drake."

"I'll walk you home." He got to his feet.

"There's no need. I doubt anyone will bother a woman with children, especially with this many people around."

"I insist." He herded them through the milling crowd and past those listening to the night's sermon on serving the members of the church.

Sophia's heart sank the closer they got to her cottage. Drake hadn't said another word since they'd left the meeting. When would she learn to keep her mouth shut and not voice her personal opinion on the lives of others?

Chapter 10

Sunday. One final week and the summer season would be declared over. Sophia stood on the cottage porch and stared toward the lake. Time had passed so quickly.

Spotting Theodore strolling in her direction, she grabbed the bag containing her swimsuit, ducked around the corner of the cottage, and took the back way to the marina. She would have to tell Theodore she would not accept his marriage proposal, but this wasn't the time. She needed to send a telegraph informing her parents first. They wouldn't take the news well, especially her mother.

She stopped by the telegraph office and sent the telegram. Knowing her mother, she'd hear back by evening.

Intending to enjoy her day off regardless, she set off at a brisk pace for the beach. A myriad of sailboats dotted the lake's surface. It wasn't until she saw the flags that she realized a race was in progress.

She shaded her eyes, trying to locate Drake's yacht. Surely he. . . *Wait, you ninny, it's a sailboat race.* She tapped her finger against her lips. What did his sailboat look like? She couldn't recall having seen it before.

Joining the crowd watching the race, she asked a young woman if she knew which belonged to Drake Moreland. "Why yes. That's his, the one with blue stripes. He's in the top three," she replied.

Sophia wished she'd known about the race. She could have wished him good luck. Suddenly a man approached her from behind.

"Splendid finding you here."

Only startled slightly, she tried to keep her features impassive so Theodore wouldn't read her feelings on her face. "I came to practice my swimming. This is all quite exciting."

"I was surprised not to find you at your cottage."

"Did we have an appointment?" She put her hand on her hat to prevent it from falling as she peered up at him.

"No." He shrugged. "But as my betrothed, I thought you'd wait on me. I'm aware it's your day off."

She almost told him then and there, but the crowd's yell drew her attention back to the race. Drake had pulled into second place as the boats rounded a large buoy. She clapped and jumped up and down. He was going to win.

"Mr. Wesley has procured Drake's services for us all to dine and enjoy a cruise our last night here."

"I do not plan on attending."

"You really must get over your fear of the water, Sophia. I am an avid seaman and intend on purchasing a new yacht at the first opportunity. One much larger than the one I sold. I'll expect you to host many a party on its polished decks." He cut her a sideways glance. "It's a good idea you've decided to practice your swimming."

"I doubt I'll ever be good enough to feel comfortable on a boat, Theodore. Maybe you should find a wife who is."

"Nonsense. You'll learn."

She opened her mouth to tell him of her decision when once again the crowd went wild. Drake had pulled into first place. *Drat.* She'd missed it because of Theodore's constant babble.

"I expect you'll attend the winner's dinner with me? They have it every year. All the sailors will be there, but the winner will be the star of the event."

"Yes." She had a suitable gown, although it was two years old. She would not be indebted any further to Theodore.

"Moreland came in first!" Someone yelled.

Sophia grinned and joined in the shouting and blended with the crowd as they flooded the marina. When Drake docked, many hands shook his or clapped him on the back. She did her best to step forward to offer congratulations, but Theodore's grip on her elbow held her back.

"Stand aside, Sophia. You'll be crushed."

"He's my friend. I want—"

"Betrothed women do not have male friends." He scowled and pulled her farther from the crowd. "You may offer your congratulations tonight at dinner."

She yanked her arm free. "Do not handle me in such a manner."

"Do not act as if you have no social graces." His face darkened. "I think your family has been outside the proper circles for far too long."

She fought back the urge to land her bag upside his boorish head. "I feel a headache coming on. I'll see you this evening."

"I'll escort you home."

Giving an exasperated sigh, she increased her pace, wanting to be rid of his company as soon as possible. When they reached her cottage, she marched up the stairs, mumbling, "Thank you." She glared and slammed the door.

Drake would never have treated her in such a manner, no matter the circumstance.

Drake adjusted his bow tie and grinned at his reflection in the mirror. He'd won. The first-place prize would help make financial problems during the winter virtually nonexistent. Why, he could actually contemplate having a wife now. He almost wondered what he would do with himself if he quit working at the restaurant and carousel. Boredom was not something he experienced on a regular basis.

Satisfied he looked sufficient to be the center of attention at dinner, he strolled off the yacht and down the dock to where bright lights burned. Every year, the winner's dinner was held in the ballroom of the hotel, being the only place big enough for all those who usually attended. Rich or poor, idle or working class, all would be there dressed in their finest clothes. Other than the Illumination, it was the highlight of the season. He intended to enjoy the evening to the fullest by asking Sophia to dance.

He stepped through the double doors of the ballroom to cheers. His face hurt from smiling for hours. Still, he doubted he'd stop anytime soon. God had granted him another lifelong dream.

His gaze roamed the room for sight of Sophia. He spotted her and Theodore standing near Mr. and Mrs. Wesley at the far end. While accepting congratulations and weaving his way through the crowd, he approached them.

"Congratulations." Sophia, beautiful in a gown of deep blue, smiled up at him.

"Thank you. Were you there?"

"Oh yes. It was very exciting."

"Well done." Theodore clapped him on the back. "You're a worthy sea captain indeed."

"Excuse me." Mrs. Wesley slipped away and headed to where Rupert and a few other boys roughhoused.

"I'm hoping to sign your dance card." Drake's attention returned to Sophia.

She glanced up at Theodore, who gave a slight nod. "I'd love that."

"Only because it's a cause for celebration, chap. Wouldn't want you stealing my fiancée away with lures of adventure." Theodore's smile didn't quite reach his eyes.

"After dinner then." Drake gave a slight bow then backed away, not wanting to push his luck with the other man. He changed direction and headed to the tables loaded with trays of food to suit every taste. He filled a plate and headed for the winner's table where the men who placed second and third sat with their wives, leaving him feeling very lonely.

His gaze flicked to where Sophia stood in line to fill her plate. She glanced his way and smiled. His heart did a flip, and he turned back to his food. It did no good to fantasize over another man's betrothed.

"That was fancy racing," said second-place winner Neal Jones, owner of the ice cream parlor. "You've improved since last year and knocked me out of first place. How'd you do it?"

"Hard work and determination," Drake said, grinning. "You

were in first for too many years. It was time someone else won."

The man laughed. "My wife will have to forgo a new dress because of it."

"Why are you not married, Mr. Moreland?" Mrs. Jones raised an eyebrow. "A young, hardworking man like you should have women following after him."

"I've been too busy to look, ma'am. But that is all about to change. Excuse me." He tossed his napkin on his plate as the orchestra tuned up to play a waltz. He approached the Wesleys' table and held out his hand. "My dance, I believe."

Sophia blushed, her eyes sparkling. "I think so." She slipped her gloved hand in his.

"Don't keep her too long," Theodore said. "I plan on twirling Sophia around the dance floor myself."

Sophia stiffened, but her smile never faded as he placed one hand on her waist and slid into a waltz. "You must be so proud."

"I am." He peered into her eyes. His hand fit as if made for the curve of her hip. "Are you all right?"

"I've a lot on my mind, is all."

"You'll be leaving next week." His heart fell.

Her expression saddened. "I'll miss this place. I didn't have a proper appreciation for the beauty and simplicity when I was young."

"Let's not think about your leaving. Tonight is enough." His gaze landed on her lips. He so wanted to know what kissing her would feel like. It would be worth a punch in the jaw by Theodore to find out.

Her lips parted, her breath coming faster, yet her gaze never left his. "I agree. Let's not think about my leaving. My heart isn't ready."

He pulled her a little closer, resting his temple against the top of her head, ignoring the glare from Theodore. He breathed deep of something floral she'd washed her hair with and thought again of stealing a kiss. "Will you be in trouble?"

She glanced at the other man, taking a step back. "I can handle him. Drake, I've decided not to—"

"Mind if I cut in?" Theodore pushed between them. "You've had her long enough."

Drake bowed. "It was the highlight of my evening. Thank you, Sophia." He tossed her a wink then strolled outside to watch the moon kiss the surface of the lake and wish Sophia stood next to him. He lifted his face heavenward. "Lord, I need to know what to do, and I need You to be very clear with me. Hit me over the head if necessary. I don't want to let something special slip by because I'm a blind fool whose mind remains stuck where it shouldn't." He turned and watched through the window as an expressionless Sophia glided by on Theodore's arm.

Taking a deep breath, he headed back to the celebration.

Chapter 11

Sophia stared at the telegram in her hand then wadded it into a ball. Her mother could insist if she wanted, but Sophia would not heed her mother's wishes to marry a man she didn't love. She wasn't sure she even liked Theodore.

Her mother threatened that her heart broke at the thought her only daughter might very well be a nanny for the rest of her life. So be it. If that's what God willed, then Sophia would make the most of it.

Still. . .she sat on the cottage porch as her mind drifted to how handsome Drake had looked the evening before with the glow of victory on his face. She smiled at the way his broad shoulders had filled out his suit. He'd looked every bit as at ease in the ballroom as he did on the water.

Mr. Wesley stepped from the cottage next door and glanced her way. "Good morning." He approached her, a serious expression on his face. "I received a telegram from your mother."

"So did I." Sophia sighed, slipping the note into her pocket.

"What's wrong with marrying the Boatwright fellow? He's not a bad chap, and you'd have a comfortable life." He put one foot on the bottom step.

"He's a boor." Tears stung her eyes. "I'd have no freedom to have my own thoughts."

He chuckled. "You're a sweet girl, but that's the way things are in a marriage."

She blinked back moisture. "Then I shall not marry."

He nodded. "Then you may remain in our employment as long as you are needed. Have you told Theodore?"

"I haven't found the right time."

"Perhaps you could continue as you are until the season is over? It might make our social engagements awkward."

She nodded. "As you wish." But not a moment more. She would inform Theodore of her decision before her foot stepped onto the ferry to return home. "I'll get the children ready for the carousel and an afternoon at the beach. Enjoy your day, sir."

"You too, Miss Blackwell." He returned to the porch of his cottage and lit a cigar.

Sophia's eyes widened.

"Mum's the word. The missus hates these things." He gave a conspiratorial wink.

Pretending to lock her lips, Sophia entered her cottage and got the children ready for the day. "We've a grand day planned. Carousel, ice cream, swimming. . ."

"I'm getting that ring today." Rupert pulled a pole with a hook on one end from under his bed. "I made this."

"That would be cheating." Sophia put her hands on her hips.

"You've plenty of money to purchase rides. There's no need to cheat in order to get a free one."

"It's the principle, Miss Blackwell. I've tried all summer. My arm isn't long enough."

"Then you'll try again next year." She took the pole from him and propped it in the corner. "One day your arm will be long enough, and you'll have a sense of pride at grabbing the ring in an honorable way."

He groaned and stomped outside. Abigail looked at Sophia and frowned. "Boys are different, aren't they?"

"Yes, my love, they most certainly are." She took the child's hand, the bag containing their swimsuits in the other, and led the children to the restaurant for breakfast.

When they finally arrived at the carousel, Sophia was informed that Drake had quit that morning, having booked several rides on his yacht before the week ended. Heart heavy, she sent the children on ahead and took a seat on the bench.

"Good morning." Alice sat next to her.

"Good morning."

"You don't sound as if it is." She crooked a brow. "Could it have something to do with the fact that handsome man isn't running the carousel?"

Sophia nodded. "He didn't tell me he planned on quitting."

"Why would he? You're betrothed to another." She patted Sophia's hand. "Although one wouldn't know that from the swimming lesson."

"Mr. Boatwright insisted I have one." Sophia exhaled heavily. "It was marvelous."

Alice laughed. "Yes, I could see how hard it was for you to allow that man to teach you. You have feelings for him, don't you?"

"Yes, but nothing can come of them. We want different things in life. He's so focused on money, it's all he thinks about." She glanced up to see Rupert stretch for the ring. He slipped but caught himself. "He said my marrying Theodore wasn't any different, and he's right. I'm not getting married for anything less than love."

"Good girl." Alice sat back. "I had love once, but he died in a carriage accident. I never got lucky to find love again, so here I am. It isn't a bad life."

"No it isn't." If she'd sought employment in a shop or factory, she'd not be spending time on Martha's Vineyard or eating in a fine restaurant. Yes, there were worse things than looking after a wealthy couple's children.

After five rides, Sophia deemed it enough. "Ice cream." She tried to keep some spark in her voice but feared she failed miserably. Time was rushing away from her. In a few days' time, she'd be back on the mainland and have no opportunity to see Drake again.

Her heart leaped as she thought she'd caught sight of him then dropped when she realized it was another man. She ordered their treats and pretended to enjoy the ice cream but mostly stirred the spoon in circles. She needed to stop acting like a ninny. "Ready to go swimming?"

The children nodded and raced for the changing tents. Sophia smiled and handed them their suits. "I need the two of you to stay right here while I change. Understand?"

"I'll watch them."

Sophia whirled and stared into the smiling face of Drake. "I thought you were working."

"Not for a few hours." His smile widened. "When I saw you

heading for the beach, I couldn't let you go into the water without your teacher close by, could I?"

She laughed. "No, sir. Any respectable teacher would want to watch their student on their first solo attempt."

"I'll be right here when you get out."

⁓

Sophia had actually seemed pleased to see him. More pleased at least than she looked to be while dancing in Theodore's arms the night before. Drake couldn't help but feel a bit of hope rise in his heart. When the three emerged from the tents, Drake took the large bag from Sophia and headed to a spot on the beach that wasn't too crowded.

"Will you not be swimming?" Sophia asked.

"No. This way I won't have to worry about changing before my client arrives. I'll sit here and watch." Which wouldn't be a hardship at all. While he preferred holding Sophia in his arms, keeping her in his sights was the next best thing.

The children raced for the water, Sophia lagging behind. Abigail shrieked as the cold water splashed up her legs. Rupert, trying to be brave, lifted his arms shoulder high and waded deeper.

Sophia stepped into the water and froze. She glanced over her shoulder. "I don't remember it being this cold."

He wanted to tell her it was because he'd held her in his arms, but he held back because of the number of people around them. If he could help it, he wouldn't do anything to tarnish her reputation. "You'll adjust soon enough."

Inch by inch, Sophia entered the water, her gasps reaching his ears. He chuckled and leaned back on his arms.

Two young men chasing each other through the water

darted in her direction.

Drake was sprinting for the water as they knocked both Sophia and Abigail off their feet. Sophia's dark head disappeared under the surface. "Imbeciles!"

"Sorry, sir." One of the boys helped Abigail back onto her feet.

Drake entered the water, feeling around for Sophia. She emerged a few feet away, sputtering and spitting water.

She faced the boys, pulling Abigail to her side. "You, young sirs, are careless. You could have harmed this child." With her swimsuit limp around her legs and her hair fallen from her cap, she sloshed her way to the bank, dragging the little girl behind her.

"Are you all right?" Drake took her arm and helped her.

"Perfectly fine. It took a moment to let go of my panic and realize my feet could touch bottom." She rubbed her shoulder. "I may have a bruise, but no lasting damage. Are you hurt, Abigail?"

The child shook her head. "I'm going to build a sandcastle." She scooped damp sand in her hands.

"How sad that a five-year-old is less afraid of the water than I am." Sophia plopped to the sand.

"Fears are nothing to be ashamed of, but they can be conquered."

"What are you afraid of?"

Her leaving in a few days, but he couldn't tell her that. She wasn't free for him to tell her how he truly felt. "Not accomplishing my goals."

"Ugh." She fell back onto the sand, knocking her bag over and spilling some of its contents. "Why did I even ask? Well, that's an unreasonable fear since you've purchased a yacht and seem to have bookings lined up."

He leaned over, staring into her face. "That isn't what I'm

afraid of," he whispered.

"Oh?" Her eyes widened as a shadow fell across them.

"What's this?" Theodore glared down at them.

"Hello." Sophia sat up. "Drake saved me when a couple of boys knocked me down in the water."

"I once again owe him a debt of gratitude." His gaze flicked to Drake then returned to Sophia. "I had no idea you planned on going swimming."

Drake straightened and transferred his attention to Rupert romping in the shallow water.

"I am a nanny, Theodore. It's my job to keep the children entertained." She held up her hand for him to help her to her feet. "Drake happened to be here, thank goodness."

While Drake might appear to be watching the children, his senses were alert to the anger radiating off the other man. If he should make one uncalled-for move toward Sophia, he'd find himself on his back in the sand.

Theodore pulled her up. "As your betrothed—"

"Please do not start that again." Sophia started shoving their items back into the bag. "Rupert, Abigail, time to change into our clothes. Thank you again, Drake."

He nodded and stayed seated as if Sophia's story of them happening upon each other were true. Far from it. He'd seen her and the children at the ice cream parlor and followed them. She was the lantern, he was the moth who couldn't help but be drawn to the light. "I'm glad to have been of help. I do hope to see the two of you at the Illumination tonight."

"I don't attend such things." Theodore curled his lip.

"I'll be there," Sophia said. "I wouldn't miss the last night for anything."

Drake listened as they trudged to the changing tents. He should head for his yacht but was reluctant to leave until he knew Theodore wasn't going to act aggressively toward Sophia. When he heard Rupert laugh and Theodore respond in kind, he decided danger had passed and got to his feet.

A crumpled wad of paper, half covered with sand, contrasted sharply with its surroundings. Drake picked it up to throw it away and noticed it was a telegram. He unfolded the paper and smiled.

Sophia had no intentions of marrying Boatwright. Drake slipped the telegram into his pocket and set off for the marina, a spring in his step and a whistle on his lips.

Chapter 12

Excitement filled the air as Sophia made her way to purchase more Japanese lanterns. Mrs. Wesley insisted their cottages be lit brighter than any on the island.

Residents and guests alike bustled to and fro, stood on ladders to hang their lanterns, and called out cheery greetings to each other in friendly competition. With cheerful colors everywhere one looked, the island resembled a circus. Despite having to attend the Illumination with Theodore, she couldn't help but have a spring in her step. The only cloud hovering on such a wonderful day was that summer was almost over.

Drake waved as he sped by on a bicycle. Sophia had managed to entertain Rupert without the lure of the carousel lately. It wasn't the same without Drake there, and she didn't want to get into more deep conversations with Alice about her feelings for Drake. She'd see him that evening and then the next evening on his yacht. It would have to be enough.

At the shop, she couldn't resist purchasing another of his frames, this one covered with tiny pebbles in every hue of tan and brown. She didn't know what photo, if any, she'd put in them, but she desperately wanted something to remember him by. Armed with the frame and several lanterns, she headed back to the cottage.

"Wonderful." Mrs. Wesley clapped. "We're sure to have the most. Why, you'll be able to see the lights from our cottage on the shore."

Sophia wasn't sure about that. Many lanterns adorned all the cottages she passed. She set them at the woman's feet then took half to hang on her cottage. She stood at the foot of the ladder and contemplated how she'd climb high enough in a skirt while holding a lantern.

"Need help?"

She smiled and turned to see Drake on his bicycle. "I most certainly do." He always seemed to know when she needed him. Her heart lurched knowing how much she would miss him.

He hopped down and scurried up the ladder. "Hand me one."

Stretching, she handed him a blue-and-red lantern. "I can't believe the excitement in the air."

"It'll increase the closer we get to the singing. That tabernacle is going to resound with worship. Are the Wesleys going?"

"Surprisingly, yes. So is Theodore." She handed him another lantern, this one green and yellow. "They've not attended a single meeting but will go to the Illumination."

"It's a big social event. You'll see a lot of faces that didn't attend a meeting."

It pained her to think that so many thought only of attending parties and not the true meaning behind the Methodist meetings. "Thank you for your help."

He hung the last lantern and climbed down. "You're welcome. I'll see you tonight. I've been chosen to light the first lantern." His eyes held a strange sparkle as if he knew a secret. "Give Rupert some ginger in his tea before the yacht ride tomorrow. It will help settle his stomach." He flashed a smile, mounted his bike, and sped away.

What a strange encounter. Sophia shrugged. It was no concern of hers what he might have going on in that handsome head of his. Perhaps it was excitement over being chosen to start the evening's proceedings.

"That man seems to be everywhere you are." Theodore came around the corner of the cottage.

"Were you spying on me?" Sophia frowned.

"Perhaps." His eyes flashed. "Should I have cause to worry?"

"I really need to—"

"Theodore," Mr. Wesley called. "Come give me a hand, will you?" He gave Sophia a warning look.

She sighed and entered the cottage as Theodore went to help her employer. She'd come so close to telling him she couldn't accept his proposal. It would have to wait until Mr. Wesley was nowhere around. Hopefully she could tell him while others were present. His temper would flare at her rejection, and sometimes the look in his eyes frightened her. She suspected he kept on his best behavior for now, but after they were officially wed. . .

She laid out her best day outfit and checked for stains or tears. It no longer bothered her that her clothes were a tad outdated. Drake didn't care, so neither should she. Theodore's opinion didn't matter. She would be clean and respectable at the Illumination, which was all that was required of her. Thank goodness the Wesleys had never insisted on a uniform for their nanny.

After an idle day, Mr. Wesley had Theodore light their lanterns while the family watched. Sophia clasped her hands under her chin and smiled as up and down the row of cottages lanterns flickered to life. "It's like a fairy tale. It's so beautiful."

Theodore smiled indulgently down at her from the top of the ladder. "You are so like a child at times, Sophia."

If any other person had said that to her, she wouldn't have felt as if it were meant to be condescending. "I hope to never lose my wonder at new things."

"It's quite adorable." He climbed down. "I meant no offense. You look lovely."

"Thank you." She smoothed her deep brown skirt. "We'll most likely be sitting on the ground, and this will show dirt the least."

"Heaven forbid. Fetch some quilts." He shuddered.

"Already taken care of." Mrs. Wesley joined them. "The lanterns look quite wonderful." She narrowed her eyes at a cottage a few doors down. "I do believe they've got two more than we do."

"It's not a competition, dear." Her husband took the quilts from her. "Shall we? We want to get a good seat for the fireworks."

They made their way to the large, steel tabernacle and spread the quilts on the lawn. Sophia sat behind the Wesley family, Theodore beside her. She settled her skirt around her and squared her shoulders, determined to enjoy the evening.

Peddlers wandered past with everything from flavored ice to books until some hired police ran them off. No peddling allowed inside the fence.

"Riffraff." Theodore's lip curled. "This is the type of thing you enjoy?"

"Very much." She pulled some coins from her pocket and dropped them in the offering basket being passed around.

Theodore waved it away.

"With all your money, one would think you could give to the less fortunate." Sophia kept her gaze straight ahead.

"Very well. If it means so much to you." He called the young man passing the basket back to their spot and dropped in a few coins as well. "You are so easily pleased, Sophia."

"I wish you'd stop comparing me to a child. I am a grown woman with thoughts of my own."

He laughed and reclined on an elbow. "You are also very entertaining."

She sighed. It would be a long night.

Drake searched the crowd for Sophia, finally locating her next to Theodore. When would she tell the man of her decision not to marry him? He fingered the telegram in his pocket, his fingers itching to hand it back to her and let her know he knew the contents.

What if he'd misunderstood the message? She had said she didn't want to wed Theodore, but her mother strongly insisted. Sophia could very well be obedient enough not to disappoint her mother. After all, a lot of her worries would be eased, along with some of the financial burden on her parents.

Some of the hope growing in his heart diminished. It would do no good to get his hopes up—she would still leave in a few days' time. But he had one more day to spend in her company and vowed to make the most of it.

Mr. Wesley caught his eye and waved him over. His glance

colliding with Sophia's, Drake made his way through the crowd to where they sat as a band played the beginning notes to a hymn.

"I hope you're enjoying yourselves," Drake said, still keeping his gaze on Sophia despite the thunderous look on Theodore's face.

She nodded and ducked her head, starting a conversation with Abigail.

"I trust everything is ready for our boat ride tomorrow," Mr. Wesley said. "It's our last night on the island. I want it to be spectacular."

"I've ordered the food and drink you asked for. I'm as ready as I can be to grant your wish for a wonderful last night." He'd hired the restaurant's chef to prepare tomorrow night's meal. The Wesleys would not be disappointed. He was counting on them spreading the word to their friends for next summer.

"Join us, Moreland. You're quickly rising in the same social circles. Before you know it, you'll own a home on the mainland and vacation here same as us."

"I don't think I'll live anywhere else, sir, and I'd love to join you." He sat on the other side of Sophia, tossing Theodore a cheeky grin.

The man's face darkened, and he leaned behind Sophia. "You and I are about to have an altercation."

"Let's wait until after the ride tomorrow, shall we? We wouldn't want anything to interfere with the family's enjoyment." Drake's grin widened, and he leaned back on his arms.

Theodore wasn't the only person growing angry. Sophia's dark gaze darted from man to man, her frown deepening. She muttered something about who acted like a child now, then took a deep breath and sang along with the words to "Rock of Ages."

Drake joined in as the others in their group remained silent and listened. Hopefully the words would take root in their hearts and they'd attend the meetings next year. Many a soul received salvation each summer. To Drake, that was the highlight of the season, not any parties.

Tears trickled down Sophia's cheeks as they started in with "Amazing Grace." Theodore rolled his eyes and plucked at a blade of grass.

"I remember this song," Mrs. Wesley said. "We sang it at church when I was a child. Perhaps we should attend again. It would be good for the children." She turned and glanced at Sophia. "You could teach them some Bible stories in the meantime."

Sophia nodded but continued to sing, closing her eyes. By now Theodore had a questioning look on his face as he stared at her. "What is she doing?"

"You've never seen a person worship before?" Drake's eyes widened. He knew the man wasn't religious, but not to recognize worship seemed hard to believe.

"Right." He shrugged. "My wife-to-be has a lot of sentimental notions. Most women do, I suppose."

Drake bit his tongue to keep from blurting out the contents of the telegram. Whether or not Sophia chose to discuss it with the man was up to her. As he'd just realized, she might very well go along with her mother's wishes. Drake intended to have fun in the meantime. If Theodore thought another man was interested in Sophia, he might be a bit nicer in his attentions.

By the end of the festivities, the two Wesley children had fallen asleep. When Sophia went to lift Abigail, Drake scooped the child up instead. "I'll carry her. She's too heavy for you."

"You overstep your bounds," Theodore said. "I should be the one helping."

"Then you should have offered immediately." Sophia folded the quilt they'd sat on.

"I see I will need you to show me gentler ways when we're married."

Her head snapped up. She opened her mouth to say something then shook her head. "It's late, and I'm tired. We'll talk more tomorrow."

With Abigail's head cradled on his shoulder, Drake led the way to the Wesleys' cottage. At Sophia's insistence, he carried her inside and laid her on her bed while Mr. Wesley did the same with Rupert.

"Good night, gentlemen." Sophia closed the door behind them.

Theodore stepped up to Drake the moment Mr. Wesley joined his wife at their cottage. "Do you have intentions toward my fiancée?"

Drake crossed his arms. "Since there is no ring on her finger, I'm not convinced there is a wedding in the near future." At least not between him and Sophia.

"I plan on officially proposing on the yacht tomorrow night." He matched Drake's stance. "Not that it is any of your concern. Miss Blackwell is above you, sir."

"I have come to believe that she doesn't think the same as you."

He narrowed his eyes. "She has a lot to learn."

"She's perfect as she is."

Theodore blinked like an owl. "Tomorrow will reveal all." With a hitch of his chin, he marched away, his shoes beating a heavy rhythm on the walkway.

Yes, perhaps tomorrow evening would reveal more than any of them knew. He cast a glance at the cottage in time to see the curtain fall back into place. So Sophia had seen them. He grinned and shoved his hands into his pockets. Good. He wanted her eyes wide open before she made her decision.

He'd definitely made his.

Chapter 13

Sophia stood on the dock and watched Drake's boat bob up and down in the water like a child's toy. Not that by any means it was small, but she rather preferred her feet on solid ground. Noticing the dock did not signify solid anything since she could see the water through the planks of wood, she stepped back onto the ground.

"Come on. We haven't all day." Theodore took her arm and ushered her forward.

"I feel a headache coming on." Her stomach churned.

"Don't be silly. It's perfectly safe."

Drake leaned over the railing. "I won't let you drown, Sophia. Trust me."

Her gaze locked on his. "Promise?"

"Good grief." Theodore stormed ahead of her and up the gangplank. "You're worse than Abigail."

The child skipped past Sophia and onto the yacht, followed by the rest of her family. Rupert slipped his hand into Sophia's. "I'll help you. It's as simple as one foot in front of the other."

"That simple, huh?" She gave him a trembling smile.

"Yep. Mr. Moreland is a good captain. He'll take care of us."

"Very well then. Lead on, kind sir."

"I promise," Drake whispered as she moved on shaky legs past him.

She chose a seat near the back and slipped on a life preserver. His words didn't erase her fear but did ease the ache in her stomach a bit.

Theodore sat beside her and stretched his arm on the seat behind her. "See how easy it is? All you have to do is sit still and enjoy the wind in your hair and my company." He patted his pocket.

Oh Lord. She could make out the shape of a small box. He planned on making an official proposal. Nausea churned in her stomach. She should have sipped ginger tea along with Rupert. Why must Theodore make her last outing on the island worse?

Her gaze drifted to where Drake untied the mooring. She would rather have spent the time solely in his company and risk her heart breaking more when she left. She sighed and stared over the railing as the yacht's sails caught wind and they drifted away from land.

"Here you go." A few minutes later, Drake handed her a cup of tea. "Ginger. You look a mite green."

"Once again you are my hero." She smiled and took a sip. "You added sugar."

"You seem the type to enjoy sugar in your tea." He grinned and moved to check on Rupert.

"That man is a boor." Theodore glared. "He doesn't know his place."

"You didn't seem to mind when you sold him this yacht." She took another drink to keep from telling him who the real boor was.

"Any man who will try and take another's girl is not a gentleman."

"Drake has been nothing but a gentleman, Theodore."

He leaned over to peer into her face. "Must you always argue with me? I once thought it cute. Now it's quickly becoming annoying."

"My apologies for having a mind of my own." She lifted her chin. "Perhaps you should choose another to be your wife, Theodore."

"Nonsense." He straightened against the seat back. "You and I are suited well enough." Planting his hands on his thighs, he pushed to his feet and joined the Wesleys.

Good. Sophia needed room to breathe and think. She lifted her face to the breeze and closed her eyes. The yacht came to a stop and rocked as a mother might rock an infant.

"Hungry?"

She opened her eyes to see Drake handing her a plate of lobster and rice in one hand and holding a second plate in his other hand. "This is a surprise."

He grinned. "I plan on catering to the upper elite. Good thing I like seafood. Mind if I join you?"

"Please do, and thank you for the tea. It settled my stomach. Now I'm ravenous."

"I'd do about anything to bring a smile to your face, Sophia." He sat and balanced his plate on his knees.

She smiled and ducked her head. "You always manage to know

what I need when I need it. I will miss you so much, Drake." She blinked back tears.

A shadow crossed his face, and he turned away. He ate the rest of his meal in silence then stood. "Just set your plate by your feet. I'll gather the dishes later." He strode away and raised the sails again, sending them speeding across the lake's surface.

What had she said to silence him and bring sadness to his features? Surely he would miss her too. They'd spent a lot of time in each other's company over the course of the summer.

Abigail sat next to her. "I want a boat like this when I'm big."

"It is rather beautiful, isn't it?" Sophia took a moment to admire the polished decking under her feet and the freshly painted cabin. "I think you'd make a fine captain."

"It's like flying when we go fast." Abigail stood and spread her arms.

"Why don't you sit down? You're making me nervous."

She glanced sideways at Sophia. "I'm not scared. Try it, Miss Blackwell."

Sophia took a deep breath and stood.

A smaller sailboat cut in front of the yacht.

Abigail screamed and plopped to her seat.

Sophia gasped and fell backward over the railing. She gulped in water as the lake closed over her head. She flailed until remembering the life preserver would help her float. She bobbed to the surface like a cork as Drake dove into the water.

"I've got you." Drake wrapped an arm around her waist and swam them both to the ladder.

"I'm fine. I remembered what you taught me." She coughed.

He turned her to face him. "We need to talk, you and I."

"About what?" She waved her arms gently in the water. "I didn't mean to fall in, Drake. I wouldn't—"

He put a finger on her lips to quiet her. "Shhh." He leaned closer.

"Are you all right, Sophia?" Mrs. Wesley peered over the railing. "Help her up, Mr. Moreland. She'll catch her death of cold."

Moment broken, Drake said, "Right away, Mrs. Wesley. After you, Sophia."

She climbed awkwardly up, her skirt impeding her progress until Mr. Wesley pulled her over and helped her stand. Drake followed just in time to see Sophia march up to Theodore. She shoved her wet hair from her face then planted fists on her hips.

"Why didn't you go after me? A fiancé would jump into fire for the woman he loved."

"This suit cost a fortune, Sophia. You're being unreasonable. Did you hit your head?" His brow furrowed.

"I did not hit my head, but it's definitely time I came to my senses."

"A selection of women's clothing is in the cabin," Drake said, stepping between them. "Why don't you go change and continue this conversation later?"

She directed her gaze to him. "Why do you have women's clothing?"

He grinned. "I have women's, men's, and children's for such an occasion as this. Nothing fancy, but it's dry."

"Very well." Head high, she marched into the cabin, Mrs. Wesley on her heels.

Drake shot Theodore a hard glance. "You should have jumped in after her."

"You're the captain and responsible for the safety of your passengers." He flicked a speck of lint from his shoulder.

"You aren't worthy of that woman. At least you had the sense to stop the boat after I jumped in."

"Of course I would. I did own it once, if you recall." He shook his head and took a seat.

The man was utterly clueless and the most self-centered person Drake had ever met. He caught Mr. Wesley's thoughtful gaze. The man glanced at the cabin, to Theodore, then to Drake, a knowing light coming to his face. He smiled and nodded before sitting next to his children.

When Sophia emerged in a yellow dress two sizes too big for her, she marched past Theodore and took a seat as far away from him as she could. Every attempt by the man to draw her into conversation was met with stony silence.

Drake grinned and steered the yacht toward shore and the impending conversation with Sophia. He pulled the vessel up to the dock, where Theodore jumped out and secured the boat to keep it from floating away.

He held up a hand to help Sophia.

She slapped it away. "Let me be."

"But darling—"

"Don't 'darling' me." She turned to Drake. "What did you want to tell me?"

"You want to talk now? Here?" His eyes widened, and he motioned his head to where the others stood, curiosity on their faces.

"Come, dear." Mr. Wesley grinned at Drake then led his family away. "You too, Theodore."

"I do believe I'll stay." Theodore's face darkened. "Please continue, Mr. Moreland. I'm anxious to hear what you have to say to my betrothed."

Sophia stomped her foot and stared at him. "Enough is enough. I'm not going to marry you, Theodore." She exhaled slowly. "What a weight has been lifted from my shoulders."

"What?!" His face darkened. "Explain yourself."

"I wanted to tell you, but Mr. Wesley asked me to wait because of social obligations. I'm sorry, but my heart belongs to another."

Drake took her hands in his. "Whose heart, Sophia," he asked, huskily. Dare he hope?

"You, you silly, stubborn, clearly clueless man." She cupped his cheek. "Couldn't you tell?"

"You didn't like my goals. . . . You said you'd miss me."

"I wanted you to stop me from leaving." Tears ran down her cheeks. "I wanted God to tell you I was made for you."

"Excuse me." Theodore knocked on the hull. "Have you forgotten I'm here? I demand an explanation."

"There's nothing to say." Sophia kept her soft gaze on Drake's. "I am staying on the island whether this man will have me or not."

"Go away, Theodore." Drake pulled Sophia into his arms. "I'm about to kiss this woman. Something I've wanted to do for a very long time."

Footsteps pounded away as he lowered his head and claimed Sophia's lips. She tasted as sweet as the sugar he'd put in her tea and felt as soft as the lake water on his skin. He pulled her closer and deepened the kiss until they were both breathless. He lifted his head. "Will you marry me? Right now, I have nothing more to offer you than this yacht. I live here, but I'll get us a place soon—"

This time it was her finger on his lips. "Hush, silly. I'd live on the beach if it meant living with you. Yes, I'll marry you."

Epilogue

Three months later

I cannot believe you're having the wedding ceremony at the carousel," Sophia's mother said. "Why, all of society has left the island. It's growing cold. And living on the yacht. . ."

"Drake has found us one of the cottages, Mother." Sophia took her mother's hands in hers. "I'm happy."

With a sigh, her mother nodded. "I can see that, and you are lovely." She turned Sophia to see her reflection in the mirror.

Her mother's wedding dress, modified to fit Sophia's thin frame, fell in cascades of silk and ruffles. The veil shimmered against Sophia's dark updo. "I feel like a princess."

A knock on the door drew their attention. Sophia's father entered, a grin across his face. "You're the prettiest bride this island has ever seen." He handed Sophia a jeweler's box. "A gift from your mother and me."

Sophia opened it to reveal a diamond bracelet. "Oh Father,

can you afford this?"

"Theodore might not be the husband you wanted, but he is a shrewd businessman and kept up his part of the bargain in letting me oversee some of his investments. We can afford it."

"So that's why he wanted to marry me?" Her eyes widened.

"Are you angry?" Her mother frowned.

"I should be, I suppose, but no. I have found the man God planned for me. If I hadn't taken the job as nanny for the Wesleys, I wouldn't have come to this island and met this wonderful man." Thank goodness she'd realized what a mistake marrying Theodore would have been and waited for Drake to receive God's nudge. Sophia smiled and held out her hand. "Will you fasten it for me?"

Her father clasped the bracelet on her wrist. "Are you ready?" He crooked his arm.

"More than ready."

He led her and her mother to a waiting carriage. A brisk breeze sent shivers down Sophia's spine, but the warmth of her love for Drake would keep her from being too cold. Still, her mother draped a white wool shawl around her shoulders.

With a flick of his wrist, her father drove them to the carousel, where a crowd of islanders smiled and waved. Sophia stood, trying to catch a glimpse of her groom.

"Sit down, dear. He'll be waiting at the front of that throng." Her mother patted her arm before letting Sophia's father help her out of the carriage.

While Sophia was helped down, her mother strolled to the front of the crowd. A violin began the wedding march. Sophia took a deep breath and moved toward her husband-to-be.

Drake stepped into sight, handsome in a dark suit. "You look beautiful."

"You aren't so homely yourself." She smiled then turned to the pastor.

"Dearly beloved. . ."

She barely heard the words, so focused was she on Drake. When the pastor pronounced them man and wife, she closed her eyes as Drake lifted her veil and gave her his first kiss as her husband. Amid cheers and yells, he led her to the carousel and lifted her onto a white horse.

He climbed onto the one beside her and motioned for the operator to send the ride in motion. Then he leaned over and gave her a second kiss as her husband.

"I love you, Mrs. Moreland."

"I love you, Mr. Moreland. Thank you for finally coming to your senses and asking me to marry you."

He laughed. "I can't wait to spend the rest of my life with a woman who always has to have the last word."

She joined in with his laughter and pretended to seal her lips with a key that she tossed over her shoulder.

Dear Reader,

Oak Bluffs in Martha's Vineyard is home to one of the world's oldest carousels. Only two of the ones crafted by Charles Dare are thought to be in existence today, and this is one of them. Hand carved with manes and tails of real horsehair and glass inserts for the eyes, the carousel drew visitors in droves. In 1870 when the carousel left Coney Island, Oak Bluffs was known as Cottage City because of the cottages that sprang up as a result of the Methodist meetings held on the island each summer.

I don't know whether they held races or hosted a fancy dinner, but from the research I've gathered, there were many opportunities for all social classes to mingle, the greatest being the Methodist meetings. Forgive my liberty in adding one more.

I've strived to insert as many historical facts as possible into this story of a place tourists once flocked to in the summer—and still do. I may have taken a few liberties for the sake of the story, but the carved horses and carousel are as true to fact as I could make them. So are the meetings, which would mark the end of the summer season with much fanfare and draw crowds of thirty thousand.

God bless,
Cynthia Hickey

Cynthia Hickey grew up in a family of storytellers and moved around the country a lot as an army brat. Her desire is to write about real but flawed characters in a wholesome way that her seven children and nine grandchildren can all be proud of. She and her husband live in Arizona where Cynthia is a full-time writer.

The Art of Romance

Patty Smith Hall

To the editors at Barbour who work hard at
making me a better writer. God bless you!

Chapter 1

Riverside, Rhode Island
1895

J ane, you must remove every speck of dust from the carving's surface or it will delay the painting."

"Yes, Papa." Pressing her lips together, Jane Wells picked up a clean rag and wiped it across the surface of the carousel horse's engraved ribbons. Preparation may be as important as the actual painting, but she'd been at work on this carving for three days! At this rate, they'd never finish. Finally, she couldn't hold in the words any longer. "Why exactly did you take this job, Papa, when all you seem to do is complain about it?"

J.T. Wells stepped out of the shadows, the briefest hesitation in his steps a reminder of the stroke he'd suffered two years ago. She had almost lost him then, and in some ways she had. Gone was the loving man who'd raised her after her mother had died. In his place was a man filled with bitterness at his plight, as if he blamed God Himself for the stroke that had crippled him.

"Of course I couldn't turn it down. When someone the caliber of Charles Looff offers you the chance to paint one of his world-renowned carousels, you seize it." He puffed out his chest, his face a purplish shade of red. "This carousel will seal my legacy."

Jane dropped the cloth around the wooden stallion's neck and hurried over to her papa. "Calm down. You're going to put yourself in bed if you don't take it easy."

He glared at her. "Then don't ask such stupid questions."

She nodded, the familiar ache settling under her rib cage. He couldn't help his outbursts. The doctors had told her as much. Still, the knowledge didn't stop his words from hurting her.

"I'm sorry, Papa." Jane took his good arm and led him to a row of benches nearby. "I'm just a bit frustrated with our progress."

"True genius takes time, my dear. These horses must be our very best work."

"Of course." She helped him get settled then turned back to her work.

Grabbing the rag once more, she focused on the rivets along the saddle. What must it be like never to be able to paint again? She glanced back at her father. He'd been so talented in his youth, painting portraits for the wealthiest families in New York. Then he'd seen his first carousel and knew his true calling.

She walked a short distance and shook out her rag. Tiny particles of dust floated in the air. Would she ever be free to be known as a carousel painter in her own right? To build a career of her own? Or was God punishing her for their deception?

Tossing the towels to the side, Jane walked over to the horse. "Mr. Looff has outdone himself this time. The details on this stallion are remarkable."

"I wouldn't expect anything less from a master craftsman."

Her father pushed forward with his good arm to get a better look. "But I have to agree with you, Jane. He's created a masterpiece this time."

She drew in a shallow breath, dreading her next question. "Will you be painting today?" She didn't like to push, but the doctors had advised her to do so. It might be the only way to get him back to work.

"Why would you ask me that?" His voice held a sharp edge of bitterness.

"I thought you might like to. Doctor Morgan said—"

"I don't care what that man says." He lifted his affected hand slowly to his lap. His fingers, once so nimble, were drawn in toward the palm of his hand. "I will never paint again."

She sat next to him. "But Papa, you might discover that you can if you just try."

"So everyone will realize I'm an invalid?" He shrugged away from her. "I could paint circles around you in my day."

Another blow to her battered heart. She stood and walked back to the carving. "All right then. I'd better get some work done or Mr. Looff will be none too pleased with us."

Jane was in the middle of arranging her brushes when Papa called out, "You know I didn't mean that, Jane dear. You're so talented in your own right, and I'm. . ." He fell back against the bench. "I don't know what I am anymore."

Her heart ached for him. "It's all right. I'd probably feel the same way if I were you. Now why don't you get comfortable and help me pick out the colors for this fine stallion. Bold colors, I think. Maybe a turquoise blue to set off his fine black mane?"

"Very well." He shifted to his side, leaning to get a better look. "He'll see more of this world than I will in the years to come."

"But think of all you've already seen and done."

"I know." He released a heavy sigh. "Still, it feels awkward to watch the world leave me behind."

"Yes." She understood. Jane had put everything she'd hoped for herself—her schooling, the possibility of a husband and children—on hold. Now, years later, she had no regrets. Well, she conceded, there was one.

There was a knock at the door. "J.T.?"

Mr. Looff. But they weren't expecting him today. Jane turned to her father and whispered, "Why is he here?"

He shrugged one shoulder. "It is the man's building. I suppose he can visit anytime he wants."

Maybe, but this wasn't a good time, not with Papa moving slower than normal today. If they were to keep up the illusion, she would have to act quickly. Hurrying over to the bench, she helped her father to his feet, brushed a kiss against his cheek, then hurried back to where the horse stood. By the time Papa reached the door, she was scrubbing the intricate patterns on the animal's head.

"Charles, to what do we owe this pleasure?" Papa's voice boomed throughout the empty shell of the hippodrome where the carousel was housed. "I thought you were in New York this week."

"We cut our visit short." Charles Looff walked into the room, his gaze taking in everything from the cut-glass windows to the multicolored tapestry on the walls. "One of the children caught a cold, and my wife thought it best to come home." Jane felt the man's gaze turn to her. "How is the work coming along?"

"Splendidly," Papa boasted. "Jane finally wiped the last speck of dust from that magnificent stallion you created, and we were deciding on colors when you arrived."

"It has taken longer than expected to prepare the horse, hasn't it?"

"Yes, but even the smallest speck of dust can effectively ruin a masterpiece." Papa paused for a long moment. "You wouldn't want that."

"No." Looff lowered his voice but not enough to keep Jane from hearing. "You know the importance of this project, J.T., and while it's admirable that you're training your daughter to follow in your footsteps, I can't help but wonder if she's up to the task."

Heat flooded Jane's face. Of course the man would question her abilities. She would too if the shoe were on the other foot. But then, Charles Looff likely wouldn't lie as she and her father had these past two years, pretending she was an apprentice when in truth she was doing all the work. Not that the craftsman would ever learn the truth if she could help it. She stole a glance at her father. Papa's reputation was all he had left, and she would do anything in her power to protect it. Still, it would be nice to be recognized for her own work.

"I completely understand your concerns, but let me assure you, all the real work will fall to me."

Jane grimaced. How did Papa do it? How could he be so blatantly deceptive to the man's face? Even now, two years later, she choked on the words. How had their lives come to this?

"I would hope I'd do the same for my daughters, though I'm relatively certain none of them want to learn how to carve wooden animals." Looff hesitated for an uncomfortable moment. "But I won't pay her, as she is still just an apprentice."

"Of course not." Papa shook his head. "I wouldn't dream of asking you."

Maybe Papa wouldn't, but Jane would. And why shouldn't she? She worked hard, sometimes twelve or thirteen hours a day, painting in a room with little ventilation and only her father to talk to on the days he decided to join her. How could she plan for a future without funds of her own?

"I dropped by to tell you there's a newspaper reporter I'd like you to meet who is interested in writing an article about the carousel." There was a smile in the man's voice. "I've known the young man all of his life and think he'll do a fine job of it. Of course, it would be beneficial to the both of us, J.T."

A reporter? Dear heavens. That's all they needed at the moment. It was difficult enough keeping Papa's disability a secret without some nosy reporter prying into their personal business. The results of such an interview could prove disastrous.

Her father glanced at her, hope in his pale gray eyes. He used to thrive off a good discussion with a reporter, but there was too much at risk now. She shook her head slightly.

Disappointment clouded his expression as he turned back to Mr. Looff. "I'm sorry, Charles, but a reporter right now would be too much of a distraction. I need to focus on producing the most beautiful carousel the world has ever seen."

"Understandable," Looff replied. "I myself don't particularly care for reporters, but I do know one or two I can trust. And they do have some worth. Think of all the business such an article would generate." He broke into a smile. "We'd have more work than we'd know what to do with."

Exactly what Jane feared. It was one thing to help her father reach retirement and secure his reputation but quite another to commit to their deception years in advance. No, she could barely stomach lying their way through this job. She gave another slight shake of her head at her father's pleading look.

Papa's mouth pursed in disappointment. "I'm sorry, Charles, but the answer is no."

Mr. Looff's gaze slid to her then back to Papa. Had he seen her shake her head? Possibly. He probably thought she was just a spinster busybody her father should ignore. Jane lifted her chin. Well, she didn't care what the man thought. Papa and his reputation were her only concerns.

Which led her to ask the man a question. "Mr. Looff, have you given any more consideration to hiring an assistant for my father?"

"Aren't you his assistant?"

Jane glanced at her father. She had tried to talk him out of such a cockamamy idea, but he was determined. All great artists asked for assistants. She doubted Looff would hire one, but this was one thing she could do for Papa. "I am, sir, but in order to mix the paint properly, I need—" She caught herself. "I mean we need someone who can lift the barrels easily. Neither I nor my father can accomplish that."

"Blast it all," Looff whispered under his breath. "Fine then, I'll figure out something. When will you start the actual painting?"

Jane glanced around. "Two, three days at the most."

He waved his hand. "Fine. I'll think about it and get back with you."

"Thank you." With that piece of business done and with no reporter to contend with, Jane grabbed her dustrag and went back to work. The sooner her father could retire and they could stop lying, the better for everyone.

Chapter 2

I'm sorry, Thomas. I know you were counting on an interview with Mr. Wells, but he won't agree to it." Mr. Looff took his place behind the large mahogany desk in his library. "I want to help you, and I see how such an article would promote my new carousel, but I can't force the man to do it."

Thomas West sank down into the Queen Anne chair, his hopes of landing the coveted reporter position at the *East Providence Examiner* fading quickly. "Did he give you a reason why?"

Looff sat back in his seat, drumming his fingers against the padded armrest. "Oh, he made up some excuse about needing to focus."

Understandable, Thomas surmised. Everyone in Riverside knew Looff's latest carousel was intended to be the climax of J.T. Wells's life's work. He just figured after two years of silence the man would want to talk. It had been a long shot, he knew. A chance to finally put his journalism degree to use. Thomas glanced down at his ink-stained cuticles. No matter what happened today, he refused to run the printing press another minute.

"There is something that frustrates me," Mr. Looff said. "I can't swear by it, but it seems to me that Wells's daughter might have something to do with his decision."

A daughter? Thomas sat up a bit straighter. He hadn't come across anything about a daughter in his research of the man.

Mr. Looff steepled his fingers. "Miss Jane Wells. Her father is teaching her the craft of painting carousel horses." His forehead wrinkled in thought. "Though I've seen her working on my carvings more than J.T."

That was strange. From everything Thomas had read about the man, Wells enjoyed the solitude of his work. "Are you concerned he won't do a good job on your carousel horses?"

"No." Looff shook his head. "But there's more to this situation that I don't understand."

"What do you mean?"

"Well. . ." He paused, almost as if wondering if he was betraying a friend, then continued. "When I asked J.T. about having you interview him this afternoon, he looked at his daughter as if he couldn't make the decision for himself."

"Mother does that with me sometimes when she wants my opinion."

"Yes, but you're the man of the house. Of course your mother would seek your advice." Mr. Looff sat up in his chair. "But asking a daughter? That's the silliest thing I've ever heard of."

Thomas smiled. The man might think differently were he to visit their home. Since his father's death fifteen years ago, his mother, God bless her, had ruled her home with a firm but loving hand. But there was no sense correcting the man. He was from the old country where men were men and women had no say.

Mr. Looff gave Thomas a weak smile. "Still, it would have been nice to have someone working with J.T. every day who could shed some light on this puzzle."

"It would have been a great help to me too." Disappointment seeped into Thomas's voice, and he admonished himself. The Looffs had treated each member of Thomas's family as one of theirs since his mother joined their house staff soon after his father's death. While others less fortunate had wanted for food and clothing, his mother's job had provided more than enough for her family. When Thomas graduated with honors from high school, Looff sent him to college alongside his own sons.

Yet what did he have to show for all of his efforts? Five years typesetting the printing press at the *Examiner*. How would he ever repay Mr. Looff for the money the older man had invested in him?

He needed this interview not just to prove himself but to provide for his mother and sisters, and to pay back the kindness the Looffs had shown them.

Lord, please show me a way to do this. Open a door.

"And now Miss Wells is demanding an assistant for her father." The older man fell back in his chair. "I thought she was supposed to be his assistant, but no. Neither of them is capable of lifting the paint barrels."

Thomas had an idea, a brilliant idea. "I could."

Looff glanced over at him. "You could what?"

"Be the Wells's assistant."

Looff's brow furrowed. "Why would you want to do that?"

Thomas studied his mentor. In all the time he'd known the

man, he'd never known him to lie. But this wasn't lying as much as going undercover, was it? "To get my story."

"I don't know if I like the sound of that."

"It's not illegal." Unethical, perhaps, but every great newspaperman had gone undercover at least once in his career. Besides, Looff had questions the Wellses refused to answer. "What I'll do is go in to assist Mr. Wells each morning and find out exactly what they're hiding from you. And maybe, if I'm very fortunate, I'll get enough for my story."

Looff's gray brow arched up. "And just how do you propose to do that?"

"I don't know." Thomas drew a small pad of paper and a pencil from his jacket pocket. "Maybe if I knew a little bit about them, like what do they do when they're not here painting? Where are they staying while they're here?"

"They leased a cottage in town. I remember overhearing Miss Wells say something about being close to a doctor in case something happened." Looff shrugged. "Whatever that means."

Why would they need a doctor? Thomas wrote the question down with a space to answer it later. "What else can you tell me?"

"They work every day. They're at the hippodrome before I arrive in the morning and are still at work when I leave at night."

"And Miss Wells? Does she have a beau?"

Looff scoffed. "I seriously doubt it. She's pretty enough, mind you, but oh so serious. Her biggest priority seems to be her apprenticeship to her father." He shook his head. "I fear she doesn't have her father's talent."

"Does anyone else work at the hippodrome when the Wellses are there?"

"No. I had all the glasswork and tapestries in place before they started. Everything else is finished except for the carousel."

"So, the only other person working there will be the assistant." Thomas smiled. This was better than he'd expected. "What would I have to do as an assistant?"

"The biggest challenge is mixing the colors. We're painting over sixty horses, not counting coaches and chariots, and each must be unique in color and color combinations. Because of the vast amount of paint being used, it was delivered in large tubs that are difficult to carry." The older man leaned forward on his forearms. "Do you think you can do it?"

Shifting a few vats of paint? He'd done harder jobs at the newspaper. "Sounds fine to me."

"One more thing."

"What's that, Mr. Looff?"

"It's just a rumor really, but around two years ago, people noticed that J.T.'s work improved dramatically. He started using a more colorful palette. And, more significantly, he was capturing the essence of the animals." Looff paused as if gathering the right words. "There's no other way to explain it but to say that the horses' manes move with the light, almost as if they were real."

Thomas registered the awe in Looff's voice, as if the man truly believed Wells had brought the horses to life. Did he learn a new painting technique? What had happened two years ago that made J.T. the master he was today? And what part did his daughter play in all of this?

Chapter 3

The day had not started out as Jane had hoped. First, she'd woken up late, having worked at the kitchen table past midnight, writing out the paint combinations she wanted to use on the first six horses. Then there was no warm water for her to wash her face and hands. Then their cook, Grace Gentry, was out of sorts after an argument with her father, so Jane was left with a bowl of congealed oatmeal when all she really wanted was a strong cup of coffee and a hot-cross bun.

"Is there bread in the cupboard?" She wedged her spoon into the hardened oats. "I'd like to make some toast."

Grace jerked around, her wooden spoon pointed at her. "What's wrong with the oatmeal?"

Jane had enough of being yelled at by her father. Well, she was no child. She was mistress of this house until Papa decided to marry again. Holding on to the spoon, she picked the bowl up from the table. "I don't think it's edible, Grace."

"My stars! You can't eat that." The older woman stomped her foot. "I'm sorry, Jane. I don't know what's wrong with me this morning."

Pushing back from the table, Jane walked over to the garbage pail and raked the oatmeal from the bowl. "It's all right, Grace. I'm not hungry anyway. A strong cup of coffee will be just fine."

"That I have." Grace pulled two cups from the cupboard and poured steaming coffee into each before handing one to Jane. After adding milk and sugar to hers, she sat down across from Jane. "Maybe this is what I need to set me to rights this morning."

"Maybe." Jane dropped two sugar cubes into her own coffee then reached for the milk pitcher. "Has Papa already left for the hippodrome?"

"I haven't seen your father this morning," Grace said, then whispered against the rim of her cup. "Nor do I want to."

Hiding behind her coffee cup, Jane smiled. She'd long suspected Grace had tender feelings for her father, as he did for her. They were perfect for each other really. She loved to give him all the attention he wanted, and Papa respected her kindness and practicality. If only they both weren't so stubborn. "I heard you arguing again last night."

"We weren't arguing." She hesitated. "We were discussing."

Jane took a sip. "Rather loudly."

The cup clinked as Grace set it on her saucer. "That man just infuriates me sometimes."

Jane could empathize. "What was it last night?"

"He was complaining about something you were doing with the carvings, and I'd just had enough. I told him he should be grateful for your help, and if he didn't like what you did, he should do it himself."

Jane set down her cup and reached for the older woman's hand. "I'm sure he didn't like hearing that."

"No." Grace sniffed. "But how does he ever hope to recover if he won't even try? It's like he's giving up."

Jane had asked herself that question many times over the last two years with no answer in sight. But she couldn't give up hope. "I'm almost certain I saw him move his hand yesterday."

Grace's eyes widened. "You did? How? When?"

"I'd asked him if he was going to paint, and his fingers moved, almost as if he were holding a brush. I don't even think he realized he was doing it."

"But that's wonderful. That means—"

Jane shook her head. "We mustn't get our hopes up. Until Papa is ready to try again, we must let him move at his own pace."

"Of course." Grace's face was alight with joy. "Still, it's a start."

Yes, but whether her father would take advantage of it was yet to be seen. If only he'd put his anger away and try to heal. He may never be the painter he was before, but she and Grace didn't care. Having him back healthy and whole was enough.

Maybe then he and Grace would marry and she could. . . Biting the tip of her tongue, Jane winced. There was no use thinking about what might be, not yet. What was it that Pastor Kelly had said in his sermon last week? Oh yes, God has us where we are for a reason.

When will I get the chance to stand on my own two feet, Lord?

She waited for a moment then sighed. No answer. Well, she had more to think about than her situation. The first horse was ready for painting today. A flicker of nervous excitement coursed through her. Something about a paintbrush in her hand made her come alive.

Jane took one last sip then rose from the table. "I'd better hurry. Papa will be—"

The sound of shuffling behind her interrupted her. Grace glanced up then flew out of her chair, almost tripping over her feet. "John?"

Jane turned, her heart lodging in her throat when she saw her father. He was pale, his hair disheveled, the slight limp in his right leg more pronounced. The corner of his mouth drooped as if the thin threads that held up his smile had been severed. His right arm hung awkwardly, the movement Jane had seen just yesterday undetectable.

Grace wrapped his good arm over her shoulders and helped him to the table. "Are you hurting, my dear?"

"No." The word slurred past his lips.

A heavy weight bore down on Jane. One step forward, two steps back, the doctors had warned her. If only. . .what? She didn't have time for "if onlys."

"We need to go for a doctor," Grace said as she settled Papa into a chair. "I can go."

"I'll go by on my way to the hippodrome." Jane grabbed her hat and reticule from the table. "I'll be back as soon as I tell Mr. Looff we can't work today."

"You have to." Papa managed to rasp out, his good arm flailing about. "Money." He puckered his lips as best he could. "Reputation."

"But Papa," Jane started then noticed the wild look in his eyes. She drew in a deep breath. She hated dishonesty of any kind, yet she'd lied these past two years to protect her father. She bent down to meet her father's gaze. "Why don't I tell Mr. Looff the truth? That you've had a brain seizure that has weakened your hand and I've been painting in your place for the last two years?"

"Forbid!" Papa's body shook wildly, yet his voice rattled the cupboards.

"Jane, please," Grace begged. She knelt beside Papa, holding his face in her hands. "John, you have to calm down or you'll have another attack even worse than the last."

But Papa wouldn't stop. "No. No. No."

She was so tired of battling with him. "All right, Papa. I won't tell Mr. Looff the truth." But one day the truth would come out, and what then? Any hope of salvaging their reputations would be destroyed.

She looked at the timepiece pinned to her bodice. Eight o'clock. She'd have to hurry if she hoped to catch the doctor before he left on his rounds. Pinning her hat into place, she turned to Grace. "Could you send me a note once the doctor has been here?"

"Yes." Grace filled a spoon with coffee and gave it to Papa. "What about the bill?"

"I'll take care of it." Though how, Jane pondered, was anyone's guess.

"I can send a note to the doctor if it's too much trouble to stop by to see him. You're just so busy." Grace's worried eyes peered up at her.

Jane shook her head. "No. The walk through town will give me time to come up with an excuse for Mr. Looff."

"Tell him the carvings need further preparation so there's no need for your father to be there today."

That would make Jane appear incompetent. Yet it couldn't be helped. She kissed Papa's cheek then gave Grace what she hoped was an encouraging smile before hurrying out the back door.

Once she was down the sidewalk, Jane stopped, her shoulders slumping under the weight of their circumstances. Another setback. How much more could Papa bear?

And what excuse would she give Mr. Looff? Certainly not that story about further preparation. The man would question why her father hired her on as an apprentice. So what could she tell him?

The hippodrome was within her view before she came up with a plan. As no two horses could be identical, each paint color had to be individually mixed. Using the color chart she'd designed last night, she would begin mixing the paints today. It would be difficult. The barrels were particularly hard to maneuver, and it might take her most of the day, but she could do it.

As she walked into the courtyard where the carousel was housed, a man about her age was leaning against the railing closest to the door. Even bent down as he was, there was an easy grace about him, his gray pinstriped suit complimenting his wide shoulders. He wore his bowler low on his brow as if to shield his eyes from the sun. His chest moved in a slow rhythm, steady and peaceful.

Maybe he was a beggar. Jane chided herself. How many beggars wore nice three-piece suits? Whoever he was, she didn't want to disturb him.

Quietly, she walked to the door and put her key into the lock. "Miss Wells?"

The key slipped out of Jane's fingers, making a soft ping against the pavement.

"I'm so sorry." The man leaned down to retrieve the key. "I didn't mean to startle you."

132

Jane swallowed and backed up a step to put some space between them. "You didn't. Scare me, I mean. I thought you might be asleep, but who would nap up against a building?" Why was she babbling on as if she didn't have an ounce of sense in her head? "What I mean is yes, I'm Miss Wells."

He took off his hat, and she wondered at the golds and warm browns that made up his thick shock of hair. His gaze met hers, and her breath caught in her lungs at his cocoa-colored eyes. "Thomas West at your service, ma'am."

Breathe, you ninny! "Nice to meet you, Mr. West."

He placed his bowler back on his head. "You too."

"Do we have an appointment?"

"I take it Mr. Looff hasn't been in touch with you."

Mr. Looff? Oh dear, he hadn't arranged a surprise interview with a reporter, had he? "I'm sorry. My father is under the weather today, so if you'll excuse me, I have work to do."

"That's why I'm here." One side of his mouth lifted into a crooked smile. "I'm your new assistant."

Oh rats! She never expected Looff to actually hire an assistant. No one else had over the years. It had just become one of her father's unfulfilled demands. "Mr. Looff didn't tell us."

"He must have figured my appearance today would serve as an announcement."

"I guess." But Mr. West didn't quite fit her image of an assistant. For one, he dressed better than she'd expect from someone who lugged barrels of paint around for a living. Not that it mattered. As long as he could lift, she shouldn't care whether he'd graduated college or sixth grade. Yet she couldn't stop herself. "Where did you study?"

His brows rose slightly, as if her question caught him off guard.

"Syracuse. Class of '92."

Good heavens, he might as well be an Ivy Leaguer. Jane's suspicions flared. "Why would a Syracuse man take a position as a painter's assistant?"

He chuckled, a melodious sound that caused a lovely shiver down her spine. "I guess you could say I'm suffering for my art."

Jane perked up. "You have an art degree?"

"A bachelor of arts." He glanced around, then shoving the key into the lock, he turned it and opened the door. "Are you all right? You look a bit flushed."

"It must have been the walk." Jane felt warm even though a refreshing breeze was coming off the Providence River. Maybe she should have seen the doctor too. There could be something going around.

Jane stepped inside and turned on the electric lights. The soft glow made the colored sandwich glass windows twinkle as if touched by tiny rays of sunshine. Beautiful surroundings for the carousel she'd planned but difficult to work in. "Could you get two of those lanterns and bring them closer to the horses?"

"Of course."

Unpinning her hat, she set it and her reticule on a nearby bench then looked around. "Where's the key?"

Holding two lanterns in one hand, Mr. West held it up with the other. "I have it. Remember?"

Of course, he has it, you ninny. He opened the door for you. Jane's cheeks flushed with heat. Papa's condition must worry her more than she realized.

He set down the lanterns then handed her the key.

"Thank you."

He smiled, one that reached his eyes. "You're welcome."

Jane's stomach did a funny little flip as he gave her a slight nod then stepped away to place his hat on the bench behind her. She hurried to her workstation to gather her apron. Then, thinking about Mr. West's suit, she retrieved another one. Walking back to him, she held it out. "You're going to need this."

He stared at the bleached linen. "Why?"

Was he serious? She shook it at him. "Unless you want to get paint all over your nice clean suit, I'd suggest you wear it."

Instead of taking it, he simply stood there. "I'm not the apron type."

Jane blinked. "But your clothes. . ."

He glanced down then back at her, a crooked grin tugging at one corner of his mouth again. "Better my clothes than that thing." He grimaced. "It's got ruffles."

"Well, yes. That's because it's mine."

"I'm certain it looks fetching on you, but me?" He shook his head, shucking off his suit coat and laying it beside his hat. "No thanks."

"Suit yourself." Jane returned the apron to its place. What had possessed Mr. Looff to hire this man? Maybe he had seen something in Mr. West, a spark of mad genius that would account for his unreasonable response to the apron. If only Papa were here to meet their new assistant. He'd know how to size up the man.

"Where is Mr. Wells?"

Of course, the man would want to know where her father was. It was probably the very reason he'd applied for this position in the first place. How would he respond if she told him the truth, that for all practical purposes, she was J.T. Wells? Jane pulled the apron's strings tight around her waist. "Papa is under the weather today, so it'll just be the two of us working."

"I hope it's nothing serious."

She glanced down at her watch. The doctor should be at the cottage by now. Hopefully the news would be good and she could stop worrying. For now, there was work to be done. "Let's get started."

Chapter 4

Jane Wells wasn't anything like he'd expected.

Not that Thomas had had any concrete expectations. Mr. Looff had been brief in his description of Jane. Mousy, hardworking, bossy where her father was concerned. Not the talent J.T. was.

Yet Thomas sensed there was more to Jane than met the eye. He followed her across the room to where dozens of large canisters sat neatly stacked against the wall. Miss Wells studied the piece of paper she'd pulled from her pocket then walked closer to the barrels, reading the labels on each container.

Thomas's interest was piqued. "What are you doing?"

"Looking for white paint." She moved on to the next barrel.

"Why?"

"To use as a base." She straightened, her gray eyes wide with bewilderment. "Any freshman art student would know that."

How did he respond to that? The closest he'd been to an art class was the article he'd written about a local museum. "It's been a long time since my freshman year."

He half expected Miss Wells to *humph* at him, but her lips twitched, and he caught a brief hint of a smile. "Well, I start with a white base then mix in the colors until I get just the right hue for each horse."

"How many horses are on the carousel?"

"Sixty-one." Jane shifted through the smaller pots until she apparently found the one she wanted. "There are also two giraffes, two carriages, and two chariots."

"Sounds like a great deal of work."

She turned her cool gaze on him. "If you're not up to the task. . ."

Thomas shook his head. He had expected to work with the father, but maybe this was better. Getting information from Miss Wells would be far easier. He rolled up his shirt sleeves. "Just tell me what needs to be done, Miss Wells."

She pointed to a stack of blankets. "Lay those down beneath and around the carvings. We don't want to get paint on the floor."

"You seem to know what you're doing." The wool blankets scratched Thomas's arms as he carried them to where the horses stood. "How long have you been an apprentice to your father?"

Miss Wells took one of the blankets from him and spread it out on the floor. "I've always helped Papa with his work, but I've been more involved the last two years."

"Why's that?"

One blond brow arched as she studied him. "Do you always ask so many questions?"

He shrugged. "If you don't ask, you won't learn."

Her brows knitted together as she gave that some thought. "I've never thought of it that way. But then, I never went to college."

"You didn't?" The expression on her face, one he'd seen in the mirror whenever he'd doubted himself, tore through him. "I mean, college is nothing compared to real life experience."

"I've had plenty of that," she muttered under her breath as she moved to the next canister.

Exactly what had she meant by that? Thomas watched her as she went from one wooden container to the next. Jane Wells didn't look old enough to have much life experience, but there was something about the way she carried herself, almost as if waiting for the other shoe to drop, that gave him pause. What had caused the anxiety inside her?

"Would you please stop staring at me?"

Thomas blinked. She was observant too. He would have to be on his guard. "Sorry about that. I like to study people."

"If you would move this over to the carvings." She pointed to a rather large barrel of what he supposed was white paint. As he leveraged it into his arms, she spoke again. "I study people too."

It was an innocent confession, yet for some strange reason, a sense of accomplishment flooded through him. Miss Wells didn't seem the sort to reveal many things about herself, but she had trusted him with this.

Securing the barrel in his grip, he followed her. "What is it about studying people that you like?"

She didn't answer right away. Instead, she laid out the brushes and smaller pails he assumed they would need today. By the time he pried off the last paint lid, his starched shirt was limp and soaked with sweat.

Miss Wells hadn't fared much better from their exertions. Thomas stole a glance at her. She continued working, though her face glistened with a fine sheen of perspiration and her cheeks glowed a lovely shade of pink. He found himself drawn to her, though he wasn't sure why.

Giving the brushes one final pat, she turned to him. "The horses need to be wiped down one last time to make certain I got every last speck of dust."

He frowned. "I don't understand. I thought we were just mixing paint."

"We are, but in order for us to know if we've combined the correct colors, we have to test them on the wood. Dust soaks up the paint and makes it clump together, so. . ." Her words drifted off.

"We have to dust the horses."

"Correct." She gave him a wide smile that did funny things to his heart. "Now, if you'll hand me one of those towels, we can get started."

Thomas picked up a couple of clean cloths he'd dropped next to the paint cans and handed one to her. He'd need to get Miss Wells talking if he wanted anything to report to his editor, but about what? Too many questions about her father might raise her suspicions. Maybe he should focus on her first. "Have you always wanted to paint?"

"Not always." She moved the toweling in long strokes up the animal's neck. "When I was a little girl, I wanted to be the president. Then I wanted to be a teacher or a professor." A chuckle escaped her lips. "I even toyed with writing one time but decided to leave that to Alcott and Twain." She glanced over her shoulder at him. "As I began working with my father, I learned about the seedier side of writing."

"The seedier side?"

"Newspaper reporters." There was a hint of bitterness in her voice that put Thomas on alert. "Those men don't think anyone deserves an ounce of privacy."

Which answered his question as to why she'd been so against an interview in the first place. He'd have to tread lightly if he had any hope of writing this article. Thomas wiped down the saddle. "You sound as if you've had experience with them."

"No."

It must be her father then. Thomas made a mental note to find out more about what happened. "So you decided to paint instead?"

She stopped and stared at him. "I've never met anyone so full of questions, Mr. West."

Maybe if he shared something about himself, Miss Wells would open up. Thomas flashed her an easy smile as he continued to work. "I've always been inquisitive."

He thought he saw a wisp of a smile. "Really? I couldn't tell."

Teasing, was she? That had to bode well for him. "My ma said I drove her crazy asking questions when I was a boy, but I couldn't help myself. I've always wanted to know how things work." He glanced over at her. "What about you? Did you ask your parents lot of questions?"

"Another question." But there was laughter in her voice this time. "I probably asked my fair share, but Papa never seemed to mind. It's just been me and Papa for years now." She scrubbed at the horse's withers. "Mama died when I was six."

"I'm so sorry." Then he added, "My pa died when I was nine."

"That must have been hard, being a boy and all."

"No different than you losing your mother, I'd suspect."

She gave a slight shrug. "Maybe."

He chuckled. "You're not much of a talker, are you?"

"No, I guess not." Thomas heard the smile in her voice. "I must not have much to say."

From where Thomas stood, she had more to say than she thought. "Everyone has an opinion, Miss Wells."

"True," she answered thoughtfully. "Yet most opinions are better kept to ourselves."

He couldn't help himself. He laughed. "I believe you have more sense than all the men in Washington DC combined."

She chuckled, a low, throaty sound that made him relax. Which was odd. He'd never had a woman as a friend. Most were too interested in marriage and babies. But with Jane Wells, it felt easy to slip into friendship. She was intelligent and had a sense of humor, with a quiet work ethic that did her proud. And it wasn't just that she was a means to an end. Strangely enough, he wanted her friendship.

A friendship he could keep until she found out the truth behind his presence here.

The thought sobered Thomas. Maybe it was for the best. Once he delivered this story to Mr. Delano, he wouldn't have time for anything but work.

Still, he liked knowing he could get Jane to talk. She would be quite an asset to his story. Thomas shifted sides so that he faced away from her. "So how long have you wanted to paint carousel horses?"

Their cloths brushing against the grain of the wood was the only sound in the hippodrome, and Thomas wondered if she'd finally had enough of his questions. But then she spoke in a low whisper as if meant only for her ears. Yet he'd heard her, and her answer startled him.

"Never."

Chapter 5

N ever."

The word was out of Jane's mouth before she could stop herself. Thomas West and his stupid questions. Why couldn't the man simply do the job he was being paid to do and leave her alone?

Grabbing a clean towel, she rubbed it roughly between her hands. It wasn't that she didn't like painting carousels. There was an excitement in making the wooden carvings come to life with just a stroke of her brush. To see her finished product and watch as children stepped onto the platform and carefully chose a horse brought her great joy.

But was it her calling? She thought so at times, even prayed about it. How was she to know for certain? Was it in her excitement of picking out paint choices or the satisfaction of seeing a horse finished? She wished she could ask Papa, but she couldn't share her feelings with him. She stole a glance at Thomas Wells. Then why, for heaven's sake, had she revealed herself to this man?

"What do you want to paint?"

Jane couldn't take any more of his questions. Best to set an example of their working relationship. "You are not paid to be nosy, but to assist me and my father."

He hesitated then gave her a brief nod. "Yes, ma'am."

Her shoulders slumped. She had given up the luxury of social etiquette long ago. The last two years had been devoted to caring for her father and saving his reputation. There was no time for frivolity, only the demands of work and Papa.

Why wouldn't her father be honest about their situation instead of demanding that she lie? Yet she couldn't fault him. What would she do if her body rebelled against her and she could no longer paint? To be denied the one thing that was so vital to her, it was like her next breath. No, she couldn't condemn her father. He was acting out of fear.

Why did You allow this to happen, Lord?

It wasn't the first time she'd asked the question, yet God had been annoyingly quiet on the subject. Dropping her dustcloths on a nearby bench, she walked to where Thomas had stacked the pails and reached for a container of navy blue. "I could use your help."

"Certainly." Throwing the towel over the carving's neck, Mr. West brushed his hands against his pants as he hurried toward her. "What do you need?"

She pointed to a medium-sized vat. "The one containing black."

"As you wish." He moved forward, lifting the heavy container as though it were a sack of feathers. The muscles of his shoulders bunched under his linen shirt, and Jane couldn't help but compare him to Da Vinci's sketches of the human body. If she were to paint Thomas, he would be Atlas, carrying the weight of the world on those strong, dependable shoulders.

"This is getting kind of heavy."

His statement jolted her out of her thoughts, and she pointed to the spot next to her brushes. "Beside the bench will be fine."

Jane followed him, her gaze trained on the floor. So the man was nicely built. She could probably walk down the streets of Riverside and see as much, not that she had ever noticed such a thing. Maybe her father wasn't the only one under the weather.

Once he set down the container, he went to work on opening the lid. "So your first horse is going to be black."

"Not just black," she scoffed. "A blue black the color of midnight."

"I didn't know midnight was a color."

He didn't know midnight was a. . . She glared at him. "How did you ever graduate with an art degree?"

"Ma prayed a lot." His deadpan answer almost made her laugh.

"She must have been in constant prayer."

His laughter sounded like tenor bells in her ears. "Are you questioning my education?"

"Not as much as I am your professors." She popped open the small vat's top to reveal a rich navy blue. "Didn't anyone tell you that everything is made up of color? Or is that something you just understand from life experiences?"

"Touché, Miss Wells." He winked at her. "What I meant was I've never heard anyone describe the night sky as a color. It's very. . .poetic. But why blue black?"

"Because I've found it gives the horse's mane movement."

He blinked, remembering what Mr. Looff had said. "But it's a carving."

Really, Mr. West was the most inexperienced artist she'd ever met. "And as an artist, it's my job to make the carving come alive, to make the observer feel like it's living, breathing flesh."

"You mean, it's your father's job."

This time she was confused. "I don't understand."

"You said it was your job, but really, it's your father's."

"Oh yes." Dear heavens, she'd been so distracted by him, she'd almost let the cat out of the bag. How could she recover without lying? "It's really a shared position. I paint the bodies of the horses while Papa puts on the finishing touches."

"Yet he gets all the credit for it."

Jane didn't answer him. What could she say? It was true. Papa felt he didn't owe Jane any credit. Not when she'd discovered how to make the wooden animals come alive, nor when he'd received critical acclaim for the technique. She would have her day, Papa often reminded her. Just not now.

She poured a small amount of the blue paint into a good-size pail. "Now, if you'll pour some of the black paint in here."

His arms tightened, muscles straining against the edge of his rolled-up sleeves as he tipped the barrel slightly. A rush of excitement ran through her. It was always this way when she began to mix the colors to the perfect shade. She didn't know if painting carousels was what God had called her to do, but it was still a blank slate, ready to be brought to life by the creativity He gave her. For the moment, that would have to be enough.

Mr. West set the barrel upright. "Is that enough to get started?"

She glanced into the bucket then back up at him. "You didn't fill it up."

"Is that not what you wanted?" Wiping his forehead with his bunched-up sleeve, he started to pick up the barrel again. "I figured you'd want some room."

Jane did, but it was her method of mixing equal parts of blue and black paint that gave the horses their midnight coloring. Her father thought it was wasteful, but the uneven coloring of horses painted first one color then the other bothered her artistic senses. Yet this man understood. Maybe he was a fellow artist like herself. "Yes, thank you."

He replaced the container's lid then tapped around the edges to secure it. "So navy blue mixed with black looks like midnight?"

Then again, maybe she was wrong. "Haven't you ever been outside and looked at the night sky?"

"Of course I have. I just haven't studied it like it sounds you have."

"Well, you're missing out. When there's not a cloud to be seen and all the stars in the heavens are twinkling, it's as if God is putting on a show just for you."

Mr. West's soft smile made her stomach flutter. "You turn a nice phrase, Miss Wells. I can understand why you considered being a writer."

For some strange reason, his compliment pleased her. "You know, if we're going to work together, you should really call me Jane."

He wiped his hand on his shirt then held it out to her. "Then, please, call me Thomas."

"All right, Thomas." She took his hand. He gave hers a gentle squeeze without crushing her fingers the way some men did. Unlike hers, his palms were calloused, his long fingers stained at the tips with patches of black. Indigo ink, Jane would guess. "Do you work in inks?"

He released her hand, wiping his against his pants as he hurried to retrieve her brushes. "Sometimes. But I'm not ready to show it to anyone yet." He eyed her with a wariness that she understood. It was always difficult to reveal a new piece, even to family and friends. What if they hated it? Or worse, to spare your feelings, told you it was brilliant?

"It must be wonderful to be able to draw. It's something I've always dreamed of doing."

Thomas's gaze caught hers, pinning her with his gentle intensity. "Is that what you'd rather do than paint carousels? You want to draw?"

Oh dear. In her excitement at discovering another artist, she'd forgotten about their circumstances and protecting her father. "I'm my father's apprentice, but I'd like to try my hand in other mediums."

"Oh." Something in his brief response didn't ease Jane's conscience. She hated this heavy cloud of deceit she was buried under, but what could she do? Not only would the truth ruin their reputations, but it might put her father's life in jeopardy. Jane thought back to this morning. One small disagreement had sent Papa to his bed and scared both the women who loved him. No, no matter how wrong it was, she must protect her father. Once this job was over, once Papa retired with his reputation intact, then and only then could she tell the truth.

As for Thomas, best to keep him busy answering her own questions. "I know you graduated with an art degree. What about your family?"

"Let's see." His face lit up with a smile. "There's my ma, Ellen.

She's worked for the Looffs as their housekeeper since my pa died. Then I have two younger sisters, Lilly and Rose. Lilly is a maid at the hotel in town, and Rose is a waitress at the Silver Spring House down by the shore."

"Do they have those seafood bakes I've heard so much about since we arrived?"

Thomas's chest puffed up with pride. "The best in Riverside. You should take your father there sometime."

If only she could, but Papa didn't like to stray too far from their cottage after work. Jane shook her head. "I don't think he'd like that." She pressed her lips together. "So you're the creative one in the family?"

"I don't know about that." He rubbed the back of his neck, and Jane couldn't help wondering if he felt as vulnerable as she did, always wondering when she'd be good enough for her father. She knew she was good, but his constant complaints about her work wreaked havoc on her confidence at times. He snapped the dusty rag in frustration. "As hard as I try, I can't seem to get a break."

Jane could sympathize with him. They had been fortunate Papa had always been able to make a good living, but that wasn't true for most artists. It must be especially hard for a man whose entire worth was based on the figures in his ledger. "Have you sold any of your work?"

"A few pieces, but nothing substantial." He straightened. "I'm hoping this leads to a more permanent position."

But there would be no position after this job, not even for her. "I'm sorry—"

He must have read her expression, because he interrupted. "Not with your father but someone else."

"I'm sure Mr. Looff—"

"Not him either, though he has already done a great deal for me, sending me to college." Thomas shook his head. "No, I want to be considered on my own merits, not some misguided sense of response." He smiled at her then. "We Wests might not have much, but what we do have, we've earned through hard work and the grace of God."

Her arms crossed over her waist, Jane couldn't help but admire Thomas's determination. He would need it to make his living in the art world. "It sounds like you're destined to make something of yourself, Mr. West."

"You think so, Miss Wells?"

Jane nodded, for once glad to be able to tell the truth. "I most certainly do."

Chapter 6

One week later

The note from Grace had a sense of urgency to it. Jane hurriedly locked up the hippodrome then turned, mapping out the fastest exit from the amusement park. Grace had been vague, only saying that the doctor had reexamined Papa, but that there was something they needed to discuss.

Lord, let it be good news for once.

What was Grace keeping from her? They had been so encouraged last week when the doctor had ruled out another stroke, believing Papa was merely exhausted and needed a few days in bed. Had he taken a turn for the worse? Was he. . . ?

She couldn't finish the thought. Instead, she picked up her skirts and broke into a run. Minutes later she collapsed against the kitchen door, gulping in lungfuls of air. She pushed the thick tangle of hair from her face, her pins scattered along the sandy path that led to their little seaside cottage.

Turning the handle, Jane pushed the door open. "Grace, where are you?"

The older woman bustled into the room, looking startled. "Jane, what are you doing home so early?" She stared. "Dear heavens, what happened to you?"

Pressing her hand to her side, Jane bent and drew in another deep heath. "I got your note and ran home."

"You did?" Grace took her hand and led her to the table. Once she had her settled, Grace set a kettle of water to boil then took the chair beside her. "Darling girl, I never meant to worry you. I'm sorry."

"It's not your fault. I obviously read more into your words than I should have." She took Grace's hand in hers. "So, what did the doctor say? How's Papa?"

Grace pushed a strand of hair behind her ear. "He's fine. Dr. Espy didn't find any reason to suspect that John had a stroke. In fact, he saw some signs of improvement."

"Thank God!" Jane touched her forehead against the cool surface of the oak table, her eyes burning with unshed tears. She sniffed then sat up and gave Grace a weak smile. "Your note was so serious. I thought something was wrong, especially when you said you needed to talk to me."

The kettle whistled, and for the next couple of minutes, both women prepared their cups of tea. As Jane added the last lump of sugar, Grace said, "Your father should talk to you, but I'm so excited, I'm fixing to burst."

Jane reached over and patted the housekeeper on the shoulder. "I don't know what it is, but you've got me excited."

"You've met Dr. Espy?"

Jane nodded. "He recently joined Dr. Morgan's practice."

"Yes, and such a smart fellow. He graduated from Harvard just a few years ago." Grace took a sip of her tea. "Anyway, he did a thorough exam of John and saw what you did. Your father can move his affected hand."

Joy welled in Jane's chest then as quickly dissipated. "What does that mean?"

"It means there's a chance he can recover enough to paint again."

"How?" She hated being the voice of reason, but someone had to be. "It's taken him two years to move his fingers."

"Yes, but Dr. Espy has a plan." Grace traced the outline of her teaspoon. "He knows of exercises and techniques that have been proven to help stroke victims regain the strength they lost."

"Why have we never heard of this? We would have certainly tried it if we thought it would help him."

"It's relatively new, but Dr. Espy says the research is interesting."

If it worked, it would give them the miracle they'd never expected. Papa might even paint again. Oh, what that would mean to him! Jane sniffed back the tears. "What did Papa say?"

Grace bit her lip, but her eyes were alight with laughter. "John was so excited. I thought he'd jump out of bed and dance a jig." She hesitated, her cheeks turning a lovely shade of pink. "He asked me to marry him."

"Grace! How? When?" Laughter bubbled up, filling the space between them. She leaned over and threw her arms around her dear friend. "I knew it was only a matter of time before he asked you."

The older woman sat back, blotting her eyes with the hem of her apron. "I'd begun to wonder if he would ever ask me."

"Oh, I knew he would." Jane sniffed again, overcome with happiness for Papa and his bride-to-be. "Papa may not show it, but he knows how blessed he is to have you in his life."

Grace giggled. "I can hardly believe it's really going to happen. Your papa wants to be married before we leave for the sanatorium."

What? "A sanatorium?"

"Dr. Espy recommended one in Flagstaff that specializes in helping people who've suffered from brain seizures."

Flagstaff? Arizona? But that was halfway across the country. It might as well be on the other side of the world. What about their contract with Mr. Looff? Was Papa finally ready to tell him the truth, that it was Jane who'd painted the carousels for the last two years?

The thought was a welcome relief. "When is Papa going to talk to Mr. Looff?"

Grace stared down at the tabletop, her lips pressed into a thin line. "I've tried to talk to him about this, but he's stubborn, you know." She reached over and took Jane's hand. "He feels that you've done such a wonderful job these last two years, he sees no reason for you to stop now."

"But Grace. . ." There were dozens of reasons, the most important being that she had been forced to lie. If she continued painting the carousel after her father left, then the world would know the truth. What about her hopes and dreams? They would be lost once people learned of her deception. Her reputation would be ruined.

Yet this might be Papa's only hope of regaining the life he'd lost. Was she that selfish to take it from him? No, she'd do whatever it took to help him. Jane gave Grace's hand a squeeze. "Have you given any thought about what you're going to wear to your wedding?"

"Oh Jane." Grace leaned over and kissed Jane on the cheek. "I know you hate this lying business as much as I do, but I fear if we don't go along with it, he'll take a turn for the worse."

"I know," Jane said. "It's why I've gone along with him these last two years." She sighed then slumped back in her chair. "I just hope Mr. Looff doesn't start asking questions."

"We're leaving you to deal with a mess, aren't we?"

They were, but what could Jane say? For the first time since the stroke, there was hope. And if by some miracle Papa regained the ability to paint, he would need Mr. Looff's commendation. All she had to do was finish this project.

Then she could begin her life anew.

Jane plastered a smile on her face. "When do you need to leave?"

"This Friday. John is scheduled to check in by Wednesday of next week."

Jane thought back over the note Grace had sent her. What had there been to talk about? Papa had already made up his mind without asking her opinion or discussing how to handle Mr. Looff. He just expected her to accept his decision.

"We don't have to do this now," Grace said, as if reading her thoughts. "We could wait for an appointment, but from what Dr. Espy said, it could be up to a year. The only reason your father is getting in now is that Dr. Espy learned of a cancellation just this morning."

Jane shook her head. "This may be Papa's only chance, and if we don't take it, we'll regret it for the rest of our lives."

"But the contract—" Grace started.

"I'll handle it."

"You're a good daughter, Jane."

No she wasn't. She had her own reasons for wanting Papa

to recover. First and foremost so that she could stop lying to everyone.

Thomas's face flashed through her mind. In the short time she'd known him, he'd made quite an impression on her with his outspoken and honest views. He worked hard yet still found time to make her laugh. And he loved his family. Although she'd only known him for a week, she had quickly come to view him as one of the few people she could call her friend.

What would he say when he learned of her deception?

"I couldn't be prouder if you were me own son." Edwin McDaniel beamed as he handed Thomas his pay envelope. "I only wish you could write your articles and then come down here and typeset them yourself."

Thomas chuckled along with the man. A bruising Scot, McDaniel had been a champion prizefighter before settling down into marriage and the stability of running the printing press for the *Providence Examiner*. "I don't think Mr. Delano would take too kindly to that."

"As if the man takes kindly to anything," McDaniel scoffed. "If he had any sense in that educated brain of his, he would've hired you as a reporter when you graduated college."

"I don't fault him for that." Thomas glanced around, the smell of fresh paper and ink filling his nostrils. The clinking of the metal letters as the typesetter set the page filled him with a sense of excitement. One day soon, it would be his writing being set.

Thomas offered his hand to McDaniel. "Ed, I've learned a lot about the newspaper business from you. Thank you."

" 'Tis nothing I did." The old Scot's face turned ruddy. "You were a fast learner, boy. One of the best. And now ye're moving up."

Thomas gave him an uncomfortable smile. He hadn't told the brawny man about the deal he'd made with Mr. Delano. If, and only if, Thomas secured an interview with the elusive J.T. Wells would he be considered for a job at the news desk. If he failed, he'd be back typesetting for good. It was a gamble, one Thomas couldn't afford to lose.

Ed held out another envelope. "Me and the fellas thought ye might need something to tide ye over until your first paycheck."

"You don't need to do that." Thomas pushed the envelope away. "You've got families."

"So do you," Ed said. "I know ye give half your wages to your mother. Ye'll be needing a little extra for all those lunch meetings and dinner parties ye'll be attending."

"None of those kinds of things just yet." No, just backbreaking work, hoping each day he might get the opportunity to talk to Mr. Wells. "Besides, I've got a job to hold me over." The confused look on the man's face pushed Thomas to confess. "It's for the article."

Ed's smile broadened. "Ah, already hard at work."

Truer words were never spoken. Yet he couldn't complain. Thomas rolled his shoulders back, hoping to relieve the knots there. Jane pushed herself just as hard. Between planning out color combinations and doing the preliminary painting, she was in constant motion, like a whirlwind on the open prairie.

Ed gave him a gentle poke in the ribs. "Is there a girl involved?"

Thomas blinked. "Why would you ask that?"

"I don't know. You just were thinkin' so hard, and then there was that look."

Thomas crossed his arms over his chest. "What kind of look was that?"

"You know." Ed gave him a crooked smile. "That droopy cow-eyed look we lads get when there's a handsome woman involved."

Thomas chuckled. "I can assure you it's nothing like that. We're simply friends."

"Ah, boy." The older man clapped an arm across Thomas's shoulder. "Even I can see she's already leading you on a pretty chase."

Thomas rolled his eyes. Let the man believe what he wanted. If he met Jane, he'd learn the truth. Jane Wells was not the type to lead any man on. Her answers to his questions were always straightforward and honest without the flirtatious air most marriage-minded women employed.

Still, he couldn't deny the best part of the job was Jane. She was interesting, with a quiet determination that spoke of inner strength, and she was far more talented that Mr. Looff gave her credit for.

"Boy." Ed interrupted his thoughts. "I think someone's looking for you." He nodded toward the door where a clerk stood, trying to get Thomas's attention.

Thomas walked over to the young boy who was no more than fifteen. "Are you looking for me?"

The boy nodded. "Yes, sir. Mr. Delano wants to see you upstairs. Right now, sir."

Thomas waved goodbye to his old boss then followed the boy upstairs, the sounds of the newsroom greeting him, sending a thrill of anticipation through him. It had always been like this for him. Even as a young boy, his fingers were constantly smudged with ink from reading the newspapers the Looffs had discarded. Was this how Jane felt when she spoke of colors and textures? He smiled at the thought, enjoying the knowledge that they shared this feeling.

The room was bursting with activity, from the clacking of typewriters to the low hum of people talking. Thomas followed the boy down a row of desks to a makeshift office in the far corner of the room.

"Mr. Delano," the boy said as he showed Thomas into the room. It wasn't much as offices went, with only a simple oak desk, two chairs, and a bookshelf. Nothing compared to Mr. Looff's quarters. Yet there was an energy to the room, due in large part to the man behind the desk.

"West, will you take a seat?"

It wasn't a question so much as a command. Thomas pulled back the chair and sat down. "You wanted to see me, sir."

"I hear you're going after the interview with J.T. Wells." Delano chomped on his unlit cigar, never lifting his head as he studied a paper in his hands. "You do understand what happens if you fail."

"I'll become a permanent fixture in the typesetting room."

The editor lifted his gaze. "Do you know that Wells hasn't given an interview in over two years?"

"I'm aware of that fact, but I have an opportunity most reporters don't."

"You mean your connection with Charles Looff." Delano sat back, studying Thomas as if seeing him for the first time. Which could well be the case. In all of Thomas's years in the typesetting room, Matthew Delano had never made a visit. "Have you secured an interview?"

"Not yet."

"And you won't. More experienced reporters than you have tried and failed to corner the man. Very few people have seen him in the last couple of years, and those are only the ones who are close to him." He pulled his cigar out of his mouth, glanced at it, then popped it back in. "What makes you think you'll succeed?"

"I've been hired on as Mr. Wells's assistant."

That got Delano's attention. "You've gone undercover?" He thought for a moment then nodded. "That might just work. What have you learned so far?"

That J.T. Wells was as elusive as always. Not once in the last ten days had he bothered to show up at the hippodrome. It was almost to the point where Thomas had considered another option—that Jane might very well be the talent behind the name. But the way she spoke of her father and the reputation he'd built as a carousel painter over the years gave him pause. Jane wouldn't lie. At least he didn't think she would.

Thomas couldn't tell any of this to his editor. "Nothing yet, but as I've said, I spend ten hours a day with Miss Wells. I'm sure to uncover something."

"So, you're romancing the daughter?" Delano chuckled. "I've heard she's a nice enough woman, even if she's not that pretty."

Thomas bristled at the editor's cruel remarks. "Jane is a good sort, and extremely talented in her own right. And I'm not romancing her as much as I'm offering her friendship."

Delano nodded. "Well, I'll say this for you. You're tenacious, which is exactly what you need to be to become a great reporter." Leaning on his desk, he steepled his fingers together. "How much are you making as an assistant?"

Not near enough. Between supporting his mother and paying for his room and board, there was usually nothing left over.

"What if I keep you on the payroll while you're undercover?" He named an amount that was more than triple what Thomas had been making. "But I want to see your notes, and I'll expect you in here once a week to give me an update on where you're at with the article. Is that understood?"

It was more than Thomas could hope for. At least for the moment he could put away some money in case he didn't get the interview. He had no intention of going back to typesetting, no matter what happened.

For him at least it was sink or swim.

Chapter 7

The lavender with just a drop of daffodil yellow gave the ribbons the jaunty feel Jane wanted. Paying close attention to the indention that separated the ribbon from the horse's body, she painstakingly drew a fine line between the two then made broad strokes to fill in the ribbon.

Today had been more difficult than she had thought. Of course there had been wonderful moments too, like Papa and Grace's wedding this morning. Papa had looked so handsome. The last two years had felt like a distant memory as she watched her father, his expression one of hope and joy, stand at the altar, waiting for his bride.

And Grace. She had raced up the aisle with an eagerness that had made the poor pastor blush! When she'd asked Grace about it later, she'd said she couldn't keep her John waiting.

Yet it had been their vows, so sweetly and honestly spoken,

that caused the ache in Jane's chest even all these hours later. *"To love and to cherish, for richer and for poorer, in sickness and in health as long as we both shall live."*

Jane lifted her brush and sighed. Marriage had never been something she'd considered, not that it had ever come up. She'd never had a beau, and once her father had his stroke, she didn't have time for one. What would it be like to have someone who would love and honor her all the days of her life?

The door clicked open. She lifted her head and smiled as Thomas came toward her, shucking off his coat as he walked. "I gave you the day off."

"I decided I didn't want it." He tossed his jacket on the bench then shook out a length of dark cloth. "Ma heard I needed an apron, so she made me one." He looped it over his head. "See. No frills."

Her lips twitched. "Very nice."

"I thought so." He glanced past her to the carving. "What are you doing?"

"Trying out colors." She stepped aside, giving him a clean view. "What do you think?"

Thomas studied it for a long moment then glanced at her, a smile playing along his lips. "It's a pretty shade of purple."

Jane looked at the horse through fresh eyes. "It is, isn't it?" She glanced up at him then started to turn away but found she couldn't. She enjoyed watching him too much. "I'd love to paint you."

A bashful grin kicked up the corners of his mouth. "I couldn't sit still long enough for that, but I have had my picture taken." He hurried over to his coat, pulled something small from his front pocket, then returned. He held it out to her. "See."

The tintype was recent, and it wasn't just of Thomas, but also of two young women flanking him on either side. None of them smiled, but there was a joy in their expressions that Jane couldn't help but envy. "Your sisters?"

Thomas nodded. "The dark-haired one is Lilly. Rose is the one with the dimple in her chin. Ma had it made right after I graduated from college. She thought it might be the last time she'd get all of us together in one place."

"It's a lovely picture." She handed it back to him. "I always wanted a sibling, but Mama almost died having me."

He took the picture and dropped it in his pants pocket. "That sounds like a lonely existence."

"It wasn't." At least most of the time it wasn't, but there had been moments in the last two years that she'd wished she'd had a brother or sister to lean on, someone to share the responsibility. Well, there wasn't any sense in hoping for something that could never be. "We need to get to work."

"Is your father coming in today?"

Jane closed her eyes. Of all the questions Thomas asked, this was the one she dreaded the most. It reminded her she'd lied to this man. She studied the paint drops as if they held the mysteries of the world. "Not today."

"He's been under the weather for a while now." The concern in his voice pricked her conscience. "Maybe it's time you called in a doctor."

Jane grimaced. If only he knew. But then why shouldn't he? Not everything of course, but what would it hurt to share her memories of today with him? "He's not coming in because he was married this morning."

"Married, huh?" He watched her, and Jane felt as if he was staring into her very soul. "Is that why you gave me today off?"

"Maybe." That, and she wasn't certain how she'd react after leaving the train station today. It hadn't been as hard as she thought. Both Papa and Grace looked so happy and full of hope, Jane couldn't help but feel comforted.

"Are you happy about it?"

"Of course I am. Grace has been with us as long as I can remember, and they love each other. I only wish it had happened sooner."

"Then why aren't you off celebrating with them?"

Jane shook her head. Another one of his questions. Why couldn't he leave well enough alone? She scrambled for an answer. "A newly married man doesn't want his grown daughter tagging along on his wedding day."

"No, I guess not." He chuckled, the husky sound warming a place inside her she never knew existed. "Where are you staying tonight?"

Jane blinked in confusion. "Why would you ask that?"

"It's your father's wedding night." Color crept into his cheeks. "And as you just said, a man doesn't want his grown daughter tagging along on his wedding night."

Heat flooded her face, and she stammered. "No, I mean. . . Yes. . . What I mean is, Papa and Grace are staying at a hotel tonight."

"Oh." Thomas rubbed the back of his neck, clearly as uncomfortable as she felt. "I didn't mean to embarrass you."

"It's just that. . ." A giggle escaped. "I guess I'd better get used to the idea that my father is a newlywed."

"It does give the rest of us unmarried folk some hope."

"Papa was certainly full of that today." She glanced up, meeting his dark eyes. "I haven't seen him this happy in years."

"Why is that?"

She should have expected Thomas would ask. But should she tell him, at least part of the truth? The answer surprised her. "The last two years have not been very kind to Papa."

Thomas's dark brow bunched, and for a brief moment she wanted nothing more than to reach up and smooth it. "But he's been at the height of his success during that time."

Yes, a fact Jane was certain hadn't been lost on her father. Was that why he was so critical of everything she did? She hoped not. "Yes, well, success doesn't always equate with happiness."

"No, I guess it doesn't."

She thought he'd dropped the subject, and she had turned and started back toward the horse she was working on when he spoke again.

"Are you happy, Jane?"

Why had he asked Jane that question?

Thomas stared down into her pretty gray eyes, wishing he knew all the secrets hiding there. There was a wariness in them now, something that held her back from finding her own happiness. Suddenly it was important that he discover what it was.

"I'm happy."

But the words rang false. There was no joy in her voice, no contentment with the life she lived. "You're not being honest."

Her head snapped back as if she'd been punched. Then her shoulders slumped, hardly enough for anyone to notice, but Thomas had been in close quarters with her for days now and had grown aware of her changing moods.

She pressed her lips together as if to stop the tremor in them.

"A person can't be happy all the time."

"That's true," he agreed, stepping closer. He reached out and took her hand in his, surprised by the spark of awareness from the touch. "But I can tell something is troubling you. I thought you were happy about your father."

"I am. It's just that. . ." Her eyes went wide, as though she'd surprised herself. She took a steadying breath and continued. "Have you ever done something you know is wrong, but you did it to protect someone else?"

It wasn't the response he'd expected, nor did he expect the sharp prick to his conscience. Wasn't that what he was doing here, pretending to be something he wasn't, deceiving Jane so that he could provide for his family?

At least he could be honest with his answer. "Yeah, I have."

"Really?"

He nodded. "I'm not proud of the fact, but it's the only way I could get what I needed to provide for my family."

"You padded your résumé to get this position."

"What?"

She stared at him, her expression serious. "I know you've never been an assistant painter before, and I doubt very seriously you're a painter at all."

Thomas crossed his arms, watching Jane's mind at work. "How did you come to that conclusion?"

"It was relatively easy," she answered, giving him a ghost of a smile. "You don't think in terms of colors, but in black and white, and there were the ink stains on your fingers. Most painters have colored pigment on their hands."

She was certainly observant, much more than he'd given her credit for. But what would she do with that information? "Are you going to sack me?"

Jane shook her head. "You've always been honest about wanting to provide for your mother and sisters, and I admire that. Plus, you're a quick study." She hesitated. "I don't know how I'd do without you."

"That's a relief." Thomas couldn't lose this opportunity to interview Jane's father. He couldn't go back to typesetting after this. "So what about you? What have you done out of love for someone else?"

Her face went pale, as if the question had stolen all the color out of her life. Whatever it was that she'd done, it bothered her immensely. Would she trust him enough to confide in him? For a second, he thought she might, but then she turned and walked to where she'd set up her brushes and paints for the day.

"Jane. . ."

"You ask too many questions, Thomas." She picked up her brush and dipped it into the purplish mix. "It's annoying."

"I'm just concerned about you." Which surprised him. When had he started caring about Jane Wells? He was here for an article and the possibility of providing for his family. Yet he couldn't deny Jane mattered to him. Quite a bit, if he were honest.

All of a sudden his story didn't seem so important.

Chapter 8

Jane took a deep breath and massaged her forehead. *Please, Lord, I don't need a headache today.* Her stomach growled, and she felt a slight wave of nausea, though why, she wasn't sure. Her attempt at cooking dinner last night had ended up in the trash pail. And her coffee. Another wave of nausea struck. How did she manage to turn perfectly good coffee into muck at the bottom of the pot?

"Are you okay?"

She glanced up to find Thomas staring. It was the first question he'd asked her since their disagreement on Papa's wedding day. Since then they hadn't talked much except for "yes" and "no," a situation that irritated her to no end.

And he was waiting for an answer. "I'm fine."

"You don't look fine." He gently took her arms and led her to a nearby bench. "Have you got a cold or something?"

"No." She rubbed between her eyes with the tips of her fingers. "It's just a little headache."

"Maybe you ought to go home and lie down."

She shook her head then regretted it. The cottage was simply a bunch of useless rooms without Papa and Grace to fill them. "I'd rather stay here."

Thomas knelt down in front of her. "Then tell me what I can do to help."

Before she could respond, her stomach answered for her.

His eyes lifted to meet hers. "When's the last time you ate?"

Jane didn't answer, too ashamed to admit she didn't know how to boil water without burning it.

Plucking the paintbrush from her fingers, he laid it on the bench then reached for her hat and reticule. "Come on. I'm taking you out to lunch."

"You don't have to do that. I'll be just—"

He tenderly took her chin between his thumb and forefinger and lifted her eyes to meet his. There was concern there, but also some other emotion. Anger? "I don't want to fish you out of a paint vat just because you haven't eaten. Is that understood?"

Jane nodded, her heart thumping like a bass drum in her chest. For the last two years, she'd spent most of her time caring for her father without any concern for herself. Yet this man saw a need in her, took charge, and supplied an answer. She took the hat and reticule he offered then stood and followed him.

Once outside, she drew in a deep breath, the tang of brine dulling the pain in her head. Maybe Thomas was right. All she needed was a good meal to set her to rights.

Thomas offered his arm, and she took it, her fingers skimming over the taut muscles. "Why are you starving yourself like this?" he asked.

"Do I look as if I do without food?" She hesitated. Might as well tell him the truth. "I don't know how to cook."

"But you have food?"

Was he concerned she couldn't afford groceries? Why? "I have plenty of food. I simply can't cook. You see, Grace. . ." Jane stopped herself. If she told him the truth, that Grace, her father's brand-new wife, was with her father, heading west for rehabilitation, Thomas would have all sorts of questions. Questions she couldn't answer. "Grace usually cooks, but she was off with Papa last night. I was left on my own."

"If she knew you don't cook, why didn't she make you something before she left?"

"Maybe because she thought a twenty-four-year-old woman should know how to boil water." Jane chuckled. "Don't think ill of Grace because of my deficits."

"I don't think badly of Grace. I don't know her." He patted her hand. "And I'm sorry if I overreacted. I don't like to hear of someone going without food."

A comfortable silence settled over them. Yet Thomas's strong reaction caused questions to come to mind. She stole a glance at him. "Have you ever gone without food?"

His arm tensed beneath her touch, as if she'd uncovered some shameful secret. "Why do you ask?"

"You seemed angry when you found out I haven't eaten, like you knew how that felt."

"You've very observant."

"That's what artists do. We observe and try to capture what we see in our medium." She gave him an encouraging smile.

"So, did you go hungry?"

He nodded, the tension slipping out of him slowly. "After Pa died, things were tough. There was no money coming in, and Ma had four mouths to feed. We did without a lot."

The thought of the boy Thomas going without food pricked her heart. She already knew the answer, but she asked anyway. "Food?"

He nodded. "There was barely enough for one of us, and Rose was so sickly back then."

Thomas had given his food to his sisters. He'd never say so, but she knew as sure as she knew the rhythm of her heart. Providing for his family and securing their future was his chief goal. It was why he had taken the job as her father's assistant. She held his arm tighter, in awe of his kindness and selflessness. "Where are we going to lunch?"

He smiled then, and Jane felt as if her heart would burst. "The Silver Spring House. It's got one of the best shore dinners around." He leaned closer to her. "I'm kind of partial to one of the waitresses there."

Jane nodded. Of course he had a beau, maybe even a fiancée. When she glanced at him, there was amusement in his eyes. "You're teasing me."

"You make it so easy." He chuckled. "Rose works there."

"Is she working today?"

"Yes." He took her arm as they turned down the main boardwalk that led to the shore. "I'd hoped she would go to college, but she was determined to work instead."

"You have to give her credit for knowing college wasn't for her."

"I know, but she's so intelligent." He led her down the sidewalk to the wharf. "Both of my sisters are. I just want more for them than being in service."

And Thomas thought that he could make better decisions for them than they could for themselves. She sighed. "Is that what they want?"

He slowed their pace. "What do you mean?"

Dropping his arm, Jane stopped and glared up at him. "Just because you want something doesn't mean it's the right choice for them. You need to encourage them to make their own decisions about their future. Just like they encourage you."

He stared off into the ocean behind her. "I never thought of it that way."

"Most men don't." She retook his arm. "I know my father never has."

"Really?" Thomas turned them toward a large colonial-style white building with a bright red tin roof. "I would have thought that, as an artist, your father would be more progressive in his views. He did make you his apprentice, didn't he?"

Only out of necessity, not because he thought she deserved it. "Dear heavens, no, Thomas. Papa is as old-fashioned as they come. I may be a grown woman, but he still makes all the decisions."

"I can't imagine you sitting by while he decides everything for you."

She shook her head. She had fought constantly with her father, begging him to let her be his apprentice, but it was only after he'd fallen ill, when he had no choice, that he'd allowed it. Since then, she'd been too worried any upset would cause a relapse. Now, she wondered if going along with him had been such a good idea.

"So, let me ask you. What would you decide for yourself if you had a chance?"

Her chest tightened, the answer clear in her mind. She would own up to their deception. First, she'd tell Thomas then Mr. Looff and anyone else she'd deceived over the last two years. If her father got angry, good. He needed to understand how much this bothered her.

Jane glanced over at Thomas. Telling this man would be the hardest. To see the disappointment in his eyes. She could bear almost anything, but not Thomas's disapproval.

Of course, she couldn't say any of these things, at least not until Papa was stable. But Thomas was waiting for an answer, and there was no other choice but to give him one.

"If I could decide one thing for myself," she said, "I'd tell Papa I don't want to be his apprentice anymore."

"Lunch was extraordinary." Jane patted her lips with her napkin and sat back in her chair, looking for all the world like the cat who ate the canary. "I can't believe I've never tried lobster before."

"Neither can I," Thomas said, taking one last sip of his coffee. More than the food had been extraordinary. Jane approached her meal with the same quiet intensity with which she painted the horses. Everything about their lunch had entertained him. The surprised look in her eyes when she spooned up her first bite of red chowder. The way her lips curled up in a buttery smile as she conquered the lobster. How her eyes fluttered closed when she bit into the boiled corn. For the first time since he'd met her, she truly seemed to enjoy herself.

He liked this relaxed and happy Jane. He liked her very much.

Yet her answer to his question still bothered him. If she didn't want to be her father's apprentice anymore, why didn't she simply quit? It seemed easy enough, but then things weren't always as they appeared. There was more to this story than what Jane presented to the world, but what was it? Why did she feel the need to keep it a secret?

Thomas pushed the thought aside. For now, he wanted to enjoy this moment with her. "Would you like some dessert?"

"After that feast?" She shook her head then leaned forward slightly, a playful gleam in her eyes. "What do they have on the menu?"

Thomas leaned forward also, and the world narrowed to just the two of them. "My favorite is the homemade chocolate cake."

She shook her head. "I shouldn't."

But something in her expression told him she'd like a piece anyway. "What if we share a piece? It's big enough for two."

Her cheeks turned a delightful shade of pink. "Is that proper?"

"Probably not, but let's do it anyway."

Thomas waved down Rose, who bustled over to their table. "How was lunch?"

"Good, as usual. Even the waitress was nice," Thomas teased. "I might even leave her a tip today."

"No more wooden nickels, big brother." Rose gave him a loving shove. "I've got my eye on a new hat at the millinery, so I need all the tips I can get."

"Don't worry. If he doesn't give you one, I will," Jane said, playing along.

"Thank you!" She eyed her brother. "Has Jane met Ma and Lilly yet?"

Thomas felt suddenly warm. "Are you here to take my order or order me around?"

"Like that could happen," Rose scoffed as she pulled out a small pad of paper and a pencil. "Let me guess. Chocolate cake."

Thomas nodded. "And two forks. Jane's never had it."

"Sharing your cake. Must be serious." She leaned down close to Jane, her gaze studying him. "He never shares his cake with any of us."

"Could you hurry? Or I'll have to report you to the manager for slacking on the job, brat." Last thing he needed was his sisters pushing him on Jane. Maybe she didn't fancy him that way, or she wanted to remain friends. The thought made his heart sink.

"She's lovely," Jane said as Rose hurried into the kitchen. "She seems to love her big brother very much."

"She loves to provoke me is what you mean."

"Well, maybe that too." There was laughter in her voice. "You're very close to your family."

He nodded. "Though they can drive me crazy at times. Like Rose. Why does that girl need another hat? She's got a half a dozen in her closet."

Jane shrugged. "Most women have several hats."

"You don't. You wear the same hat every day."

Her cheeks warmed to a rosy pink. "You noticed?"

He smiled at her confused expression. "I'm observant, remember?"

Before she could respond, Rose returned with their slice of chocolate cake topped with whipped cream and a fat red cherry. Thomas handed Jane a fork. "Ladies first."

She eyed the cake, turning the plate from side to side, moving it this way and that. "I don't know where to begin. It's like ruining a masterpiece."

Leave it to Jane to compare sweet confection to art. "If you don't hurry, I'll be forced to be rude and steal a bite."

"All right then." She turned the plate once more then sank her fork into equal parts whipped cream and cake. She held up the fork, a look of triumph in her expression. "The perfect bite."

He laughed then stopped as his breath caught at the sight of her, her eyes dancing with merriment, the corners of her mouth kicked up into a shy smile. She was beautiful, nothing like the "plain Jane" Looff had described that first day in his office. But she was more than beautiful. She was interesting and accomplished, determined, and loyal to her family. Everything a man wanted in a woman. Everything he wanted.

I love her.

"Thomas, if you don't eat some of this cake soon, I won't be able to stop myself." Jane covered her mouth with her fingertips. "It really is wonderful."

It really was, this feeling. Absolutely extraordinary. He watched her take another bite then loaded his fork. He hadn't planned on falling in love, but then, whoever did? He'd gone in hunt of an interview and found Jane instead.

His article. His euphoria dampened. How would Jane feel if she knew the truth, that he'd only taken this job to get information about her and her father?

Chapter 9

The chatter of typewriter keys banged out an irritating beat as Thomas hurried through the newsroom to Mr. Delano's office. Usually the sights and sounds of the newsroom settled him as they had since his days of writing for the college newspaper. But today they had the opposite effect. He felt off-balance and slightly confused, and it was all because of Jane.

Delano's secretary stood before Thomas stopped in front of her desk. "Mr. Delano has been held up downstairs but said for you to go right in. He should be back in a few minutes."

"Thank you."

Thomas let himself into the office then took a seat, his thoughts going a mile a minute. All he wanted was the opportunity to prove himself, to make a better life for Ma and the girls, and this story about Jane and her father was his ticket. With this job, his mother could retire. He might even be able to swing college tuition for

Lilly and Rose. Surely Jane would understand that.

"You should encourage your sisters to make their own choices like they encourage you."

The door opened, and Matthew Delano blew into the office like a gale-force wind. "About time you showed up, West. I've been looking all over town for you."

He must not have been looking too hard, Thomas thought as the man threw a stack of papers on his disorganized desk and sat down. "What did you want to see me about?"

Delano pulled a newspaper from the top of the pile and flung it across the desk. "You know anything about this?"

Thomas scanned the print, his chest tightening as he found the small announcement in the right-hand corner. "You mean about J.T. Wells's marriage?" He tossed the newspaper back on the desk. "I heard about it."

"I figured you had, considering all the time you've been spending with Wells and that daughter of his." Picking up the paper, Delano shook it at him. "I have a man undercover with the Wellses, and I have to read about the man's wedding in the *Times*."

"I'm not a writer for the society page."

"You're not anything yet!" Delano bellowed. "And you won't be if you keep information like that to yourself again."

"I didn't have permission to share it."

Delano cocked a bushy eyebrow. "Permission? No one gets permission. If reporters did that, the paper would just be full of advertisements." He leaned over his desk like a buzzard on a tree branch. "You're going to need to lose some of your scruples if you hope to make it as a reporter."

Thomas didn't reply. He'd known Delano was a cutthroat newspaperman when he'd taken a job at the *Examiner*, but was that the kind of reporter he wanted to be? There had to be writers who held on to their integrity rather than get a story for the price of their conscience.

"Well, have you got anything for me yet?"

Thomas met his boss's hard gaze. "I don't know. There's a story there, but it's not the one I thought it was. It's more about Jane than her father."

"The daughter?" The large man clipped off the end of his unlit cigar then stuck it between his teeth. "The one you're romancing?"

Thomas started to object then figured there was no point. "She's his apprentice, and Wells is still a no-show. The horses are being painted, so it makes me think he's been painting them at night."

Delano chomped on his cigar. "Have you caught him at it?"

"I've been out there a couple of times in the evening, but he's either not arrived or locked himself inside."

His boss shook his head. "Sounds like a nutcase to me."

Or someone who has a secret.

"For Pete's sake, Rome was built in less time." Delano's expression was hard and unforgiving. "You need to figure out a way to catch him in the act. Steal the key from that lady friend of yours. Anything to force the man to give you an interview."

Thomas didn't answer right away, shocked by Delano's suggestion. "If you'll give me some time, I can get the interview without"—he paused—"using such tactics."

Steepling his fingers over his rounded belly, Delano sat back in his chair. "Has anyone else been there when you showed up?"

"Why do you ask?"

"Just an old rumor I heard about Wells being sick." Delano studied him across the desk. "Do you know anything about that?"

No, but it did explain Wells's reclusive behavior and Jane's protectiveness of her father. "When did this illness happen?"

"A little over two years ago."

Two years. About the time Jane took on the role of her father's apprentice, a position she took very seriously. The detailed prep work she performed on each horse, the color charts she spent hours poring over, her late-night visits to the hippodrome. It even explained her father's reclusive behavior.

Why hadn't Jane told him about her father's illness?

Why would she? Jane had been protective of her father since the first moment he'd met her. Which made him wonder. Just how much work had J.T. Wells done on Looff's carousel, and how much had been Jane's?

Jane painted under her father's name.

Yet why would she do it? Why would she sit in the background and let her father collect the accolades for her work? An answer came to him, but the only one who could give him the truth was Jane.

"Anything you'd like to tell me, West?"

Thomas glanced across the desk at the older man. He didn't trust Delano enough to share his thoughts until he had some answers. Even then, he'd do everything he could to protect Jane. She was his friend, maybe something more, though he wasn't ready to examine those feelings yet. When he wrote this story, it wouldn't be at her expense.

Delano shook his head. "I don't need a reporter who's soft. If you can't get the story, I'll give it to someone who can. Maybe Jameson."

Thomas gritted his teeth. Jameson was like a bull in a china shop. Jane deserved better, and he hadn't lost hope she would consent to an interview in the end.

Thomas stood and glared down at his boss. "Get my desk ready. I'll have your story by the end of the week."

Loading her brush with a lush crimson, Jane put the final touches on a rein around the horse's neck. "You look lovely in red, my dear. It brings out the golden flakes in your eyes."

She laughed at her silliness, the sound a pleasant echo against the walls of the hippodrome. Once the carousel was finished and the musical apparatus in place, the children would swarm to it like bees to a newly bloomed flower.

Maybe Thomas was right and there was a poet somewhere inside her.

Thomas. Her lips curved into a smile as she pushed an unruly curl behind her ear. Their afternoon together had been an unexpected surprise. Never had she talked and laughed so much. In those few short hours, she'd discovered their shared interest in Mark Twain and politics and that he shared her faith. She saw firsthand how important his family was to him and even enjoyed the bantering between him and Rose.

Yet it was the chocolate cake she remembered or, rather, the way he studied her while she ate. As if he thought her the most fascinating woman he'd ever met. A thrill went through her at the memory. No one had ever looked at her that way before.

Her brush depleted, she set it down beside the container then checked the lines. She had to hurry. Thomas would be here soon, and she still needed to clean up. It was getting more and more difficult to keep the truth from him. These last few weeks she'd come to know him as a friend. As more than a friend, she admitted to herself. He made her laugh, which was something she hadn't done a lot of since her father had become ill. She'd even come to love his questions.

What would it be like to be Thomas's wife?

A ridiculous question, she scolded herself. A man like Thomas wouldn't take kindly to being deceived, and that's all she'd done since they'd met. Maybe she should tell him the truth, that her father's fear of losing his reputation had caused her not to be forthcoming with the truth. Yet even to her ears it sounded like a weak excuse. No, she needed to finish this job and secure her father's reputation. Then her father would retire and she could move on with her life.

What would that life look like?

Replacing the paint lid, she tapped it into place. She'd travel, of course. Papa had promised her the payment from this job so she could start anew. Maybe London or Paris. All of those museums to wander through and relish. Finally, she would be free to study the masters up close. Even if Thomas wasn't a painter, he'd appreciate such a visit. It was easy to see them strolling beside the Seine, finding a place to set up her easel. She'd certainly draw him. His clean-cut jaw and ruggedly male features would look magnificent in charcoals, but could she capture the depths that lay behind his expressive dark eyes?

Heat flared in her cheeks. She shouldn't be thinking about Thomas this way, but her heart wouldn't listen. Is this what being in love felt like? She didn't know. Papa had never broached the subject with her, and while she loved Grace, it didn't seem appropriate to ask her. But she'd seen her new stepmother around her father. Patient when he didn't deserve it, kind even when he flustered her. And loving, always loving and wanting only the best for him. If what she'd seen of Grace was anything to go by, she was very much in danger of falling completely in love with Thomas.

That would be a disaster. Her heart would break when he learned the truth and walked away from her.

Jane grabbed a small canister of golden yellow and marched over to where another carved horse stood. It was better to work than to ruminate on what she could never have. And she'd never have a life with Thomas, not after he learned the truth about her.

Glancing down at the watch pinned to her bodice, Jane opened the paint can then retrieved her narrow brush from the table. There was enough time to complete one more set of ribbons before Thomas arrived. Within minutes she lost herself in the delicate brushstrokes. *A little girl,* Jane mused, *will think she's holding satin strands of gold as she rides her steed.*

Something clattered to the ground behind her, and she whirled around, tiny drops of paint spraying a wild pattern across the floor. In the doorway stood Thomas, a grim expression on his face.

Jane tried to clear the lump from her throat and failed. There was no reason to believe he suspected anything. "I didn't hear you come in. You're late."

"No I'm not." He walked toward her, his boots chewing up the concrete as he chipped away at the distance between them. "I've been standing at the door for a while."

Jane's heart slammed against her chest. "How long?"

"Long enough to know the truth." He took the paintbrush out of her hand and tossed it aside. "That you're the one painting the horses. You're painting under your father's name."

Chapter 10

It's not what you think."

How many times had Thomas heard that, only to find out later it was exactly what it looked like. Same thing went for the articles he'd read when he was typesetting. The truth came out, and it was exactly as described in the story.

Thomas studied her. All the way here, he'd been at war with himself, certain he'd misjudged the situation. But Jane had gotten sloppy and left the door unlocked. The evidence was right there in front of him. He needed to hear Jane's explanation. But would Jane tell him the truth now? Or would she continue to perpetrate a lie?

"I. . ." She started then dropped down on the bench near them. Her head down, her hands trembled in her lap. "I'm so sorry. I've known since the beginning this was a bad idea."

Not knowing what to do, he sat down beside her, her skirts

brushing up against his thigh. "You want to tell me how all of this started?"

Jane lifted her gaze to meet his, her eyes brimming with unshed tears like the ocean at high tide. "My father has always aspired for more. To be the best husband and father. The best painter." She sniffed. "I couldn't have asked for a better papa. After Mama died, he lost his focus for a while, and it damaged his career. Mr. Looff gave him the opportunity to paint carousels, and he was building quite the reputation when the first stroke hit."

"The first?" So, the rumors Delano had heard were true. "How many has he had?"

She shook her head. "We're not certain. The doctor feels that he may at times experience small seizures we're unaware of." Jane slipped a handkerchief from the sleeve of her shirtwaist and dabbed at her nose. "He feels it's only a matter of time before one of these seizures. . ." Her voice broke on the last word and she couldn't continue.

"How long has he been unable to paint?"

Jane sighed, her shoulders slumped as if she carried a large burden. "He hasn't picked up a paintbrush in a little over two years. Papa hated being seen as weak after what happened when Mama died. I was the only one who knew the truth, so Papa asked me to become his apprentice."

"But you're not an apprentice anymore."

She shook her head. "I guess not, as I've been the one doing all the painting over the last two years."

Gracious, right during the height of J.T. Wells's popularity. Thomas glanced at the finished horses that had been placed onto the carousel, each animal almost lifelike, as if Jane's paintbrush had breathed life into them.

"Papa has agreed to retire after this job. His reputation as an artist will be beyond rebuke."

"But it's all been a lie, Jane." He took her hand in his and gave it a gentle squeeze. "You're the one who's brought brilliance to his work. It should be you getting all the praise and accolades from Mr. Looff."

Jane scoffed. "That's ridiculous."

"Is it? Your father's reputation as a painter didn't take off until you took over the majority of the work."

She jumped to her feet and paced across the room. "That's not true. Papa was widely known before he became ill. He always had work."

"But nothing compared to his fame now." How could he make her understand? Thomas stood, blocking her way when she walked back to him. "Why are you afraid for people to know the truth? That you're the one who makes the carousel come to life?"

"I don't care about that." Jane shook her head. "Why can't you understand? If word of this got out, Papa's reputation would be ruined." Her voice broke. "It would kill him, Thomas."

Reaching for her hand, Thomas pulled her into his embrace. She tensed at first then slowly relaxed, finally resting her head against his shoulder. What a burden she'd had to bear, and all for the sake of her father. He rested his chin on the top of her head. She deserved so much more than her father had given her these past few years, yet her first concern was for him, his reputation and his health.

Anger flared, not at her but at her circumstances. He knew right then and there he couldn't write the story he'd planned to write. The story that needed to be told was of selflessness and of a daughter's love. It might not sell many newspapers, but people needed to read it just the same.

Yet if she didn't want him to, he wouldn't write it at all. He'd never betray her like that no matter how much he needed the position. Even though he didn't need her permission to write the story, he would ask her for it.

She lifted her head but remained in his arms. "You won't tell anyone, will you? If word got out. . . My father." Her words caught on a soft sob.

Thomas had no doubt he'd regret his next words, but for Jane he'd move mountains if he must. Cupping her face in his hands, he touched his forehead to hers. "You have my word."

"You look chipper this morning," Grace said from her post at the oven as Jane walked into the kitchen. "You're happy this morning."

"Maybe I'm glad you're home." Jane sat down and forked a sausage onto her plate. "I had to make an appointment with the seamstress to have my gowns taken in, I've lost so much weight since you've been gone."

"I'm glad to be home too, though I do miss John." Grace placed two pieces of toast on a plate and brought it to the table. "Once he was admitted, there was no point in me sitting in the hotel, doing nothing. So we decided I should come home."

"Well, I'm glad." Jane smiled over her cup of coffee. "This house is lonely with the two of you gone."

"And yet there's a little sparkle in your eyes." Coffee dripped onto the table as Grace pointed her spoon at her. "You've met someone."

Jane choked on her coffee, her heart beating a mad rhythm in her chest. She'd never hear the end of it if Grace found out she'd fallen in love with Thomas. "Good heavens, when do I have time for such nonsense?"

That stopped Grace for a moment, and then she snapped her fingers. "It's that assistant of yours. That Thomas fellow, isn't it?" Satisfied, she sat back in her chair. "I should have guessed by the way you wrote about him in your letters. He sounds like a nice lad."

"He's not a 'lad' but a man. A very handsome one." Jane dug into her scrambled eggs. "Not that I see him as anything but a coworker."

"A coworker, huh?"

"Of course, that's what he is."

Grace picked up her coffee cup. "But you talk about him all the time. In your letters, that is."

"You're just imagining things."

"Hmm." Grace reached into the pocket of her apron and pulled out some folded sheets of paper. Opening them, she began to read. "His mother works as a housekeeper for Mr. Looff while his sisters work in town. Mr. Looff sent him to college to learn a trade, but he decided he wanted to be an artist, and his family is encouraging him in that." She looked up. "Would you like me to read more?"

"No." Jane reached out to take the letter, but Grace pulled it away. "Why are you carrying around my letter anyway?"

"Believe it or not, your papa and I missed you." She folded the letter and tucked it away. "He wanted me to read your letters every Sunday when I went to see him, so I got into the habit of tucking them in my pocket."

"Oh. That's sweet." She hadn't been sure Papa would even think of her, let alone miss her. If he knew what had happened, how Thomas had discovered the truth about them, he wouldn't be too happy. "How is Papa? Has he seen any improvement yet?"

"A bit, but he's still got a long way to go." Grace took another sip of coffee. "Now, about Thomas. How is he going to support a family on an artist's wages?"

"Papa provided for us quite well over the years."

Grace let out a feminine snort. "Much better since you've taken over the day-to-day work."

Thomas had said much the same thing last night. Jane lowered her gaze. "I wish you wouldn't say such things. It would hurt Papa."

"Jane." Grace set down her cup then reached for Jane's hand. "Your papa might not be able to paint anymore, but he's not blind to the truth. It bothers him something fierce that he's taking the credit for your talent."

"Then why won't he let me tell Mr. Looff the truth? Then he can retire, and we can put this all behind us."

"I asked him that when we first arrived in Flagstaff." She patted Jane's hand. "He wants to be certain you're taken care of in case something happens to him."

"And his reputation?"

Grace gave her a crooked grin. "He is a man, pet. One who feels he was cut down in the prime of his life. And he resents it." She let go of Jane's hand and sat back. "It may be wrong, but that's how he feels."

Jane pondered that thought. Is that how Papa truly felt, as if his opportunity to prove himself had been snatched away? It would explain his obsessive need to protect his reputation. She could even understand his desire to take care of her. But to lie about it? "Does he realize how much damage we'll suffer if the truth comes out?"

Grace shrugged. "He believes no one would ever suspect a woman could create such a stir in the art world." She must have noted the disbelief in Jane's expression, because she leaned over and rubbed her back. "Silly, I know, but that's the way things have always been, Janie-girl."

Hurt and anger intertwined inside her. All these years, Papa had led her to believe that the art world would be open to her, that her work on the carousels would be accepted.

Had he lied to her too? The thought left her raw and uncertain of anything.

"You'd better get going if you want to be at the hippodrome before your handsome Mr. West gets there."

That snapped her out of her thoughts. "Thomas isn't my anything," she said.

Grace pushed back her chair and stood. "I recognize that look, Jane. It's the same one I used to wear around your father."

"Thomas is our employee." Jane rose, carrying her half-eaten breakfast with her. "And a good friend."

"That's how it starts, you know, when you become sweethearts." Grace retrieved a large kettle of steaming water from the stove and poured it into the wash pan.

Jane took one last sip of her coffee rather than reply, her feelings a tangled mess. Best to be quiet than give Grace something to write to Papa about. "Let me know if you get a letter from Papa today."

"I will." Grace cleaned off the plate then dropped it into the soapy water, winking at her as Jane put on her hat. "You have a good day."

Grabbing her reticule, Jane hurried out of the kitchen, Grace's laughter chasing her down the footpath. The woman had a knack for knowing exactly what Jane was feeling without a word being spoken. A good thing most of the time, but not today.

Once outside, Jane turned up the sandy path that led to the amusement park, her thoughts racing around in her head. Was Grace right? Did her father truly believe a woman didn't have a place in the art world? Then why had he encouraged her all of these years? Was it all part of a plan to keep her painting carousels for him? If he was well enough, she'd ask him, but a confrontation at this point in his treatment might bring on a setback.

The door to the hippodrome stood ajar when she arrived. Stepping just inside the door, she found Thomas putting down wool blankets under the horse she'd planned to work on today. Jane leaned against the doorjamb and quietly watched him.

Telling Thomas the truth had lifted a huge burden from her shoulders, giving her the freedom to be herself with him. They had talked late into the evening last night, and their conversations felt more personal. Grace had not been mistaken this morning. Jane had fallen in love, and for the first time in a long time, she felt happy.

"Are you going to stand by the door all day?"

Thomas's gentle teasing broke through her thoughts, and she moved farther into the room. "I might."

He laughed. "You're in a good mood today."

"Confession does the heart good." Jane stepped closer, pinching the tip of each clothed finger and pulling until her glove slipped off. "Of course, breakfast helped."

"You cooked?"

Her lips tilted up in a smile. "No, Grace was waiting up for me when I got home last night."

Wiping his hands on his apron, he walked toward her. "Is everything all right?"

Jane nodded. "She and Papa thought it would be best if she came home after he was admitted. We'll go out and visit once this project is finished, but until then, she's here to stay."

"At least you won't starve."

"That's true." She set her gloves and reticule on the bench then walked over to their day's work. But looking at the horses, she couldn't help thinking of what Grace said. "Is it difficult to think that a woman could paint these carvings?"

He picked up the edge of a blanket and straightened it. "Where did that come from?"

Grabbing an apron, Jane unfolded it then tied it at her neck and waist. "Something Grace said this morning."

"Why are you worried about it?"

"It's not what Grace thinks." She sighed deeply, her feelings still hurt from what Papa said. "It's my father. He doesn't believe a woman can be successful in the art world."

Thomas shook his head. "He's probably afraid someone would discover the truth about you."

She didn't blame him for his low opinion of her father. "Papa isn't like that, not really."

The blanket whipped into the air with a pop. "Obviously he doesn't know what he's talking about," Thomas said.

"That's the thing. He does know." She clenched her hands into the folds of her skirt. "On the way here, I tried to come up with the name of one female artist and couldn't. Not one."

He dropped the blanket. "Maria Martin Bachman."

Jane blinked in bafflement. "Who?"

"Maria Martin Bachman." Thomas replied. "She was a

scientific illustrator who painted many of the backgrounds for Audubon's *The Birds of America*." He leaned forward as if to share a secret. "He even named a woodpecker after her."

What anger she had felt melted in the light of his smile. "How do you know that?"

Thomas cocked his head to the side. "Art history class."

A bubble of happiness lodged in her chest. She didn't deserve to have someone like Thomas in her life. "I've never heard of her."

"Sounds like your father hasn't either." Thomas settled his hands on her shoulders, his touch warming the cold places in her heart. "Jane, you're an amazing artist. Don't ever question that."

She felt flushed with joy at his comment. When had Thomas's opinion become so important to her? Did it even matter? She turned his words over in her heart. *An amazing artist.* "Is that truly what you think? That I'm an amazing artist."

"No." Thomas leaned his head against hers, his gaze holding her a willing captive. "I think you're the most wonderful woman I've ever known. There's no doubt in my mind about that."

Jane's heart did a little flip in her chest. No one, not even Papa, believed in her the way this man did. She leaned forward with every intention of brushing a kiss against his cheek, but he turned slightly. Their lips brushed, and then Thomas pulled her closer and settled his mouth over hers.

Chapter 11

Thomas had kissed a few women in his time, but nothing in his experience had prepared him for Jane. He slipped his fingers into the softness of her hair, tilting her head to the perfect angle to kiss her again. Her lips parted on a gentle sigh, and he deepened the kiss.

His Jane—that's how he'd thought of her these last few days—was talented and beautiful, kind and patient, rare traits in today's world. She'd put aside her own aspirations to care for her father.

Yes, she'd been dishonest, but to protect her father, not for her own sake.

I need to tell her about the article.

Thomas broke the kiss, the contented look on her face when he lifted his head a threat to his control. He wasn't ready to let go of this moment. Taking her hand in his, he gently tugged her around to the other side of the carousel.

"They were putting this in when I arrived this morning." He pointed to a thin iron pole hanging from the corner to just beyond the ride. Rows of metal rings, each a different color, circled the pole. "Do you know what that is?"

Tilting her head back, she studied it, her smooth forehead furrowed as she tried to figure out what it was. How he wished he could soothe the tiny lines with his lips. Finally, she glanced up at him, her gaze full of questions. "I don't have a clue."

"It's a game called Catch the Brass Ring." Stepping up on the edge of the carousel, he leaned out and grasped one of the rings from the pole. "The riders reach out and try to grab a ring. Whoever gets the brass one wins."

"What do they win?" Her eyes were bright with amusement, and Thomas had to stop himself from kissing her again.

"Most times, it's a free carousel ride, but the men who installed it said some people keep them." He flipped the ring over in his palm. "Those who keep it see it as a sign of good fortune." He reached into his pocket and pulled out a second ring. "I got this one for you."

Taking it from him, she turned it over and examined it then glanced up at him. "But this is the brass ring. You should keep it."

"I want you to have it." Thomas covered her palm with his hand. "If anyone deserves the best life has to offer, it's you."

She glanced down at their joined hands then back up at him. "That's sweet of you."

"I only want the best for you, sweet Jane," he replied, brushing a kiss against her cheek.

Even if the best didn't include him.

◝◞

"Mr. Looff will be with you shortly." The butler gave Jane a slight bow before excusing himself.

Jane glanced around the room. In one corner, a large oak desk sat with two comfortable-looking Queen Anne chairs in front of it. Along three of the walls, tall bookcases filled with leather-bound novels reached up to the ceiling. There was another collection of chairs and a sofa cluttered around the fireplace, where she imagined the family gathered in the evenings.

Jane walked over to the desk and sank down into one of the plush chairs as the library door clicked shut. Mr. Looff's note this morning had been brief and to the point. *"Come to the house this morning at nine. Urgent business to discuss."*

If only Papa were here to attend. She rocked backward and forward. The letter from Papa this morning was encouraging, almost cheerful. The exercises were difficult, but he'd seen some improvement. And as she'd noticed in the last few letters, there was no mention of their work.

Jane stood and walked around the room, trying to calm the butterflies in her stomach. What could Mr. Looff need to speak to them about? Was he unsatisfied with her work? Or was it something else? Her breath caught. Had he discovered their deception?

The library door swung open, and Mr. Looff bolted inside, his steps bold and enthusiastic, much like the man himself. He stopped then glanced around the room, his gaze coming to rest on her. "Ah, Miss Wells. Just the one I was hoping to see."

Jane swallowed, willing herself to remain calm. "Good morning, sir."

"Please, sit down." He walked over to the bell pull and tugged on it. Almost instantly, a maid appeared. "Mary, could you please bring us some coffee. And see if Cook has any more of those apple cinnamon cookies I like so much, would you? Thank you, Mary."

She bobbed a curtsy. "Yes, sir."

"Now." He turned and joined Jane near the desk. "Sit, sit. Make yourself comfortable."

This was not how she'd anticipated this meeting going. From everything her father had told her, she'd deduced that Charles Looff was a very unpleasant man. Yet the gentleman sitting before her was all smiles and kindness.

Dear heavens, how much trouble was she in?

"Miss Wells, you're probably wondering why I asked you to meet me here today."

Jane sat at the front of her chair as she had as a child when waiting for a punishment. "The question did cross my mind."

He opened a drawer and pulled out an envelope. "I received this a few days ago. It's from your father."

"A letter from Papa?" Jane felt as if she'd been punched in the gut. What could Papa possibly hope to accomplish with a letter?

Looff pulled out the folded papers and opened them. "It's very interesting." He glanced over the top of his glasses at her. "He says he's been unable to paint for quite some time now."

Oh dear. Why did he do this? Now she'd have to explain everything to Mr. Looff and pray he didn't kick her out on her ear. "He had a stroke a little over two years ago that affected his right side."

"Why didn't he say anything?"

The door opened, and a servant with a tray loaded down with a coffeepot, cups, milk and sugar, and a plate of cookies walked into the room. Jane thought about how to answer his question as their coffee was poured. The wrong word would destroy her father's reputation.

Looff dismissed the maid then turned back to her. "I shouldn't have asked you that question. I know your father well enough to know that he's a proud man. It must have killed him to not be able to paint."

"It was difficult for him." Jane added quickly, "But he was involved with every aspect of preplanning and color design."

"And you've painted the carousels for the last two years."

She nodded, feeling like an unruly child caught in the act. "Papa is an excellent teacher."

Steepling his fingers over his waist, Mr. Looff gave Jane an understanding smile. "You're very protective of your father."

"Of course I am. He's a wonderful man." Her voice cracked. "I love him very much."

"As any good daughter would."

The room went quiet as if both of them were uncertain what to say. Would Mr. Looff dismiss her father without pay? Would he speak out and ruin what little reputation they had left?

"I stopped by the hippodrome late last night. You've done a beautiful job with my carousel, Miss Wells."

Of all the things he could have said, Jane hadn't expected a compliment. She lowered her gaze to his desk. "Thank you, sir."

"I should have known it wasn't J.T.'s work." He leaned back in his chair. "His work didn't have the depth and richness your painting has. Have you given any thought about what you'd like to do with your talent?"

"I've had my father to consider."

But he continued on with his questions. "Why has your father never spoken of your talent before now? Surely he had to know you would make an enormous splash in the art world."

"I don't know about that, sir. People have a pretty narrow view of female painters." Except Thomas. He not only believed in her as an artist but wanted the very best for her despite everything she'd done. A smile threatened the corners of her mouth as she remembered their kiss last week. Her first kiss, and it had been everything she'd always hoped.

"Miss Wells, do you like painting carousels?"

Jane blinked, her thoughts so muddled by Thomas, she couldn't think straight. "I beg your pardon, sir."

Mr. Looff sat up in his chair, a thread of excitement in his voice. "I'd like to offer you a job, Jane, as the creative director for all of my carousels."

Creative director for Charles Looff? Jane sat back in her chair and mulled over the possibilities. She would have the creative freedom she'd longed for, a steady income, and a chance to put down roots. She could marry if she wanted.

Marriage. She'd never considered it until she met Thomas. If she took this position, they could continue working together. The idea of being with Thomas every day left her with a serenity she hadn't felt in a long time.

Jane's thoughts ground to a halt. What about Papa? Would he resent seeing his daughter offered the job he'd always wanted? Or would he be happy for her?

"You're worried how your father will react."

Pressing her lips together, she nodded.

Mr. Looff reached for the candy jar that sat on the edge of his desk, and after offering her one, took a peppermint for himself. "I've known your father for a long time. Knew your mother too. A charming lady. She was talented also. Some of her charcoals were amazing."

This was news to Jane. "I never knew my mother drew."

He nodded. "She gave it up soon after they were married. She said she didn't have the time to devote to it between managing the household and caring for you." He popped the peppermint into his mouth. "But I saw how frustrated your father became whenever anyone mentioned your mother's work. J.T. didn't ask her to, but Evelyn gave up her drawing to keep the peace with your father."

Jane hated to admit it, but that sounded like something that could happen with her father. "Poor Mama. How could she give up something she obviously loved?"

"Because she thought it was what was best for their marriage, and she loved him."

"That doesn't really help me, Mr. Looff."

"Then may I give you a piece of advice?" He leaned forward. "Take the job. Give your father the opportunity to be the man I've always thought him to be." He held up the letter. "He wants you to succeed, Jane. This is proof of that."

Still, she wasn't certain. Maybe Thomas could help her make up her mind. "I'd like to talk it over with a friend of mine before I decide, if that's all right with you."

"Of course, dear. I want you to be happy with this new opportunity."

There was a knock on the door, and an older woman walked in, her dark hair and eyes vaguely familiar to Jane. "Mr. Looff, I'm sorry to bother you, but Mrs. Looff would like to speak to you for a moment about the tapestries. She has some questions about the color designs."

"If you'll excuse me, Jane." Looff stood and walked around his desk. "When I get back, we'll discuss your salary and future projects I'll be working on. I want to make sure you have all the facts for your friend." He turned to the woman. "Ellen, would you freshen up Miss Wells's coffee?"

"Yes, sir." She reached for the pot as Looff walked out the door. "Here you go, ma'am."

Jane stole a glance at the woman while taking a sip. "Excuse me, but do we know each other? You seem very familiar to me."

The woman sat down in the chair beside her. "I think that's because you're the Miss Wells my son has been talking about for the last few weeks."

"Mrs. West." Jane held out her hand to her. "It's so very nice to meet you. Thomas has told me so much about you."

"Please, call me Ellen." She took Jane's hand. "So I hear you know exactly how to manage my son."

Thomas had talked to his mother. About her. A man wouldn't do that unless he felt something for a woman. Jane let that news settle over her. He cared about her just as she did him.

"I met Rose last week when Thomas took me out to lunch. She's a very sweet girl, and I saw how devoted he was to his sister."

Ellen shook her head. "That boy worries too much over us. 'Tis best if he gets his career settled before he interferes in his sisters' lives."

"That could take awhile. Even the best painters take years to establish themselves."

"Painter?" Ellen's puzzled expression confused Jane. "My son is a writer."

"That can't be right. He told me. . ." Jane stopped, going over their conversations in her head. In all their time together, she'd never seen the first painting, not even a drawing that he'd done. In fact, he'd never actually told her he painted. She'd just assumed it when he'd taken the job as her assistant.

He did say he was an artist, though one could say writing was an art form. Why hadn't he just been straightforward about his writing? Yes, she was a little disappointed, but that was her own fault. "What does he write?"

Ellen sat up a bit taller. "Right now he works the press at the *Providence Examiner*, but a position for a reporter has opened up, and Thomas is doing his best to secure it."

Jane sat, numbed by her answer. A reporter. Someone who made their living from digging up dirt on unknowing victims, ruining people's lives and damaging reputations.

And she'd been silly enough to share every last secret with Thomas, believing that he might care for her. *Stupid woman.* All he'd wanted was a story, and she'd given him a juicy one. Once word got out about her father, both of their reputations would be destroyed. Mr. Looff would rescind his generous offer, and her father. . . She sucked in a breath. This would destroy Papa.

She had to stop Thomas. Jane stood and started for the library door then, realizing she'd been rude, turned to find Ellen staring at her. "I need to find Thomas, but he took the day off, and I've no idea where to look for him. Do you know where he might be?"

Worry creased the area around Ellen's dark eyes, a mirror image of her son's. "He had an appointment with his editor this morning about a story he's writing."

So he hadn't finished it yet. She still had time to get him to change his mind.

"What do you mean you can't write the story I asked for?" Delano glared at Thomas from across his desk. "All I wanted from you was a piece about an insignificant carousel painter, not an interview with President Cleveland."

"I'm not going to give Jane another reason to hate reporters," Thomas argued, leaning forward in his chair. "And the story I want to write is the kind of story people will be able to relate to. Something our readers will remember months, maybe even years, from now."

Delano leaned back, his arms crossed over his chest. His expression revealed nothing, but there was definitely interest in his gaze. "All right then. Tell me what makes this story so different?"

Oh no. He wasn't saying anything to his man until he'd talked to Jane and told her the truth. How would she react? Would she forgive him for not being completely honest? If anyone could understand what someone would do for their family, she could. He intended to marry her if she'd have him, but first they had to get over this hurdle.

Lord, please help Jane forgive me.

Thomas looked at the editor. How much could he share without saying too much? "The story isn't just about J.T. Wells, but his daughter and how they work together to paint beautiful carousel horses."

"Why would Wells do that? He's the celebrated painter, and his daughter, well, she's nothing."

Thomas drew in a deep breath, trying to calm his anger. Delano was fishing for answers and thought nothing of using Jane as bait. Yet if he didn't give the newspaperman something to chew on, he'd be back at the printing press or, worse still, out on the street. "That's confidential, sir."

The office door banged open, ricocheting off the wall. Thomas jumped to his feet, surprised to see Jane standing in the doorway. "Jane? What are you doing here?"

"I would ask you the same question, but I already know the answer." She glared at him so sharply, he could feel the knife wounds. Suddenly she shifted her gaze to the editor. "Mr. Delano?"

At that moment, a spindle-necked clerk pushed his way passed Jane. "I'm sorry, sir. This woman flew by me like she owned the place. I'll get her out of your way." He grabbed Jane by her arm and dragged her toward the door. "Really, miss, you'd make this easier on yourself if you'd just leave."

"Let her go before I take you outside." Thomas pushed his chair back so hard it toppled over. In two short strides, he stood over the clerk, his fist clenched at his side, ready to strike. "Is that understood?"

The man dropped Jane's arm and backed away. "I have it on strictest orders to keep people away from Mr. Delano."

"I'm sure Delano will discuss your failure at a later date, but for now I'd suggest you leave. And shut the door behind you."

The moment the door clicked shut, Thomas turned to Jane, his hands running down the length of her arms. "Are you all right, sweetheart? He didn't hurt you, did he?"

Jane pulled away from him, leaving him strangely bereft. "The only person in this room to hurt me today is you, Thomas West."

Her words were like a punch in the gut. "Sweetheart, I wanted to tell you that day at the carousel when I gave you the brass ring." But then he'd kissed her, and the wonder of the moment, the joy of holding her in his arms, the gentle press of her lips on his, had robbed him of the ability to breathe, much less think straight.

She didn't answer but turned her attention to Mr. Delano. "I believe Mr. West has come here to sell you a story about my father."

The man studied her for a moment then gave a brief nod. "It has been discussed."

He felt her stiffen beside him. This wasn't the way he'd wanted to tell her about his job. No wonder she was so angry. Jane had spent the last two years protecting her father. This was more than a simple deception. This was betrayal. "Jane, if I could speak with you for a moment—"

She shook her head then turned her attention back to Delano. "Sir, I'm not sure what Mr. West has told you, but I can assure you that my father has never granted him an interview in all the time he's worked with us. I would go so far as to say the two have never met."

The man glared at him. "Is that true, West?"

He couldn't deny it. Thomas nodded. "I've spent most of my time working with Miss Wells."

Delano's bushy brows lifted slightly as if deciphering the information. Finally, he said, "Then there's nothing for you to worry about, Miss Wells."

"Thank you, sir," Jane breathed out a soft sigh, her shoulders sagging in relief. Then she turned to him, her gray eyes chips of ice. "Mr. West?"

He knew what was coming, but his heart, that wretched thing, held on to a thin strand of hope. "Yes?"

"We are no longer in need of your services."

He'd barely had time to recover before the door slammed behind her as she left the office. Thomas was still reeling when

Mr. Delano broke the silence. "She's the painter, isn't she?"

Tired of the lies, Thomas nodded. "Her father had a stroke two years ago, which left him unable to paint. Jane's worked on the carousels ever since."

Delano chewed the tip of the cigar as he eyed Thomas. "This article you want to write, how did you want to approach it?"

Thomas couldn't have heard him right. "You want me to write it?"

"I think you're the only one who can."

Thomas rubbed the back of his neck. "I don't know, sir. I don't want to cause Jane any more pain than I already have."

"Then go to the source. Ask J.T. himself to verify the facts." Delano smashed his cigar into the ashtray. "Go write your article before I change my mind and fire you."

Wire Jane's father. Why hadn't he thought of that? Thomas still wasn't certain that writing the article was the way to handle this, but having Mr. Wells's consent would help.

As he opened the door to let himself out, he turned. "Mr. Delano?"

"What?" he barked.

"Thank you." Closing the door, Thomas walked over to a secretary's desk. "Excuse me, but where is the closest telegraph office?"

Chapter 12

J ane walked to the end of path, the smile she'd plastered on during breakfast slipping away as the reality of the last month sank in again. It had been two weeks since she'd seen Thomas, fourteen days since she'd exploded at the news that the man she'd fallen in love with was just a conniving reporter.

I'm no better than he is.

She opened the garden gate, taking the path that led into town. Grace needed to post a letter to Papa, and Jane had volunteered to take it to the post office for her. Maybe today she'd get a reply from her father. After her meeting with Mr. Looff and her argument with Thomas, she'd scribbled a long letter to Papa, telling him everything that had happened since he'd been gone.

Writing the letter had given her time to calm down and think, and the truth didn't comfort her. She was no better than Thomas, and probably worse, considering she'd deceived people for years.

She'd soothed her conscience by telling herself it was to protect her papa, but in the last few days, she'd realized the truth. She'd been protecting herself from the possible critics, those people who had no use for a female painter.

Standing at the corner, Jane drew in a deep breath, the tangy scent of brine and salt water filling her lungs. She closed her eyes, needing a peace only God could provide.

Lord, please forgive me for my deception. I've hurt people by not being honest with them or myself. Help me to do what is right in Your eyes.

She opened her eyes. For the first time in a long while, it felt like her world was in focus. With a sudden sense of peace, Jane started back down the street toward the post office. She'd barely made it two steps before a woman she wasn't familiar with waved at her from across the street.

"My dear." The lady hurried over to talk. "I can't wait to take my grandchildren to the carousel when it opens in a few weeks. I hear you've done a splendid job on the horses."

"Thank you," Jane answered, slightly perplexed. How did the woman know she'd been the one painting the horses?

At the post office, then on the way to the hippodrome, Jane was stopped several more times with well wishes and congratulations. It was almost as if everyone in town had listened in on her conversation with Mr. Looff two weeks ago.

Jane was standing across from the amusement park when a tug at her skirt drew her gaze downward. A little girl, maybe six or seven, stood there, her clear blue eyes shining with excitement as she stared up at Jane. "Is it really true? Do the horses look like they're moving?"

Jane felt lost. "What horses, darling?"

The girl's childish giggle warmed her heart. "The horses on the carousel. Papa read it in the newspaper this morning."

The newspaper? But Delano had assured her he wouldn't publish an article about her father. She squeezed her eyes shut. But he hadn't promised not to write about her! Dear heavens, she needed to read the article before she figured out what to do. She bent down to the child. "Do you know where I could purchase a newspaper?"

The girl pointed to a drugstore across the street. "Mama always gets ours from Mr. Gant."

"Thank you, dear." Jane stepped off of the curb, but the girl stopped her. "What is it?"

"You never answered my question. Do the horses really look like they're moving?"

Jane gently tugged on the child's braided pigtail. "You'll have to come to the carousel and find out for yourself."

The little girl's braids bounced as she nodded then skipped away. Jane hurried down the street to the drugstore, stopped once more by Pastor Kelly, who told her how much he admired the way she'd honored her father. Handing the druggist two pennies, she hurried down the street to the park.

As she sat down on the bench and unfolded the paper, Jane prayed. *I don't care about me, Lord, but please let it be gentle with Papa.*

Then she started to read.

Thomas had been honest. He was an artist. His words were a tapestry of color and emotion that drew her in from the first line. He'd written of their work but also of the bond between her and her father, about the love they had for one another and Jane's desire to protect him after a stroke had robbed him of his life's work. But it was more than that. Love for her and understanding of the situation could be found in every sentence, every syllable.

She couldn't have painted a more compassionate picture.

And she'd sent him away.

A tear dropped onto the newsprint, and she sniffed. She had to find him, tell him she was sorry, that she understood. He wanted to provide for his mother and sisters as much as she'd wanted to protect her father.

But where could he be? The newspaper office was the obvious place. She'd start there and then move on until she found him. But first she needed to get Mr. Looff a message telling him she'd be late.

"Jane!"

She looked up from the paper to see Mr. Looff walking toward her, his hat skewed at a jaunty angle. "Good morning, Mr. Looff. I was on my way to your office."

He pulled the folded paper from under his arm and opened it. "Isn't this a wonderful article?" He slapped it on his open palm. "I knew that boy could write. He'll have his pick of positions now."

Positions, as in plural, which meant he might live in Riverside. "But Thomas wants to work for the *Examiner*."

"Not according to his mother. Mr. Delano offered another reporter the spot on his staff even after he published Thomas's article. Not that it matters." Mr. Looff smiled wide. "He's on his way to the city for an interview with the *New York Times*."

Jane's heart fell into her boots. "When did he leave?"

"I walked with him to the train station. He should still be there." He glanced at her, putting a steadying hand on her arm. "My dear, are you all right? You've gone as pale as a sheet."

"I'm fine. I just need to get to the train station before Thomas leaves." Jane started back toward town then turned. "I'm going to be late, Mr. Looff."

He gave her a knowing smile. "Not if you hurry."

Thomas stood at the edge of the train platform, his leather suitcase beside him as he waited for the ten forty-five to arrive. Porters, prepared for the first wave of summer visitors, stood ready with their handcarts to transport luggage to waiting carriages. At the far end of the platform was a young couple, the man's arm draped casually over the woman's shoulders as their children played alongside.

That could have been me and Jane.

Thomas drew in a steadying breath and turned away. His article had come out in the *Examiner* today, though what good it had done, he didn't know. While Delano had agreed to publish it, he reneged on his offer to make Thomas a reporter, giving the job to "a friend of a friend." No matter. He didn't want to work with the likes of that man anyway.

His only alternative was New York. Away from home and his family. Away from Jane.

Jane. Not that she cared a bit where he was as long as it was far from her. It had been two weeks since she'd confronted him in Delano's office, but it felt more like two years. There wasn't one thing he missed most about her; he missed everything. Like the way he felt her smile from across the room or her rich laugh or the look in her eyes when he'd kissed her.

He cleared his throat. Best to forget about those things. He hadn't heard anything from her—not that he expected it. He'd betrayed her in the worst possible way.

A distant whistle signaled the train's approach. Leaning down, he picked up his suitcase.

"Where are you going?"

"Jane." He turned to find her a few feet away, looking as prim and proper as the first day they'd met. "What are you doing here?"

She took a step closer then hesitated. "I could ask you that same question."

He shifted the suitcase to his other hand. "I'm going to New York to look for a position as a reporter."

A tiny line formed between her brows. "I'm sorry about the position at the newspaper."

Thomas shook his head. "Delano thinks I'm too soft to do any serious writing." Because he wanted to know, he asked, "Did you see the article?"

"Of course I did." She gave him a ghost of a smile. "It's all everyone in town is talking about this morning. It's on the front page."

"Really?" That surprised him. From the way Delano had talked, he figured it would be buried deep in the back of the paper.

"Yes, really. Mr. Looff is over the moon about it." She took another step toward him. "He's certain it will draw people from up and down the Eastern Seaboard to the park once the carousel is finished."

"That's good," he replied. "But his is not the opinion that matters the most to me."

"It isn't?" Her gray eyes widened.

"No." Thomas paused, almost too afraid to ask. But this was Jane, his Jane, and he wanted to know what she thought. "Did you like it, Jane?"

She came closer, and it was then he noticed the gloves crumpled up between her hands. She seemed vulnerable and unsure of herself, and it took everything inside him not to reach out and comfort her. "I thought it was the most beautiful piece of writing I've ever read."

"Even Mark Twain?" he quipped.

She relaxed a little. "Even Mr. Twain, though I do believe you made me and Papa out as much better people than we are."

Her father, maybe, but not Jane. "I'm glad you liked it."

The air around them vibrated as the train whistle blew again. The platform beneath them shook as the train slowly rolled into the station. People poured out of the ticket office to board.

He felt her hand on his arm. "Don't go."

"Jane—" he started, but she interrupted him.

"I was wrong about everything, Thomas. I never should have gotten angry with you like I did." She pressed her lips together, a nervous little habit she did whenever she was uncertain of herself. "I may not have liked how you went about getting your article, but I understand why you did it. We both wanted what was best for our families."

"But I shouldn't have misled you."

"You mean like I misled you and everyone else we've done business with the last two years." She shook her head. "I was just as wrong as you were, and I'm not going to let it ruin what we have together."

His throat grew thick. "I don't want that either."

"All this keeping secrets and pretending to be what we're not has caused a lot of heartache." She took his suitcase, dropped it down beside her, then reached for his hand. "From this moment on, I'm going to be completely honest with you about everything, no matter how it affects me or my father."

It felt like a sacred vow. Thomas squeezed her hand. "And from this moment on, I promise never to keep anything from you, whether it be good or bad. I'll always tell you the entire truth."

Her face brightened as if he'd promised her the moon. "Then don't go. We have a carousel to finish."

He gave her a crooked smile. "You mean you have a carousel to finish. You fired me."

Cocking her head to one side, she propped her hand on her hip. "Can't a woman change her mind?"

Thomas threw back his head and laughed. "You really are something, you know that? That's why I love you so much."

Her breath snagged. "You love me?"

Cupping her cheek in his hand, he lifted her gaze to meet his. "I'll always tell you the truth, remember?"

"I know. It's just. . ." Her face broke into a beautiful smile. "I love you too, Thomas. So very much."

Joy burst through him. He stared into her face, memorizing the shape of her nose, the tiny mark beside her eye, the fullness of her lips. Then he lowered his head and kissed her. It didn't matter if the whole world saw them. He loved Jane, and by some miracle, she returned his feelings.

When he lifted his head several moments later, Jane had a dreamy expression on her face. "You really are a great kisser."

"I'm not your first?" His words were teasing, though the thought turned his stomach sour.

"Of course you are." She nestled against his chest. "But it's lovely to know I have the best kisser in the world."

Thomas rested his chin on the top of her head. "I should put that on my résumé."

She tilted her head back to look up at him. "You're really going to New York?"

"It's the only thing I can do." He drew in a deep breath, the scent of her lavender shampoo invading his senses. Leaving her now when they'd finally revealed how they felt would be difficult. But if he wanted to marry her, he'd need a way to support them both. "I need to be a reporter, sweetheart, and the only way that's going to happen is if I look for a position in New York."

She nodded then stepped back enough to slip her hand into the pocket of her dress. She held out the brass ring he'd given her. "Here."

"But that's yours."

She shook her head. "No, it's ours, and I'm giving it back to you with all of my heart." She pressed it into his hand, the metal still warm from her touch.

Thomas leaned down and kissed her again, promising himself that one day soon, he'd replace their brass ring with a wedding band.

Epilogue

The lines outside of the Crescent Park Amusement Park trailed down the sidewalks leading from town, scores of men, women, and children all waiting for the opportunity to glimpse Looff's latest masterpiece.

Inside the gates, Jane stood waiting too. Thomas's train was due later that afternoon, and she was eager to see him. He'd settled into city life nicely three months ago, landing a job at the *New York Times* after the editor there read his article in the *Examiner*. He didn't report the hard news as he had hoped, but he found his niche writing human-interest stories that encouraged a nation mired in recession and facing an uncertain future. Jane had clipped each one, then mailed them to her father, hoping they would encourage him as much.

The gates were about to open. A tingle of excitement shot up her spine. Would the children enjoy the carousel? Would they find it as enchanting as she did?

Someone laid a gentle hand on her shoulder, and she jumped. "Really, Grace. . ." But her words scattered as she turned then threw herself into Thomas's arms.

"Miss me?"

"Yes." She lifted her face to be kissed then realized they were attracting attention. Taking his hand, she walked him over to a private garden Mr. Looff had put in for employees to enjoy.

Once they were out of view, Thomas took her into his arms. "Did you miss me, or did you just miss kissing me?"

"Both."

Her answer must have satisfied him, because he tightened his arms around her and pulled her in for a kiss. When he lifted his head, they were both breathless. "I've missed you so much, sweetheart."

Jane smiled against his chest. "It's just been a week."

"Seven days too long, if you ask me." He dropped a kiss on her forehead then stepped back, nodding toward the crowd. "I guess Mr. Looff is pleased."

"More than pleased. Tickets to the carousel sold out a month ago."

"Of course they did." He took her hand and threaded it through his arm. "Everyone wants to see your masterpiece."

"You mean Mr. Looff's. He's been interviewed by newspapers from all over the country since your article came out."

"Well, you and I know the truth. You're the Maria Bachman to his Audubon." There was a teasing glint in his eyes.

Well, two could play at that game. "I wonder if he'll name a woodpecker after me."

Thomas barked with laughter. "I miss our talks. Which is why there is someone I want you to see." He led her away from the garden and the crowded gates, across the midway to the hippodrome.

She glanced up at him. "Why are we meeting here?"

"It just seemed like the right place." He opened the door and led her inside. The carousel was all lit up, the strands of light glittering off the beveled glass. The horses stood silent, as if waiting to be let out of the paddock to run free, their ribbons and reins colorful and enchanting. It was everything Jane had dreamed of and more, because here was where she found Thomas.

"Jane."

A knot formed in her throat at her father's voice. "Papa?"

Letting go of Thomas's arm, Jane lifted her skirts and ran to where Grace and her father stood. She stopped just short of her father, then overcome by love, threw herself into his outstretched arms.

"Papa, you're home."

"Yes, dear girl, I'm here. And so proud of you, I could almost burst." He shifted Jane to one side. "You did a magnificent job."

She brushed a stray tear away. "But how are you here? I thought you were going to stay in Flagstaff awhile longer."

"I was but—" He broke off, glancing at Thomas as he joined them. "It seems your young man had something very important to discuss with me."

Jane glanced between the two men she loved most in the world. "What could be so serious that you needed to talk in person?"

"I'm afraid that's my fault." Taking something from his coat pocket, Thomas dropped to one knee in front of her. "Jane, I couldn't understand why New York didn't feel like home to me, and then I realized it. You're my home. Wherever you are is where I want to be. I want to build a home with you, have children with you, and grow old beside you." He nodded to her father and Grace. "I brought your father home because I wanted his blessing." He held out a band with a brilliant blue stone. "I love you, Jane. Will you marry me?"

She couldn't speak but could only nod furiously before she threw herself at him. Thomas kissed her temple then her hair before finally brushing a gentle kiss against her lips. Short seconds later, she broke off the kiss, her cheeks blazing as she remember the spectacle they were making of themselves in front of Papa and Grace.

"Do you want your ring?" Thomas whispered.

"Of course I do." Jane held out her left hand. He slipped it on, kissing her hand softly before letting her go.

She studied it for a moment then looked up at Thomas. "Is this. . . ?

"Our brass ring. I had it melted down and made into rings for us. The wedding bands are safely at my apartment back in the city."

"So I'll always have it with me." Jane admired it on her hand then glanced up at Thomas. Her love. Her future.

"Always. Just like my love." He sealed the promise with a kiss.

Multipublished author **Patty Smith Hall** lives near the North Georgia mountains with her husband, Danny. When she's not writing on her back porch, she's spending time with her family or working in her vegetable garden.

Carousel of Love

by Teresa Ives Lilly

Lying lips are abomination to the LORD:
but they that deal truly are his delight.

PROVERBS 12:22

Chapter 1

Exposition Park, Conneaut Lake, Pennsylvania
1910

"O uch! My ankle." Tamara Brand fumed and stared at the tall, ginger-blond-haired man hovering over her. From her seated position on the hard pier bench, the man seemed almost a giant. Even if he did have gorgeous blue eyes, which dared to compete with the open sky, she wasn't about to smile at his gracious apology.

If I ever meet the owners of Bessemer and Lake Erie Railroad, I will be sure to give them a piece of my mind.

"I'm sorry I was so clumsy, miss. I never meant to hit you with the suitcase." The man fanned a newspaper back and forth over her. "Please don't try to stand up. You might collapse."

It was difficult not to faint from the pain that wrapped around her ankle, but her irritation with the ridiculous situation agitated Tamara even more. She sat up straight and waved away his impromptu homemade fan.

"Please stop waving that paper! I never collapse or faint." Her words came out through clenched teeth.

The man tucked the newspaper into his pants pocket and lifted his flat cap, which Tamara had seen only last week in the latest *Ladies' Home Journal* referred to as a "newsboy," off his head and allowed unruly curls to spring loose. He wiped his arm across his forehead to erase the beads of sweat from his brow.

"I'm sure you need a doctor. This suitcase hit you pretty hard."

Tamara wished she could lift anything to give herself some relief from the July sun, but the unbreathable petticoat under her silly silk dress clung to her legs. She instantly regretted allowing Thelma to convince her she must arrive at Exposition Park Resort wearing this monstrosity. Tamara grasped the railing that protected her from falling into the cool waters of Conneaut Lake and pulled herself into a standing position, a short gasp of pain escaping her lips.

The other passengers were already off the ferry and traipsing toward the red-roofed Penn Pavilion Boathouse, where they'd be whisked off to their prospective hotels. Tamara watched them disappear, leaving her alone with the tall, handsome stranger.

"It's quite all right. I'm sure I'll be fine." She lifted a gloved hand above her eyes and squinted, noting the distance she'd have to walk just to get to the pavilion. She felt concern crease her forehead. Normally it would be considered just a short brisk walk, but with a throbbing ankle, she wondered if she'd make it at all. Tamara leaned on the injured leg and sucked in a breath then shifted all of her weight onto the other foot. The movement caused her to topple sideways. She quickly righted herself. If her foot didn't hurt so much, she would probably stomp it in vexation.

The man moved forward, ready to help, but pulled back at her glare. By the concern on his face, she assumed she must have turned pale from the pain. "Miss, you need to sit down." He hooked his thumbs behind his suspenders, cocked his head, and stared at her ankle. Tamara knew he was only trying to determine how to remedy the situation, but she felt like a goldfish in a bowl being watched by a big tabby cat.

Tamara's cheeks flushed, and she knew the heat of Pennsylvania's summer sun did not bring it on. She wasn't accustomed to wearing dresses and skirts that stopped just a few inches below her knee. Yes, it was the style, but modern styles were not for ladies' maids to wear. Society would rebuke her severely for dressing in such a revealing way if they knew her true identity. It didn't matter that her legs were covered by a new pair of black hose. Just knowing a man was staring at her ankle not covered by a long, sensible skirt made her squirm uncomfortably. She drooped back down, crossed her arms, and squeezed her eyes, fighting back the tears of frustration forming against her will.

The man pulled a white handkerchief from the pocket of his tan, cotton-blend knickers and handed it to her. She accepted it, dabbing her eyes for a moment, then scrunched it in her hands as a wave of pain shot up her leg.

The man crouched down in front of her and spoke quietly, as if she were a child. "If you promise to stay right here on this bench and not try to walk again, I'll find a way to transport you to your hotel. I assume these are yours?" His arm swooped toward the three large trunks and four hatboxes the ferryboat captain had set on the dock earlier.

"Yes, they're mine." Her voice trembled at the falsehood. She was glad to know it wasn't getting any easier to tell a lie. "And, yes.

I promise not to move. As you can see, I am currently unable to even stand on my foot."

The man's shoulders slumped in what Tamara assumed was self-blame. "All right. I'll go and get some help. Where are you staying?"

"The Hotel Conneaut," she whispered in awe. She could hardly believe her own words. Was she really going to stay in the grand hotel? The Hotel Conneaut was known for its spacious verandas, which extended the entire length of the hotel, overlooking Conneaut Lake and all the other wondrous attractions of Pennsylvania's Exposition Park.

The man nodded. "Only the best, I see." His voice dripped with sarcasm, which made Tamara lift her head. Her eyes locked with his, and she wondered what was behind his words.

"I'm Blake Conner, by the way." He held out a hand, and Tamara set her smaller one into his large grasp.

"Tama... I mean, Miss Thelma York." The words barely escaped her lips before she noticed the change in the man's attitude. He seemed to grow rigid right before her eyes.

"York?" he asked incredulously.

She nodded. Everyone knew the name York. They were one of the wealthiest families on the East Coast. Tamara shuddered to think of the risk she was taking, impersonating the daughter of a famous millionaire.

The man crossed his arms over his chest. A smile of sorts spread across his face, and he bowed in front of her. "It's a pleasure to make your acquaintance, Miss York." He seemed to put an unusual emphasis on the name, and she felt his bow was somehow a mockery. "Of course, it distresses me to meet you under such unfortunate circumstances. I'm afraid I'll have to leave you alone to find help, which leads me to wonder why you don't have a maid with you?"

Tamara gulped. She'd assured Thelma the lack of a maid would be a huge problem for this plot the debutante had come up with just to avoid being shipped off for the summer to a remote resort by her father.

"My maid was taken ill right before I boarded the train in New York. I felt it only right to send her back home. When she regains her health, she'll join me here." The explanation sounded plausible, although her heart was pounding as the web of lies grew thicker. "I'll be fine here by myself, if you'll only hurry." She tried to interject the haughtiness for which Thelma York was known. "I don't know what's worse, the pain in my ankle or the heat."

Finally, with several backward glances, the man made his way toward the Penn Pavilion Boathouse. She watched his back until he disappeared.

Tamara took a deep breath and released it, allowing her shoulders to drop, then returned to her original contemplations. *If I ever meet the owners of Bessemer and Lake Erie Railroad, I will be sure to give them a piece of my mind. Surely if they hadn't placed that ad in the* New York Times, *Mr. York never would have seen it and decided the Hotel Conneaut in the Exposition Park Resort was the best place to send Thelma for the summer while he traveled abroad. And if he had not pressed Thelma into coming to the resort, she never would have hired me to take her place.*

Tamara raised her trembling hand and tucked a loose wisp of autumn-brown hair into the Saratoga hat she wore. Boasting ten large flowers, the hat was stunning but, for her, too weighty. She felt if she tilted her head, the hat, which was securely attached to her hair with numerous pins, might cause her to tumble over.

If only she were home now, sitting on her front porch enjoying the summer sunshine instead of sweltering in clothes that didn't even belong to her, waiting for help from a man who obviously disapproved of her. At least he disapproved of Thelma York. It was all her fault though, because she agreed to work as Thelma York's maid for the summer. She just didn't know it would mean being sent to a resort to impersonate the New York socialite.

Lord, please forgive me for agreeing to this terrible ruse, but with Mother so sick, what could I do? We need the money.

Blake stomped toward the Penn Pavilion Boathouse, his hands clenched. He wasn't sure what he was more upset about, his hitting the young woman's leg with a suitcase or her pretending to be someone she wasn't. And of all the people in the world, he couldn't believe she claimed to be Thelma York. He had just seen Thelma at a debutante ball last month when he was visiting his aunt in New York.

Blake almost laughed at the comparison between the high-society, sneering Miss York and the sweet face of the young woman he'd just left sitting on the Conneaut Lake pier. Surely she couldn't imagine she'd be able to impersonate anyone as well known as *the* Thelma York. On the other hand, Thelma had been away at school for some time, and her photo hadn't appeared in any of the social pages in over a year.

What would make her do it? Why would anyone want to impersonate. . . His thinking halted as the reality of his own deception sank in. *Am I doing the same thing? I'm not trying to be someone else, but I am trying not to be me.* After all, he had come to Exposition Park and taken a job as a carnie to hide from his mother. She meant well, but he was tired of her pushing every eager, husband-seeking debutante who came along at him.

As a matter of fact, Blake was pretty sure he'd been invited to his aunt's recent party just to encourage an alliance between himself and Thelma York.

Blake lifted his cap again and ran a hand through his hair. For now, there was nothing he could do about the situation. He was the cause of the young lady's injury. No matter who she claimed to be, as a gentleman, it was his responsibility to take care of her until he was sure she would be all right.

He scanned the area, trying to decide what would be the best way to transport her to the hotel. He'd only been at the resort for a week and was still getting used to the crisscross of roads intersecting with the midway. Not only was the area confusing, but being a carnie could be a complex job. He was glad he'd only be running the carousel. It was one of the easiest jobs on the midway.

A bitter laugh escaped his lips. He, Blake Conner, son of one of the richest families in Stamford, Connecticut, was unable to handle anything very complex. Reared in a life of leisure, he was the prince of society, drifting along carelessly. However, since coming to the park, he'd learned he would need something more substantial on his résumé than "wealthy bachelor" to stand on his own. He hoped that doing some physical labor for the summer would help him gain the real-life experience he needed.

Just then, Blake noticed a horse-drawn wagon sitting outside a two-story building. He recognized it as the carryall wagon other carnies used to move equipment, food, prizes, and just about anything else they might need to take from place to place within Exposition Park.

Blake dashed toward the wagon, jumped onto the front

buckboard seat, and snapped the reins. The horse jolted in surprise but quickly settled into a slow walk. Blake began to weave the wagon through the crowd. One thing he knew was horses. He'd been riding since the age of two, playing polo since the age of eight, and was known for his equestrian jumping skills. All those skills didn't help at the moment, though, because he couldn't push the horse to go any faster without trampling people in the crowd.

For a moment, Blake wished he had a buggy or the new Ford Model T automobile his father had given him on his twenty-fifth birthday. *You left all that behind,* he reminded himself, so this wagon and old nag would have to suffice.

As he drew the horse close to the pier, Blake's eyes searched and lit on the young woman's hat. He recognized the mastery of the hat, having seen many women in Connecticut and New York wearing similar ones, but pursed his lips at the sight of it set on the petite woman's head.

That hat was meant for the real Thelma York. She would have worn it boldly, daring anyone to even crease a smile at the audacity of the overabundance of flowers. This woman, on the other hand, was too small and timid for the miscreation. Did she actually have Thelma's hats and clothing in those boxes, or had she purchased look-alikes? Thelma wore only the newest gowns, made for her in France, and her accessories were always one of a kind. There was no way this girl could have copied them.

He shook his head. No matter what he imagined, none of the images made any sense. Finally, he jumped down and strode the length of the pier. As he drew near, the young woman tilted her head back slightly and lifted her hand to the hat rim as if she expected it to fall off her head. His blue eyes locked with her mesmerizing green eyes, which were now rimmed in red. Signs of recent tears still lingered there.

"Is your pain worse?" he asked anxiously, stepping closer.

She lifted his handkerchief to her eyes and dabbed. "No, I suppose I'm just being foolish. I was sitting here wondering what would become of me if you never returned. I must say, I was beginning to worry." Her lip trembled, causing Blake's stomach to tighten in distress. He was raised in a world where the appearance of being a true gentleman was important, but most of his friends only wore it as a cloak over their true character. He, however, took the role seriously. A lady in distress needed a Prince Charming to save her, but if she was pretending to be someone she wasn't, did the rule still apply?

He glanced at her face once more. The tears she wiped away were real enough. Until he knew more, Blake decided, it was his job to treat her with respect.

He stepped closer, squatted in front of her again, and explained, "I'm sorry. I had to go all the way to the entrance of the midway before I found that wagon." He pointed at the sad-looking animal and wooden contraption. "It's not a carriage for Cinderella, but it's the best I could find on such short notice."

He watched her face and was surprised to see her eyes light up. Had she been the real Thelma York, her lip would have curled, and she would have demanded her own chariot to carry her to the hotel.

"That will do nicely." Her voice softened, "At least it's not a pumpkin. Isn't that what Cinderella's carriage started out as? Besides, I'm used to—" Her words came to an abrupt halt.

Blake recognized the faux pas. Thelma York had never ridden in a wooden wagon drawn by an old horse. This was a clue to the woman's identity. *Obviously not a society darling. I can't think of a single debutante who has ever ridden in a wagon like this.*

"I don't think I can walk that far." Her words drew him out of his musings.

His eyebrows drew together in concentration. He stood up and took a few steps away. "I'll have to carry you."

Her eyes opened wide in true surprise. This was not the coy way Thelma would have acted.

"Perhaps I could just lean on you." Her eyes dropped in what Blake believed was true embarrassment.

"No, until you've had a doctor look at that ankle, I don't want you to put any more weight on it. I'm hoping it's just a bruise, but if anything is broken. . ."

Her head wagged back and forth. "I'm sure nothing is broken."

Moving quickly, Blake bent over and scooped her up. She was light as a feather. "Just place your arms around my neck," he suggested. He felt her push on his chest at first, and then she choked slightly on her own breath intake and finally did as he bid.

To keep her from feeling further humiliation, he kept up a steady conversation as he carried her to the wagon.

"I'll get you settled at the hotel. When the doctor comes to see you, I'll retrieve your trunks and boxes. How long did you plan to stay at the resort?" He took a few steps and almost stumbled on the uneven pier. "Perhaps you should hold on?"

The woman gingerly placed her arms around his neck, but she tightened her grip. Her touch seemed to send a shot of electricity down his back.

She answered his original question. "The rest of the summer."

"Good. I was afraid you'd only come for a day or two, and this injury might affect your fun."

A trill of laughter escaped her lips. "With three trunks and four hatboxes, did you really believe I only planned to stay a day or two?"

Blake placed her on the front seat of the wagon and shrugged. "High-society women are always prepared for any occasion." He stared at her, hoping she would admit the truth about her identity. He saw her bite her bottom lip and press the handkerchief to her eyes once more.

So, she isn't ready to confess, and neither am I. For now, I'll keep her secret, and I'll stay close to her until I know why she claims to be Thelma York. A sweet girl like her can't be up to no good. There must be some desperate reason behind it.

Blake climbed onto the wagon beside her, picked up the reins, and gave them a flick.

"Didn't you say you were staying at the Hotel Conneaut?"

She nodded. Blake steered the horses down the boardwalk, through the tree grove in front of the hotel, and stopped by the veranda.

"When your ankle is mended, I hope you'll allow me to give you a ride on the carousel, Miss York."

"Is that your job, running the carousel?" She seemed intrigued.

"Yes, for the summer at least." He realized he must be careful about what he told her until he knew more about her. "I'll go in and make sure your room is ready." He hopped down from the wagon and moved toward the hotel, shame filling his heart.

Lord, how can I judge her for impersonating someone when I too am living a lie?

He turned back and glanced at her. Even with the outrageous hat, she was one of the prettiest girls he'd ever seen. "Will you be all right, Miss York?"

She smiled and waved him on. "Yes, I'll be enjoying the view. I've never seen such a lovely grove, and just look at the lake." Her hand swept around, indicating the entire area.

Blake made his way into the hotel and stopped at the front desk to check her reservation and pick up her key. He gleaned from the manager that Thelma York's father had made the reservation for his daughter and paid for the entire summer. Which was fine with him. What better way to spend his summer than with an intriguing, not to mention lovely, mystery woman?

Tamara sat in the wagon with a smile on her face as she imagined herself free from the burden of trying to impersonate Thelma York. She would be happily riding a lovely carousel with Blake Conner by her side. How she wanted this ordeal to be over and done! When Thelma had pressed for Tamara to pretend to be her, it sounded like a peaceful, lovely summer, but the reality of wearing Thelma's clothes, acting like Thelma, and trying to appear to be a wealthy debutante was much more overwhelming than she'd imagined. Her conscience ached each time she told a lie.

Mother would never approve, and I know my deception is not pleasing to God. I can only hope that when the summer is over, He will forgive me.

Chapter 2

Your room is ready," Mr. Conner informed her when he returned to her side. "I've asked the porter to get your luggage from the pier. He can use this wagon."

A young man walked up to the wagon, tipped his hat to Tamara, and stood waiting. Tamara felt sorry for him. All that luggage had become quite a nuisance to her, and knowing it was all made by Louis Vuitton made her nervous. She didn't want any of it to get damaged or lost. She pulled her reticule closer. Thelma was generous with the money she gave Tamara to use for tips, and this man was certainly going to earn his.

Tamara glanced at Mr. Conner. She wondered if she should tip him. If he hadn't smashed her ankle with a suitcase, he would have left after helping her off the boat at the landing. But now he'd gotten a wagon for her, checked her into the hotel, and provided a porter for her cases.

Mr. Conner's voice interrupted the questions swirling in her mind. "There's a doctor on hand who will check your ankle. However, you'll have to put up with my help a bit longer. I'll carry you to your room now."

Tamara's cheeks flushed. "Can't I try walking?" She pulled back as the man reached his arms out again.

He dropped them back to his sides and shook his head. "I'm sorry, Miss York. I don't think you can put any weight on your ankle, and I know of no other way to get you to your room. It's only a few steps into the hotel. Your room is on the first floor."

Tamara noted a tone of irritation in his voice. As Thelma York, she should take control and put the man in his place. As Tamara, she felt she needed to repay him for his kindness, but the pain in her ankle caused her to tense her lips.

"I appreciate your help." She lifted her arms. He picked her up again, and she wrapped her arms around his back, her hand sweeping through the unruly curls on the nape of his neck.

When Mr. Conner had taken a few steps, she glanced over his shoulder and watched the young man steer the wagon away. He didn't appear strong enough to lift even one of the boxes Thelma insisted she bring. But there was nothing she could do about it at this point. With a quiet sigh, she leaned into Mr. Conner's chest and allowed him to carry her into the hotel.

Once in the room, he placed her on the foot of the bed. "Shall I stay with you or go get the doctor? I left a message for him, but I believe I can hurry him along."

"I think the sooner I see him the better. It's been a long day, and I would like to rest." Remembering who she was supposed to be, she flung a hand up, pressing the back of it to her forehead, mimicking one of Thelma's dramatic actions.

She noted the frown cross his face, but in a most gentlemanly way, he bowed and turned to leave the room. Tamara wasn't sure what had caused the mood change, but the throbbing in her foot kept her from contemplating it any longer. She watched his back as he left the room. There was something slightly familiar about him, but she only noticed it as he walked away. There was nothing about his face she recognized.

Tamara had planned to check into the hotel and keep as low a profile as possible, perhaps stay in her room for the entire summer. That way she was sure no one would discover the truth. There was always the chance Thelma wouldn't uphold her promise to keep herself out of the public eye. If that happened, someone was sure to put two and two together. Tamara didn't want to get in trouble for posing as Thelma York, even if she was being paid for it. She especially didn't want her mother to hear about it. The doctors weren't sure how long she needed for recovery. They suggested it could be as long as two months. Three weeks had already passed when Thelma pressed Tamara into taking on the pretense by offering her a larger sum of money. Tamara had jumped at the chance because her low wages as a maid would not pay for one more week of the sanatorium's bill, even combined with her father's income from the farm. Tamara knew her mother would do whatever it took to regain her strength and get back home to her quaint country house, garden, and church choir as quickly as possible. Until then, Tamara felt sure she had to do something drastic to help. Thus, the agreement with Thelma seemed a godsend at the time.

Images of her home flitted through Tamara's mind. It wasn't far from where she was now, only a short trolley ride. Of course, she mustn't consider visiting until she was no longer playing the part of Thelma York. And staying out of the limelight was of utmost importance at this point. However, attention had already been drawn to her, thanks to the accident on the landing. The clerk at the front desk, the bellboy, a porter, a doctor, and Mr. Conner, the carnie, would all remember her as Thelma York. She tried to stand up, but pain shot through her ankle. She wilted down to a sitting position again and slipped off the tight shoes and black hose she was wearing. Releasing the pressure gave her a little relief from the pain.

A knock on the door interrupted her musings. Mr. Conner's voice, although muffled, announced his presence.

"Yes, come in." Tamara quickly dropped her dress over her legs.

The door opened, and Mr. Conner entered her room followed by an older gentleman carrying a black bag.

"This is Doctor Burroughs," Mr. Conner explained, stepping aside and allowing the other man access. "I thought you might prefer to have someone else here while he examines your ankle, so I came back." These last words were whispered, and he gave a small wink.

Surprised, she nodded and answered with a gentle smile. It was kind of him to think of her comfort. Being alone with a strange doctor would have been most uncomfortable indeed. In her whole life, she'd only been to a doctor once when she had the chicken pox. Otherwise, she'd always been healthy.

The doctor grabbed a chair and pulled it close to the bed. He lifted her foot and began to examine her ankle. Several times she grunted in pain and barely recognized that Mr. Conner sat on the bed beside her and took her hand in his.

The doctor finally finished the exam, released her foot, and adjusted his glasses. "The good news is, your ankle isn't broken. But it is badly bruised. I'll prescribe something for your pain. You'll need to keep your foot elevated for the next few hours, and you'll need to take it easy for the next few days."

Tamara didn't speak. She closed her eyes, fighting back tears of pain and frustration. The doctor picked up his bag and pulled out a prescription pad. Tamara shook her head when she saw it was a US Treasury Department prescription form for medicinal liquor.

"I don't drink and wouldn't want to have any alcohol, even for pain. Is there any other choice?"

The doctor's eyes registered surprise, and too late, Tamara recognized her mistake. Most society men and women would probably jump at the chance to get a prescription for alcohol.

The doctor scribbled on the prescription pad, tore off the page, and handed it to Mr. Conner.

"Thank you, Doctor," she whispered, her eyes beginning to close from the fatigue that had set in from the pain and stress of her injury and situation.

With a grumble and a bow, the doctor picked up his bag and left the room. As he stepped out, the porter stepped in with a dolly filled with Thelma's suitcases and hatboxes. Tamara pointed at one corner where she wanted the porter to put all the cases. Before she could ask for her reticule to tip the man, Mr. Conner pulled the necessary cash out of his own pocket, hurrying the porter out of the room and leaving himself and Tamara alone.

When Tamara opened her eyes, Mr. Conner was standing beside the bed looking down at her. Once again, he wore a frown.

How she wished he would smile. His scowl only reminded her of her deception.

"Miss York, I can take this prescription and get it filled for you."

"Please call me Thelma. I hate to ask it of you, but I am obviously in need of help. I can pay you." Tamara watched a stormy black color fill his eyes.

"I don't need your money. It's my fault you're hurt, and it's my responsibility to help you."

Tamara wanted to take back her words. She could see she'd insulted him. He was standing ramrod straight now.

"I'm sorry. I didn't mean. . ." Her voice dropped. "I do appreciate your help."

He crossed his arms over his chest and stared at her for a few seconds. She felt heat flow into her cheeks under his scrutiny. Finally, he dropped his arms and shook his head as if trying to shake out something bothering him. "If I am going to call you Thelma, please feel free to call me Blake." He turned and started to leave.

"But I can ask the clerk to send a bellboy. . . ." Her voice faded again. It seemed every time she spoke to the man, she said something that instantly caused his smile to flip.

This time Blake held up a hand to stop her from speaking further. She scooted back on the bed and shrugged herself onto the pillow. She was tired, and her ankle was throbbing. "Here, let me put a pillow under your foot. While I get your prescription, you should sleep."

Tamara's eyes felt heavy. She knew she should take charge or flirt with the handsome man as Thelma would do, but she was just too tired. By the time Blake left the room, she was sound asleep.

~☙~

Blake marched to the small pharmacy, which was housed in the park, holding the prescription in his hand. He wasn't sure exactly what to do. He knew the young woman in the hotel room was not Thelma York, yet he was getting ready to have a prescription filled for Thelma York.

Was there any chance there might be two Thelma Yorks? No, not in New York. Yet somehow this girl didn't seem like someone who could be doing anything illegal. There had to be a good explanation for her subterfuge.

Blake decided that getting her ankle healed must be his priority. It didn't matter who she claimed to be. For several days, she would be restricted in her activities. He'd have time to look into the situation, perhaps make a few phone calls to New York. He'd also keep a close eye on her, escort her around the park, if she'd let him.

He smiled at his thoughts. Any girl in New England would swoon if Blake Conner asked to spend a day or more escorting her around a fairground. However, as Blake the carnie, there was little chance of a lady like Thelma York, or a girl pretending to be Thelma York, even agreeing to be seen with him.

When the prescription was filled, he paid for it and hurried back to the hotel. He rushed by the hotel clerk without speaking.

Blake knocked on her door a few times. When she didn't respond, he used the key, which he still needed to give to her. He entered the room and saw her still sleeping on the bed, right where he had left her. This was an opportunity to search her reticule to look for an answer, but Blake didn't have time. He had to get to work. He set the bottle of pills on the nightstand then jotted her a note and set it beside the bottle.

> *Dear Miss York,*
>   *I hope you'll allow me to call on you later and see how*
> *your healing is progressing. I will ask the front clerk to deliver*
> *a meal to the room later today. If you need anything, ask for a*
> *bellboy to come and find me at the carousel.*
>
> *Blake*

He gazed at her for several seconds. She looked so young. Although she was no younger than the real Thelma York, she had an innocence about her that confused him and made him want to protect her. But would he be doing the right thing by helping her perpetuate her ruse?

Blake placed the room key beside the note and left the room. He strolled back to the carousel just in time for his shift. It wasn't hard work, just tiresome. The carousel was beautiful, having only been installed in the park recently. It was a Muller Harton carousel, with three rows abreast. Unlike other carousels, this one not only had horses but also other animals and two chariots. The music came from a band organ, which played as the carousel turned.

Each day Blake had to check all the horses and all the gears, make sure everything was in working order, and then run the carousel as the crowds gathered, awaiting their turns. On a usual day, he was content with the job and his anonymity. But today he wanted to be at the hotel, waiting for news about the girl claiming to be Thelma York.

The hours seemed to drag by. He was glad to see his replacement, Jack, arrive.

"What's the hurry, Blake?" Jack shouted over the din of the

crowd when Blake jumped off the carousel's platform. "Big date?" The heavyset man held a cigar between his teeth and chuckled.

Blake turned and stared at him. "What? Oh yeah. I mean, no."

Jack laughed. "Uh-oh! You've got it bad." He clambered onto the platform to take Blake's place. "I told you not to get serious about any of these summer gals. They's all the same. Just come here for a bit of summer fun and romance. Not looking for anything permanent."

Blake didn't hear all the man had to say. He was jogging down the midway toward the hotel, but he knew one thing for sure. He was not romantically interested in anyone who was pretending to be someone else, even if her eyes were the shade of emeralds.

Tamara awoke with a start and a moan. She moved her ankle, and the dull pain reminded her of her injury. The room was darker now. She could tell it was dusk. She pushed herself into a seated position and looked around the room. There was a light on the nightstand, so she turned it on.

Immediately her eyes fell on a bottle of pills and a note. Tamara lifted the paper and read, and a smile flitted across her lips. It was kind of Blake, but as Thelma York, she needed to be careful how she reacted. Thelma would care little for the man's generosity. Tamara had worked for Thelma long enough to see how she treated anyone she felt was an underling. That was one of the main things she dreaded about playing this part. Tamara could not think of one time she'd ever heard about when Thelma York was considered kind by anyone. Selfish and haughty described her best.

There was more than one reason Tamara was concerned about

being seen. Not only might someone realize she wasn't Thelma York, but there was also a good chance someone might recognize her as Tamara Brand from the town of Harmonsburg, which was only two miles from Exposition Park. Although she hadn't been home in two years, since she'd been working in New York as a governess first and then as Thelma's maid, she might still run into an old school chum, and that worried her.

It was strange to think she was now staying at the Hotel Conneaut, just miles from where she grew up. Yet she'd never been to Exposition Park before. Her father was a farmer and didn't have money to spare for such frivolous activities. As soon as she finished school, she had set out to get a job and had ended up in New York.

A knock on the door startled her. Tamara looked up. "Come in?"

No one entered. After a moment or two, another knock. Whoever was on the other side of the door wasn't taking any chance of barging in unwanted. Her legs were already dangling over the side of the bed. Moving hurt, but not as much as earlier. She pushed to a standing position and then, lifting her hurt leg, jumped toward the door like a one-legged jackrabbit.

When she opened the door, a bellboy stood outside the door holding a tray, and Blake was behind him. His mouth quirked into a brief smile. She didn't wait for either of them to speak. She just hopped back to the bed as the two men entered the room.

The bellboy set the tray on the foot of the bed, gave a small bow, and turned to leave. Blake handed him a tip and closed the door behind him.

He hesitated a moment before he spoke. "If you want me to

leave, I will. I just happened to arrive at the same time as your meal."

Tamara swallowed. "It's fine. I wanted to thank you for all your help."

"There's nothing to thank me for. You wouldn't be in this situation if it weren't for my clumsiness. I feel awful and want to do whatever I can to make it up to you." He flashed her a smile, showing his perfectly even, white teeth. It was strange how certain things he did reminded her of the so-called "gentlemen" who flocked around Thelma. But Blake's true kindness assured her he could never move in Thelma's group.

"You've already helped me so much. I think the debt is well paid. Speaking of debt, I've noticed you paying the tips to the porter and bellboy. Please hand me my reticule so I can pay you back."

"Miss York, I may only be a carnie, but I assure you I can pay a few tips. Besides, as we already discussed, your mishap was my fault."

"Yes, but if it hadn't happened, I would still have had to tip the porter and bellboy."

She watched the way his body straightened into a frigid stance. *Oh no, I've done it again.*

She moved back and squirmed into a comfortable position. "Would you push the tray closer please? I need to eat so I can take a few of these pills. My ankle feels a little better but not much." She hoped that would suffice to ease the mood. If she could find a way to repay him, she would. For now, she wouldn't speak of it.

Blake stepped forward and moved the tray closer to her. "May I sit with you for a few minutes?" he asked.

Tamara lowered her lashes. "Yes, that would be nice."

Blake pulled the chair close to the bed and sat down.

While Tamara ate the delicious sandwich and salad, Blake told her all about Exposition Park, the midway, the rides, and the different buildings where they sold ice cream and other wondrous treats. She forgot how bored Thelma would have been. Tamara ached to see it all for herself.

"Unfortunately, I'll probably be off my foot for several days and won't get to see much of the park," Tamara said sadly when his description ended.

"That's part of what I came to talk to you about. I asked at the front desk, and they happen to have some rolling chairs. I would gladly stroll you around, at least up and down the walkway in front of the hotel. If you do well in the morning, I'm pretty sure we can get you to the carousel later in the evening. It's not far from here."

Tamara knew she should refuse, keep to her room, but the draw of seeing the lake and some of the park was more than she could withstand.

If I keep myself covered up, wear a hat that hides my face, no one will notice me.

Tamara smiled and agreed to allow him to come for her in the morning.

"I don't want to interfere with your work," she said.

"My shift is late afternoon until a bit after dusk. I'd love to take you down to breakfast, and then we can go for a morning stroll."

"In that case, I'd enjoy the stroll very much."

◡◝

Blake made sure Tamara ate everything on her tray and took her pills. Then he left her room with a small chuckle to himself.

Wouldn't the other carnies be impressed if they knew I just spent the evening in a wealthy debutante's hotel room!

All the way back to the carousel Blake tried to come up with ways he could find out the young woman's true identity because, strangely, more than anything, he wanted to get to know her better.

Chapter 3

Tamara was able to hobble to the bathroom and get cleaned up the next morning. She struggled to open one of the borrowed cases to find a golden-wheat-colored silk day dress with a reasonably long train. The sleeves were made of four layers of lace, which hung to her elbow. She slipped into the dress, glad the great clothing designer Paul Poiret had released women from corsets with his dresses. She would never have been able to put a corset on by herself. She found the matching hat and white gloves and slipped them on.

She was unable to squeeze her foot into her brown laced shoes with silk bows on the toes, so she put the one on she could and then sat on the edge of the bed to wait. Her Bible was on the bed beside her where she placed it after reading her morning chapter from Proverbs.

Several minutes later, she heard a knock and called out for

Blake to enter. He pushed open the door she'd unlocked earlier. She inhaled deeply when he stepped into the room. He was such a handsome man.

"Good morning, Miss York." Blake pulled off his newsboy cap and gave a slight bow.

"I thought we agreed to call each other by our Christian names."

"We did, but what will people think? You're a very wealthy woman, and I'm just a carnie." Blake spoke in a tone that sounded as if he was making a joke.

Her face flushed as she squirmed under his watchful eye. He seemed to see through her, into her soul.

She remembered the Bible verse she'd read earlier. *"Lying lips are abomination to the Lord: but they that deal truly are his delight."* She wanted to tell Blake who she really was, but she'd promised Thelma to keep the secret, and earning the money to help pay for the sanatorium for her mother's care was dependent on that promise.

Blake reached out his hand. She placed hers in his. He pulled her to her feet then allowed her to lean on him. He placed an arm around her waist and lifted slightly so she didn't have to put much pressure on her foot. She hobbled to the rolling chair he'd left in the hallway.

"This is so kind," she gushed as he pushed the chair down the hallway and into the hotel restaurant. The square tables were covered in white linen, and the chairs were Brentwood. Each table had a vase with yellow flowers and a lovely water carafe set on it.

"It's so beautiful," Tamara said.

Blake pulled a chair out from the table and pushed the rolling chair in. Within minutes they were both enjoying fresh-squeezed orange juice, eggs, bacon, and toast.

"Did you know Samuel Clemens once stayed in a town near here?" Blake asked between bites. Tamara tilted her head in feigned ignorance. She couldn't let on that she knew the story about Mark Twain.

"He stayed on Lake Conneaut, pretending to be a man called Mr. Turner, but he couldn't get away with it. His true identity was revealed at a debate in a town called Harmonsburg. No one can ever get away with a pretense like that." His gaze bored into her. Tamara turned her head so he couldn't see the truth in her eyes.

"Have you ever read *Tom Sawyer* or *Huckleberry Finn*?"

Tamara lifted her face again. "No, I've had little time in my life for reading." She covered her mouth, realizing her mistake. Thelma York had nothing but time on her hands. Of course, she would never waste any of it reading anything other than ladies' fashion magazines. She set down her fork and blurted out in a haughty voice, "I mean, I don't care for that type of reading."

She watched a frown cross Blake's face. "That's too bad. They're both wonderful adventures that take place on the Mississippi River."

"Well, perhaps it would be interesting."

A waiter interrupted further conversation when he poured more coffee into their cups. Tamara tried to keep the look of awe off her face. Sitting in the Hotel Conneaut restaurant, eating a meal and drinking coffee, had long been a dream of hers.

"I saw a copy of *Tom Sawyer* in the hotel store. Since you'll be confined to this chair for a few days, I could purchase it for you to read while you rest on the veranda."

Tamara set down her cup of coffee and stared at Blake. Everything in her wanted to jump at the suggestion, but

Thelma York would never do such a thing. Still, she was here, and Thelma was not.

She tried to look bored. With a wave of her hand, she said, "I suppose that would be all right. It might help to pass the time."

Blake pushed back his chair and stood. "I'll just run over and get the book. Then we can go out onto the veranda and get you settled in." He reached over, lifted her hand, and placed his lips against the back. She smiled as he walked away and pulled her hand up to touch her cheek. She wondered if he felt the thrill that passed through her with his kiss.

"I am Thelma York. I am Thelma York." Her lips moved as she repeated the words over and over. She had to remember she was only at the hotel because of the agreement she made with Thelma. More importantly, her mother may need to be at the sanatorium four more weeks.

Blake could not believe he'd pressed a kiss on the young woman's hand. As Blake Conner, the action would have been expected. As a carnie, on the other hand, it would be seen as trying to rise above his position, something the real Thelma York would have recognized and pointed out to his embarrassment. In fact, any girl from that class would have known it. He could only assume then that this "Thelma" was not from their social set.

He closed his eyes for a moment, trying to conjure a vision of Thelma's friends. The red lips and short, bobbed haircuts they all flaunted flashed through his mind. But not one face as pure as the girl's he just had breakfast with was revealed.

He needed to be careful. There was some reason this girl was impersonating Thelma York. Until he knew why, he didn't want to expose her, and he preferred not to reveal who he was. They both had their reasons for secrecy. He knew his but couldn't imagine hers.

Blake strolled into the hotel store, found the copy of *Tom Sawyer*, paid for it, then headed back toward the hotel restaurant, only to stop and step closer to the wall when he noticed someone he knew across the room. Clarence Viscount regularly attended the same events, parties, and gatherings he did. The man was not his friend. Actually, they were more like enemies because Clarence seemed to take pleasure in inserting himself into Blake's sphere of friends and then causing dissension in the group. Viscount's most recent episode was one reason Blake decided to leave New York.

Blake's shoulders sagged. Clarence might not recognize him, but it would be better if Blake was nowhere near the hotel.

He hurried back to the table, holding up the book. "I got the last copy!"

The young woman's reaction startled him. She set her lips in a thin line and said, "I suppose it won't be awful, having a handsome escort for the day." She leaned closer and batted her eyelashes in the way he'd seen Thelma do hundreds of times. Her attempt at flirtation was laughable, which was another clue she was not one of Thelma's set. All the girls in that group knew the art of flirting. Blake stared at her, trying to see into her soul. Then he remembered Clarence.

"I was thinking, it might be nice to go to the swimming pavilion and sit on the observation deck instead of the veranda. There's a nice breeze."

Without waiting for her to agree, he grasped the rolling chair and began to push. He strolled her out the front door, across the veranda, down the front walk, and along the lake's edge. When they reached the pavilion's observation deck, he found a shaded corner where they could watch the swimmers in their voluminous black bathing suits and bathing caps.

Blake noticed her eyes fixed on the swimmers. "Do you swim?"

She shook her head. "Not very well anyway. I've always wanted to become proficient, especially since I've been near the lake most of my—"

Blake cocked his head. He was sure she'd just slipped up and told something about who she really was, but he acted as if she hadn't said anything unusual. He pulled a deck chair closer and sat down.

"I have some time before I have to be at work. Would you like to take turns reading aloud from the book, or shall I leave you alone for a while?"

"I'd like you to stay."

Blake opened the book and began to read. " 'Tom Plays, Fights, and Hides. . .' "

They spent hours taking turns reading aloud from the book, laughing at Tom's antics. When it grew close to the time Blake needed to go to work, he suggested taking her back to the hotel veranda. "But I'd love to give you a ride on the carousel later tonight. When I finish my shift, I can come get you with the wagon."

"I'm rather fatigued." She opened her reticule, pulled out an embroidered hanky, and patted her forehead. "Perhaps it's best I return to my room now. My ankle is beginning to ache again."

Blake stood immediately, concern in his eyes. "I'm sorry. I should've taken you back in hours ago. And here I am, asking you to venture out again this evening." He placed the book in her lap, turned the chair, and began to push her toward the hotel.

Tamara wanted to jump at Blake's suggestion, but she hesitated. No matter how handsome he was, he was definitely not someone Thelma York would give the time of day to. But she'd spent the entire day with the kind, gentle man and didn't think she could refuse his invitation. As he pushed her chair, she bit her bottom lip, trying to decide what to do.

Many people were milling around the area. Ladies with parasols in new-style tea dresses strolled beside men on the walkway in front of the hotel. The summer heat wasn't unbearable yet, although Tamara was glad she wouldn't be confined to the heavy black skirts and high-collar blouses she would have been expected to wear as Thelma's maid.

I have to uphold this charade, so it's best I'm not seen often, and especially not with a man from the working class.

She bowed her head. *Lord, I don't want to continue living this lie. Please show me what to do.*

When they reached her room, she handed Blake the key. He opened the door and pushed the chair in.

"Would you like me to help you onto the bed? I can send for room service to bring you a cold glass of lemonade."

Tamara felt her face flush. The previous day her pain had been so great, the fact that Blake carried her to her room and placed her on the bed didn't register. But today she was aware of his closeness.

"The lemonade sounds refreshing; however, I'm sure I can get onto the bed alone." She pushed herself up to a standing position, hobbled to the bed, and sat down.

Blake moved to the door. "I'll send the lemonade—and

tonight?" His blue eyes held hers, willing her to agree.

Against her better judgment, Tamara's head moved up and down. "That would be nice." She twisted her hands together in her lap, not sure she was doing the right thing. Blake was so kind, not like the men who usually flocked around Thelma York. The rich set took delight in scorning those below them. She couldn't imagine Blake being cruel to anyone.

With a small bow, Blake left the room. Tamara lifted her leg onto the bed, placed her foot on a pillow, and leaned her head back with a sigh. So far this "vacation" she'd agreed to was turning out to be much more complex than she ever imagined.

A bellboy delivered a cold glass of lemonade then left. Tamara sipped the drink, set it on the nightstand, and then fell asleep underneath a hand-crocheted shawl. She pressed the hand Blake had kissed against her cheek. In moments she was fast asleep.

Chapter 4

Tamara sat up straight on the hard buckboard bench, her head turning back and forth as Blake weaved the wagon through the crowds down the midway. It was better than a candy shop, with all the lights, sounds, and activities going on around her. They passed the Dreamland Ballroom, a two-story building recently added to replace the bowling alley that burned down in 1908. She remembered reading about it in the local newspaper.

Her eyes lingered on the building, wondering if she would ever have a chance to see the inside. With her ankle still hurting, dancing was out of the question. Besides, she barely knew the steps to the latest dances. That was something Thelma was good at. She could dance all night long.

Many women in their walking dresses and lavish hats glided through the park, some of them on the arm of a young man. Tamara couldn't see herself doing the same. Even if she were to stroll with a man while pretending to be Thelma, she would be too afraid of meeting someone who would recognize her as Tamara or someone who knew the real Thelma.

"Look over there." Blake pointed at a group of what looked like Indians.

"Who are they?"

"Just an ordinary family, dressed up in Indian costumes. Indians were the ones who named Conneaut Lake and roamed this area years and years ago, so the park set up a 'dress-up station' where visitors can try on Native costumes. Would you like to try one on?"

Tamara stared at the group longingly but shook her head. "Not with my ankle still hurting. Perhaps another day."

"Well, even if you don't, you can always purchase some Native knickknacks at the Cozy Corner souvenir shop." Once more Blake's arm swung out, pointing at a building. This one boasted postcards, ribbons, little boats, and glass plates, along with many Native items. Tamara couldn't afford to waste any money on trinkets, and she didn't want to spend the money Thelma had given her for tips. She smiled. "Perhaps another day."

When they arrived at the carousel, Blake tied the horse to a post. Tamara watched the carousel go around and around. She laughed at the children who slid to the side of their horses, or other animals, and reached out, trying to grab the golden rings.

Blake stepped up beside the wagon and held out his arms. Tamara scooted over and off the seat, into his waiting grasp. She felt the warmth of his hands penetrating through her dress. Blake set her on the ground but kept an arm around her waist. She leaned on him for support to keep her full weight off her injured ankle.

They moved together toward the carousel. Tamara could feel her cheeks burning from the excitement his holding her brought. She was glad dusk had come and gone. Even with the carousel lights, it would be hard for anyone to recognize her. Still, she tilted her head forward and hid under her hat.

There was a short wait, but within minutes it was their turn to get on the carousel. If her ankle hurt, she wasn't thinking about it. She'd always wanted to ride on a carousel.

"Do you want to ride on a horse or another animal?"

"A horse, of course." She laughed. "One that goes up and down."

Blake lifted her onto one of the middle-row horses. Then he mounted the one beside her. The music began, and the carousel moved gently, her horse going up and down, forward and back, as if it was stretching ahead to win a race. The ride moved slowly around and around, lulling her into a peaceful, dreamlike state.

Tamara relaxed. Her injured ankle dangled off the side of the horse. She'd never ridden on a carousel before and was positively transfixed.

"You like it?" Blake's voice pulled her from her reverie.

Her head bobbed up and down. "Yes, it's rather glorious." Her words rang out, no hint of the Thelma York impersonation. For this moment, she was Tamara Brand, farm girl and lady's maid, taking her first carousel ride and enjoying every minute.

"I always imagined what it would be like to ride a carousel. Trying to look at anything outside of the carousel makes me feel dizzy even though it's not revolving very fast."

"Just keep your eyes on me then." Blake reached over, took her chin gently, and turned her head to face him. Their eyes locked for a lovely moment.

The horses began to slow. Tamara felt a tug of disappointment until Blake leaned over and whispered, "Don't worry about getting off. I've given the carnie the sign to let us go once more."

Tamara sat up straight, grasping the pole, which anchored the horse onto the floor. "Thank you, Blake. This has been a wonderful treat."

In minutes the other animals were filled with new riders, and once more the music began. Tamara was transported into the fairy world of lights, music, and the gentle motion of the carousel.

At first Blake wasn't sure bringing this girl to the carousel was the best choice. If she was anything like the real Thelma York, she would be sure to snub him for even thinking of it. But once they arrived, he could see from the look in her eyes that she was thrilled to take a ride.

Riding a carousel had always been one of Blake's fondest childhood memories, which was part of the reason he'd come to Exposition Park and applied for the job as a carnie. He'd made a point of hinting to the hiring agent he'd like to work on the carousel. The man had eagerly accepted Blake and given him the job of his choosing. Carousels were not only for the young children. Many of the young debutantes enjoyed the carousel, and the agent said that having a handsome man running the ride was good for business because, as he stated, "The younger girls pretend to swoon when a good-looking carnie helps them onto their horses, and the young women feign interest, but they really hope the man will hold their waist just a moment more than is proper.

It gives them something to remember and dream about the whole winter."

After Blake lifted this young woman onto her horse and swung up beside her, he gave the carnie a hand signal, and the ride began. Blake watched the joy filling her whole being. She was definitely not Thelma York, or even one of Thelma's friends. Those girls were trained in the art of indifference. Not one of them would have shown, in any way, that she was enjoying the ride. Whereas, this one was like a butterfly set free from its cocoon.

After the second ride, Blake lifted her off the horse, carried her all the way back to the wagon, and set her on the seat. He stepped back and smiled up at her. She flashed her lovely smile at him. He inhaled and felt his heart skip a beat. This young woman was not the perfection of beauty which Thelma York claimed to be. Instead, she was like a fresh morning daisy, lovely and pure, much more to his liking. Unfortunately, he knew she was not the type of girl his mother planned for him to marry someday. Of course, his mother wasn't the one who would choose his wife.

Blake ran his hand through his hair. *What am I thinking about, Lord? A wife? All I know about this woman so far is that she's an impersonator, and not a very good one at that. I must get her to tell me why she's here, pretending to be Thelma.*

Blake leaned toward her, lifted her hand, and pressed it to his lips. "If there is anything you ever want to talk about or want to tell me, you can trust me." He tried to give the words deeper meaning with a soulful glance.

He noticed her hand shake slightly as she pulled away and pushed a strand of loose hair off her cheek, and she turned her eyes away from him. He moved around to the other side of the wagon.

It's too soon. She isn't ready to reveal her identity yet.

Tamara stared at her reflection in the mirror and frowned. *So this is the face of a liar.* She laid her head down on her arms and sighed heavily. *Lord, please let me hear that my mother is well again soon so I can stop this charade.* She'd just spent a very pleasant evening with the carnie, Blake, especially during the carousel ride. She knew her behavior had been nothing like Thelma's would have been. Not that Blake would know that. Still, there was something different about Blake. He didn't seem like the type of person she would imagine being a carnie. He seemed, well, a bit too sophisticated.

Tamara pictured the way Blake carried himself. His manners toward her were impeccable, much like the men who swarmed around Thelma in New York. Although she knew their true characters were revealed late at night, during their evenings of drinking and dancing. On several occasions, Tamara had been required to stay nearby in case Thelma needed anything. Tamara had worked hard at staying out of sight so the young men wouldn't notice her once they'd had a few drinks.

She shook her shoulders, trying to swipe away the unpleasant memories from her mind. The time she'd spent working for Thelma had been the most difficult in her life, but she'd been paid well. When Thelma asked her to take her place at the Hotel Conneaut for the summer and offered to pay her a larger salary, Tamara was only too glad to get away from Thelma's male acquaintances.

Tamara ran a brush through her hair. She'd been the one to

brush Thelma's hair in the evenings, before the parties and after. No one had brushed Tamara's hair for her since she was a young girl living at home. It was one thing to pretend to be a wealthy debutante, but another to face the mirror at the end of the evening and know she was only and always a servant.

Chapter 5

Clarence Viscount slumped down in a chair, nursing a hangover from overindulging the night before at the Crystal Room. Sitting on the front porch of the Hotel Conneaut was not as pleasant as staying in bed and being waited on by his manservant, but he'd left the man in New York, sure he'd only be gone a day or two. All Clarence could do was ask himself over and over again why he'd come to this out-of-the-way place.

Yes, Thelma York had indicated she might be headed here for the summer. Once she disappeared from the New York social life, he was sure he was the only one who knew where she'd gone. However, doubt niggled at him when he recalled the suppressed, excited glitter in her eyes as she whispered her plans for his ears only.

The one thing he knew about Thelma was she could not be trusted. He wanted to be her favorite suitor, but he doubted he was. And for that reason, he'd come to the Hotel Conneaut. He hoped to find Thelma alone and offer her his companionship without competition.

Clarence slapped his legs. He'd been here several days and had not seen even a glimpse of Thelma. He knew she was staying in the hotel, because he slipped an exceptionally large tip to the manager, who then gave him a look at the register. Thelma York's name appeared on the page, but the man refused to share her room number with him.

He spent the previous evening at the Crystal Room keeping an eye out for the debutante. If Thelma were anywhere near Exposition Park, she would surely show up at the only place to dance. Thelma loved to dance. Although he danced and drank until the early morning hours, he was no closer to finding Thelma York than when he arrived.

Clarence decided today would be the last day he'd waste at the resort. If Thelma was here, she was keeping herself too well hidden, which meant for some reason she didn't want to be found. He leaned his head back, his temples aching. He thought about all the lovely girls he'd danced with the night before. Although there were many amusing young women at the hotel, none of them were as interesting as Thelma, nor as wealthy.

Clarence rose to his feet and stumbled down the porch, headed toward the bathhouse with the notion of taking a morning swim. Several steps down the walkway, he swayed slightly, bumping into someone.

Bleary-eyed, he looked up. It took several seconds before his mind could make sense of what he was seeing. The face of Blake Conner on a man dressed as a midway carnie.

"Blake? Blake Conner? Is that you?"

"Yes, Clarence."

"What are you doing here, and dressed like that?" He swung his arm up and down in front of Blake.

Blake cleared his throat. "I'm a working man this summer."

Clarence broke out in uproarious laughter. "That's too funny, old man. Now tell me the truth. Why are you rigged out in such a way?"

"I told you the truth, and you don't believe me. So why don't you tell me why I'm here?"

Clarence cleared his throat and stared at Blake. In his practiced droll tone, he answered, "I assume you're here for the same reason I am. Thelma York."

Blake looked at him like he was crazy. "Thelma York? What would Thelma York be doing here?"

Clarence shrugged. "That's my question. She indicated she'd be spending the summer here. She was acting rather secretive, maybe hinting she didn't want to be here completely alone. I assumed she was telling me about it exclusively, but I take it she told you as well."

"Not at all," Blake said. "I haven't seen Thelma since I left New York. This isn't the type of place where Thelma would spend her time. I'm sure she's still somewhere in New York. Probably went to the coast for the summer like everyone else. If I were you, I'd look for her closer to home."

Clarence stared at him. "You seem awfully eager for me to leave, yet you haven't satisfied me with an answer as to what you are doing here." He stepped closer, almost pressing his nose against Blake's.

Blake stepped back and let out a sigh. "As I stated earlier, I'm a working man. I wanted to get away from Connecticut and New

York for a while, so I got a job here at the resort. I'm working as a carnie on the carousel. It's great fun." A wide grin spread across Blake's face.

Clarence crossed his arms over his chest and snorted. "That's the most preposterous story I've ever heard—a man of your wealth working as a carnie. I'll believe it when I see it." He leaned closer to Blake again. "I can see what you're doing. Think you can run me off that easily? Think you can keep Thelma all to yourself? Well, you'll find I'm not so easy to get rid of."

"Clarence, I can only assure you that the Thelma York you and I both know is not at this resort."

Clarence stomped off, leaving Blake standing alone in front of the hotel.

Now, what am I going to do, Lord? Blake turned away from the hotel and strolled down the walkway. He'd planned to see if his Thelma York impersonator wanted to have breakfast with him again, but now he'd have to be exceptionally careful. He knew Clarence would be watching him like a hawk. If he saw Blake with a woman, Clarence was sure to ask around and find out her name.

Until he could discover why the young woman was using Thelma's identity, he didn't want Clarence to know anything about her. There was no saying what he would do, but he was sure to expose her. For all Blake knew, Thelma herself was at the bottom of the ploy.

Blake strolled out to the edge of the lake. A slight breeze helped to cut through the heat. He was glad to be able to dress in the casual carnie clothes. He'd mentioned to Clarence about going to the coast for the summer, something he himself had done each year before, but this lake was much more peaceful. Even with all the people visiting Exposition Park, it was still less crowded and less stifling than the East Coast. Blake felt this was sure to be his favorite vacation spot from now on.

Tamara set her Bible down on the nightstand. Her favorite time to spend with God was in the early morning, before all the troubles of the day rushed in, especially now. However, even reading the Word couldn't erase her guilt over the lie she was portraying. She tried to rationalize away the guilt. So far she hadn't met anyone who knew the real Thelma York. Therefore, it didn't seem to matter much that she was pretending to be her. She wasn't hurting anyone by doing this favor for Thelma, and she was helping her own mother.

She dropped her head into her hands. *Lord, even if it's for a good reason, I know I'm not doing the right thing. Please help me to figure out a way I can fix this situation.*

Tamara stood. Her ankle was much better today. She probably still needed to stay off it for most of the day, but by tomorrow it should be fine. She wasn't sure why that made her feel so sad. Surely it couldn't have anything to do with all the attention she was getting from Blake.

She walked over to the window, pulled back the curtain, and gazed out at the lake. It was sure to be a lovely day, but Tamara couldn't help looking forward to the evening, when Blake would take her to the carousel again as he'd promised the night before.

Thinking about him lifting her onto the carousel and riding beside her brought a flush of heat to her cheeks. He was one of the handsomest men she'd ever seen.

Since they'd met, he'd been courteous and attentive, more so than she would have imagined a carnie to be. She wondered if it was because of her name alone. Thelma York was a millionaire's daughter. Did Blake hope to get something out of spending time with her? A reward from Thelma's father? Was there any chance he didn't know the name and was spending time with her because he liked her? Would a carnie in Pennsylvania even know anything about a socialite in New York?

Suddenly she leaned forward and pressed her nose against the glass window, straining her eyes to focus on one man she saw walking away from the hotel. When he turned his head slightly, she pulled back and bit her bottom lip.

She was positive he was one of Thelma's most persistent admirers, Clarence Viscount. She wasn't worried he'd recognize her. He wasn't the type to ever look at the help. If he was here, though, it could only be for one reason. He believed Thelma was here.

Peeking from behind the curtain, she squinted her eyes, trying to convince herself it wasn't Clarence. When he stopped again, she could see his profile perfectly. She leaned forward, her mouth gaping when he stopped to speak to someone.

Why is he talking to Blake?

She watched them as they spoke. She could almost see the way Blake tensed up.

What could Clarence and Blake have to talk about?

Now Tamara was even more concerned. Did the two men know one another? What did Clarence say to Blake to make him so tense? Why was Blake walking away from the hotel now? She'd hoped he might join her for breakfast again.

She had no answers, but for now she'd need to be very careful so Clarence Viscount didn't find out who she was pretending to be.

Tamara pulled back again and sat on the bed. She wasn't sure what to do. She didn't know if she should even go to the dining room. Clarence wouldn't recognize her, but if he was looking for Thelma York, someone might point her out, even though the only people who'd met her as Thelma so far were the manager at the front desk, the porter, the bellboy, the doctor, and Blake.

Tamara realized her hands were shaking. She decided she had to eat, no matter what, so she pinned a hat on her hair, which was swept up into a high bun. She slowly made her way to the hotel lobby and into the restaurant. She kept her head tilted in such a fashion that her hat blocked a full view of her face. She asked to be seated at a far back table that overlooked the lake. From that vantage point she could also see the tennis courts. If Thelma York were really here, she would probably be out playing tennis every day. At least if anyone asked why she wasn't playing, she could use the excuse of her bruised ankle.

As she gazed out the window, the waitress poured her a cup of coffee. "Miss York? Miss York?"

Tamara didn't acknowledge the woman at first then remembered who she was supposed to be. Startled that someone else knew her false name, she glanced up. "Yes?"

"There's a man who has been asking around the hotel for you. I assured him you were staying here. He seemed upset he hasn't been able to meet up with you."

Tamara wanted to slink down and slip away. Instead, she sat up straighter. "I'm here for rest. I don't want to meet up with anyone!" She lifted her chin slightly. "I would appreciate it if you don't mention anything about me to him. I'm surprised the staff at such a prestigious hotel would be discussing their guests with anyone."

Tamara saw a tinge of fear flash across the woman's countenance. She cringed inside, hating herself for causing such a reaction, but she knew it was the only way to ensure the woman's silence.

"I'm sorry, Miss York. I never meant—"

"I'm sure. I won't say anything about it, this time."

The woman bobbed her head. "Thank you." She slipped away quickly.

Tamara tried to take a sip of her coffee but couldn't swallow. Her heart was racing. This subterfuge had taken on a new aspect. How was she to continue as Thelma York but avoid Clarence Viscount and perhaps others who might come looking for Thelma as well?

Chapter 6

Blake knocked on the hotel door and waited. A few seconds later, the young woman peeked out.

"Good evening, Miss York. Are you interested in joining me for dessert? I know a wonderful place on the midway that sells ice cream, sodas, and milk shakes."

Blake waited. She was silent. He wondered what the problem was. "Is your ankle worse?"

"No. I would like some ice cream."

"Wonderful! Do I need to get the rolling chair or the wagon?"

"I think I can walk." She opened the door farther, slipped her head out, and looked around. Blake wondered what she was searching for.

"Are you alone?" she asked.

"Yes. I usually am. I don't really know anyone here at the park except for the other carnies."

"But I saw you. . ." Her voice dropped.

"Saw me?"

She bit her bottom lip and stared at him. Blake decided not to press her. He wondered if she had seen him talking to Clarence Viscount earlier in the day. If she knew Clarence, she should know him as well. They'd both attended events with the real Thelma York on many occasions. He stared at her, trying to decide if there was something familiar about her, but nothing came to mind.

Blake stepped aside and held out his arm. "Shall we go? I believe the carousel awaits us as well."

She placed her hand in the crook of his arm and allowed him to escort her down the hallway and out the door, her lavender perfume enveloping him. He was glad to see that her ankle was definitely better, but having her lean on him had been pleasant. The air was warm, and fireflies danced in the sky.

They strolled down Park Avenue and stopped at a white-brick building sporting a large sign: Ice Cream, Milk Shakes, Soda Water. After waiting a short time, they headed toward the carousel, each with an ice cream cone in hand.

"This is one the best ice creams I've ever had," Blake said as they stood beside the carousel, watching the horses go by. "The last time I had any ice cream was at the coast."

Tamara tilted her head. "The coast?"

"Yes, everyone in the city heads to the coast for the summer. I was just telling Clarence—" His mouth clamped shut as his eyes met hers. She blinked at him, innocence but also curiosity in her beautiful green eyes.

"Clarence?"

"Yes, um, a fellow carnie. We once worked at a fair on the East Coast." He looked away, trying to hide the shame he felt. Even if this girl was pretending to be Thelma York, he wasn't proud of his own pretense. "Are you ready to ride?"

Tamara nodded and allowed him to lead her onto the carousel. This time they chose to sit on a chariot instead of a horse.

"Do you know much about this carousel?" Tamara's question allowed Blake to relax. She didn't seem suspicious, so he assumed his slipup went unnoticed.

"Yes, a bit. I know that there are twenty-three jumping horses, thirteen standing horses, and twelve other animals—a goat, a hippopotamus, three bears, two cats, one giraffe, three rabbits, and a llama, besides this chariot."

Her head swung around as she seemed to be counting the horses. Finally, she nodded. "That is exactly right. How do you remember it all?"

"I have plenty of time to count them over and over when I run the carousel."

Blake watched her press her head back against the seat and close her eyes. "I could stay on this ride all night long. There's something so soothing about it."

Blake took a deep breath. Seeing her in such a vulnerable state brought out the protector in him. She was such a beautiful young lady. Not a thing like the real Thelma York, who was a beauty in her own stoic way. This girl was more like a fresh breath of country air, and he imagined she would be even more appealing dressed less like a high-society woman and more like herself. He was sure the outfit she had on tonight was one Thelma wore recently.

How does she have Thelma's clothes?

"On a night like this, I can't help but feel thankful to God for creating such a beautiful world." Her voice pulled him from his thoughts.

Blake moved closer so his leg pressed against hers. He could feel the heat from her penetrate his skin. It was like a warm blanket covering him. The heat reached all the way to his heart.

If only she would tell me who she really is.

Blake whispered, "Thelma, I hope you feel you can trust me."

Her head moved gently up and down. "I do."

"You can tell me anything. If you need help. . ." His voice lifted slightly with anticipation.

"Yes." Her lips trembled. Her eyes opened and locked with his. He was sure she was about to speak, but the carousel slowed and came to a stop. The passengers began to dismount from their horses. The movement broke the mood between them.

Pushing herself up and away from him, she shook her head. "I'm sorry. I'm afraid I was daydreaming a bit." She moved with a jerk, almost jumped off the platform, and would have stumbled had Blake not caught her in his arms and carried her several steps away from the carousel. "Careful, you don't want to reinjure your ankle."

She didn't pull away. For a moment, she actually nestled her head against his shoulder and whispered, "Thank you, Blake."

Blake tried not to use the name Thelma for her very often. He wished he knew her real name. He wanted to tell her how lovely she was, how her eyes made his heart beat faster, but he felt he couldn't speak of those things until he knew who she really was.

He set her down and loosened his grip. She stood on her own two feet, staring at him, her face infused with pink.

Blake took her hand and placed it in the crook of his arm as they strolled back to the hotel. It was a quiet night by the lake as the water gently lapped the beach shore. When they reached the hotel veranda, she turned to him.

"It's been a lovely evening, again. I can't expect to take up all your nights. You know, my ankle is almost completely healed. You mustn't feel obligated."

Blake took her hand in his, pressed his lips against the back. "I don't feel obligated. I've enjoyed every moment we've spent together, and unless you have other plans, I'd love to take you to the carousel every evening."

With an endearing smile, she answered softly, "I have no other plans."

Chapter 7

The following morning, Tamara sat on the hotel porch relaxing. She'd received a note from her mother saying she was getting better. Tamara told her mother she was at the Hotel Conneaut with Thelma and she should send any messages to the room under that name. Another falsehood she was not proud of. Tamara hoped her mother's note meant she would soon be able to stop playing the part of Thelma York.

Tamara sighed. She'd made a commitment to Thelma, but the longer it went on, the more she wanted to send Thelma a letter asking her to end the charade. However, Thelma had been adamant Tamara agree to the entire summer so she could sneak off to the coast without her father finding out. Tamara wondered how Thelma would keep out of the limelight for that long.

Just then someone sat on the chair beside her. Tamara had her hat tilted down but lifted her chin slightly, immediately regretting her action. Clarence Viscount nodded at her with a half smile.

The man lay his head back and moaned. "What a morning. Too much sunshine if you ask me."

"You prefer an overcast day?"

His eyes focused on her, bleary from the previous night's indulgences. From the sideline of Thelma's parties, Tamara had seen this young man in this condition several times.

His eyes stretched open a bit. "Do I know you?" His words slurred.

"No, I'm sure you don't."

"Hmm, something about you looks familiar. My name is Clarence Viscount." He sat up, leaned closer, and peered at her face. Tamara pulled back from his offensive breath and stood up.

"If you'll excuse me, I have some letters to write." She took a step, but he stood up and blocked her way, stumbling and almost knocking her over.

"We've just met. Can't we go for a stroll by the lake? Find a lemonade stand? Personally, I could use something stronger."

Tamara moved around him, feeling the tension in her ankle in the movement. Through clenched teeth, she answered, "Thank you, no." She strolled away, trying to appear nonchalant, her limbs shaking. When she reached the hotel door, she looked back over her shoulder. Clarence had slung himself back on the chair and once more sat with his head thrown back.

Relief coursed through her. Tamara made her way to the dining room and asked for the same seat by the window where she'd sat the previous day. In minutes she was enjoying her orange juice and waiting for breakfast.

"So, this is where you snuck away to."

Tamara's head popped up in surprise. Clarence stood beside

her. "May I join you?" He sat in the chair across the table from her without waiting for a reply. "I just need to know where I've met you or my head will hurt all day thinking about it."

Tamara set down her glass. "I can assure you, sir, you do not know me." She searched the room for a way of escape.

Clarence continued as if she hadn't spoken. "I'm sure I should remember someone as beautiful as you." He reached across the table, lifted her hand, and clasped it between his. Tamara had seen him do this with Thelma many times.

"You'll have to excuse me." Tamara pulled her hand away, pushed back her chair, stood, and briskly exited. She hurried to her room, where she sagged onto the bed and lay praying the summer would go by quickly.

Blake saw "Thelma" rush out of the dining room and head toward her room. He wanted to follow, but curiosity caused him to go to the dining room instead. He stood outside the door, looking over all the Brentwood chairs until his eyes lit on Clarence. His hands clenched.

Blake strolled across the room, pulled out a chair, and sat across from Clarence.

"Morning, Viscount. Still hoping to find Thelma here?" His voice took on the dull drawl his crowd tended to use. "I can assure you Thelma York is not within one hundred miles of this hotel."

Clarence scratched his head. "So it seems, but that doesn't mean there aren't some lovely women here. I've been enjoying the evenings at the dance hall, and I just now met a most provocative young woman. I'm sure I've seen her before, but she's playing the coy game. Only a matter of time, old man, before I run her to ground."

Blake shook his head. "Not quite your league of ladies here. Most of them are fresh off the farms." His insides cringed at his own crude words. "I've even considered jumping ship and heading for the coast, where I'm sure to find Thelma hidden away, pining for a real man."

Blake noted the flash of anger in Clarence's eyes. Blake knew Clarence wasn't one to leave a challenge unaccepted.

Clarence threw down his napkin on the table and stood. "Guess I'll check out today. There's sure to be more action on the coast. But if I were you, old man, I'd just stick around here and play on your carousel. You know the women on the East Coast won't care to go with a man they hear has been getting his hands dirty working at a carnival." He tossed back his head and laughed.

A year ago, a month ago, a week ago, Clarence's words would have made his blood boil, but since meeting the young woman posing as Thelma York who didn't seem to mind him being a carnie, Blake wasn't sure the young women in New York were the type he wanted in his life after all. His mother had been pushing him to get engaged. Not one of the debutantes could hold a candle to. . .

Lord, please help me discover her real name.

Tamara splashed cold water on her hot cheeks. This was silly. She couldn't stay in her hotel room all day. She wanted to go swimming. Surely Clarence wouldn't be able to find her in the black bathing suit that matched those all the other female hotel guests would be wearing.

She timidly slipped from her room, covering her face with a

hat and scarf, then scurried down the hall. She stopped when she noticed Clarence leaning against the front desk, talking to the manager. Since his back was turned, she hurried out the front door.

She lifted her parasol and strolled leisurely down the path leading through the tree grove in front of the hotel then along the edge of the lake. She reached the bathhouse and, without a glance back, entered.

ℕ

"So, you want to check out?" the manager asked, a frown spreading across his face.

Clarence nodded. "Not quite enough action for me here." He turned his head and caught a glimpse of the woman he'd met earlier as she hurried out the front door. "Excuse me, do you happen to know that woman's name? We met this morning, but circumstances didn't give us time for formal introductions."

The manager tilted his head to see beyond Clarence then straightened. "Yes, that is Miss York." He turned back to his register. "Now, what can we do to convince you to stay on with us?"

"York? That's odd. I know some Yorks back east."

The manager shrugged. "That's Thelma York, from New York."

Clarence's mouth dropped open. "Thelma York? Surely you jest."

"Not at all. Her father wired ahead and secured one of our best rooms. I made a point to look him up. Very wealthy man. In the society papers all the time."

Clarence clenched the edge of the counter. "Yes, and so is his daughter, so I'm not sure who you're trying to kid. That young woman is not Thelma York. I happen to know Thelma York personally. I will, however, look into this imposter."

"Well, I looked up photos of Mr. York, not his daughter." The man pulled at the collar of his shirt, and Clarence could see the man's hand tremble.

"I guess I'll have to stay a few more days." Clarence pushed the register back across the counter and scooped up his key again. "I've got some investigating to do."

Clarence stomped out of the hotel, his eyes searching the area. When they finally lit on the imposter's parasol, he began to hurry. She was heading toward the bathhouse. Once she was dressed in the standard black bathing suit and black cap like all the other women, he'd never be able to pick her out of the crowd.

Tamara stared at her reflection in the bathhouse mirror. Her cheeks were flushed with excitement. It had been years since she'd been in the lake. She didn't feel comfortable swimming too far out, but she could wade around. For just a moment, her fear of being seen by Clarence Viscount disappeared. She skipped out the bathhouse door and crashed straight into a man's chest.

"So, we meet again, Miss York." The man's voice dripped with sarcasm.

Tamara's eyes locked with his.

Clarence leaned closer and snarled, "That is your name, isn't it?"

Tamara bit the inside of her cheek. She scanned the area, searching for a way to get away from him, but Clarence grabbed her hand and pulled her toward a lounge chair. "We're going to have a nice long talk," he said.

Tamara tried to pull her arm away, but Clarence held tight. She tried to plant her feet, but the pressure from his tug sent pain through her leg. He gave a sharp pull, and her ankle twisted.

"Oh!" Tamara crumbled to the ground, tears rushing to her eyes.

"What's going on here?"

Blake's voice filled Tamara with relief at first. However, she was concerned Clarence would tell Blake she wasn't Thelma York. She tilted her head up. "Blake, I've hurt my ankle again!" Her lips pressed together in pain, and her head began to spin.

Blake pushed Clarence away, bent over, and scooped Tamara into his arms. She pressed her face against his chest, tears flowing freely now.

"Whatever you've done to her, you'll pay, Viscount!" Blake called over his shoulder as he carried her to the first aid building on the midway.

Once she met the doctor, he wrapped her ankle, and the pain began to subside. Finally, Tamara's mind cleared. Suddenly she sat up straight, staring at Blake.

"How did you know that man's last name is Viscount?"

Chapter 8

Blake clenched his teeth. He hadn't wanted her to discover his relationship to Clarence Viscount, but he was also tired of the lies between them. It was time for him to come clean. Then perhaps she would too.

"I'll tell you all about it once we take care of you. The doctor wants you to put your leg up again."

She slapped her hands on the chair. "Grr, I'm tired of this ankle. I'm beginning to wonder if it will ever get well."

"I'm sure it will get better soon. You'll be dancing in New York in no time."

Blake saw her eyes drop and a pink flush cross her cheeks.

"Can I help you to your room?" Blake took her hands and lifted her to her feet. She sighed and leaned on his arm as they made their way to the hotel. With each step she took, Blake could see her wince in pain.

"That scoundrel will pay for this," Blake's voice growled out.

She shook her head. "Please, Blake. He doesn't matter."

"But what he did was. . . Well, I can't think of a word for it, but he deserves some type of punishment."

"That's what forgiveness is for. Don't we all deserve some kind of punishment in our lives for our sins?"

They reached the hotel porch. "I'd like to continue this conversation. Would you like to sit out here? I'm sure we can find some pillows to elevate your leg."

She nodded. "I do hate spending the whole day in bed. It's very boring."

"Well, until I have to go back to the carousel, I can keep you company." Blake held her arm and helped lower her onto a lounge chair. He waved for the porter and asked for two glasses of lemonade and a pillow. In minutes Blake was ensconced in a chair beside her, and they were both sipping their cool drinks.

"Now, please continue with the conversation about the punishment we all deserve."

"Isn't it true? The Bible says, 'For all have sinned, and come short of the glory of God.' If we've all sinned, then we all deserve punishment, but God has forgiven us, so we should forgive others."

Blake ran his hand through his hair, wondering how a girl who was so blatantly lying about who she was could talk so reverently about God and forgiveness.

She set her hand on his arm. "So forget doing anything to Clarence Viscount. I'm sure he believed he had a good reason for what he did."

Blake set down his glass of lemonade on the small stand between the chairs. "Have you met this Clarence Viscount before?"

He watched her face turn pale.

"No. That is, I've seen him before in New York. And you? I heard you call him by name. Do you know him?" She leaned forward.

"I—I heard someone call him by name by the carousel the other night." Blake's stomach twisted at his own words. Here they were talking about God's forgiveness, and he was lying to her.

Would it matter if I told her who I really am? Does she already know? If she knows who Clarence Viscount is, she must know me.

"I've been in New York before. Have you ever seen me?"

The girl gulped but shook her head. Blake felt she was lying.

"You've had enough excitement for the day. Why don't I get you settled in your room? I'll come back with the rolling chair tonight and take you to the carousel. That is, if you aren't getting tired of riding the carousel every night."

She sat up straight. "Not at all. I love the carousel." She pressed herself into a standing position, took his arm, and hobbled along beside him to her room. Before closing the door, she tilted her head with an enchanting smile. "I'm looking forward to riding the carousel later."

He wasn't sure why, but Blake felt like dancing. Instead, he took two steps backward and leaned forward in a bow. "Until then. . ."

She giggled and closed the door. Blake turned and jumped in the air, clicked his feet together, and almost bounced down the hallway. When he reached the hotel's front door, he suddenly stopped, turned back toward her room, and felt his jaw drop.

Lord, I don't even know her name, but I'm pretty sure I'm falling in love with her.

Tamara laughed gaily as Blake pushed the rolling chair down the midway, pointing out interesting sights and making little jokes. The colors of the park at night dazzled her, and she forgot her burden of pretending to be Thelma York and really enjoyed herself for a while. As they neared the carousel, Blake stopped pushing the chair.

"The line seems especially long. There may be a problem with the carousel. I'll go check on it. May I leave you alone for a moment?"

Tamara smiled. "Of course."

Blake pushed her closer to the side of the walkway then scuttled off.

Tamara strained her neck, trying to keep an eye on Blake, but he disappeared onto the carousel platform. She sat back in the chair and took a deep breath of the cool evening air. This was the type of night she loved most and had missed when living in New York, working for Thelma.

Just then, a small boy stopped by the chair. She noticed his cheeks were stained with tears.

"Are you lost?" She leaned closer, softly grasping his hand. She assumed he was about six years old. His large brown eyes stared at her as he nodded.

"What's your name?"

"Charlie," the boy hiccuped. "I gotta find my sister. She losted me." His tears began to flow again. Tamara opened her arms, and he flung himself into her embrace, his shoulders shaking.

"Well, who do we have here?" Tamara felt relief shoot through her at Blake's voice. With her ankle twisted, she'd wondered what she could do to help this boy.

"This is Charlie. He must've gotten separated from his sister. What can we do to help him?"

Blake squatted in front of Charlie with a grin. "Hmm, I suggest we start with an ice cream cone."

Charlie's eyes lit up. "But Julie says ice cream will give me a tummy ache."

Blake stood, ruffling Charlie's hair. "I think Julie will be okay with you having one small ice cream cone. Do you like vanilla or chocolate?"

"Chocolate."

Tamara could see that Charlie was no longer upset. Since the first moment she met him, Blake continued to impress her with his kindness, but his behavior in general was nothing like that of the other carnies. Most of them were a rough bunch, but Blake had a sophistication that set him apart from all the rest.

"How about you help me push this lovely lady to the ice cream stand?" Blake moved behind the chair. Charlie grabbed onto one side, and they both began to push. Within minutes they were each eating a chocolate ice cream cone.

"What now?" Tamara whispered so only Blake could hear.

"I figure by now his sister is looking for him and is probably at the lost and found booth. I wanted to give her time to miss him and get there. I'm pretty sure she'll never lose him again."

Tamara stared at him, impressed with his reasoning.

Blake led them toward the lost and found booth. As Blake surmised, Charlie's sister was already there, glancing around frantically. When she caught a glimpse of her brother, she plunged through the crowd, scooped up the boy in her arms, and through tears and laughter, begged him never to wander off again.

Charlie squirmed out of his sister's arms and stood beside Blake, hands on his hips. "Julie, you losted me, but I got to have ice cream, and it doesn't hurt my tummy." He nodded to emphasize his point.

Julie glanced up at Blake's tall, strong stance and gulped. "Thank you for finding him and for the ice cream." Her voice trembled.

Tamara was about to speak some comforting words, but Blake unfolded his arms and grinned.

"I'm just glad he told us he was lost."

Julie fidgeted with her purse. "Can I pay you for the ice cream?"

Blake held up his hand and shook his head. "No, it was my treat. Just promise to keep a closer eye on Charlie from now on."

Julie nodded vigorously.

Before the brother and sister left, Charlie ran over and gave Tamara a hug. She had to wipe her eyes several times to keep tears from spilling out. When they were alone again, Tamara smiled at Blake.

"The way you handled that situation was wonderful. How did you know just what to do? Are the carnies trained to deal with lost children?" Tamara was surprised to see Blake's shoulders droop at her compliment.

"No. I just did what I believed was best. I imagined my own sister and what would've helped her most."

"Well, I believe you hit the nail on the head. I don't think Charlie's sister will ever lose him again."

Chapter 9

Blake watched Clarence Viscount stomp back and forth in front of the carousel. He knew he had to wait for the other man's anger to subside before he could talk any sense into him. Finally, Clarence stopped.

"So now you see. This whole thing is a big cover-up. That girl in the hotel, who is calling herself Thelma York, is just a ploy set up by Thelma to fool her father. And I've wasted so much time here when Thelma's been at the coast all along."

The urge to laugh pressed at Blake's ribs, but he knew better than to upset Clarence any further. "If you remember, I did suggest that very thing to you."

Clarence squinted at Blake through his morning-blurry eyes. "You've known all along the girl isn't Thelma, so why haven't you done anything about it?"

"If you must know, I've been hoping she would tell me the

truth herself. I'm just glad to know she isn't some insane person who thinks she is Thelma. This is just like Thelma though. She's put this young woman into a role she's not fit for."

Clarence ran a hand through his hair. "Indeed. She's just her maid, Tamara Something-or-other. How could Thelma do this? If anyone finds out I spent time with a maid, I'll be the laughing-stock of New York."

Blake felt his hands clench. He figured he'd done this more often since meeting Thelma's substitute than any other time in his life. This time it was to keep himself from punching Clarence in the face.

Blake spoke to him in a harsh voice. "I hardly think spending time with a kind young woman would be any reason for your friends to laugh at you." But Blake knew the truth. The group he and Clarence ran with in New York would, in fact, laugh at them both for their interest in Thelma's maid.

At least I know her name now, Blake comforted himself.

"I'm just glad Thelma answered my call and told me the truth before I did anything stupid."

Blake glared at him. "Chasing Tamara to the swimming area, causing her to twist her already injured ankle, wasn't stupid?"

Clarence straightened and stared down his nose at Blake. "Water under the bridge. I'm off, old man. Time for me to head to the coast."

Blake watched Clarence's back as he walked away. A sense of relief washed over him. If Clarence left right away, he wouldn't have time to approach Thelma's maid and expose her. Blake still hoped she would come to trust him enough to tell him the truth herself.

But should I tell her the truth first?

Blake tried to imagine the maid's reaction to finding out he was one of New England's wealthiest and most eligible young men. She would no longer look at him with her endearing smile. Instead, she would back away, eyes lowered, and never allow herself to be seen with him again.

He slammed his fist into his palm. *No! I can't let that happen. She mustn't find out yet. I have to find a way to tell her once I assure her I love her.*

"Yes, Clarence Viscount checked out today," the manager informed Blake. "I had hoped to encourage him to stay the full summer. It's hard to rent the best suites."

Blake nodded, trying to show some sympathy and still get the information he wanted. The manager closed the registry. "He did ask questions about Thelma York, and now he's leaving. I wonder if they had a lover's quarrel."

Blake clenched his fists at the thought.

"Where you want these?" A gruff voice pulled their attention. The manager glared at the man holding a stack of New York newspapers. "Right here on the corner of the counter, as usual," he snapped.

"W'al, you never knows. Some folks change their minds, and I can't reads 'em." The man placed the stack of papers on the mahogany counter and sauntered out the front door.

Blake's eye caught the photo on the front page. A lovely blond debutante, waving at the camera, smiled from the page.

The manager frowned and reached for the paper, his scowl deepening. "It never ceases to amaze me how they can't find anything more important to report about in a place like New York

City than a rich debutante's doings." He squinted and read the caption, "New York's Most Lovely Deb, Thelma York, Spending the Summer on the East Coast." Just then, some motion pulled Blake and the manager's attention off the paper. Miss York's maid was making her way out the front door.

"Good morning, Miss Y—" The manager's voice stalled. His eyes dropped to the paper once more then refocused on the hotel guest.

Blake winced. He knew the manager had just discovered the ruse.

"Good morning." The young woman smiled. She hobbled slightly but moved out the door to a chair on the front veranda.

The manager looked back at Blake. "Who is that young woman? Why is she impersonating Thelma York?" Blake could see how upset the man was by the way he ran his hand through his hair.

"Who is paying the extravagant bills for her, and what should I do about it?"

"Don't do anything yet. Give me a chance to look into it."

The manager gave a wan smile. Blake wasn't sure he'd convinced the man to wait, but he was sure that Tamara Something-or-other's charade had come to an end.

Tamara settled onto the lounge chair, setting her large hat beside her. A waiter offered her a glass of lemonade, which she eagerly accepted. The day promised to get rather warm. She stretched out her leg and gently swirled her foot. Her ankle was feeling much better.

If only I can keep from twisting it again. When my ankle is completely healed, I can take the trolley to Harmonsburg and see Mother. She'd received a letter earlier in the day, informing her that her mother had returned home, fully recovered. *Then I'll contact Thelma and ask her to allow me to end this charade.*

"Hello!" Tamara lifted happy eyes at the sound of Blake's voice.

"Hello." She lifted her hand and gave a welcoming wave. She caught her breath as she watched him walk toward her in his careless, easy fashion. He was the epitome of the perfect gentleman and country boy mixed in one.

Blake sat on the chair beside her. "I've got the day off and wondered if you'd like to see more of the park. I can get the wagon to escort you around." He offered her a charming smile.

Tamara adored the way his ginger hair curled slightly by his ears and his blue eyes lit up. He looked like a naughty child planning to skip a day of school to go fishing. She glanced at her ankle. Riding in the wagon would give it the rest it needed, but she'd still be able to enjoy the day.

"Sounds wonderful, but is that what you want to do on your day off?"

"Sure, I can't think of anything better than driving a lovely lady around a park for the day." He leaned over, picked up her hand, placed it in his, and gave a gentle squeeze. Their eyes locked for moments. "We can really get to know one another."

Tamara pulled back and stared down at her lap. She felt the heat on her cheeks. Blake's intense gaze made her feel shy. His words worried her. She wanted to get to know all about him, but she wasn't able to tell him anything about herself, not until she spoke to Thelma.

"I happened to see Charlie and his sister Julie this morning. They're staying at the Lakeside Inn. I hope you don't mind, but I suggested they join us later this afternoon at the café on the upper floor of the boat pavilion for lunch and a swim. You never did get that swim you wanted the other day. Did you?" The corners of his eyes crinkled, and he gave a quick wink.

Tamara giggled even though her cheeks grew warm again. "I'd love for them to join us, and I would like to finally take a swim with you."

"And this time, there will be no interruptions. Clarence Viscount is probably halfway to New York by now."

Tamara hoped that was true. Yet she also hoped she'd be able to reach Thelma before Clarence met up with her. The whole situation felt impossible.

"After swimming, we can take a canoe out on the lake." Blake's words drew her back into the conversation.

Tamara clapped her hands together. *This truly will be a perfect day. When I get back to the hotel, I'll call Thelma and tell her I'm done pretending to be her. Then I can tell Blake the truth about myself.*

She glanced up at him and wondered if he would still be interested in her once he knew she wasn't the rich debutante she pretended to be.

Blake stood. "Are you ready to go now?"

Tamara nodded. She allowed him to pull her to her feet then placed the oversized straw hat with its large pink rose blossoms on her head. How she hated the thing, but there was nothing she could do about it. She had to wear a head covering, and this was one of the least objectionable Thelma had packed for her.

She tried to tilt her head up, but the hat teetered dangerously, slipping to one side.

"Perhaps I should stop by my room first and change hats." She fumbled to keep the dratted thing in place.

A loud guffaw escaped Blake's lips. "I believe that's a good idea." He patted her hand gently and led her into the hotel.

Tamara decided he was mocking her, which she deserved. But he was awfully cute when he laughed. She hoped the day would end with another ride on the carousel together.

Chapter 10

Charlie's laughter filled the afternoon as Blake guided the horse through Exposition Park. Intrigued by all the rides, Charlie's head swished back and forth as he tried to see everything. Tamara couldn't help joining in. Seeing the entire park was marvelous. They drove by the Blue Streak roller coaster, the Ferris wheel, and the carousel. They all enjoyed the treats Blake willingly bought. Tamara wondered how he could afford to be so generous on a carnie's salary.

On their way to the bathhouse, a horn blasted, and Blake pulled the horse's reins sharply to stop from smashing into a 1910 Paterson Touring automobile. After a moment, while everyone took a deep breath of relief, Blake ran his hand through his hair. "I wish they wouldn't allow automobiles in the park. They're best kept on the road."

The others nodded in agreement, but Charlie's wide-open eyes lingered on the vehicle. Blake could tell the boy was frightened.

"Did you ever hear about Dr. Horatio Nelson Jackson's transcontinental trek in an automobile?" Blake tried to divert Charlie's attention. Charlie shook his head.

"Well, seven years ago, a year before you were born, there weren't very many paved roads yet. Most of them were in large cities, but Dr. Horatio Nelson Jackson, along with his chauffeur-mechanic, Sewall Crocker, traveled four thousand five hundred miles across the United States in a twenty-horsepower automobile. Along the way, Horatio bought a dog named Bud, who enjoyed the trip immensely."

"Is that far?" Charlie asked.

"Yes, very far. And it took about sixty days." Tamara watched the joyous emotions flit across Charlie's face as Blake finished his story.

"Wow, I want to do that when I grow up." Charlie bounced up and down on the seat. Blake reached over and tousled the boy's hair.

"By then automobiles will have taken over completely. No one will ride horses or drive wagons anymore."

Tamara's heart ached. The automobiles she'd grown used to seeing in New York were lovely, but her country heart preferred the slow pace of a horse-drawn wagon. She'd ridden a few times in the automobiles driven by Thelma's chauffeur, but she didn't care much for the experience. Horses and carousels were enough excitement for her.

By the time they reached the café, the ice cream and cotton candy were somehow forgotten, and they settled down for a lovely lunch. The sounds of laughter filled the building, swimmers coming and going.

"Are you two looking forward to swimming?" Tamara asked the children.

"We don't know how to swim," Julie said.

Blake patted her shoulder. "That's okay. I know how, and I can teach you."

Tamara smiled at him. She loved the way he included Charlie and Julie in everything, never brushing the children aside as if they were pests. None of Thelma's crowd would ever do that. Yes, she was sure now. She didn't wanted to spend her life with a New York man. She'd be happy and content with a man from the country or a kind summer carnie.

The rest of the afternoon was one happy blur. The swimming and then canoeing were glorious. Tamara's ankle no longer hurt. Even though he helped Julie and Charlie with their swimming, most of Blake's attention was diverted in her direction.

When the swimming was done and they'd dropped Charlie and Julie at their hotel, Blake continued to give her his attention. In fact, he scooted closer to her and allowed her to hold the reins, his hands on hers, guiding her.

She would have laughed if it wasn't so sweet of him. Little did he know she'd driven a wagon most of her childhood.

Oh, if only I could tell him all about myself, but I don't want to ruin this spectacular day. I'll call Thelma tonight, and then I can tell Blake all about it tomorrow.

"Would you like to go to see George M. Cohan tonight? He's singing in the Dreamland Ballroom. Have you heard his song 'The Small Town Girl'?"

Tamara gulped. Was Blake's emphasis on the words *small town* supposed to mean something? Did he know who she really was?

"I—I think that would be lovely. Yes, I've heard the song

before." Her voice trembled slightly.

"Okay, we'll ride the carousel first then head for the Dreamland."

"But my ankle may not be ready for dancing."

"I prefer to sit and listen, especially when it's someone as famous as George M. Cohan. You know, he was raised in vaudeville before writing and performing songs."

She shook her head. Knowing all about famous singers was not in her scope of life, nor did she think Thelma would know such things. The girl loved to dance but couldn't name the songwriters or the names of the songs.

Blake leaned close to her and whispered, "Besides, I'd rather sit beside a lovely girl like you anytime."

Tamara dropped her eyes, a tiny smile flitting across her lips.

"I'll take you back to the hotel now. You can prop that ankle up for a few hours. But we'll take the path along the lake. It's so peaceful."

Tamara settled back with a deep contented sigh. They rode on, knee to knee, in silent companionship. When they arrived at the hotel, Blake jumped down and reached out for her. Tamara slipped across the seat and slid into his arms. Blake held her a moment then set her on her feet. He bent forward and pressed his lips on hers for just a fleeting moment. Then he stepped back.

"I'll walk you to your room," he said.

She blinked several times then took his arm, and they began to stroll into the hotel. They'd just passed the front desk when suddenly Tamara heard words that made her heart stand still.

"There she is, Officer, the girl who's impersonating Thelma York!"

Chapter 11

Blake tried to block Tamara from the oncoming man, but the officer, dressed in the dark blue uniform of the park police, sidestepped around him and grabbed her arm.

"Miss, you need to come with me." With his free hand, the officer touched his broad-brimmed gray felt Stetson then rested his hand on the wooden baton hanging from his belt.

Blake saw her eyes fill with tears.

"You are Officer. . . ?" Blake asked.

"Beasley."

"Officer Beasley, how dare you manhandle this woman."

The officer glared at Blake and spat out, "Get out of my way, carnie. This girl's been living in the hotel, in the most expensive suite, claiming to be Thelma York. The whole time, the real Thelma York's been on the East Coast."

Blake straightened. "I'm sure there's a reasonable explanation, which she will tell you, once you let go of her. You're going to bruise her arm!"

Something in Blake's tone made the officer release his grip on Tamara. She moaned and moved closer to Blake, rubbing her arm.

The officer twiddled with his whistle for a moment, the whole time glaring at them. "I'm waiting to hear your story."

Once more Blake spoke. "Officer, is this the way you treat a young lady? Can't you see she's trembling? She's suffered an ankle injury this week, which can be confirmed by the manager as well as the hotel's doctor. She needs to sit down. I'm sure a table in the dining room will suffice. She can tell you her story there."

The officer grunted in agreement, and they all moved into the dining room. Blake led them to a table, assisted her into a chair, then sat next to her. He slid his hand across the table to cover hers.

Once the officer was seated with the manager beside him, they all turned their eyes on the young woman. Tamara.

"Please start at the beginning," Blake encouraged.

A single tear slipped out of Tamara's eye. She blinked. This was no time to start crying. The worst had come, and she needed to stay strong. For a moment, she lowered her head, whispered a soft prayer for God to help her, then began to explain. "Yes, Officer Beasley. My real name is Tamara Brand. I have been staying at the hotel, impersonating Thelma York."

The officer and manager gave one another conspiratorial nods.

"But it's not what you think!" she almost shouted when she noted the looks the two men exchanged. "Thelma York is paying me to impersonate her."

Once she spoke those words, she could see the look of disgust and unbelief on the two men's faces. She hated even to look at Blake. She didn't want to see what he was thinking, but she turned her head to him. She was surprised to see a smile on his face.

"Go on, Tamara. Tell them the whole thing," Blake encouraged her.

"Up until last week, I was working in New York as Thelma York's personal maid. When her father told Thelma he wanted her to come to the Hotel Conneaut for the summer while he traveled, she wasn't happy about it, so she asked me to take her place. Someone had to be here because she knew her father would telegraph a few times during the summer and check up on her. So my job was to spend a quiet summer here and not let anyone guess I wasn't the real Thelma. Then she would be able to go to the coast without her father knowing about it."

The manager sat back, arms crossed. "Humph! How do we know this is true? I've sent a telegram to Mr. York but haven't heard back from him yet."

"I'm sure you can call and speak to the real Thelma York," Blake insisted.

"We will do that, first thing in the morning," Officer Beasley said. "Is there anyone here who can confirm any of this?"

Blake jumped in, "Yes, Clarence Viscount spoke to Thelma York today. He'll tell you the same story. Thelma told him all about it. I personally have known all along she wasn't Thelma York." He turned and looked at Tamara. He knew she probably had questions about how he knew she wasn't Thelma and why he'd kept it a secret all this time.

The manager wagged his head back and forth. "Clarence

Viscount checked out today. By now he's back in New York. He's the one who told me she wasn't Thelma York, and he wasn't very happy about it. I doubt he would want to tell us anything to clear her."

Blake sat back with a sigh. "Officer, she's told you what she knows. I suggest we all get a good night's sleep, and tomorrow we can make the needed phone calls."

The officer sat forward. "I'll have to take her to jail?" His words were more a question than a statement. His eyes met Blake's.

"I don't think that will be necessary," Blake said. "I'll vouch for her. She won't disappear tonight."

The officer coughed. "That sounds reasonable, but may I ask who you are?"

"My name is Blake Conner from Connecticut." He stared at the officer as the man's eyes grew large.

"*The* Blake Conner from Connecticut? Your father is Earl Conner, the industrial tycoon?"

Blake nodded.

Officer Beasley crossed his arms over his chest. "How are we to believe that?"

The manager spoke for the first time. "I think I can help. I have a little hobby of collecting articles about some of the wealthiest families in the United States. I probably have a photo of the real Blake Conner. I'm sure I can have something to show you in the morning."

Officer Beasley stood and announced they would all meet again in the morning after breakfast to make the necessary identifications and phone calls.

"But what about this girl?" the manager protested. "She isn't the real Thelma York. She's only a servant."

The officer slammed his hand down on the table. "It doesn't matter tonight. We can clear it all up tomorrow."

The manager stood up, glared at Blake as if memorizing his face, then stomped out of the room, clearly upset that a maid would be allowed to stay another night in the best suite. The officer shook Blake's hand, gave Tamara a curt nod, and walked out of the room, leaving Blake and Tamara together in silence.

After a few moments, Blake stood and pulled Tamara to her feet.

"It's getting late. You need to get some sleep."

She lifted her face, her lips trembling. "I'm sorry, Blake. I wanted to tell you, but I made a promise to Thelma."

He shook his head. "It doesn't matter. I know how Thelma can be."

"But I want you to understand. My mother was sick, and I needed the money to pay for her to stay at a sanatorium. She's better now. I was going to go see her tomorrow. She. . . I. . . My family lives in Harmonsburg."

Blake tilted his head, gazing at her.

Tamara's eyes met his for a moment, and then she looked down. *So, he was pretending to be a carnie, while I've been pretending to be a wealthy debutante.* It was hard to believe that such a situation could be, but it didn't matter. Now that the truth had been revealed, she had to accept that they came from totally different worlds. She could feel the space between them grow. She stepped away, facing him.

"As soon as you hit me with the suitcase and I had to start relying on you, I realized I was doing the wrong thing, but I didn't know what to do about it. There were so many times I wanted to tell you who I really was. So you knew all along I wasn't Thelma?"

"Yes, I've known it all along. I was hoping you would eventually trust me enough to tell me who you really were."

"Can you ever forgive me?" Her voice quivered.

Blake reached out and pulled her into his arms and pressed a kiss on her forehead. "Tamara, I forgive you, but can you forgive me for letting you believe I was just a carnie?"

"Yes, I forgive you." She pressed her hands against his chest, stepping backward. "But you know you mustn't kiss me."

"I'm sure you can tell I care a great deal for you, Tamara. Now that our true identities have been revealed, we can really get to know one another."

She shook her head. "The truth changes everything. You're a rich man, pretending for the summer to be a poor man. When the summer is over, you'll go back to being a rich man. I, on the other hand, am a poor girl who can never be a rich girl, nor can I ever be the debutante your family will want in your life." Tears began to stream down her cheeks.

"None of that matters. My family will love you."

She took another step away from him. "You know that's not true. I've seen the world you come from, and I won't ever belong there. Please, I want to go to my room now."

Blake wanted to argue with her, but it had been a long day, and they both needed to rest.

"Very well. I'll walk you to your room."

She took his arm, and they made their way to her room. All memories of carousels and moonlit paths were forgotten. She wasn't sure how he felt, but she carried a heavy heart.

∽◯

As Tamara lay on the bed in the dark, a bit of a breeze blew through the open window. She could hear the crickets and the lake lapping the shore. It was a sad and beautiful sound. She closed her eyes, trying to press out the last half hour of unpleasantness.

Oh Lord. How did things ever get so out of hand? I believe Blake has forgiven me for the part I was playing, but can You forgive me?

Her room was silent. As the tears rolled down her cheeks, she felt a comforting warmth spread through her chest, and she knew now the lie was over. God had forgiven her.

∽◯

Back in his room, which he shared with three other carnies who were already asleep, Blake sat on the edge of his bed, head leaned into his palms. All he'd wanted was a quiet summer away from the drama of Connecticut and New York, but what a mess it had all turned out to be. Surely nothing good could ever come from living a lie. He slipped down beside the bed and prayed.

Lord, I'm sorry for lying to Tamara. I should have told her from the beginning who I was, and that I knew who she was. Please, Lord, forgive me.

Blake spent a good amount of time on his knees, talking to God. He'd forgotten how refreshing and cleansing it felt.

Unable to sleep, Blake headed to the front desk and sent out several telegrams. When he was satisfied he'd done all he could, he returned to his room and climbed into bed.

Blake admitted to himself that he'd enjoyed the time he'd spent as a carnie and didn't regret meeting Tamara, but he did have to wonder if he'd never taken on the role of carnie if he ever would have met her. Somehow he believed Tamara would still have been his destiny.

She may not be the wealthy debutante my mother would approve of, but she's the only woman I will ever love, Lord.

Chapter 12

Tamara sat up and pulled a blanket around her shoulders. The evening breeze from the night before was gone, replaced by a cold wind rushing through her window. The lake's water was choppy, and she could see a storm brewing outside.

That's just great. A fine way to start what will already be a difficult day. She stood, stretched, walked to the window, and pressed it shut.

She knew she needed to get dressed and meet Blake and Officer Beasley in the restaurant. She hoped they had been able to reach Thelma. Although she'd considered it many times, Tamara hadn't tried calling Thelma since she'd arrived at Conneaut Lake. She knew Thelma. The girl would be living a whirlwind life, busy playing golf and tennis, swimming, dancing. Chances of her being anywhere she could be reached by phone or even telegram were slim. Tamara was surprised Clarence had been able to contact her as quickly as he had.

The only thing that brightened her mood was knowing she no longer needed to dress in Thelma's clothes. She'd made sure to slip a few of her own personal items into the trunks. She had one navy blue skirt with a white blouse, which would suit her perfectly today.

Tamara sat on her bed and opened her Bible. She usually read a psalm and a proverb each day. The words were uplifting, but her mind kept running back to Proverbs 12:22. *"Lying lips are abomination to the Lord: but they that deal truly are his delight."* Now that she'd spoken the truth, she could feel His delight in her again.

Being in right standing with You is all that really matters to me, Lord.

A knock on the door pulled her attention away from the Bible. She set it on the bed, stood, and walked to the door. She knew before opening it that Blake would be standing there. She wanted to see him, but she also still felt ashamed.

"Good morning, Tamara." Blake's voice was friendly. He smiled at her with a quick wink. "I'm so glad to be able to call you by your real name. I didn't like calling you Thelma."

Her shoulders sagged. "I'm sorry." She sat on the bed and ran her fingers along the edge of the Bible.

He stepped into the room. "I didn't mean to upset you."

"I'm not upset. I know God has forgiven me for pretending to be Thelma and lying to you and everyone here, but I feel some-how. . ." She wasn't sure how to finish.

"Tamara." Blake moved closer to her. "Look at me."

She tilted up her head.

"Remember, I knew the first moment we met you weren't

Thelma, and I've never held the pretense against you. I knew there was an explanation, and, knowing Thelma, I figured she'd trapped you in one of her schemes. You were doing the best you could to help your mother and to appease Thelma."

She gazed into his lovely blue eyes, wishing she could just float away into them. "Nothing should ever give us a reason to lie. I won't allow my mother's illness or Thelma to be my scapegoat. I take responsibility for this, and I promise you, myself, and God I'll never do anything like it again."

Blake pulled her close to him. His chest felt so comforting. For a moment, she let herself lay her head there.

"Remember, I was lying about myself the whole time too. The great thing is, when we were together, we were dressing like people we weren't, but we were actually being ourselves. I've gotten to know you, the real Tamara, and you've gotten to know me, the real Blake."

Just then there was another knock on the door. Blake stood, strode to the door, and opened it.

"Yes?" he asked the bellboy standing there.

"A police officer told me to tell Miss Brand he's waiting for her in the restaurant."

Blake thanked the boy and shut the door.

"Are you ready to go?"

Tamara stood, straightened her skirt, and nodded. "I only hope they've been able to reach Thelma and she's straightened this whole thing out. I have a feeling that officer still wants to take me to jail." She caught her bottom lip between her teeth.

"Don't worry. I sent out telegrams last night. One to Thelma, one to Clarence, and one to my father. I'm confident the entire situation will be cleared up this morning."

Tamara could feel tears threatening to fall. "You are such a kind man. I don't know what I can ever do to repay you for your help."

Blake leaned over and whispered, "Promise me a carousel ride when this is all over."

Tamara's hand trembled in his as they walked to the restaurant. His other hand was clenched at his side. He couldn't stand knowing she was nervous, and his anger toward Officer Beasley rose again.

"That officer shouldn't be allowed on the streets. He obviously has no idea how to treat decent people."

A small laugh escaped Tamara's lips. "Decent people? Decent people don't lie and stay in an expensive hotel, pretending to be someone else. He had every right to treat me the way he did. I'm just glad you were able to keep him from arresting me."

Blake stopped walking and turned her toward him. "No one is going to arrest you. This whole thing has been a big mistake, but no laws have been broken. If Thelma doesn't contact us soon, I might have to consider twisting her arm a bit." He chuckled, actually enjoying the idea.

"Blake! Don't say such things." Tamara pulled away and continued to walk.

Blake moved to her side again and held up his hand. "I promise not to say such things if you promise to stop worrying."

She nodded.

Blake took her hand again, lifted it to his lips, and pressed a warm kiss on the back.

∽

The officer was surprisingly kind enough to let them order breakfast and didn't start the conversation until they'd all been poured a cup of coffee. However, he didn't wait much longer.

"I hope you have a plan to sort this whole thing out, Mr. Conner," he began. "We've sent a telegram and tried to find Thelma York, but so far we haven't heard anything."

"I've sent some as well. It could take a day or two to find her, or Clarence. Once we reach them, either can clarify the issue." Blake took a sip from his cup, his eyes never leaving the officer's face. He didn't plan to allow the man to start browbeating Tamara. "I expect to hear from my father today as well."

Officer Beasley cleared his throat. "I'm wondering if we should allow Miss Brand to continue staying at the hotel under false pretenses until we hear from Mr. York."

Blake slapped the table. "The room's already paid for."

The officer ignored Blake's outburst. "I believe you told us your home is nearby, Miss Brand?"

"Yes. All I have to do is take the trolley. Will that be all right? I'll be available for any further questions."

"I don't think that's all right at all!" Blake's voice rose.

Tamara turned and faced him. "Blake, I appreciate your support in this, but honestly, I'd love to go home. I don't want to stay here any longer."

Blake's eyes bored into hers. Finally, he let out a breath. "Then that's probably the best plan."

Officer Beasley agreed after writing down her address. Then they all finished their food in awkward silence.

Once he was finished eating, the officer rose, bowed, and left the table. Blake turned to Tamara.

"I'd like to help you do whatever it takes to get you home today. I'd feel better riding along on the trolley with you."

"I'm not sure what to do with Thelma's trunks and hatboxes. There's no room in my home for them."

"The hotel can store them for a few days, until Thelma contacts them. Just put everything inside the trunks and boxes. I'll have a porter take care of them. How long will that take?"

Tamara calculated. "About an hour."

Blake took a final sip from his coffee, set down the cup, and pushed out his chair. He then stood, stepped behind her chair, and pulled it out for her to rise.

She smiled sadly at him, and they walked side by side to her room.

Tamara was used to packing Thelma's belongings, so she made quick work of the job then stood beside the window overlooking the lake. She'd wanted to enjoy the summer here at the Conneaut Hotel and Exposition Park, but it had been a doomed hope from the beginning.

She knew she'd probably never return to the hotel or the park. This had been her one and only chance to experience the luxuries and entertainment offered here. Once back home, she would need to look for a new job because she was never going back to being Thelma's maid.

For a moment, she closed her eyes to squeeze back the tears and remembered the pleasure she'd experienced riding the carousel with Blake beside her. The feelings they'd shared together on the carousel had been genuine, of that she was sure. She would hold those moments as a special, unsullied memory.

When the porter knocked on the door, she quickly dabbed a handkerchief under her eyes. No one must know she'd been crying.

She opened the door. Blake stood behind the porter, always on hand to help. He no longer wore the clothes of a carnie. He was dressed in the casual but refined sporting clothes the men in Thelma's set wore daily.

The difference made her feel shy, but he stepped into her room and directed the porter until all the cases were out of the room. Only she and one small bag were left behind.

"Now, are you ready to start for home, or do you feel like getting something to eat at the Boat Pavilion café?"

"I couldn't eat a thing." Her voice was a soft whisper. She noticed his smile drop to a frown.

"Tamara, as you can see, I've given up the carnie job, but I hope that won't affect our relationship. I'm still Blake, and you're still Tamara."

She gave him a wan smile. "Seeing you as who you really are changes everything, Blake. Surely you understand that."

Blake moved to her side and lifted her hand.

"Please don't say that, Tamara. The only thing that's changed for me is I finally know your real name."

She wanted to leave her hand in his, but now, knowing their difference in station, she pulled back. "Blake, you're one of the wealthiest bachelors on the East Coast, and I'm a maid. I think that says it all."

Blake turned to face her, placing his hands on her upper arms. "Don't say that, Tamara. I'm still the man who wanted to spend every evening with you, and I believe you are still the woman who wanted to spend your nights with me on the carousel." He leaned forward, pressing his lips against her forehead.

Tears slipped unbidden down her cheeks now.

"I need to go home, Blake."

He leaned back, pulled out his handkerchief, and dabbed at her eyes. "I'll take you home, dear. But this conversation is not over."

He took her hand and placed it in the crook of his arm. His heart felt heavy as they strolled out of the room, past the front desk and the manager, who didn't even acknowledge Tamara, across the veranda, and toward the trolley station.

Chapter 13

Tamara sat while Blake stood on the trolley as it rolled along the rails, leaving Conneaut Lake behind. She kept her eyes focused on the passing scenery outside the window, trying to avoid any further conversation. At this point, she wasn't sure what to say to him or how to react to his proposal that they act toward one another as if nothing had changed.

Mother will know what's best.

Tamara remembered watching the progress of the trolley being built several years earlier. It was started in Harmonsburg and went all the way to Exposition Park. There'd been many problems, and it took almost a year longer than expected to complete. In fact, one trolley car had come in painted with the name of the town spelled "Hamonsburg" instead of "Harmonsburg." Her father had gone to town in 1907 to be one of the first to ride the trolley. It cost fifteen cents to ride, and the price hadn't changed since then.

She watched as they passed fine fields and forests with enough buildings between the lake and Harmonsburg to make the trolley ride interesting.

"Quaint area." Blake broke the silence between them.

"It's peaceful in the country. Not like city life."

Blake scowled. "I grew up in Connecticut, in a quiet area. I prefer taking long strolls through natural parks than walking down New York City streets."

Tamara turned away from him. He didn't understand the difference between her small hometown country life and his Connecticut home. Perhaps bringing him along was the best thing. He would see her parents' little farmhouse and realize where she came from and how impossible continuing a relationship with her would be.

When the trolley slowed and came to a stop, Blake held out his hand and helped Tamara to her feet, and they stepped off the trolley together. Before they could take another step, a police officer approached them.

"You Blake Conner?"

"Yes?"

"Just got a telegram. You need to hop back on the trolley with the girly here and head back to the hotel. Seems there's a situation, and Officer Beasley wants you both there right away."

Blake blew out a breath of frustration then turned to see Tamara's reaction. From the way she stood with her arms akimbo, he knew she wasn't very happy.

"Can't we even go see my parents first?" Her eyes pleaded with the officer as she spoke.

The man shook his head. "Nope. I was told to tell you this is high priority. I'm not to leave until I see you both back on the trolley." He straddled one of the trolley rails, hands set firmly on his hips, and waited.

Blake gave Tamara a half smile. "I suppose we have no choice. We have to do what this officer says." He watched as she struggled with her emotions for a moment.

Finally, she reached out and allowed him to take her hand and help her back onto the trolley, which would be returning to Exposition Park.

"And to think, here I was believing I would never get another chance to go to the lake." Tamara sighed and sat down.

And to think, I get a chance to be with you at the lake again. Blake smiled to himself.

ᔕ

Tamara was understandably quiet on the return trip. Blake watched her face and could see her holding back tears. She'd wanted to go home, to get away from the hotel and all the lies. Now she was headed right back. Had the police officer changed his mind about arresting her? He couldn't imagine what other reason there would be for them to call her back so hastily.

Once or twice she glanced up and their eyes met. He tried to comfort her with his smile. Her lips never stretched out of their pressed thin line. Blake wanted to smooth the worry lines on her forehead. He wanted to gather her in his arms and hold her until her trembling stopped.

This was not the time or place, but Blake was sure now he was never going to leave Tamara behind, whether in Harmonsburg or Conneaut Lake. As soon as this whole fiasco was cleared up, he planned to ask her to marry him and allow him to care for her always.

I love her, Lord. I need to convince her that we should be together.

"Tamara, God doesn't put up social barriers between people. Only society does that."

She shook her head. "But, when you live in a certain class of society, you end up being ruled by the barriers whether you like it or not."

Blake bent down on one knee and took her hand. "That's not what I want. I want to live the life God has for me, not society."

He saw a wistful look cross her face.

"I believe God brought you and me together, and that's what I want to pursue. Even if you won't continue to see me, I have no plans to go back to a life where I'm forced to be someone different than God wants me to be."

He saw a tear fall from her eye.

"No matter what happens at the hotel, please promise me you'll forget all about the barriers between us and follow what you think God wants for us."

He watched her lower her head and heard her whisper, "I will, Blake."

When the trolley stopped at the Exposition Park station, they stepped down and headed toward the hotel.

When they reached the veranda, Blake took her hand.

"Everything will be all right, Tamara."

He liked the way she tilted her chin up bravely.

Hand in hand, they headed into the main lobby.

"Blaaaake Conner, is that you?" A high-pitched voice rang across the lobby. Blake didn't have to look up to know the voice. It was the real Thelma York.

She glided across the lobby and wrapped her arm around Blake's, ignoring Tamara completely.

"Why, darling, I've spent a week on the coast searching for you. I hoped we could spend the summer together. What could you possibly be doing here?" Her eyes glanced past him and settled on Tamara with a piercing glare.

Blake let his arm drop and pulled away from Thelma's red-painted fingernails.

"I've been working this summer, here at Exposition Park."

"And what, pray tell, are you doing with my maid?"

Blake saw the sneer on Thelma's lips.

"Thelma, you may as well drop the innocent act. I know all about how you paid Tamara to take your place this summer. I'm surprised you believed you could get away with it."

Thelma stomped her foot and pointed at Tamara. "If she had just stayed quietly in her room and kept her head down, no one would've known the difference. Instead, she had to get noticed, not only by Clarence, but I see she also got her hooks into you."

Thelma lunged at Tamara. Blake stepped between them and grabbed Thelma's wrists just in time to stop her from scratching Tamara's face.

"That will be enough! Tamara did exactly what you paid her to do. If you hadn't gotten your picture in the paper, no one would've known anything different."

Thelma's eyes grew round, and she tried to pull away from him. "Blake, you're hurting me. What do you care about that girl? She's nothing. No matter what she's told you, she's only a country girl I hired as a maid."

Blake struggled to keep his temper. "*Nothing?* She has more character and kindness in her little finger than you have in your whole body." He dropped Thelma's hands and stepped closer to Tamara. "I would prefer you not speak anymore, except to the police. It's time you straightened this whole thing out."

Thelma's mouth opened and closed again. She'd probably never been spoken to in such a manner before. For the moment it seemed to cower her. She followed Blake and Tamara into the restaurant and sat at the table across from the officer.

"Now, Thelma. Please explain how Tamara happened to be here under what appeared to be false pretenses while, in reality, she was only doing her job." Blake's words were commanding.

Thelma stared at him. He was glad that for once she didn't try to flirt her way around him. She began to speak

"That's the truth. I hired Tamara to come to Exposition Park, stay in the Hotel Conneaut, and pretend to be me. I wanted my father to think I was here. At the time, it seemed like the perfect plan."

Blake placed his hand over Tamara's and gave a small squeeze. Thelma saw the gesture. Her eyes narrowed.

Officer Beasley scribbled notes in a small book, nodding from time to time. Blake recognized Thelma's best coy act, but nothing wiped the scowl off the man's face. When Thelma finished speaking, the officer cleared his throat. "It seems if anyone is to blame for this fiasco, it's Miss York and not Miss Brand. Although I would suggest in the future, Miss Brand, you not accept jobs of such a questionable nature."

He closed the notebook.

Blake spoke. "So may Miss Brand go home now?"

"Yes, we have all the information we need. The hotel has been paid and Miss York has cleared Miss Brand of all wrongdoing, so I consider the matter closed."

Blake and Tamara both let out an audible sigh.

"Come, Tamara, we still have time to catch the trolley again."

"But Blake!" Thelma whined. "I wanted you to show me around the park. I've heard there's an absolutely lovely dance hall, and I want you to be my partner." She froze Tamara with a stare.

"Sorry, that's not in my plans. I'm taking Tamara home to see her mother, and then later tonight, I'm bringing her back here for one last carousel ride." His eyes met Tamara's for concurrence, and she nodded.

"What? You want to take my maid on the carousel? Really, Blake, I think you've overdone this carnie pretense. Be a good boy and let the girl go home. She knows you're out of her league."

Blake clenched his hands. "Thelma, there's no league Miss Brand wouldn't fit into. Now, if you'll excuse us, we have a trolley to catch."

Blake helped Tamara to a standing position, but Thelma flung herself between them. She grabbed Tamara by the arms. "Look, Tamara. You've had your fun, pretending to be me, but it's over now. It's time for you to remember who you are. If Blake is seen with you, it will ruin his reputation."

Tamara smiled. "Thelma, I do remember who I am. I am Tamara Brand from Harmonsburg, Pennsylvania, and he is Blake Conner from Connecticut. But the only thing that matters is that we're both children of God."

Blake peeled Thelma's hands off of Tamara. "Why don't you call Clarence, Thelma? He will be only too happy to come back to the hotel and escort you." Blake watched Thelma clench her fists. Suddenly a deep voice caused them all to look toward the doorway.

"Thelma!"

"Yes, Daddy?" Blake could see the girl cower as she met the cold, steel-gray eyes of her father.

"You've got some explaining to do!"

Blake put out his arm for Tamara, and they glided out of the room.

Chapter 14

Tamara was able to laugh a good deal on the way to Harmonsburg. She felt the burden of guilt and worry lifted from her. When they finally reached Tamara's front porch, she stopped. No one in her family would notice her until she knocked on the door. She turned and tilted her head up to look at Blake.

"I appreciate you bringing me home, but I'm sure now that this whole thing is over, you have more important things to do, places to be."

He peered at her, his sky-blue eyes intense. "Do you want me to leave?"

Tamara bit her bottom lip. "No, but I can't expect you to stay. Now that everything has been revealed, you must be anxious to go back to Connecticut."

"If you remember, I came here and took the job of a carnie of my own accord. I didn't want to live the life I had in Connecticut or New York. My mother kept pushing girls like Thelma on me. She wanted me to mingle with the debutantes, but that life was empty and boring. Remember our conversation earlier. I want to live the life God has planned for me. I can't serve God and live that old life. What I want, and what I think God wants for me, Tamara, is a woman like you."

"But I'm nothing. I mean, in comparison to the women in Connecticut and New York."

"How can you say that? You are God's child, which makes you worth far more to me. Don't you understand? I love you, Tamara."

Blake took her arms and drew her close to him. He reached under her chin, tilted her head up, and pressed his lips against hers.

When he broke the kiss, Tamara stood still. She couldn't take her eyes from his face.

"Do you love me, Tamara?"

"Yes, Blake. I love you more than I've ever loved anyone."

Blake led her to the wooden swing on her front porch. He turned her around and had her sit, and then he knelt in front of her and pulled out an emerald-cut diamond ring. "Tamara Brand from Harmonsburg, Pennsylvania, will you marry me and make every day of my life perfect?"

A tear of joy slipped down her cheek, and Tamara whispered, "Yes, Blake. I will marry you."

Blake slipped the ring on her finger and kissed her again. He sat on the swing beside her, and she leaned her head onto his chest, her eyes closed.

Thank You, Lord, for bringing Blake into my life.

Epilogue

The crowds were gone, and Exposition Park was closed until the following summer. A few travelers stayed at the Hotel Conneaut, but for Tamara and Blake, none of that mattered. This lovely fall day, with the maple tree leaves turning their splendid shades of yellow, gold, and red, was the day they'd been anxiously awaiting.

Tamara's mother adjusted Tamara's veil then walked with her to the pathway where her father stood. Although Blake's mother had wanted Tamara to purchase a wedding dress from one of New York's finest establishments, Tamara felt beautiful in the dress her mother had worn for her own wedding.

Several rows of chairs were set along the path, on which lay lovely pink and white rose petals, all leading to the carousel where Blake stood.

In Tamara's mind, there was no better place to get married

than in front of the carousel that had given her and Blake so much joy together, no matter how unconventional it seemed. The mixed crowd of Connecticut's wealthiest, New York's most stylish, Harmonsburg's country folk, and Exposition Park's carnies was quite a sight to see, but Tamara and Blake wanted everyone they cared for to be there and celebrate with them.

Tamara's hometown pastor performed the simple wedding. After they both said "I do" and their guests strolled away to the reception area in the hotel's ballroom, Tamara and Blake stepped onto the carousel platform. Blake lifted Tamara onto a lovely golden-maned horse then mounted the lion beside her. In moments the music started. The carousel began to go around and around.

"Will you try to reach the golden ring?" Blake asked.

"I don't need the golden ring, Blake. I already won the greatest prize."

"And what's that, sweetheart?"

"Truth and love."

Blake leaned closer to her. "Tamara, I have just one more question."

She gave him her full attention as the carousel began to slow.

"Will you promise me that we will return to Exposition Park every summer and ride the carousel together?"

The music had stopped and the platform was still. Tamara slid off her horse into Blake's waiting arms. She pressed a gentle kiss onto his lips and whispered, "Always, my love."

Teresa Ives Lilly has been writing for more than twenty years. Her articles have appeared in a variety of magazines. She has created and published over two hundred unit studies which are used widely in the Homeschool and Public School arena. She has written and published more than twenty-five novellas with publishing companies Lovely Christian Romance and Forget Me Not Romances, a Division of Winged Publications. Her novel *Orphan Train Bride* was a number one bestseller on Amazon. Teresa loves to hear from her readers.

The Carousel Wedding

by Susanne Dietze

For Dad, who rode the Balboa Park carousel when he was a boy and who helped me with my research. For this and all the ways you've helped and supported me, thank you. I love you!

But ask now the beasts, and they shall teach thee; and the fowls of the air, and they shall tell thee: Or speak to the earth, and it shall teach thee: and the fishes of the sea shall declare unto thee. Who knoweth not in all these that the hand of the LORD hath wrought this? In whose hand is the soul of every living thing, and the breath of all mankind.

JOB 12:7–10

Chapter 1

Balboa Park, San Diego, California
1922

J une Lowell was about to get fired.

If she was not behind her desk at the Natural History Museum in eight—no, make that seven—minutes, according to the watch pinned to her coat, her boss, Mr. Willard, would show no mercy. But how could she leave now that the carousel was taking its inaugural spin?

The two jumping horses whirled past, as did the donkeys, frogs, cats, and other menagerie animals—all lacking riders so the workers could note its balance after moving it to Balboa Park this morning from Coronado's Tent City. The workers who'd seen to the task stood back and watched, grinning like children.

June pushed her spectacles higher up the bridge of her nose and smiled too. Carousels had a way of making one feel young again. Even if one never rode them anymore.

One of the workers, a tall, lean, hawk-nosed fellow with wavy hair the same maple-syrup brown shade as hers, trotted to her side. "Look at it, June."

"Look at *you*, Kelly. I'm so happy for you." This was the first job her twenty-one-year-old little brother had taken that brought a smile to his face. Since their parents had died in an automobile crash five years ago, he'd hawked newspapers and polished shoes to help pay for his schoolbooks and recreation. But now that the carousel had found a new home here—at the park where June worked, no less—Kelly had a part-time job that was steady, to his liking, and allowed him time to focus on his college classes so he'd be ready for law school next year. God had provided this job for Kelly, no question about it.

And He'd provided June's current job too, which enabled her to support them both and pay for Kelly's college courses. Her work at the Natural History Museum was reliable, interesting, and—oh, she really must get back to it. One last longing look at the giraffe on the outer rim of the carousel and she sighed. "I'd better go. Meet you here at five?" The streetcar stop was mere yards from the carousel.

"Yep, I'll be here—wait, Sis. There she is." His gaze latched onto an approaching bob-haired brunette in a beige dress. When the young woman waved at Kelly, he responded with enthusiasm.

June nudged his shoulder. "Who's your friend?"

He blushed ever so slightly. "That's Evie. *You know.*"

Not personally, but she'd heard all about the object of Kelly's affections since he met her at the carousel a few weeks ago, when it was still in Coronado and he was learning how to operate it. "She's pretty."

"Miss Howard's the bees' knees, all right."

"Miss. . .Howard, did you say?" June stared at Evie, who'd

stopped to admire the carousel—no, someone had stopped her. A blond man in a boater hat, the sort of fashionably dressed fellow Kelly sometimes referred to as a sheik. It was difficult to see Evie's face now that she'd turned away, so June couldn't search her features for a resemblance to the Howard she knew. "Is she perchance related to Martin Howard?"

"That's right. She did mention he's affiliated with the museum. You know him?"

Did she ever, not that they'd exchanged more than friendly chitchat in the museum halls. Nevertheless, whenever she saw the kind marine zoologist, or thought about him for that matter, a cloud of butterflies took flight in her stomach.

She strove to tame that reaction, however. Her boss, Mr. Willard, had implemented a strict no-fraternization policy between the office staff, such as herself, and the naturalists and scientists who worked with or for the museum. Therefore, if she wanted to keep her job, she had no choice but to admire Martin Howard's kindness—and that delightfully unruly curl of dark hair that flopped over his forehead—from a distance.

"I know Dr. Howard a little, I suppose."

Kelly rocked on his heels. "Will you put in a good word for me with him?"

"I don't know him *that* well, Kelly." She and Dr. Howard had spoken about church, jazz, the weather, and museum exhibits, but he'd never mentioned a sister. She pushed her glasses up again. "If it comes up, I can try, but he's not at the museum every day. He spends most of his time at the Scripps Institution for Biological Research."

"When you see him, just mention I'm not a bad apple." Kelly stared at Evie. "Evie's so excited for the carousel. I'm going to invite her out for a spin and a soda Saturday after work."

The moment he said it, though, June was gripped with the unhappy knowledge Evie would decline Kelly's invitation, because the man with the boater lowered to one knee before her. He spoke, and then Evie squealed and nodded.

"No." Kelly gaped in disbelief as the man withdrew a small box from his coat pocket. Evie tugged off her left glove to receive what was undoubtedly an engagement ring.

Her poor baby brother. Ready to ask Evie on a date, only to watch her receive a marriage proposal. From all he'd said, Evie had encouraged him, given him hope. But clearly, things were not as they'd seemed. She took his arm. "Kelly. I'm so sorry."

"Oi, Lowell, we need you to check the balance," shouted a lean man in a tweed cap. Kelly's boss, by the disapproving look on his face.

That look reminded her of her own supervisor and how much she'd like to keep her job. "I'm sorry, dear, but I have to go. We'll talk about this at home."

He didn't respond, but she knew he'd heard and understood. Praying for Kelly's fractured heart, she pressed her cloche hat to her head so it wouldn't fly off, and ran toward El Prado, the wide promenade running through the park. How many minutes did she have left? She didn't dare pause to consult her watch. Usually she enjoyed taking in the gorgeous architecture surrounding her, the Spanish Colonial Revival buildings constructed twelve years ago for the Panama-California Exposition, but she didn't dare focus on anything but getting back to the museum.

Feet aching from her heeled shoes, June burst into the exhibition hall and rushed through the door that led to the offices. In seconds she reached the small room where she worked alongside one other typist, Gladys King. Raven-haired Gladys looked up, brows upraised in a question. "One o'clock on the nose. Good thing you got here before the big cheese did."

June removed her hat and took her seat. "I stayed too long to admire the carousel, but oh Gladys, the saddest thing happened right as I left."

"Something broke when they moved the carousel?" Gladys's hand went to her mouth.

"No, I meant something with Kelly. Oh, Mr. Willard. Hello."

Their balding, jowl-cheeked supervisor stood in the threshold, file in one hand, and his open pocket watch in the other. After consulting the time, he snapped it shut with a decisive click. "Good to see you both on time."

June might have cut it close today, but she and Gladys both were punctual and efficient and had yet to be tardy. Much as June liked her job, she wished Mr. Willard didn't seem so hard-pressed to catch them breaking a rule. Hoping to sweeten his mood, June cast him a smile. "Was your lunch satisfactory, sir?"

He didn't answer but handed her the file. "Type this up. An exhibit proposal by Dr. Howard."

As usual, the mention of Martin Howard's name stirred up the butterflies inside her. She tamped them down, however. They were neither professional nor constructive. "I'll have it ready as soon as possible, sir."

"And you, Miss King?" Mr. Willard peered at Gladys's desk. "Still working on the press release for the saber-toothed cat exhibition?"

When Gladys nodded, Mr. Willard told them to carry on and left.

June opened the file Mr. Willard had given her. She'd never

typed anything for Martin Howard before. His penmanship was as crisp and neat as his suits. That made her task easy. But first she knew Gladys would want the rest of the story. Sure enough, once the sound of Mr. Willard's footsteps on the tiled floor faded and his office door clicked shut, Gladys scooted to the edge of her seat. "So, you were saying? What happened to Kelly?"

Setting the pages on her typing stand, she leaned toward Gladys. "Kelly's had his eye on this young lady, Evie, and from what he's said about their friendship, he's had reason to hope she'd agree to an outing. Well, she arrived at the carousel today, but then this other fellow appeared and *proposed* to Evie."

Her friend's mouth popped open. "As in marriage? Did Kelly tell that fella to scram?"

"He couldn't when Evie said yes." June's stomach ached, seeing it again in her mind.

"Poor boy." Gladys might be closer to Kelly's age than June's, but she treated him as a younger brother too. "I can tell by the look on your face there's more to the story though."

"One curious thing. Evie is Dr. Howard's sister." June sipped the remnants of her cold coffee from this morning.

"*Your* Dr. Howard?"

June sputtered and had to wipe coffee from her lips. "He's not *my*—Gladys. Honestly."

"When will you admit you're keen on him?"

"I'm not." June wouldn't allow herself to be. Even if—well, never mind. She had one priority: working to keep her brother in school. Why dream about a future she couldn't have?

She inserted a sheet of paper into the typewriter, placed her hands in position on her keys, and tapped out the first few words of Dr. Howard's proposal, but she could feel Gladys's gaze on her.

Clearly her friend didn't believe her, so she looked up. "I'm *not*, Gladys. Anyway, all I wanted to tell you was *our* Dr. Howard's little sister got engaged today at the carousel."

Gladys looked up at something over June's head, and her lips parted. Mr. Willard? June inwardly winced and spun to face him.

But it was Martin Howard, broad shoulders set off by the slender-cut, gray, three-piece suit he wore, looking at her with his dark brows knit together. "What's this you were saying, Miss Lowell?"

Her lungs stopped working. Had he overheard the part about his sister being engaged, or the earlier part where Gladys announced that June carried a torch for him? Neither was good. *Oh Lord, help me hold my tongue in the future.*

Meanwhile Martin Howard, that curl of chestnut hair she liked so much flopping onto his forehead, waited for her answer, and she had no idea what to say to him.

Of all the things Martin Howard thought about June Lowell, being tongue-tied was not one of them. Not that she was a chatterbox like his sister, but when he encountered her at the coffeepot or passed her in the hallways, they always conversed on a number of topics. He knew her well enough to recognize her as dependable, kind, and intelligent. He'd thought he and June Lowell were friends. Or at least friendly. Now she looked as if she wished to run from the room.

At last she swallowed, hard enough for him to see the jarring movement in her throat. "You, ah, overheard?"

"That a sister of Dr. Howard is getting married, yes, but if you meant me, I'm afraid you have me confused with someone else. I have but one sister, and she's not engaged."

Miss Lowell stood, her hands smoothing the front of her brown frock. "Pardon my error, Dr. Howard. My brother is acquainted with an Evie Howard. He told me she's your sister."

"What a funny coincidence. My baby sister's name is Evelyn, but as I said, she's nowhere close to being engaged, so they cannot possibly be the same person. Anyway, I came by to ensure you'd received my exhibit proposal."

"Oh yes." June sat down, her cheeks flushing. " 'The Regenerative Powers of Starfish and Its Ramifications.' I've only now started it."

"I usually type things myself, but my arm is troubling me today." An understatement if he ever uttered one. "Remnant from the war."

"I didn't know." June's hazel eyes went wide.

"I don't make a habit of talking about it." Maybe because in doing so he'd be forced to relive the horror of the explosion before he was almost swallowed by the frigid North Atlantic.

June nodded, taking his hint that he wasn't in the mood to discuss it. "I'm always happy to type anything you need, Dr. Howard. Anything."

Did Gladys snicker? Hard to tell, the way she now hid her mouth behind a mug.

Martin shook his head. "Thank you, but typing is good exercise for that arm. Most days." He started to leave, but two steps away, something popped into his mind. He turned around. "Miss Lowell, you said something about this Evie being at the carousel?"

"Yes. It moved into the park today, and I took my lunch there to watch the men set it to rights while I ate. There was a marriage proposal."

His stomach sank as he put facts together. "The carousel is Evelyn's favorite thing. She's mad for it. I wouldn't be surprised that she came to watch things today as well. But a proposal? What did they look like, the couple who got engaged?"

"Her hair is dark and short. He was fair-haired, well-dressed. Boater hat."

Those words could describe anyone, but. . . "Evelyn has bobbed hair. And the man sounds like Bernard Galbraith."

She shrugged. "I am not familiar with him."

Martin wished the same for himself and Evelyn. That fortune hunter had been sniffing around Evelyn for weeks. His stomach clenched, and so did his fists, which brought a fresh ache to the old war wound in his arm. He forced his hands to relax before the pain worsened.

Miss Lowell's eyes crinkled at the corners. "I'm so sorry to ruin her surprise."

"On the contrary, I'm gratified for the warning."

He'd shocked the ladies, saying that. But what was Evelyn thinking? She scarcely knew Bernard Galbraith and refused to listen to Martin's or Aunt Beulah's concerns about the fellow. All they knew of him was that he worked at his uncle's imports shop, running it while the uncle was on the continent, and whenever Martin had dropped by the shop for a friendly chat with Bernard, the store was closed—no way to run a business.

More troubling, though, was Bernard's recent pursuit of a fresh-from-the-schoolroom heiress that had tongues wagging about him being a fortune hunter. When that lady's father sent Bernard away, Bernard immediately turned his attentions to Evelyn—an heiress herself. When Martin asked about Bernard's job or past, Evelyn grew furious and insisted he stop, but Martin would be a fool to ignore his suspicions where Bernard was concerned.

Meanwhile he was undoubtedly distracting the ladies from their work. "Forgive me. I'm taking up your valuable time."

"Nonsense." Miss Lowell smiled.

"Never," Miss King echoed, but her gaze was on June. Odd.

"Martin!" The feminine holler was accompanied by the staccato rapping of heels against the hall tile. Evelyn rushed toward him, blue eyes wide. "There you are. I have the best news. Oh, hello." She peeked into the room at Miss Lowell and Miss King. Martin was about to introduce them properly when Evelyn clutched his lapels. "Bernard just proposed! Look!" She waggled her left hand in front of his face then twisted it so the ladies could see the emerald set in a gold band. "We're getting married at the carousel."

"Slow down, Sis. Married on the carousel?"

"Not *on* it, silly. In front of it, so the first thing we do as husband and wife is go for a whirl. That's sure to make this wedding the talk of the town, don't you think?"

"If that's what you want." To be the talk of the town, that is. "I want you happy."

"Best wishes." Miss Lowell stood and extended her hand. "I'm June Lowell. I think you know my brother, Kelly."

Evelyn's face grew even brighter. "Kell the Swell, I call him."

"He thinks quite highly of you," Miss Lowell said.

Gladys King stood and introduced herself. "Best wishes. When's the blessed event?"

"Soon. Say, does anyone know if I need to reserve the carousel for half an hour? Who do I talk to about that?"

Miss Lowell shifted her stance. "Kelly will know who to ask. He's employed at the carousel now. I'll ask him tonight."

"Thanks ever so much." Evelyn bubbled with excitement, and it was hard for Martin not to smile. He'd promised their parents to see her happy, hadn't he?

Pity Bernard Galbraith wasn't with her right now though. He'd have liked a frank talk with the man.

Evelyn slipped past him into the office and peered at Miss Lowell's desk. "Look at this calendar. You're an organized sort, aren't you?"

"Since the museum is expanding into the Commerce and Industries Building next door," Miss Lowell explained as she adjusted her spectacles, "there's a lot to keep track of around here."

"Speaking of which, we're taking them from their work, Evelyn. Why don't we go outside and discuss the plans? Surely Aunt Beulah and I can help." Aunt Beulah, however, would be torn between her pleasure at Evelyn marrying and her distaste of the groom.

"You're both too busy. You with work, and Auntie B with planning the women's luncheon at church. I'll handle it all."

Will-o'-the-wisp Evelyn plan a wedding? "But there's a lot to do."

"*Pfft.* How much work can it be anyway?"

Miss King resumed her seat. "There are flowers, an officiant, a dress, cake and punch. Oh, and invitations."

"Bills," Martin added.

Evelyn rolled her eyes. "Fine. But that doesn't mean you need to worry about it. I'll hire someone to help me." She smiled at the ladies. "Either of you know who to ask for a job like this?"

"I do." Miss King gestured at Miss Lowell. "June's planned a few parties."

"Really?" Evelyn's eyes went wide.

Miss Lowell shook her head. "Those were small affairs. A Christmas party and a reception here at the museum."

"Small is good. We want our wedding to be intimate. Bernard called it *exclusive*."

Martin wouldn't call marrying at a public place like the carousel *intimate* or *exclusive*. It would draw plenty of attention.

Evelyn clutched Miss Lowell's arm. "Would you help a girl out? It wouldn't be much, I promise. Just the things your friend mentioned. Flowers and a cake and reserving the carousel."

Miss Lowell pressed her lips together. Was she determining how to say no without upsetting Evelyn? Martin couldn't allow her to feel forced. "It's all right, Miss Lowell. Truly."

Then again, he'd been praying for a steadying influence on his spontaneous, carefree sister. A true friend who cared about Evelyn, not her inheritance. June Lowell had all the characteristics he'd want in a friend for his sister. She was kind, dependable, and diligent. And if she was helping Evelyn with wedding plans, she'd be spending time with his sister.

Was this the Lord's answer to his prayer?

Chapter 2

Once Dr. Howard and his sister had gone, June gaped at Gladys. "Why did you tell them I'd be happy to help plan a wedding?"

"You're welcome." Looking smug, Gladys started typing. "Did you see how happy he was when you said yes? Your Dr. Howard—"

"He's not *my* doctor, Gladys. You must stop saying he is."

At June's exasperated tone, Gladys looked up. "What's got you in a dither? You now have an official excuse to talk to Dr. Howard. Sounds like you'll be paid for your time, and you never say no to extra work. Besides, you don't have to do too much. You know I'll bake the cake, so that's one thing off the list right there."

It was true she never turned down extra cash, and this didn't sound like a great deal of work. But spending time with Dr. Howard? What if that meant she started to feel more than just an attraction to him?

Goodness, she sounded ridiculous. She was far too practical to moon over a fellow. The best way to nip this in the bud was to take it to the Lord in prayer. *Lord, I'd appreciate it if You would remove these butterflies from my belly when I see Martin Howard. Thanks.*

Her pull toward him wasn't the only problem with helping plan a wedding at the carousel though. "I hope Kelly isn't too upset I'm helping Evie marry somebody else."

"I didn't even think of that. Here I thought I was matchmaking for you and Dr. Howard, but instead I'll be breaking Kelly's heart." Gladys rubbed her temple, mussing her curled coif. "Don't worry. I shoved you into this, and I'll make things right. I'll talk to Dr. Howard right now."

June's heart warmed at her friend's gesture. "No, it's all right. Kelly will understand it's a job, which is top priority in our house."

Gladys rose and wrapped an arm around June's shoulders. "Are you sure? I'm as bossy as my mother always said I was."

June returned her friend's hug. "You meant well. I know you want to see me with Dr. Howard, but there's a no-fraternization policy to consider, remember? Besides, I am not available for anything but work until Kelly's out of law school."

"That sounds miserable, June."

"It sounds like life," she said with finality. Whenever she'd taken time or money to do something for herself—well, there'd been a price to pay. Like the time a few years back when she'd splurged on ballet tickets, but then Kelly grew out of his best trousers and there hadn't been enough money to replace them for the school dance. She'd felt terrible and vowed never to forget that her job as the older sibling was to provide for him, even when it meant making sacrifices.

That meant taking whatever job opportunities came her way,

including this one. She extricated herself from Gladys's hug. "If I'm going to help with the wedding, I need to do something at once."

"Now? What's that?"

June took a deep breath. "Making sure this carousel wedding won't get me fired."

It was an exaggeration, of course, but June felt it best to explain the situation to Mr. Willard. She promised to work on the wedding during off hours, but she also wanted Mr. Willard to know she wasn't trying to break any rules if she spoke to Dr. Howard about the wedding.

It was a matter of professional courtesy, and she told Martin Howard as much the next day when he dropped by the secretarial office midmorning.

He scratched his freshly shaved jaw. "I'm sorry, Miss Lowell. I didn't realize helping with the wedding could cause problems for you here."

Unfortunately, his endearingly abashed look only made her butterflies worse. *Lord, remember, we've talked about this? No more butterflies, please?*

She swallowed down her emotions. "Mr. Willard understands I'll be helping Evelyn on my off hours, and he's fine with that." So was Kelly, although when she told him about it last night, she could tell he was devastated over Evie's engagement. That was nothing she needed to tell Dr. Howard though. "I'm meeting Evelyn at the end of the day, after work is done."

They would meet here at Balboa Park, and June had prepared a checklist of items to discuss: the wedding date, officiant, guests, and a color scheme. The carousel animals would look adorable with bows tied around their necks.

Gladys rose. "Pardon me, but I need to hand this to Dr. Abbott." The museum's director. "Be back in a minute."

Dr. Howard stepped closer to June's desk, close enough she could smell his rich aftershave. His dark eyes were so soft. "Thanks again for helping. You may have noticed yesterday how shocked I was about this proposal. Evelyn and Bernard have only been seeing each other a few weeks."

"That does sound hasty." Then again, her parents had had a short courtship, and their marriage had been rich and loving. "One never knows, I suppose."

"In any case, I'd hoped to join you and Evelyn, but I have plans with a friend who wants to see the carousel."

A lady friend, no doubt. The butterflies in June's belly swooped low, leaving a trail of disappointment in their wake. She forced a smile. "That will be lovely."

"And appropriate to his age, which I'd like to encourage." Dr. Howard rubbed the back of his neck. "Tim's twelve but runs with an older group. We met a few weeks ago just outside the park. I was looking for the imports shop operated by Bernard Galbraith's uncle, but I must've looked thirsty, because Tim assumed I was looking for a speakeasy."

"A speakeasy! Why ever would he assume that?"

"There's one nearby, and he works there, sweeping floors."

There was an illegal drinking establishment near the park? A shudder coursed through her, but she shouldn't have been surprised by the prohibited activity. Since the Eighteenth Amendment had gone into effect two years ago, there had been news of such places around town. The notion of one this close, however, was made even more horrible by the knowledge that a child worked inside it. "That place must be shut down."

"I agree, but their locations are guarded secrets. Tim asking me if I was looking for it defeats the purpose, a blunder he won't soon repeat. I wish I'd had the foresight to go along with it then so I'd know where the speakeasy was located. I couldn't have gone inside without the appropriate password, but I could've reported the location to the police. Alas, all I know is there is a speakeasy somewhere around Sixth Street."

"Despite that interesting meeting, though, you befriended Tim?"

"I'm trying to get him out of that job. I've met him after school a few times, showed him things in the museum, anything I can think of to interest him in more wholesome activities. He's intrigued by engines, so I'm hoping he'll like the carousel's mechanics. He's a good lad, truly, doing what he does to make ends meet at home. His mother is a widow."

"There aren't many ways to earn money for a lad that young, beyond hawking newspapers and shining shoes." It seemed Kelly had tried them all before finding the carousel job.

"I'm trusting God to provide something nevertheless. It's a complicated issue. My friend Calvin Faulker is a policeman, and while he works to close the speakeasies in town, I'm trying to help Tim, and I have a sense of urgency. Summer is coming, and I fear there's not much for Tim and other lads to do but get into trouble. Look at me, taking you from your work. Willard won't be pleased with me."

She hated for him to go, but she did have a few projects to work on. Still, she couldn't resist one last bit of conversation. "I enjoyed your proposal yesterday."

His brows rose. "You enjoyed a proposal for an exhibit on

echinoderm regeneration?"

"I like learning new things. What a surprise that starfish can regrow limbs."

He smiled and looked genuinely pleased, as if few people outside his field ever showed interest in his studies. "For brainless creatures, they're fascinating, aren't they?"

"I will never look at them the same way again." If she ever went to the tide pool and saw one for herself again, that is. After Kelly's graduation from law school, probably. She didn't have time for frivolity right now.

He paused at the door. "I have a request. Would you call me Martin? I'm not much for formality."

The butterflies raced through her tummy. "I'm June."

"Thank you, June. For that and for helping my sister."

"You're most welcome, Martin." Saying his name was like honey on her lips.

When he left, she sighed. *Being on a first-name basis with him is not helping these butterflies of mine, Lord.*

Shortly after five, Martin stuffed an apple into his coat pocket and exited the museum. The afternoon air carried faint strains of the tune played by the carousel's band organ, the perfect backdrop to a meeting about a wedding at the carousel. He'd feel like a fish out of water, but popping by to check in was part of his job as Evelyn's brother. Their parents would have wanted him to be involved, even if this was not the wedding they'd envisioned for their favorite child.

He strode across El Prado toward the lily pond in front of the striking Botanical Building, noted for its unique lath structure and beautiful display beds. Catching sight of the three women seated on facing benches, he headed toward them. Slender Evelyn, her dark hair fanning her cheeks, sat beside Aunt Beulah, whose iron-gray curls were pinned in a style popular some ten years past. Her hands were folded on her ample lap, a sure sign she was biting her tongue against whatever Evelyn was stating with such animated gestures. On the other bench, June sat with a notebook in her lap, posture perfect, ankles crossed just so, nodding and writing.

Aunt Beulah looked up at him and rolled her eyes. He removed his fedora and dipped beneath the brim of her black hat to kiss her cheek, as she expected. "Good afternoon, all."

June looked up and smiled. Wearing a green sweater over a white dress, she looked like one of the water lilies that floated on the pond, pretty and fresh.

His paternal aunt clutched his hand. "We were just discussing whether Evelyn should marry *in front of* the carousel or *on* the carousel, which she says was your idea."

"It was a misstatement." He waved away responsibility with a brush of his hand.

Evelyn bit her lip. "I think it would be jolly good fun, but Aunt Beulah thought the officiant might suffer motion sickness, riding backward."

"I know that would be my fate." Martin could well understand his aunt's struggle to hold back her thoughts. This sort of thing drove her mad—and Martin's parents wouldn't have liked it either. But they'd have given Evelyn whatever she wanted, whether it was a wedding on a carousel or astride mules descending into the Grand Canyon. It was Martin's job to honor their wishes. "I won't interrupt further, but I'll be back to escort you home soon, Auntie and Evelyn. I'm meeting Tim at the carousel."

"Take your time, my dear." Aunt Beulah gestured at June. "Miss Lowell has us in hand. She received tentative permission to reserve the carousel for a short time."

"My brother, Kelly, spoke to his supervisors," June explained, tapping her pen against the notebook. "All we need is the wedding date and time."

Evelyn tensed. "Bernard's uncle is in Europe, and we aren't sure when he's coming back."

"An important consideration, to be sure." June's measured tone was no doubt intended to set Evelyn at ease. "In the meantime, let's discuss the dress. Will you two shop this weekend?"

Evelyn's shoulders relaxed. "I know just what I want. A Juliet cap and veil. And the dress will be lace. Several inches shorter than floor length." Evelyn met Aunt Beulah's unimpressed gaze. "I have to be able to climb up on a carousel horse, don't I?"

Aunt Beulah muttered something about the lack of dignity these days.

That was Martin's cue. "I'll leave you to it."

June's knowing smile elicited one from him in return, and he started to whistle as he strode down El Prado toward the carousel.

A few families and couples milled about, as did a uniformed policeman with the burly physique of a football player, which in fact he'd been before he served in the war and joined law enforcement. "Calvin," Martin greeted.

His friend shook his hand. "Here to meet Tim?"

"I am."

"I assume he hasn't offered any information yet on the speakeasy."

"I'd have told you if he had."

"I can't wait for the day we raid that place."

"I agree, but the next day, another will spout up to take its place. They're like mushrooms, Cal. The root of the problem is bigger than the one speakeasy." Greed, darkness, vice—they'd been around since the fall of humanity and would persist until the Lord returned. But in the meantime, Christians had to do what they could to stand against darkness.

"I'll be praying, old sport."

"Thanks, brother." Martin's eye caught on a skinny lad with fair hair and the pronounced hands of a boy in early adolescence. "There's Tim. See you at church Sunday?"

"I'll be there."

Martin met Tim by the carousel's ticket booth, a stand large enough to accommodate one man on a stool. Martin pulled the apple from his coat pocket. "Hungry?"

"Sure." Tim bit into the fruit. Martin had brought two from home this morning, one for his own lunch and this one for Tim. Apples weren't in season, and Martin's lunchtime apple had been mushy but still sweet. It was nutritious, so Martin was glad to see the boy eat his.

While Tim chewed, Martin nodded at the menagerie-style carousel. "Did you ever ride this when it was in Tent City?"

Tim swallowed and swiped his lips with the back of his hand. "Naw. Never went there."

There were horses aplenty on the carousel, but watching the animals go around, Martin found his eye catching on the more exotic beasts.

"Which animal is your favorite, Tim?"

"The lion, I guess."

"Agreed. Although the roosters are fun."

"*Funny*, you mean. Who rides a rooster?" Tim laughed, looking like a boy instead of the rough-and-ready man-child he often presented himself to be.

"Who rides a lion either? You'd end up as his dinner."

Tim scratched his upper lip, where the faintest trace of fuzz had grown. "I pick the dragon then. Except he doesn't go up and down."

"He's not a jumper, no, but since he's on the outside you can try for the brass ring when you're on him." Martin pulled a nickel from his pocket. "Care for a spin?"

"Naw. That's baby stuff." The childlike look disappeared from his face, replaced by a harder expression that pained Martin's heart.

"I don't see any babies riding." They watched the riders go around, up and down: couples, young adults, a gaggle of school-children near Tim's age, and unfortunately, one baby. An infant, held in its mother's lap, seated on one of the chariots. "One then. But it doesn't look to be enjoying itself."

Tim snickered. "Can't blame it. Carousels are stupid."

"Now that, my friend, is not true. They are masters of engineering." Which he hoped would interest Tim, since the boy had expressed curiosity about car and airplane engines. Martin's attention shifted to those manning the carousel, especially the fellow in the center. It was hard to get a solid look because of the menagerie whirling past, but the man inside had hair the same color as June's. Her brother?

Kelly, she said his name was. Maybe Martin could introduce Tim to him, and maybe, just maybe, Tim would be curious about the mechanisms. And possibly, there could soon be an opening for someone like Tim to work at the carousel instead of the speakeasy. "My friend's brother is that fellow in there working. I imagine if we ask, he'll show us how it works."

He could tell Tim vacillated, shifting his balance from foot to foot. Then the boy pulled his cap lower on his brow. "Can't today. It's Friday."

An evening of work at the speakeasy for Tim. "I can help you find something else to do to make money."

Tim tossed his apple core into a refuse bin. "I don't want to quit."

"Don't want to or can't?"

The flash of fear on Tim's face said it all. Martin pushed down the ire rising in his chest so he'd sound calm. "Take me there, will you? I'll speak to your boss—"

"Oh no you don't. You'll tell that copper friend of yours, and then what do you think's gonna happen to me?"

"I'll protect you."

"I'm fine how I am." Tim folded his arms. "Not everyone is a bad sort, you know. The hostess, Myra, is always mothering us."

"Thank the Lord for small favors." Martin wanted nothing more than to try to convince Tim to quit. He could press the point and win the argument, but Tim could disappear from his life, along with any opportunity for Martin to help him. This was one of those situations where he had to focus on the war, not the battle. All he could do was pray and drop the matter—for now.

"If you don't want to ride the carousel, would you like to walk around a little?"

"Sure." Tim shrugged. "Down El Prado?"

Martin's hands shoved in his pockets. "Say, school's almost out for the year. Maybe we can learn how the carousel works when you're out for the summer."

"Maybe." Tim's face brightened. "Guess what came to our

school this week? A big case of shells and things. From the museum."

Ah, one of the cabinets from the museum's education program that rotated among local schools to expose schoolchildren to science. "What did you think?"

"The fossils are interesting, I s'pose, but I like the saber-toothed cat you showed me better."

"Everyone loves saber-toothed cats," Martin said as if it were obvious.

"Except you. You like ocean critters."

"Officially. But I can't resist saber-toothed cats. Those teeth are wickedly sharp."

"Glad I wasn't born a woolly mammoth."

They walked in companionable conversation as they traveled the boulevard between the former exhibition buildings until they reached the lily pond. June looked up and waved.

"Who's that?" Tim's face scrunched up.

"My friend June. I work with her at the museum. The lady in the yellow dress is my sister, Evelyn, and beside her is my aunt Beulah. Care to say hello?"

The boy stiffened. "Actually, I see some friends. Do you mind if I say hello to them instead?"

Martin did mind, because the group included older boys, including one who was clearly a young adult. Freckled and dark-haired, the man wore bright blue suspenders holding up unfashionably baggy pants, as well as a scowl.

"Who's that?"

"Vincent. My friend." Tim said it with a tone of defiance.

The one who'd introduced Tim to the job at the speakeasy. Martin's jaw clenched, but he nodded to Tim anyway. Playing the long game with Tim meant planting seeds, offering alternatives, and being available. *One step at a time, eh, Lord?*

As he watched Tim join the others, a man brushed past Martin, close enough for Martin to catch the strong odor of the gent's cologne. Bernard Galbraith. Walking right past Martin without as much as a hello when they were about to be brothers-in-law. A strong wave of dislike crested over him, but he had to work past it for Evelyn's sake—as their parents would have wanted so she'd be happy.

"Galbraith," he called after him.

Bernard spun and his eyes widened in a feigned look of shock. "Ho, old sport. Where'd you come from?"

"Right here." Perhaps Bernard had been so focused on Evelyn he hadn't noticed anything else, but Martin doubted it, the way Bernard's gaze flitted everywhere but Martin's face. "I was hoping we could talk. Privately."

"About the wedding?"

"About the marriage." Martin stared at Bernard. In his periphery, Evelyn rose from her bench and walked toward them. That didn't give him much time. "This is a big step, and you two haven't been seeing one another more than a few weeks. I want to be sure my sister will be happy."

"Calm down, old sport. We'll have heaps of money."

From Evelyn's inheritance, perhaps? "I didn't mean financially secure. I mean loved. Supported in her endeavors as well as her spiritual life, until you're both old and gray. If you love Evelyn, you'll want what's best for her."

"*I'm* what's best for her."

Evelyn reached them, grinning. "My favorite fellas together! Let's have supper tomorrow, all of us. One happy family."

"Excellent. We can talk more," Martin said.

"Sounds marvelous." Bernard offered Evelyn his arm and led her to the lily pond. Hands in his pockets, Martin followed after them. When Aunt Beulah sent him the look—the one that asked if he'd had a decent talk with Bernard just now—Martin shook his head.

Aunt Beulah glanced skyward in clear annoyance. She recovered enough to greet Bernard and Evelyn when they reached the benches. "Hello, Mr. Galbraith."

"Good afternoon, Mrs. Adkins."

"It *was*," she said. When Bernard blanched, she cracked a smile. "It's evening now, I daresay."

"Ah, you're as witty as you are lovely, Mrs. Adkins, and may I say that shade of blue is utter perfection on you."

"You may." Aunt Beulah didn't look particularly flattered though.

Bernard bowed before June as if she were a grand duchess. "We haven't had the pleasure, ma'am. I am Bernard Galbraith."

"June Lowell." She introduced herself before Martin could do the honors. "I'm helping with the wedding."

"Of course, and we're grateful, aren't we, darling?" Bernard smiled at Evelyn. "So much to do in so little time."

"Speaking of time," Martin said, sparing a quick glance at Tim, who was still with his group of friends, "did you select a date?" The longer the engagement, the better, as far as he was concerned.

June tapped her pen against the notebook. "We'd like to know as soon as possible so we may secure the venue and the officiant."

"We have a venue. The carousel."

June didn't flinch at the harsh tinge to Bernard's tone. "Yes, but they need a date so they can accommodate you."

Evelyn's dark brows knit. "June's brother, Kelly—what a lamb he is. He works at the carousel and spoke to his boss. We just have to say what day."

June opened a small notebook with a calendar printed inside. She had it open to July, a few months away. "I understand your uncle is in Europe, but Evelyn didn't think he'd be gone long. Do any of these dates work?"

He didn't look at it. "Say the word and I'll be there."

"What about your uncle?" Martin asked.

"I can't wait that long," Bernard said, gazing with syrupy eyes at Evelyn.

"I say two weeks from tomorrow then," Evelyn declared.

That soon? Martin's gaze met Aunt Beulah's then June's. "That's quick."

"Not compared to what other people are doing. Elopements are in vogue now, and that's what Bernard wanted, didn't you?"

"Did you now?" Martin didn't like the sound of it one bit. If Bernard was only interested in Evelyn's inheritance, and they'd eloped—

Well, thank God for engagements, however brief they might be.

Aunt Beulah's jowls quivered. "What foolishness, eloping."

"I knew you wouldn't like it." Evelyn rolled her eyes. "So that's why I told Bernard a unique wedding would be just as fashionable as an elopement."

Bernard chucked her chin. "Whatever you wish, my dear, so long as we're married soon."

Two weeks. Two weeks! *Lord, how do I discern if Bernard really loves Evelyn in such a brief time? How do I be the brother I need to be?*

At least there was tomorrow's dinner. "We can discuss things more tomorrow, Bernard, before dinner. Come early so you and I can chat."

Galbraith snapped his fingers, as if remembering something. "Darling, I forgot. I must go over the accounts."

"Surely that won't take all evening." Aunt Beulah's brows rose.

"Next week for supper, I promise." He winked at Aunt Beulah and then took Evelyn's hand. "Darling, shall we start our evening together on the carousel?"

Bernard had no intention of ever enduring a frank, man-to-man talk with Martin, did he? Martin's fists clenched, so he hid them in his pockets again. When he looked up, June watched him with something like sympathy darkening her hazel eyes.

Evelyn waved goodbye. "See you this evening."

"I shall wait up, so do not be late," Aunt Beulah announced as Bernard led Evelyn down El Prado toward the carousel.

June turned her attention to the group of boys circled on the other side of the lily pond. "That's your friend Tim, isn't it?"

"It is. And those are the fellows he calls friends."

"One of them looks far too old for the rest of them."

He knew who she meant: Vincent, the freckled scowler. "He's the one who recruited Tim to sweep at the speakeasy. When I consider what Tim is exposed to in that environment, I'm infuriated."

Aunt Beulah glared at the boys. "Can't you follow Tim when he goes to work? See where the speakeasy is?"

"Harder than it sounds, Auntie. Places like that wouldn't be in business if they didn't take precautions."

"Piffle. You and that policeman friend of yours should try again."

"The police also employ undercover officers, but speakeasies got their name for a reason. Once someone knows about them, they stay silent on the matter. All we know is the establishment is near the park."

Aunt Beulah gathered her purse. "I'll do it then. Play my part to help local law enforcement and pretend I'm looking for a whiskey."

He met June's smiling gaze and almost laughed himself. "You're good to offer, Auntie, but they've seen you with me, so they won't take you anywhere. And if they did, you could be arrested."

"You are a brave woman, Mrs. Adkins." June adjusted her bag over her shoulder. "Alas, I should leave. Kelly will be off his shift soon, and he and I will be catching the streetcar together."

"We mustn't keep you then. Thank you for lending your voice of reason with these wedding plans." Aunt Beulah met Martin's gaze. "No surprise, but Evelyn is not much help. Without Miss Lowell, the event would be a disaster."

Responsibility for his sister settled over Martin's shoulders like a yoke. Always had. "If there's anything I can do, let me know. I'll be in the field the first half of the week but back at the museum Thursday or Friday."

"Thank you, but I have all I need except for colors and flowers. Unless you'd like to share your thoughts on roses and daisies," she teased. When he shook his head and laughed, June bid them farewell and left in the direction his sister and Bernard had taken.

He turned to his aunt. "Will you pardon me for a moment? I'd like to talk to Tim once more before we leave."

"Of course, dear boy. I don't like the idea of him with those ruffians."

Martin didn't want to embarrass Tim, so he took only a few steps toward the group. Tim met his gaze and jogged over.

Martin explained that he was about to escort his aunt home.

"Sorry we couldn't talk more, but tomorrow's Saturday. Would you like to meet me here to organize some fossils? I'll pay you."

"Thanks, but um, Vincent has some things for us to do." Tim folded his arms. "I know you don't like me spending time with him, but I'm in charge of myself, Dr. Howard."

"What does your mother say about all of this?"

"What she doesn't know doesn't hurt her, does it?" Tim's eyes darkened, but then he looked to Vincent. The group was moving on, ambling toward the carousel. "Sorry, but I gotta go. Maybe I'll help you with the fossils next week." Tim jogged to rejoin his friends. At least Tim was willing to meet with Martin again.

Lord, grant me—or someone else—an opening with the boy.

Aunt Beulah waited, primly holding her bag in front of her round midsection. "Ready?"

"Yes, ma'am." He offered his arm.

She looked up at him with a curious gleam in her eye. "I must say, today's adventure at the park has been most illuminating."

"How so?

She gestured ahead of them on El Prado, but he couldn't tell if she gestured at Tim walking with his group, June pausing to gather something from her handbag, or Evelyn and Bernard canoodling as they ambled at tortoise-like speed. "Bernard, you mean? I'm afraid the only illumination I received in his regard is that nothing has changed. I still don't quite trust him."

"Not with Bernard, Martin. I meant *that.*" She gestured up El Prado again.

"The seriousness of Tim's situation?"

Aunt Beulah stared ahead, shaking her head. "You were always the smartest little boy. Think, dear boy."

What was she looking at? The only other person ahead was

June, and there was nothing of interest there. Nevertheless, Martin watched after June, admiring the purpose in her gait and the way her walk sent the hem of her smart dress swinging about her legs. Fetching color on her, that green of her sweater. Looked becoming with her light brown hair and hazel eyes.

Aunt Beulah's chuckle drew his gaze back.

"What?"

"I do not think it that difficult, my dear." She tapped him in the chest, in the area of his heart.

Oh. She had indeed meant June. She was under the impression he harbored romantic feelings for her.

He didn't. Did he?

Maybe Aunt Beulah found today illuminating, but Martin was suddenly confounded. He and June?

In response to the thought of her, his heart gave a mighty thump, as if it had been hibernating and was just now waking for spring.

Chapter 3

The following Friday at noon, June set aside her completed list of participants for the museum's upcoming nature walk and leaned back in her chair for a stretch. "Lunch."

Gladys glanced at the ticking carriage clock sitting on the top shelf of the bookcase behind June. "I'm going to enjoy this fine weather and take a stroll. Want to come along?"

Much as June enjoyed walking with Gladys around the park, she shook her head. "I'm meeting Evelyn today. Only eight days until the wedding."

"Oh, that's right. Don't forget to ask her about the cake filling."

"Thanks again for baking the cake. I'll ask where she wants it iced too."

"Did you get the blue ribbon she wanted?"

"I have a sample for her. Once she approves it, I'll purchase enough to make bows for the carousel horses Evelyn and

Bernard will ride after the wedding. Or zebras, rather. Evelyn finally decided which animals they'll ride. I also thought I'd tie bows around some of the trees and lampposts nearby. Do you like the color?" She pulled a sample of the light turquoise ribbon from her bag.

Gladys whistled her approval. "Is her dress this shade too?"

"I'm not sure. She couldn't decide if she wanted to wear blue or white, but I'll find out at lunch. I only need a few more details from her today."

"This engagement is too brief for me," Gladys said, rising. "But then again, if I found the right man, I wouldn't want to wait long either."

Would June? She hadn't given any thought to suitors since her parents died. And she didn't plan to until Kelly was finished with law school. That was three years away, but after he graduated, things would change, wouldn't they? He'd be working a good job and might want to move out of the flat they shared downtown. Would she think of marrying then?

Silly, thinking of her own nonexistent marriage plans when she had a real wedding to prepare.

"See you in an hour, Gladys." She fetched her lunch pail and hurried out of the museum. Crossing El Prado to the lily pond, she searched among the handful of people gathered there for Evelyn's telltale dark hair. She didn't see her, but Martin sat on one of the benches, gazing over the lily pond at the Botanical Building.

Butterflies whooshed from her stomach to her knees.

She hadn't seen him all week, since his work had taken him away from the museum. When he looked up at her approach, smiling wide, she couldn't help but smile back. My, he was a handsome fellow. Faint lines formed around his eyes and lips, proof he smiled often. She liked that in a man. She liked manners too, and he sent her pulse racing when he rose and doffed his fedora, revealing the recalcitrant dark curl over his brow.

"Hello, June. Have a seat?"

She did, trying to slow her rapid heart rate with even breaths. "Are you here to join me and Evelyn?"

"I'm afraid Evelyn's under the weather. I hope you don't mind if I stand in as substitute."

"Of course not, but poor Evelyn. It's nothing serious, I hope."

"A cold. Not horrid, but enough to send her to her bed." He gestured at the tin on her lap. "Did you bring a lunch?"

"Yes. I'll gladly share if you don't have anything to eat."

"I brought an apple and a cheese sandwich." He pulled a fabric-wrapped bundle from his bulging coat pocket. "Do you mind picnicking here?"

She shook her head. "I eat here at the lily pond when it's sunny."

"Beautiful scenery."

The pond—or rather ponds, since there was a smaller one between this larger one and the Botanical Building—was meant to serve as a reflecting pool. Sometimes algae made it look more like pea soup, but not today. "I like the lilies. Or, since you're a scientist, would you prefer me to call them *Nymphaea*?" she teased.

He laughed. " 'Lily' is a much prettier name. And I never cared for calling lotuses like those over there *Nelumbo*. Sounds like a disease."

It was her turn to laugh. "We shall leave them well enough alone then."

He bit into his sandwich, so she did the same. The deviled

ham was a tad dry, but she'd been in a hurry this morning. Washing down her bite with a swallow of not-so-cold milk, Lily pulled her notebook and pencil out of the bag propped at her feet. "Did Evelyn perchance send you with the guest list for my records?"

"She did." He withdrew a folded page from his inner coat pocket. "I'm sorry it's wrinkled."

"As long as I can read it, it's fine." The invitations were to be hand-delivered tomorrow by special messenger, but she'd asked for a copy in case an issue arose. She opened the sheet. Only twenty people were listed. Well, Evelyn had said the wedding would be intimate. Close family and friends—and the public who happened to be visiting the carousel at the time.

Oh dear. Kelly's name was on the list, along with hers, and a scribbled note alongside from Evelyn insisting June and "Kell the Swell" join the fun.

"What's wrong?" Martin lowered his sandwich.

"Nothing."

"You frowned and furrowed your brow."

"I did?" She took another bite, willing her forehead to smooth out.

"Did Evelyn do something? Or—is it me?"

She swallowed. "That's not it. Truly. You are perfect. That is to say you are perfectly fine. Both of you."

You are perfect—what a blunder!

"Then what is it? Tell me so I can be of help."

It might not be seemly to tell him this sort of thing, but his dark eyes bored into hers. *Should I tell him, Lord?*

God didn't answer with a thunderclap, but she was at once reminded of Martin's kindness. He was the sort of man a gal could trust, so she met his intense gaze.

"It's my brother, Kelly. He met Evelyn at the carousel a while back and formed an attachment. He was about to invite her out when Mr. Galbraith arrived at the carousel and proposed. Evelyn remains ignorant of his feelings, which is best, but I'm not sure Kelly will want to attend."

"Ah." He stared at his sandwich.

"Please know he has the highest regard for her and will not interfere in her happiness in any way."

"I cannot imagine him having poor manners, being your brother." He smiled.

"He's bearing the disappointment well, burying himself in his studies. He's taking college courses, you see, and will attend law school in another year. He's borne a lot to achieve this goal, and the carousel is the first job he's had that makes him smile."

"That's important, isn't it? To have a job that makes you smile?" Martin polished his apple on his pant leg. "I'm aware how blessed I am to do something I love and how I had an advantage getting here. Evelyn and I enjoyed a privileged upbringing, which enabled me to receive an education, including a doctorate, without having to labor quite as hard as your brother seems to be doing."

"Your family must be proud of your accomplishments."

His eyes darkened. "Aunt Beulah is proud but doesn't understand what I do. Evelyn thinks my work is boring. My parents are gone, and they never said much on the subject."

"They weren't the sort to discuss emotions, I take it?"

"Not with me. Maybe because I was male. It seemed expected that I'd do something valid with my time, but they never said much about me studying marine zoology, or about me joining the navy when the war came."

"I'm certain they were proud of your service, Martin."

"Probably. But while I was gone, Mama died in the influenza epidemic. Father followed shortly after from pneumonia, leaving me as Evelyn's guardian."

"Oh, that's horrible. I'm sorry."

A tip of his head acknowledged her remark. "Thankfully, Aunt Beulah moved in to help us. Evelyn is twelve years younger than I, you see, and while I've always had a sense of responsibility for her, this was different."

"I understand that feeling. My parents are gone too, and I'm also the older sibling." She'd finished her sandwich and dusted crumbs from her hands. "Our parents were killed in an automobile crash five years ago. We don't have any other relatives. It's just me and Kelly now."

"I'm sorry." He reached and squeezed her hand. A gesture of sympathy, nothing more. But it still made her fingers tingle.

"Thank you."

His eyes were shadowed by his hat brim, but there was no escaping the empathy shining from them. "We have to do our best to honor our parents' wishes and legacies, don't we? I'm trying now with this wedding business. They wanted Evelyn happy."

"She does seem giddy about getting married."

"Much as it pains me to say it though, I'm not thrilled about this wedding." Martin glanced at her. "Maybe I'd feel better if I had the opportunity to sit down with Bernard for a real talk about his intentions. His work. His plans for the future."

"You still haven't had that conversation?"

"He has excuses aplenty when we issue invitations. It's possible they're legitimate, but they ring hollow after a while. I would think he'd make more of an effort to get to know us better."

Oh dear. "What does your aunt think about him?"

"That he'll fleece Evie within the year." He looked to be considering his words, but then he shrugged. "Our parents left Evelyn an inheritance. Unfortunately, her funds make her vulnerable to fortune hunters. Bernard doesn't appear to be in need of her money—he claims to be independently wealthy and has a fine automobile, fashionable clothing, and such—yet friends of his have let slip he is always asking them for loans. Hearsay, of course, but troubling hearsay. I am not one to pay mind to gossip, but he can never describe to me just what he does at his uncle's imports shop. And he's seldom there, at least not when I drop by attempting to talk to him."

"It does sound odd." Perhaps explainable though.

His arms folded. "We are most troubled by his actions one month ago, which Aunt Beulah witnessed with her own eyes. Bernard was pursuing a naive, wealthy maiden—Kitty Dupree. Declared his undying love and devotion at a charity function my aunt attended. Kitty adored it and swore her undying affections for him, but her father returned from out of town the next day, and Kitty and Bernard were no longer a pair. You'd think the fellow would lick his wounds awhile, but instead, he fixed his attentions on Evelyn. . .within two days. Clearly his heart was not too broken."

Two days? "That does indeed sound troubling." And utterly foreign to June, who never drew masculine attention and would have no time for it if she did. The Howards' money was also a strange concept to June. She'd known they had a fine house in Logan Heights, but no more than that. There must be a lot of money, indeed, for Evelyn to be in danger of falling prey to a man who only wanted her inheritance.

"We're troubled that Bernard wanted to elope. How can I not fear his motivation isn't love but quick access to cash? He doesn't even want to wait for his uncle to return to town before the wedding. No, he wants to marry Evelyn with all haste, and I do not think the reason is because of grand passion."

"I hope you can speak to him about it soon. One would think he'd want to make a good impression on you."

"One would think."

"What does Evelyn say about your concerns?"

He snorted. "She grows furious. Says I don't understand and insists I stop, so I am keeping my thoughts to myself."

"But she could be marrying a bounder. You have to express your concerns. It's the loving thing to do."

"The problem is, even if I don't like her choice, she's of age. Of course I'd also like her to mature a little bit before she weds. Her friends are flighty, and she's so impulsive that I sometimes despair, but it's my job to see her happy. I must confess, I've been praying for her to meet someone like you. Reliable. Determined. Diligent."

Why should such praise slice her to the core? But it did. She didn't have a choice but to be reliable or diligent. Even when she craved a bit of the frivolity Evelyn indulged in on a daily basis, she had to put aside such selfishness and remember Kelly. He had to come first. She tried not to let her disappointment come out in her tone. "That's me. Dependable June."

"I admire those things in you," Martin said. "Kind June. Thoughtful June. Smiling June. Those are some of the things I like best about you."

He did? My, his smile diminished her disappointment and sent her butterflies whooshing around again. What on earth could she say to such a compliment?

She was spared answering him when he absently rubbed his shoulder, as if it ached. Catching the direction of her gaze, he offered a sad smile. "My souvenir from the war. I was aboard the USS *San Diego*—ironic, isn't it, since this is my hometown?"

The USS *San Diego* was the only American capital ship to sink in the war, although she couldn't remember whether it had hit a mine or been struck by a torpedo. He'd been aboard? "It must have been terrifying."

"It was, and fast. Thirty minutes after the explosion, the ship was gone. I received a piece of shrapnel in my arm and a cold salt-water bath in the North Atlantic from the explosion, but I lived and am grateful for it."

"Indeed." But then he twisted his head in such a way that his collar shifted, revealing a light pink scar on his neck. The shrapnel in his arm wasn't his only souvenir from the war.

One never knew what another had gone through, did one? His service and commitment to his country, as well as his family, only made her admire him more.

"Willard is watching us." Martin's observation was like a splash of cold water. Sure enough, her boss stood on the museum steps, timepiece in hand. She twisted her pinned watch to verify the time. Five till one. "I must go."

"Forgive me. I blathered on about myself this whole time."

She gathered her lunch pail and bag. "I enjoyed it. Have a good afternoon."

Mr. Willard's eyes narrowed at her as she hurried toward him. "Discussing the wedding, Miss Lowell?"

"Yes, sir." Although once she said it, she realized they hadn't discussed it at all. Not the cake filling nor the ribbon hue, only the groom. Had she broken the rules? She hadn't intended to fraternize with Martin. She had to be polite, didn't she?

Fortunately, she was seated at her desk at the stroke of one. Her gaze focused on the letter she typed, but her foolish brain kept returning to Martin and what he'd said about her.

"Smiling, kind, thoughtful June."

Even if her affection for Martin must go no further, it was nice he saw her that way. She could hold on to that, couldn't she, in the secret places in her heart?

That wasn't too selfish of her, was it?

Martin struggled to focus the rest of the day. He packed the wrong items for the museum expansion, misplaced a memorandum from Director Abbott, and forgot he'd already measured the limb regrowth of the starfish in his office.

No need to ask himself why he was so distracted. June.

Or rather his confusion over her.

Had he really told her about his ship sinking in the war? He never talked about that, but he sure had today, as well as his concerns about Bernard. He'd also almost said outright that his parents hadn't much noticed him.

In fact, he'd opened up comfortably, like a sea anemone allowing its tentacles to wave in a gentle tide. Normally when it came to discussing his troubles, he was more like that same anemone poked by a curious child's finger, closing faster than a blink.

For her part, June hadn't said or done anything to make him regret sharing with her. Instead, her calm, sweet presence invited a deeper friendship.

Martin tacked the lid on the box of display items moving to the building next door and raked a hand through his undoubtedly untidy hair—he slicked it back according to fashion for church, but the rest of the time he couldn't be bothered with sticky pomade. Just like he couldn't be bothered with relationships beyond his family, church, and those God placed on his heart, like Tim.

Was God placing June on his heart too? Not in the same way as He had those others though. Over the past few days, he'd caught himself thinking of her while collecting water samples off the pier at Scripps Institute—and while eating or brushing his teeth. Not just because she was helping with the wedding either.

Lord, Aunt Beulah was right. I think I care for June.

The admission wasn't entirely welcome. Love came with limits. Conditions. It could be withdrawn, as his parents' had been when he was twelve years old and Evelyn was born.

He hadn't known the rules then, and it had hurt him when his parents' affection shifted toward the beautiful baby girl they'd long prayed for. From that point forward, Father didn't spend time with Martin, other than to remind him of his responsibilities as an older brother. Even into adulthood, a part of him kept hoping his parents would love him a little more with each educational achievement, publication, or honor he achieved.

But of course they hadn't. It wasn't their fault that they couldn't feel more for him. Evelyn was special, which is why his parents would have wanted Martin to give her the wedding of her dreams. They couldn't deny her anything.

Their preference for Evelyn didn't hurt anymore. It was just the way human love worked. While Martin had come to learn

God's love was unconditional and constant, people were fickle when it came to love. It could be withdrawn. And while he'd thought he'd fallen in love before, it turned out the girl in question liked another fellow a lot more. It was best for him to avoid further pain in the love department.

He mulled over the situation the entire drive home but came to no conclusions beyond caution when it came to June. He had to focus on Evelyn anyway. That was his top priority.

He spent Saturday with Aunt Beulah and Evelyn, searching for opportunities to talk to his sister about Bernard or even be with Bernard so they could have a frank talk. Bernard, however, was committed on Sunday and couldn't accompany them to church, nor could he drop by for tea. But he could stop in long enough to whisk Evelyn away for dancing and insist on lobster at the wedding luncheon.

"Tell June we want lobster," Evelyn hollered as they ran out the door.

The next few days were much the same, with Evelyn occupied with dress fittings and dragging Aunt Beulah around town to build a trousseau. Since the reception was to be at the house following the ceremony, extra help was brought in to prepare. By Thursday, two mornings before the wedding, the house looked impeccable and smelled of furniture polish, by all appearances a well-ordered home.

But appearances were deceiving. Since Bernard had avoided all possibility of a private talk, Aunt Beulah let her feelings on the situation be known over breakfast. Martin had attempted to be the voice of reason, asking his sister for a few minutes of Bernard's time, but Evelyn stomped to her room and slammed the door.

"In my day, brides did not throw temper tantrums." Aunt

Beulah rolled her eyes.

"Her nerves are frayed, Auntie."

"By too much shopping? You coddle her too much, Martin."

His father's words came out of Martin's mouth automatically. "She's my baby sister."

"Who is old enough to wed now. No longer a child, but she behaves like one. Taking no responsibility for anything, making demands with no thought whatsoever about whom she's marrying. He'll take her money, and she'll be back home with us before Christmas."

"We don't know that, Auntie. Nor can we stop her."

"That doesn't mean you should give up warning her."

"Mother and Father would want her to have her dream wedding. I'm duty bound to see her happy, even if I'm not sure that happiness will last." He didn't like parting with his aunt like this, but he had to get to work, so he kissed her cheek and drove to the museum. He'd planned on stopping in to see June about the wedding plans—and to see her encouraging smile—but a colleague caught him about a display, and the day unfolded from there, one unexpected event after another.

At day's end, he'd worked a full, steady shift but felt a sense of dissatisfaction. It was past five. June would have gone home by now. Pity that he'd missed her all day. One last check on the creatures in the office tanks and he donned his fedora. He stepped out the door and collided with a small, solid form in a pale peach dress.

"June!" She smelled of a light, floral perfume and the tang of typewriter ribbon. He never would have expected the combination to be so compelling. "Sorry, I didn't see you there."

"I thought since it's after work hours, I'd see if there are any wedding arrangements I need to take care of tomorrow, if I'm not interrupting." Her gaze scanned the aquariums.

"Not at all."

"Is there anything you can think of? Everyone has accepted the invitation, even Kelly." She smiled. "He won't come to the luncheon though."

"But you will?" He wanted her and her calming presence to be there.

"I may stay in the kitchen, but I'll be there."

"You must sit as a guest, June. Please."

She smiled but didn't answer. Instead, she pointed at the tank where a four-limbed starfish clung to the glass. "Is this one of the starfish mentioned in your regeneration proposal?"

"It is. Want to hold it?"

"Will it bite?"

"It's no threat unless you're a mussel. Take off your gloves."

As she removed them, he shed his jacket and rolled up his sleeve. Cool water enveloped his forearm as he gently detached the bright orange starfish from its position. "Lay your hands together flat."

He lowered the eight-inch diameter creature on her palms. "Starfish may not have bones or a brain, but their nervous systems are complex. Each arm has an eye spot."

"It sees with its arms?"

"Light, at least, but the fact that these eye spots regenerate is amazing to consider. A lot for a humble creature, isn't it? This particular specimen is a *Pisaster ochraceus*. Ochre sea star, most common of its kind in the tide pools around here. I can't believe you've never held one."

"I've seen them before, but I always left them alone. They

didn't look like this one though. It's a pretty color."

"Sometimes they're brown or purple, which are my favorite." He took it back and gently lowered it into the tank.

"Thank you. That was fun." She wiped her hands on the towel he offered and tugged her gloves back on.

"My pleasure." He fixed his sleeve and donned his jacket. "As you know from the proposal, I'm hoping to unlock the secrets of their regeneration properties to find an application for humans. Maybe there's a way to aid in healing wounds or nerves. God's world is wonderful, at times confounding, but always exciting." He gestured for her to lead the way out. "I'll walk you to the streetcar. Busy afternoon?"

"Yes. The museum's expansion requires a good deal of paper-work. And yours?"

"Nothing exceptional. Packing display items, also for the expansion." He led her out, holding the museum door open for her. They turned right on El Prado toward the carousel and the streetcar line. "Ready for the wedding?"

"Almost. Gladys is baking the cake tonight—she's a marvel with them—and it will be delivered to the confectioner for icing tomorrow. They'll convey it to your house Saturday morning."

"Wouldn't it be easier if confectioners baked wedding cakes in addition to icing them?"

"One would think, but as I'm not in the pastry business, I can't say. At any rate, the ribbons are ready for the carousel zebras." She started to tick things off on her fingers. "Her ensemble is prepared, someone is coming to style her coiffure, the officiant is confirmed, the caterers ready, your suit was pressed, and the license is in hand."

Two days from now, his sister would be married to Bernard.

He didn't wish to spoil the pleasant walk he was having with June by mentioning the groom, however. The carousel came into sight, lit against the late afternoon sun. "I thought it didn't run on Thursdays."

"It is as of this week. Kelly isn't working tonight though. He's studying."

Why hadn't he noticed the music until now? The peppy, bright cadence of the band organ's tune?

Martin was never the spontaneous sort. Now, however, he had the sudden urge to ride the carousel. With June. To be carefree for three whole minutes. To watch her smile.

His fingertips touched her elbow. "Let's ride the carousel."

"What?" Her brows knit.

"You heard me, June." He pulled a dime from his pocket. "What do you say?"

June's breath caught. Ride the carousel?

The last time she rode this carousel was before her parents died. She'd been frolicking on the beach in Coronado with two girlfriends, Sally and Lorraine. They'd swum in the bay and eaten ice cream and ridden the carousel four times.

Whatever happened to Sally and Lorraine? June had lost contact with them over the past few years. She hadn't intended to, but from necessity her focus had shifted to work. She'd always been a dependable girl, true, but after she had to take over caring for Kelly, she became even more so. Reliable. Efficient. Indispensable to her employers.

At the time, friends from church and relatives commended her on her work ethic. But she'd never thought of it as a principle she could choose. What else could she do besides ensure Kelly graduated high school and was supported well enough to take college courses?

She'd encouraged Kelly to enjoy things, of course. To preserve his childhood as long as she could. He was twenty-one now, younger than she was when she'd had to become his sole provider. Money was always tight, so she chose not to do much of anything extra for herself.

She'd failed a few times and put herself first. That ballet a few years ago, a delightful evening. But oh, it had been expensive, and she'd paid for it in guilt for weeks when Kelly couldn't fit into his fancy clothes and they couldn't afford new in time for the school dance. All because she'd splurged on herself. The same thing tended to happen when she went out to lunch with Gladys or bought herself a trinket—inevitably Kelly would have a sudden need. Or he'd complain when she made up for her spending by buying cheaper cuts of meat or thinner socks. Generally he wasn't a grumbler, but he was young. Nevertheless, it was easier and better if she sacrificed and went without, rather than pay an emotional price later.

Therefore her automatic response to any sort of invitation was to say no. Yet a part of her wanted to come out and play. She envied gals like Evelyn who went to the picture show or had a hat for every day of the week. June didn't like having those feelings, but there they were.

If she rode the carousel with Martin, she would be guilty of fraternizing with one of the museum's scientists. She would also be going against her deeply ingrained habit of not doing anything for herself. But at this moment, she didn't care about either of those things. The golden afternoon light reminded her that summer was nigh. The band organ's jaunty tune thrummed in her veins, beckoning her, and Martin looked at her with an expectant smile that made the butterflies in her stomach take flight.

She felt happy. Light. Alive. Certainly she could enjoy a three-minute carousel ride.

So she nodded. "Yes. Let's ride the carousel."

Chapter 4

When Martin bought their tickets, June's pulse increased. They were really doing this, weren't they? They joined the short queue waiting for the current ride to end. He bent to speak in her ear so she could hear him over the band organ's loud volume. "You choose which animals we ride. Stationary or jumpers?"

Ignoring the way his closeness incited goose bumps to appear on her arms, she stood on her tiptoes to respond. "Jumpers. Any are fine."

"You've ridden this carousel before?"

"A long while ago. Before I had to become a responsible lady." She tried to make it a joke.

He turned away from the carousel so it would be easier for her to hear him. "I think that's what happened to me as well. I rode carousels wherever we found them when I was young. New York, I remember vividly. Nine years old. Come to think of it, Evelyn was nine the first time she rode this particular carousel. It was in Luna Park in Los Angeles then, but that's when she fell in love with it. After she rode it, she ran to the bench where I was watching her, begging for more tickets so she could ride all the different types of animals. I sat there for an hour, I think."

"You didn't ride it?"

His head shook as the carousel began to slow. "Our father preferred me to keep an eye on her. They expected me to look out for her back then as much as I do now."

They. "Your parents?"

"Yes, and it was my job to protect her. You can imagine how they felt when she was born after a dozen years of wanting another child. And she a girl too—just what Mother had always wanted."

His comment didn't sit well on her stomach. Surely Martin's mother was equally grateful for both of her children, boy and girl. She might have inquired further, but the current riders dismounted. When the carousel was cleared, a fellow in a newsboy cap gestured them forward and collected their tickets. Martin waved his hand at their choice of animals. "Zebras?"

She nodded, but then they were taken by a giggling young couple. She pointed at another matched pair of jumpers. "Storks."

"Those are storks?"

"Aren't you a zoologist?" she teased. "You should know what animals these are."

"You don't need me to tell you that none of these animals is scientifically correct," he teased. "The frogs are wearing clothes and the roosters are bigger than the lion. Alas, the so-called storks have been claimed. Pigs?"

"Pigs." Stepping into the stirrup, she hoisted herself sidesaddle atop the white one, adjusting her skirt. She bent down and patted one of her pig's painted tusks. "Good piggy. Go fast for me."

"Actually, your pig will rotate at a faster linear speed than my pig." He stopped himself. "Sorry. I'm not a physicist, but the science is always there, much to my family's annoyance." Tapping his forehead, Martin climbed astride his pig, which had ended on the last ride in a higher position than hers.

"Well, we don't want to go *hog wild* with science facts right now, do we?"

His laughter was infectious. "I can go *the whole hog* when it comes to such things, but you know that about me already."

Enough of the pig puns. "I know you're passionate about ocean animals. That's a good thing, not a bad one."

"You saying that is yet one more example of your kind nature, June. So what are you passionate about?"

"Not pigs," she joked. "Or storks."

"Real storks are quite interesting, but really, what makes you happy? Gladys says you're good at planning parties. I know you're good with children, having seen you lend a hand when classes visit the museum."

He'd watched her? "I do like those things. The parties require organization, that's all. But children are a delight, aren't they? One never knows what they'll say next. So spontaneous."

"Much like our carousel ride, eh?" His eyes still twinkled with mirth, but they also held an intensity she'd never before seen in the gaze of anyone who'd looked at her. It was almost like he could see into her. Through her.

June shooed away the thought. How silly she was, letting her imagination run away with her.

Then again, imagination didn't seem so bad after all. The moment the carousel began to rotate, she was young again, thrilling at the slow acceleration. Up, up, slowly at first, her pig rose in height as Martin's lowered. Within seconds, they were zipping around and around. It felt like flying.

Her heart was flying too. She'd never thought she would feel something like this, like the butterflies in her stomach had spread through her entire body, but the sensation was more than joy from doing something like riding a carousel again. It was Martin. More than liking that stubborn curl on his forehead and his courtly manners and brilliant brain. She liked him, a man who cared for his family and dealt with the challenges of life with fortitude and prayer.

She more than liked him. Her mother would have said she carried a torch for him.

"Look." He pointed to the right. The man who'd taken their tickets adjusted the metal arm where the iron rings hung with one special brass ring that could be caught by someone on the outer rim of the carousel. As they went around the circle, a little boy ahead of them with close-cropped brown hair half stood in his stirrups, reaching up for the ring.

"Did he get it?" June craned her head to see.

"I think so—no, it wasn't the brass one." They watched the boy chuck the metal ring at the stuffed clown stationed under the carousel's canopy, where the iron rings were collected for the next ride. "Next round, perhaps?"

"Perhaps."

The boy did get the brass ring on his third try, which he exchanged for a ticket for another ride as the carousel continued on, the band organ loud, the drumbeat thumping in her ears, the breeze ruffling the hair at her nape. And through it all, Martin was beside her, smiling, eyes bright. He winked at her and teased her about her pig, and she teased him back.

All too soon the carousel slowed to a stop. Her pig came to a halt high up, and Martin's was closer to the ground. He dismounted before her, hands out to assist her down. Her stomach flopping over, she rested her hands on his shoulders and slid into his arms, down until her feet planted on the carousel floor. Her back to the pig, still within his grasp, she was tempted to avoid his gaze and hide, but that wouldn't do at all, not on this carefree, joyous evening.

So she dipped into a curtsy and scrambled for another pig joke. "Thank you, gallant knight. Sir Porcine, I presume?"

He burst into laughter. "I've been called many things in my time, but that is my favorite."

She cast him a cheeky glance. "Are you sure? More so than doctor?"

"Far more so." He led her off the carousel onto the pavement. "Or Marty?"

"No one calls me Marty. Not even my mother did."

"How about—"

Her gaze lifted, drawn to someone watching her. Her boss, Mr. Willard. Her blood rushed from her head to her toes, leaving her cold, nauseated, and dizzy.

She could fib to offer an excuse for breaking the rules against fraternization—tell her boss that she and Martin were on the carousel for wedding-related reasons, but it would sound like the lie that it was. And she wasn't one to lie, was she? No, God help her.

Maybe if she apologized, Mr. Willard wouldn't terminate her employment. Maybe he'd put a note in her file, and much as she hated to mar her spotless record at the museum, a documented reprimand wasn't the worst thing in the world.

"How about what?" Martin's eyes still held that teasing, light spark. She wouldn't ruin the delightful memory they'd crafted tonight by telling him she would undoubtedly get into trouble tomorrow.

Instead, she smiled. "I'm sorry, I forgot what I was going to say. But lovely as this has been, I must catch my streetcar."

He tipped his fedora. "Then I will wait with you until it arrives."

A few more golden moments together? June couldn't deny herself that. She nodded as she started walking toward the streetcar stop. "You are above all things a gentleman, sir."

"It's the chivalric code," Martin said. "You knighted me Sir Porcine, after all."

Her laugh wasn't as robust as it had been on the carousel. Neither were her eyes as bright. What had happened? They'd just been laughing, teasing, enjoying a carousel ride that might only have been three minutes long, but it felt as if the experience had been enchanted, heightened in time and space.

At least it had for him. "Everything all right?"

She hesitated a fraction too long before answering. "Yes, thank you."

Martin wasn't convinced, but he had no choice other than to take her at her word. Perhaps she was tired after a long week of work, compiled with working on the wedding. He wouldn't press anymore, but he wanted her to know how much he enjoyed this brief but meaningful time with her.

"Thanks for riding the carousel with me."

"I thoroughly enjoyed myself. I'm surprised you haven't yet

ridden it with your young friend, the one with the unsavory job."

"Tim, yes." He glanced back at the carousel, wishing yet again the boy could find work at something honest like selling tickets there. "He didn't want to ride it the other day. He's at a tough age, one foot in childhood and the other in manhood, and unsure how he's supposed to feel about any of it. He's a good lad, truly, despite his choice of after-school job and some of the people he's associating with."

She looked up. "Don't forget, he's also associating with you. Seeds are being planted."

"I hope so."

Her steps slowed as they neared the streetcar stop. Martin didn't want the evening to end, so he stopped her where they were, several feet away from the tracks and the people milling around, waiting. "Tim mentioned his school received one of the traveling cabinets that the museum rotates through the district. Do you help with those?"

"I've typed placards, but that's all. Does he like when they visit his school?"

"I believe so. His interests don't lie in the natural sciences, but the displays are fun for him."

"I always wonder how the cabinets are received by the students, but gauging by children's reactions when they're in the museum, they enjoy them. I wish we could offer something for children here at the museum."

"Such as?"

"I haven't given it a great deal of thought, but something like a class. In the summertime." June adjusted her stuffed bag over her shoulder.

He reached for her bag. "I'll hold it until your streetcar comes."

When she complied and thanked him, he returned to the topic at hand. "I love the idea of a class. It's brilliant."

"You think so? If there's room in the budget, of course, and someone to run it. I suppose you could discuss it with Dr. Abbott and see if he's interested."

"Me? It was your idea."

She looked at him out of the corners of her eyes. "You don't mean I should propose it, do you? I couldn't."

Why not? Then again, Martin had a better idea. "How about we do it together? Tomorrow after lunch. Abbott and I are in meetings until then. Our presentation doesn't have to be anything formal, just a discussion of our idea, but I'll type something up tonight so he has it on paper." He had a typewriter at home, but she probably didn't.

"Won't typing bother your arm?"

In truth, he hadn't thought about the pain in his arm since jumping on the carousel with her. "I have to give it something to do or it stiffens up on me."

"All right then. Let's do it. For Tim and other young people like him." The thrumming *clickety-clack* of an approaching streetcar drew her attention. She turned and glanced at the straw-yellow car. "That's mine."

He hated for her to go.

Could a life change in three minutes? His had irreparably. Because now he knew his feelings for June weren't shallow or fleeting. If—and this was a large if—she returned his sentiments, was there hope for a happy life together? Or would he do something to lose her affection and have to work to earn it over and over again?

For the first time in ages, he was willing to risk the pain. He wanted to do whatever he could to make and keep June happy. Others had love in their lives. Perhaps it was like the brass ring on the carousel. Uncommon, difficult to reach, but meant to be grasped at anyway. And the reward was worth it.

Tomorrow he'd invite her to supper after the wedding. Maybe the moving pictures or a concert. Whatever she desired. And maybe, just maybe, she could care for him in return.

As the streetcar slowed to a halt, its brake shoes squealed, followed by a hiss of air and the mechanical clunk of the stairs lowering. Martin handed over her bag and gestured at the car. "Your 'cootie car' awaits, madam." Everyone called the streetcars that, a leftover nickname from the war.

She smiled again, and he memorized the adorable way it curved her cheeks and narrowed her eyes into crescent moons. "Until tomorrow, Martin."

"Tomorrow."

She climbed aboard, and he lost her in the crowd of others finding seats. The electric motor whined, and the streetcar accelerated away.

His heart full, he watched it speed out of sight.

Chapter 5

June's lunch on Friday tasted like sawdust. Her taste buds had disappeared along with her appetite since meeting with Mr. Willard in his office an hour ago—

No. She wouldn't think of it now. Wouldn't say anything either until after the wedding. She wouldn't burden Kelly, not while he grappled with Evelyn's nuptials taking place in less than twenty-four hours. Nor Gladys, who would get angry on June's behalf. Nor Martin. No, she didn't want to tell him that Mr. Willard had fired her for breaking the no-fraternization rule. He'd feel responsible somehow, even though it wasn't his fault, and his focus should be fixed on his family right now.

In the meantime, You and I will keep it between ourselves, Lord.

Kelly might be distressed about Evelyn marrying Bernard, but his appetite wasn't affected. He bit a chunk from his roast beef sandwich as they sat on one of the benches near the carousel, swallowing it down without chewing much. "Tomorrow by this time, the wedding will be over. Downright depressing, just like this weather. The 'May gray' matches my mood."

June tugged her coat collar higher up her neck. It wasn't cold, but the marine layer enveloping the park was indeed damp and gloomy. "Once this burns off, things will look cheerier. Maybe not your heart, I know."

"I'll get over Evie eventually." Kelly adjusted his newsboy cap, pulling it lower over his brow. "Though I really thought she liked me."

"I believe she does."

"As her friend from the carousel." He smiled as if it didn't bother him, but he couldn't hide the sadness in his tone. "I'm glad you got to ride it last night, by the way."

Her account of riding the carousel with Martin was what had started this discussion about the wedding and Kelly's aching heart. Kelly hadn't pressed or teased her about Martin, thank the Lord, but accepted her story that they were discussing wedding plans and did something spontaneous. Nothing more.

"You going to ride the carousel again today?"

"Probably not for a while," she said. A long, long while. If ever.

Kelly swallowed his final bite of sandwich. "To be honest, this wedding is probably a blessing for me. Evie was a distraction, and I have a lot of schooling to cram in the next year if I'm to be ready for law school. Maybe this is God's way of protecting me."

"Your attitude inspires me, little brother." She'd do well to follow his example of trusting God, but it was hard at the moment. *God, please forgive me for my selfishness. For choosing myself instead of those things You've entrusted to my care. I accept the consequences. Help me to be patient for Your provision.*

"I'd better get to work." Kelly jutted his chin toward the carousel, closed and shuttered. It would open soon, and hopefully the foggy marine layer wouldn't dissuade many people from coming to the park.

"I have a few minutes before I need to get back, so I think I'll stretch my legs."

"See you at home?"

"I'll be there."

As she bid her brother goodbye, her eye caught on a gentleman strolling from the direction of the car park toward El Prado. She knew him by his boater hat and cocky stride, even though she couldn't see his face. Bernard Galbraith.

Since they were walking the same direction and she was mere yards behind him, it seemed unfriendly not to at least say hello. "Mr. Galbraith? Sir?"

He spun around, eyes narrowed. "Yes?"

Didn't he recognize her? She pushed her slipping glasses further up her nose. "I'm June Lowell. Helping with your wedding."

"Of course." He took her gloved hand and kissed the back before she could react. She didn't much care for it, but he didn't seem to notice, wiggling his brows at her. "Tomorrow's the day."

"What brings you to the park? Are you visiting Martin?" For that frank talk, perhaps? *Lord, let it be so.*

"I avoid museums like lice. So tedious. How can you stand working there?"

"I like it, actually."

"With all those fusty old fossils?"

"The museum is much more than a collection of lifeless things. I like to think of it as a treasury of the past and present, reflected in God's creation."

Smiling almost flirtatiously, he shook his head. "You sound exactly like Marty."

"Do I? I take that as a compliment."

"At least *you* like me. He doesn't. Despite my efforts, he disapproves of me."

What efforts? Bernard avoided Martin at every turn. She was about to speak when Bernard gripped both her hands as if he was trying to save her from falling off a bridge. "I was wondering, Jane—may I call you Jane?"

"It's June—"

"I was wondering how I can impress him. Have you any insight?"

It wasn't her place, but oh well. He'd asked, and mercy if he didn't need the help. "Talk to him. Assure him you have Evie's best at heart."

"Of course I do." He dropped her hands, thank the Lord.

"But family members sometimes need to hear such things said. My family was forthright about such matters."

"And you turned out well, I daresay." His glance flickered to her shoes and back up again.

She resisted the urge to scowl at his examination. "Martin, not Marty, has been caring for Evelyn for years now, a parent as much as a brother. Speak to him, before the wedding. Perhaps now."

His glance caught on something, someone, over her shoulder. "Alas, the moment does not suit my schedule, but I shall heed your advice and talk to him tomorrow, Jane. In the meantime, I must bid you farewell."

"But—"

There was no use. He'd already gone around her. She had to turn around and call after him to bid him good day.

He didn't respond but strode toward the Botanical Building, just beyond the lily pond. An odd destination. True, numerous people visited it. It was beautiful, inside and out, and one of the largest lath structures in the world.

But she would never have pegged him as an aficionado of the banana plants, ferns, and other tropical blooms growing inside. And he was certainly in a hurry to get there.

A lithe young man, dark and freckled, with his newsboy cap low over his brow and blue suspenders holding up his baggy brown pants, appeared from seemingly nowhere, lurking by a potted palm at one of the two front entrances. It was that friend of Tim's, the one who recruited him to work at the speakeasy. Vincent.

He too was an odd person to be visiting the Botanical Building—until Bernard rounded the potted palm and clapped Vincent on the shoulder. They slipped inside the building together.

They knew each other. More than that, they appeared to be meeting together. And all she knew about Vincent was that he was up to his neck at the speakeasy.

Was Bernard involved in it too?

The unpleasant thought sprouted in her head like a weed. According to Martin, no one received a clear answer when they asked Bernard what he did for a living, although he seemed to have plenty of money. Did Bernard's income flow from the speakeasy?

Her stomach dropped to her soles.

She could be wrong. She had no evidence, just an active imagination. Perhaps she should follow. Eavesdrop. If there was nothing criminal going on, then thanks be to God. But if she could catch a few words of a questionable conversation, she must warn the Howards.

She rushed into the lath structure after them.

Warm, moist air hit her in the face, making her blink, but she couldn't see anything but green, anyway—palms and banana trees, orchids and ferns exhibited in maze-like display, preventing her from seeing much of anything but the plants immediately before her on the path. Canaries chirped from their cages, tucked into the branches of the tropical trees. The only sounds beyond the birdsong were her breaths and the spattering of water drops on large, leafy plants.

The blurred silhouettes of two faceless, masculine figures passed behind the glazed windows of the greenhouse at the north end of the building. It had to be Bernard and Vincent! She hurried to the east entrance of the greenhouse.

From the ceiling, plants hung in baskets, their thick, creamy aerial roots dangling like ropes. Ferns and fronds filled the greenhouse, along with flowering shrubs and spiky grasses. She didn't see anyone or hear anything but the drip of irrigation. They'd gone out through the door at the western end already, back into the lath structure. June hurried out, clenching her jaw. Bernard was as slippery as the wet leaves in here.

The moment she exited the greenhouse, she heard voices, loud and feminine. "A real live coffee tree, you say? My, my, and a good afternoon to you as well, sir," one woman said.

"Goodbye," said another woman.

June wound her way back through the greenery. Had the ladies been speaking to Bernard? They'd said goodbye to a man. Oh dear, had she missed him entirely?

Three women stood inside one of the entrances, all a good decade older than Beulah. "Pardon me, ladies. I'm looking for my friend. Boater hat, gray suit?"

"Right outside waiting for you, I'd expect." One white-headed woman smiled.

"And another man with blue suspenders?"

"He left too." The woman's brows knit as if she wasn't sure June should be associating with a fellow like that.

"Thank you. Good day." June left them to their visit and rushed out. Neither Bernard nor Vincent was anywhere in sight.

She had nothing to show for her attempt at eavesdropping, and if she searched any further, she would be late meeting Martin and Dr. Abbott to discuss a potential summer program for children.

Resigned, she crossed El Prado and hurried into the museum, dropping off her coat and purse at her desk. Gladys winked. "Hope the proposal goes well. Do you want me to say anything to Mr. Willard if he comes by wondering why you're not chained to the desk?"

"He won't, I don't think." June scooped up a thin file of papers. "I saw him early this morning and told him I'd be speaking to Dr. Abbott."

Gladys's brows rose. "And he didn't fire you for doing something other than typing? I'll be."

Ouch. Forcing a smile, June waved and hurried out.

Martin, the curl of hair flopping on his forehead, walked toward her down the hall. Her heart gave a little thump when he smiled at her. "There you are. I was on my way to collect you."

She had to tell him her suspicions about Bernard and Vincent, but not when he was about to walk into a meeting with the museum's director, so she held up her file. "I know you intended to type up the proposal last night, but I wrote down a few ideas too."

"Splendid. I expect they'll be far superior to my basic outline, anyway." He started to lead the way to the director's office.

"Can we talk afterward?"

"About the wedding?" He turned back.

"Yes, sort of." The groom, mainly.

Martin smiled. "Absolutely. But we'd best get to Dr. Abbott now. I think he has another meeting in fifteen minutes."

"Of course." She walked beside him down the hall.

"Nervous?"

"Not even a little." She had nothing to lose.

She'd never been in Dr. Abbott's office. The director, a kind-faced man with slicked-back dark hair, sat behind a desk piled with open books and papers. "Come in, Howard, Miss Lowell. I hear you have a proposal for me."

"We do." Martin held out one of the two brown velvet chairs facing the desk for June.

She sat on the plush chair. "Dr. Howard has informed you of the nature of this proposal? Summer programming for youth?"

Dr. Abbott nodded. "Have you something in writing for me?"

Martin handed him a typed outline and leaned back in his chair, relaxed. "I cannot speak to the costs, sources of funding, or any other practical questions, but Miss Lowell and I agreed that the concept was worth exploring."

"We already have an educational program, of course."

June nodded. "The circulating cabinets as well as receiving students on field trips. We hosted over twenty such groups this school year."

Martin glanced at June. "Miss Lowell interacts with the children when they visit."

"Do you?" Dr. Howard scanned Martin's document.

"On occasion when additional help is required. They are always well-behaved, curious, and bright. Would it not be wonderful to expand our educational outreach so it lasts all year?"

"What would this program entail?"

With steady fingers, June pulled out a sheet and handed it to him. "If the board and budget allow, I suggest a one-week, half-day session in the summer, but if that is too much, even a single-day program would be wonderful. I recommend a combination of lessons, activities, art, and even exercise outside."

"You've put a lot of thought into this." Dr. Abbott grinned.

They discussed fees or scholarships, content, and other matters before Dr. Abbott laid both palms on the desk. "It has my vote, but I must put it toward those in authority."

"Of course. Thank you for your time, Dr. Abbott." June rose and shook his hand.

Martin did the same.

And that was that. Her final act as an employee of the Natural History Museum.

"Bravo," Martin said, resisting the urge to pull June in for a quick squeeze. "I count that as a rousing success."

"I hope the board approves." Her eyes sparkled brightly, almost as if she was tearing up. How sweet she was. "So, are you working this afternoon or taking time off for the wedding?"

Leading her back the way they'd come, he shoved his hands into his pockets. "I promised Aunt Beulah I'd come home now, although I'm sure I'll be useless. Are you leaving early too?"

"Yes, actually."

"Evelyn has more errands for you? I'm sorry. Is that what you wanted to talk about earlier? You said you wished to discuss the wedding."

"Not the wedding, precisely." She adjusted her spectacles. "The groom."

"That sounds ominous." Dread pooled in his stomach. "May I walk you to the streetcar?"

"That would be lovely. First, I need to gather my things."

"Me too. Let's meet out front."

Five minutes later, they were out on El Prado. Whatever she wanted to discuss was upsetting her, causing her fingers to fidget. He'd best cut to the chase. "So something about Bernard?"

Her arms folded. "Forgive me if it's none of my business, but I saw something that concerned me. He—Mr. Galbraith—was here at the park minutes before you and I met with Dr. Abbott. He went into the Botanical Building."

"With a woman?" He knew it. Bernard was a snake.

"No, that fellow who got Tim working at the speakeasy."

He couldn't have heard correctly. "Vincent?"

"Freckled, dark-haired, those blue suspenders and baggy pants. Bernard greeted Vincent at the entry with a clap on the shoulder. I'm certain they know one another, Martin, and not because they're amateur botanists."

Martin's stomach sank as his mind raced. "The only explanation that makes sense is that Bernard is involved with the speakeasy."

By the firm set of her jaw, she'd already come to the same conclusion. "That is my suspicion, but I lack proof. Not that I didn't try."

"Try? What the—June, you didn't do anything rash, did you?"

"I tried to eavesdrop, but they eluded me and left before I could sneak up on them. I am almost certain I saw them talking in the greenhouse, but I couldn't see through the glazed glass well enough to identify them in a court of law. I did see two male silhouettes, and no one else was in the Botanical Building. I looked everywhere. I'm sorry."

"I'm not. If Bernard is doing what I think he's doing and realized you were following him, you could have been hurt."

"Just what do you think he's doing?"

"He works in imports, and his uncle is absent. I suspect Bernard is using his absence to smuggle liquor in with foreign goods." Martin's extremities began to burn. "I've got to see him—now."

Her hand was soft on his sleeve. "You must stay calm, Martin. Take time to pray over the matter, and when you are composed, with the Lord at your side, *then* go. Although I fully expect him to feign ignorance, even if he is willing to speak to you. He's avoided you for two weeks, hasn't he?"

He let out a pent-up breath, willing himself to calm down. The Lord could handle Bernard until then. "You're right. I may not get the opportunity to speak to him, but rest assured I'll tell Evelyn. Thank you, June."

"Me? I did nothing but ruin the wedding."

"You spoke the truth. To protect Evelyn before she made the mistake of marrying that rogue." Breathing was easier now, and much of it was due to June reminding him to let God work. "You're an impressive specimen, June."

"Specimen?" Her lips twitched. "Like a saber-toothed cat skeleton?"

"Rarer."

"A *Tyrannosaurus rex* skull then."

He laughed, feeling oddly lighter even though his vision still tinged red because of Bernard. It was because of June, her steady, peaceful demeanor. Her wise counsel and direction to pray. Her loveliness. "Rarer than that, I think."

He would be a fool to allow such a treasure to slip away, wouldn't he?

So here he went. He would ask her to do something together. The carousel first. Then dinner. Perhaps not tomorrow as he'd hoped, since Evelyn would undoubtedly be distressed by the news about Bernard.

He gestured at the carousel, in their line of sight. "You seemed happy when we rode on the carousel, June."

"It was great fun, those three minutes."

"Perhaps soon we can take another spin. The storks this time? Or the cats?"

Her steps slowed and her smile fell. Why? She didn't want to ride the carousel—or do anything else—with him? She didn't want to be friends?

Then she pointed. "Look. Our siblings."

Evelyn here? Sure enough, she stood with June's brother, laughing at something he said.

"See how happy she looks," June said.

The moment was lost, wasn't it? Much as Martin wished to invite June out, he had a duty to his sister and a seemingly God-given opportunity at hand. "I'm about to remove that smile."

"I think Bernard's actions are responsible for any resulting unhappiness, not you. She will heal."

"I'm supposed to make her happy though. My father's dying wish."

"Was it really?"

Martin looked down and nodded. "His last words were of her. How then can I not give her whatever she wants to be happy? Yet now I will purposefully make her desolate."

June watched Kelly and Evelyn, frowning. "You know, Martin,

life doesn't always give us what we would choose, but we have to trust that God has all things in hand."

He let that sink into his brain. "Even Evelyn."

She looked up at him. "You have a difficult conversation to have with her now. I shall pray for you both."

"Thank you." And after his talk with Evelyn, there would still be much to do. "What is involved in cancelling the wedding?"

"Perhaps there's another explanation for Mr. Galbraith's behavior, so I'll assume the wedding is still on as planned unless I hear otherwise. If it's canceled, I'll handle everything."

She started to walk away from him, toward the streetcar stop. "My landlady has a telephone. Evelyn and your aunt know how to reach me."

Chapter 6

Saturday morning dawned with a clear sky and bright sunshine. The perfect day for a wedding—generally anyway. June wasn't so sure about this particular wedding, which to her utter shock had not been canceled.

Dressed in their Sunday finery, June and Kelly had arrived early at the park with their boxes of bows to decorate and to meet the florist, unable to talk about anything else but Bernard's seeming involvement with the speakeasy. They were still talking about the wonder of the wedding going on as planned when Gladys arrived.

"You're invited?" Kelly gave her a half hug.

"Nah, but the wedding's in a public place, so there will be plenty of onlookers. Why shouldn't I be one of them?"

"Prepare to see a show," Kelly warned as June separated the turquoise-blue ribbons.

"Whaddaya mean?" Gladys reached in to help.

June quickly filled Gladys in on what she'd seen yesterday. "Martin was going to tell Evelyn—and try to talk to Bernard—last night. I expected the wedding to be canceled, but no call ever came. Perhaps Bernard has a good explanation. Like he and Vincent are cousins."

Kelly snorted. "Knowing what we do about that Vincent thug, I think it's fair to say they aren't cousins and Bernard is violating the Volstead Act somehow."

"Evelyn shouldn't marry that fella," Gladys said.

June had stayed up late and risen early, waiting for the call that never came. She found it difficult to sleep anyway, with so many things weighing on her mind. Her suspicions and suppositions about Bernard. How his smuggling would affect Evelyn. Kelly's heavy heart. Finding a new job before the rent was due. And Martin, of course. Her feelings for him had grown, despite her best intentions to regard him in a friendly light.

She'd lain in her narrow bed all night, praying, giving these worrisome things over to the Lord, only to snatch them back within minutes and start worrying again.

This is neither the time nor place, is it, Lord? Again praying for her concerns, June tied a ribbon around a eucalyptus trunk. Kelly copied her, but when he tied his ribbon, he yanked the ribbon so hard his knuckles were white. "I could stand up when the preacher asks if anyone knows any just cause—"

"I'm not sure that would help, Kelly." June fluffed the stringy bow he'd just abandoned. "She's made her choice."

Kelly crumpled the ribbon in his fist, leaving it wrinkled.

"Not quite wedding-worthy." June took the ribbon. Her poor brother, having to watch the young lady he cared for marry a fellow who probably smuggled liquor for a living. "Gladys, you don't mind finishing this while Kelly and I unpack the flowers, do you?"

"Not at all."

"If you saw what I did with the ribbon, what do you think I'll do to the flowers?" Kelly set his jaw.

"I don't want you to touch them. Just the boxes."

"Fine." Kelly walked beside her toward the florist boxes they'd left beside the carousel ticket booth. "You know what the worst thing is? She's going to get hurt by that sheik Galbraith, but there's nothing we can do or say."

"I hope it doesn't happen like that. But yes. Love can hurt bad enough, but when your loved one is suffering, it's worse."

"How would you know?" Kelly stared at her then turned a pale shade of pink. "I didn't mean it like that. I meant I never knew you had a beau."

Because she hadn't. The past five years, her life had been work and him. "You don't need to have a gentleman caller to feel things, Kelly."

Kelly lifted the sturdy lid off one of the small boxes: boutonnieres for the groom and Martin. The sweet, creamy fragrance of the white roses swirled around them, lovely but sad at the same time. "I'm sorry. I never thought of you like that. Like you might have. . .feelings."

What could she do but laugh? "Everyone has feelings."

"I guess so. I'm sorry it didn't work out for you."

"Thanks, Kelly, but it's for the best. My life is full as it is."

His brow bunched up as if he disagreed, but his gaze fixed on something over her shoulder. She turned to look and realized his expression might have something to do with some new arrivals:

the officiant; a few well-dressed but confused-looking guests; and Martin, dark hair slicked back in the current fashion, resplendent in a perfectly tailored, dove-gray suit and slate tie.

The butterflies in her stomach took flight. She wanted to run, but whether it was to him or away from him, she wasn't sure. Regardless, she needed to enquire after Evelyn. Maybe Bernard and Vincent's meeting at the Botanical Building was more innocent than she'd suspected.

Grabbing the base of his boutonniere, June hurried over. After greeting the pastor, an older, bespectacled man, June held up the white rose with the pin through its base. "May I, Martin?"

"Please."

The officiant and guests slipped away, conversing about the unique wedding venue, leaving June and Martin a moment of privacy. She had to slip her hand between his suit coat and shirt to assist with the pinning. Being this close to him, feeling the warmth of him in her fingers, was dizzying. It was a relief to finish and step back. "How's Evelyn?"

"She doesn't believe me. She phoned Bernard last night and he denied everything. He went so far as to suggest—well, it doesn't matter."

She caught the flash of regret in his eyes. "Yes it does. Tell me."

"The bounder suggested I'd put you up to concocting a story in order to thwart their happiness. Them against the world, Romeo and Juliet, all that rot. Aunt Beulah and I defended you and did our best to get her to see reason, but she's refusing to listen to anything now."

June's stomach flopped. "I didn't lie, and I do not care for him slandering me."

"Of course not. You're the finest, most considerate woman

of character I know, and I went to his house to tell him so, but he wasn't home. Or he pretended not to be. Anyway, he'll hear from me when he gets here, I assure you. But if I don't keep a firm control on myself, I might wallop him for uttering such lies about you."

No one had ever spoken of protecting her honor like that. It felt rather good. So did his words about her character. "I admit I'd like to box his ears myself."

They were smiling at each other now. Oh dear, that wouldn't help anything in the grand scheme of things. Lowering her gaze, she stepped back. "Where is Evelyn now?"

"Behind those trees there, staying out of sight until the wedding starts." He gestured with a jut of his cleft chin. "Aunt Beulah is with her."

"Bernard isn't here yet." More well-dressed people were gathering now.

"Maybe he won't come at all." Martin's tone tinged with hope. "We can ride on the carousel to celebrate."

She would like nothing more, and yet she couldn't. She couldn't have things for herself, especially not time with a man for whom she harbored romantic notions. There was always a price tag on the few occasions she took time for herself. A tight month financially because she'd spent a little on herself, a complaint from Kelly when she didn't have extra for him to be with his friends. And when she'd given in to temptation and ridden the carousel with Martin, she'd lost her job.

No, she couldn't ride the carousel again. There would be yet another price to pay, even if it was only her own heartbreak.

She had to focus on work. Stay devoted to Kelly until he finished school.

Martin seemed to read her regret on her face. His smile fell.

"Martin!" Beulah Adkins beckoned. "It's past eleven. Come escort your sister to the ceremony."

Kelly hurried to June's elbow. "The groom's not here."

That's when she saw Bernard, dressed in a form-fitting dark blue suit, sauntering into the throng of gathered guests. He grinned and joked, laughing as if he hadn't a care in the world. "He just arrived."

Kelly's body went tense. June put a hand on her brother's arm. "Don't cause a scene."

"But—"

"Leave that to me." Jaw set, Martin took a step toward Bernard.

"Martin!" His aunt trotted toward them, drawing his attention around. "Come. Evelyn is ready."

"Well, I'm not. I'd like a good talk with Bernard first." He looked ready to punch one of the eucalyptus trees.

June's stomach panged. How frustrating this must be for him, having to give his sister away in marriage to someone he held in such disregard.

His aunt shook her head. "We promised her, Martin."

"So we did. No public confrontations." Martin took a deep breath. "So I shall respect Evelyn's wishes and hold myself in check."

"Here." June reached down to the florist's boxes for Beulah's orchid corsage. "Ma'am?"

"Oh, thank you. And who is this young man?"

"My brother, Kelly." While pinning the corsage onto Beulah's lilac dress, June made the quick introductions, for Kelly hadn't yet met Martin either. Then June reached for the largest of the boxes. "This is Evelyn's bouquet." She freed the trailing bouquet of white flowers and greenery from its box.

Martin took it from her, gently but firmly, and marched off, flowers in hand.

June's gaze fell on the one last small box. "Oh dear, we haven't yet given Bernard his boutonniere."

"I'll do it." Beulah took the white rose in hand as if it was a used handkerchief. "And I'll bite my tongue raw whilst doing so."

The carousel operator—a fellow June recognized as one of Kelly's coworkers—cleared the carousel and announced it would halt for the duration of the wedding. June climbed onto the carousel and quickly, carefully tied the final two blue bows around the necks of the jumping zebras. By the time she finished and returned to Kelly's side, the crowd of onlookers had thickened, including a concerned-looking Gladys and a uniformed police officer.

Kelly led her to the back of the group of guests and sighed. "If nothing else, you did a good job. Things look nice."

She couldn't answer, the way folks were gasping. June turned. Martin and Evelyn had cleared the trees and were walking arm in arm toward the carousel.

"She's a vision," Kelly whispered.

Evelyn did indeed look lovely in her white drop-waist gown. Her dark hair had been curled in finger waves, crowned with a Juliet cap. The crowd oohed and Bernard rocked on his heels.

Martin, unsmiling, executed his duty, escorting his sister to Bernard's side, directly in front of the carousel. The officiant opened his prayer book. "Dearly beloved, we are gathered here in the sight of God. . . ."

The old words were powerful, beautiful. Would they ever be said for June at her own wedding? *Someday, Lord? When Kelly doesn't need me anymore?*

She couldn't think about it. The pain was too much. A tear slipped down her cheek.

The pastor continued on, his voice solemn. "Therefore, if any man can show any just cause why they may not lawfully be joined together, let him now speak, or else hereafter forever hold his peace."

A shiver coursed down June's spine. Would anyone speak? Kelly? Beulah? Martin? She couldn't breathe. Couldn't blink. Should she say something, herself?

"I do!" A voice cried out from behind the crowd. "I have just cause to stop this wedding!"

Martin spun. Who'd spoken?

A woman with reddish bobbed hair pushed past Kelly then two of Aunt Beulah's church friends in her haste to reach the bride and groom. Beyond her, though, Martin caught sight of a lone, lean figure leaning against one of the beribboned trees, clutching his stomach, head down. Tim?

The lad looked up then, and mercy, half his face was black and blue. Martin's nerves caught fire, urging him to run to the boy, but his feet stayed rooted by Evelyn. He'd never before felt so torn between two people who needed him.

God, I beg Your help. Be with Tim until I can.

"What's the meaning of this?" The officiant's voice drew Martin back around. "You've something to say, madam?"

The woman swiped her puffy eyes, mussing her charcoal eye makeup. "I do, padre. Bernie's supposed to marry me."

Someone gasped. The pastor gaped.

Evelyn stared at Bernard. "You know this woman?"

"No, darling." Bernard's hands rose in a declaration of innocence. "She's a madwoman, probably wandered in off the streetcar."

The woman's hands fisted on her ample hips. "Madwoman, eh? Padre, where's a stack of Bibles, because I wanna swear to tell the whole truth and nothing but. Bernie is my man."

"Bernard?" Martin was pleased his tone was so even. He wrapped an arm around Evelyn. "What's going on here?"

"Nothing, old sport."

"You lie like a dog on a rug," the woman yelled. "Not twelve hours ago you promised me you wouldn't go through with this on account of the baby, and now look at you, you double-crossing cheat."

"Baby?" Aunt Beulah's voice rose.

"Baby!" Kelly pushed past Martin. "Let me at him."

June lunged to grip Kelly's coat and held him back. "Not here."

Bernard's brows knit in anger, his gaze darting between Kelly, Evelyn, Martin, and the woman, where he finally decided to fix his attention. "Myra, I'm marrying Evelyn," he said loudly, like an actor on stage projecting his voice for those in the balcony. "Sorry to be blunt, but there's nothing between us—"

"Nothing but a baby on the way."

Evelyn shrank back "You know her name. But you said she wandered in off the street."

Myra—where had Martin heard the name? He scanned his memories. He'd heard it from Tim. "You work at the speakeasy, ma'am?"

"No." She glanced at Martin's friend Calvin, who wore his uniform and was slowly circling them from the side.

"You're the hostess at the speakeasy," Martin continued,

recalling what Tim had told him.

The pastor looked shocked. "How would you know such a thing, Dr. Howard?"

"Long story, but I'm pretty sure Bernard supplies the place with liquor."

"Look here, old sport, that's preposterous," Bernard sputtered.

"Preposter-nothing, Bernie. I'm putting my foot down at raising this baby alone." To prove her point, Myra stomped her foot.

"Perhaps we should stop here," the pastor suggested. "I will not marry you if you have been lying to your fiancée, Mr. Galbraith. Nor if there are illegal things afoot."

Thank You, Lord. You're never late, are You?

Evelyn's chin trembled. "Martin and June were right. You're involved in the speakeasy."

Bernard reached for her. "Evelyn, darling—"

"Come on, Bernie," Myra interrupted, grabbing his outstretched arm. "You didn't plan to stay married long anyway."

"Stop, Myra." He yanked his arm back. "Evelyn, dear, let me explain."

Martin's stomach revolted. He'd like to make Bernard pay for his lying and cheating, but right now his sister needed him. He gripped Evelyn's shoulders and held her upright.

She was crying now. "Were you going to be married to me long enough to get your paws on my money before you ran off with her? Is that it?"

Out of the corner of his eye, he caught sight of Tim, waving to get his attention. What could he do but reach for June? "Stay with her, please. I need to go to Tim."

She nodded, and after whispering to Evelyn that he'd return imminently, he broke away from the group to hurry to Tim.

Calvin sidled alongside. "For a fish scientist, your life is rather exciting."

"Sharks are fish too, Cal, and they're far too exciting for my tastes. Oh Tim." Martin stopped short of the boy. It wasn't just Tim's eye that was bruised and swollen, surrounded by purpling tissue. His lip was split, as was his eyebrow, which bled and would require stitching. He'd also broken a rib or two, judging by the way Tim clutched his midsection. Martin's blood iced. "What happened?"

Tim glanced at him. "I—I saw something I didn't like, so I decided not to work at the speakeasy anymore."

"And then someone did this to you?" Anger coursed through Martin, from his head down to his fists. His bad arm protested, but he didn't care. Martin felt the boy's scalp for bumps or lacerations. Sure enough, a goose egg was forming at the back of Tim's skull. "Who hurt you?"

Tim winced at Martin's touch. "He'll hurt me and Mother if I say."

Calvin laid a gentle hand on the boy's shoulder. "We can protect you and your mother."

A tear trickled down Tim's swollen cheek. "I can't say. But I ain't goin' back to that speakeasy, I promise."

"Glad as I am to hear it, they've gone too far, Tim." Martin recognized the terror in Tim's eyes, however, and determined not to press. "We'll discuss it later. But now you need a doctor."

Someone screamed. Martin turned back. Flower petals showered Bernard, from his slicked hair to the spats on his shoes. Evelyn's bouquet was upside down, in a heap at his feet. She'd thrown it at him? Martin almost laughed, until Evelyn lunged at Bernard.

Kelly and June caught her arms, but she struggled against them and oh—her elbow caught June's face, knocking June's spectacles to the ground. Enough was enough.

He glanced at Calvin then Tim. "I will be back in seconds, Tim. Don't go anywhere."

"As will I," Calvin said.

"I won't leave. I promise." The lad swiped his face with the back of his hand.

Calvin rushed alongside Martin. "Break it up, now." He blew his whistle.

Martin moved before Evelyn, bending level to her. "You can stop fighting now, sweetheart."

Her body went limp. "But I said you and June—oh June, look what I did to you." She cried harder as June retrieved her spectacles. "I'm sorry. So sorry."

"It's forgiven." June hugged Evelyn and let her cry.

"I'm such a fool."

Martin gave her earlobe a gentle tweak, just as he used to when she was younger. "We had suspicions about the speakeasy, but you couldn't have known about Myra."

Aunt Beulah offered a lace-trimmed hanky. "No one here thinks any less of you. I imagine they enjoyed watching you whack him with the bouquet as much as I did."

"Quite a good arm there with those flowers," Kelly teased. "Want to join my baseball team?"

"Oh Kelly." Evelyn laughed through her tears.

If she could laugh a little, maybe Martin could return to Tim. Calvin had Bernard in hand, questioning him about the speakeasy, while Myra clung to the pastor, her words incomprehensible through her tears. He turned to where Tim—

He was gone. Not at the tree. Not on a bench or among the

crowd or anywhere Martin could see.

"What is it?" June's eyes narrowed.

"Tim. He decided to quit the speakeasy, and someone beat the tar out of him for it."

Aunt Beulah tutted. "I just saw him, right by that tree. With that friend of his. The freckly one."

"Vincent?" Martin's heart stopped.

"Well, I don't know his name, but it was that fellow I saw him with the day we planned the wedding at the lily pond. He had Tim by the arm."

June's chin dipped. "Holding him up to help him—or gripping him to take him away from Martin and the police?"

Martin pushed down his rising panic and fury and scanned the crowd. With every passing moment, he grew more certain that Vincent had hurt Tim and had just hauled him away against his will to ensure his silence.

Chapter 7

June's heart pounded hard and fast in her chest. *Oh Lord, please protect Tim from danger.*

Before she could blink, Martin reached Bernard and gripped him by the lapels. "Where's the speakeasy, Galbraith?"

Bernard shrank into his coat. "Let me go, or I'll press charges for assault."

Martin released him but didn't move away. He glanced at Calvin. "Why isn't he under arrest yet?"

"We don't have proof of anything except that he double-timed your sister."

"What about suspicion of violating the Volstead Act? It's obvious he's been to the speakeasy, and I'm pretty sure that's where Tim's been taken, so spit it out, Galbraith, before something worse happens to him."

"Tim?" Bernard's voice cracked. "Don't know anyone by that name."

"The boy who sweeps the speakeasy floors," June enunciated, not believing Bernard's act for a second. "He was beaten this morning. Badly."

Bernard's jaw quivered. "I'm sure it's not as bad as all that. Boys get into scrapes, don't they?"

Martin snorted. "Broken ribs, black eye, cuts. He came here for help, but Vincent dragged him away, probably to ensure he doesn't talk. He could be in terrible trouble."

Bernard didn't say a word.

"You're a callous cad," Evelyn spat. "Protecting the speakeasy over a boy. You should be ashamed."

"Darling," Bernard started to plead. Before he could utter more lies, though, Kelly pulled her away so Bernard was no longer in her line of sight.

"This is useless," Calvin muttered. "He's not going to talk."

But maybe someone else would. Myra was crying again, sending coal-dark rivulets of tears stained with eye makeup down her face.

June approached slowly, pulling a handkerchief from her sleeve. Myra took it and swiped her face. June might never get the makeup out in the laundry—it was a combination of charcoal and petroleum jelly, oily and dark—but it didn't much matter. Myra needed a touch of human compassion. "Ma'am? This has been a hard day, hasn't it?"

Staring at the ground, Myra nodded. "I couldn't let him marry that fancy girl with me. . .in trouble."

June could only nod. "You're in a difficult spot. But so is Tim. Myra, will you help us find him? Tell us where to find the speakeasy?"

Myra licked her lips. "I don't know that he's at the speakeasy though."

"But it seems like the ideal place to hide him, don't you think?"

Reluctantly, Myra nodded.

"It sounds like he needs the doctor right away."

"I–I'm not sure." Myra glanced at Bernard, who was glaring at her.

June cupped Myra's damp cheek and guided her to meet her gaze. "If Tim's ribs are broken, he could have a punctured lung. That happened to my brother once. He was in the hospital for more than a week."

Martin ambled closer. Though his jaw was still clenched, June could see he understood what she was doing. "Tim mentioned you to me." Martin's voice was gentle. "He said you take care of him at work. You're the hostess."

Myra smiled for the first time but said nothing.

"Will you help us?" June tried not to beg.

Myra looked as if she wanted to, the way she was glancing between them and biting her lip. But then her trembling hand landed on her flat stomach. "I can't."

Because of her baby. Myra feared what would happen once they found the speakeasy. Anyone inside it would be arrested. Bernard could go to jail too if evidence was uncovered there that implicated him for selling them smuggled liquor.

June sent Martin a pleading look. With a knowing nod, he stepped back, allowing her and Myra privacy. "I understand. A baby needs its parents. But what about Tim? He's someone's child too. Will you tell us anything? Anything at all that will help us get him home to his mother?"

Lord, please let this work. Please.

Myra sniffled, opened her mouth. Then looked down. "I can't."

June stared at Myra for a moment. She could continue to plead her case, but it was no use. There had to be another way. She stepped away from Myra, shaking her head. Martin, the policeman, and Kelly responded with grim expressions, while Bernard suddenly looked smug.

Lord, where is Tim?

A thought flitted across her brain. "Martin?"

His brow furrowed, he hurried to her side. "What?"

"She may not have told me where the speakeasy is, but—but I just realized, perhaps you already know."

"June, no. It's near the park, but I haven't a clue where it is."

"Not precisely, no, but you were attempting to visit Bernard's shop when you first met Tim. He thought you were looking for the speakeasy. Therefore it must be quite close to the shop."

"I've thought of that, but there are numerous establishments and homes on that block. It could be within or below any one of them."

"But you were *at the shop*." She took a deep breath. "What if Bernard isn't just smuggling liquor and selling it to the speakeasy? What if he's the one running it, *inside* or below the shop?"

He stared at her for the span of three whole breaths. Did he think the idea that bad?

"You're a genius, June." He kissed her atop her cloche hat. All she could feel was the soft pressure of his impulsive gesture of gratitude, but it sent a shock down her spine to her toes.

It required incredible effort to swallow down the enormous lump that had formed in her throat and meet his gaze. "Right then. Let's go."

⁓

June had been in her share of vehicles before, but none of them were so pretty. Or fast. Martin accelerated his deep red Lexington touring car, and she lurched backward.

"Hold tight." Martin turned the wheel, and they veered right, causing her to lean toward him.

That wouldn't do. June braced herself with her feet so she wouldn't slide over the seat anymore. "We're almost there, aren't we?" Sixth Street, where Galbraith's imports shop was located, was just on the other side of the park.

"Yes. You should wait in the car though. Stay safe."

"I will do no such thing. I'm no nurse, but I can't just sit on my hands if he's in trouble." Besides, no one at the carousel needed her. The uniformed policeman, who she'd learned was Martin's friend Calvin, had called for reinforcements, and two officers had Bernard and Myra in hand. Kelly and Beulah remained with Evelyn, who'd invited the guests back to the house to enjoy the wedding food rather than see it go to waste.

Martin glanced at her from the corner of his eyes. "Then stay outside. Who knows what's going on inside there, once we find it."

The car turned another corner and slowed to a stop in front of a string of tidy businesses. A few looked as if they had apartments above them, but the one she was most interested in backed up to an alley. A few policemen had already gathered there, and one pounded on the front door.

She didn't wait for Martin to let her out of the car. She shoved her door open and stepped onto the curb.

This was it then? The brick structure with black trim and door exuded an air of elegance and sophistication. A few thickly paned windows displayed Asian objets d'art: porcelain vases and bowls, jade ornaments, a scrap of silk. Lovely things, legitimately imported to be sure. But where was the speakeasy?

No one answered the door.

Martin craned his neck to look at the upper stories then bent to examine the basement windows. "Maybe downstairs."

June started to walk away, around the shop to the narrow alley behind it. It was wide enough for a single vehicle or wagon to drive through and unload deliveries at the two large back doors. Too obvious. She kept walking.

The alley was clean. No rubbish blemished the ground or blew past her in the spring breeze—no, this alley was carefully swept. By Tim probably. A large rubbish can propped against the building in an odd place, nowhere near the delivery doors or the neighboring building's trash receptacle. Neither did anything malodorous foul the air when she approached. Curious.

June sidled up to the rubbish can. If she hadn't, she would have missed the narrow door behind it. Nondescript, plain wood, like a worker's entry, but with a tiny shuttered window in the middle.

Martin trotted toward her. "You shouldn't be back here alone, June."

There wasn't time for such nonsense. She pointed at the door. "This might be it."

He tried the knob. Locked.

"I'll try the old-fashioned way." June nudged him aside and knocked.

Martin held up his hands to argue with her when the tiny shutter opened a crack. No one spoke, but whoever it was could clearly see her, stationed directly in front of the door.

What should she do now? Ask for Vincent? Pretend she wanted to come in for moonshine? She looked at Martin, who mouthed, "Password."

She'd completely forgotten about the possibility of needing a password. Oh dear. It could be anything. Blinking her eyes at whoever was on the other side of the door, she shrugged in her best impression of abashed forgetfulness. "Sorry, mister, I forgot. Be a good egg and let me in?"

"Sorry, doll. We ain't open yet anyway." The shutter closed.

"I guess these sorts of establishments don't open at noon." Martin drew her away. "So now I get to break down the door."

Before June could register what he'd said, he'd curled his shoulder and rammed into the door with a loud thunk. When it didn't give, he tried again.

This time the door gave way with a splintering crash.

Well, *that* hurt the war wound in his arm. A shockwave of pain traversed up to his jaw and down around his chest, but it was worth it to see the door busted on its hinges.

Calvin and his fellow officers arrived just in time. Police poured inside the speakeasy, and all within was shouts and chaos. June brushed against his side, ready to march inside as well. Despite the pounding agony in his upper half, he caught her in his arms. "You must stay here."

"I shan't get in the way. Nor shall I faint from shock at whatever dissipation goes on in there. I'm no simpering miss."

"I never suspected you were, June, but it might not be safe."

"Safe enough for you though?"

"I'll be back in a moment. With Tim. Please stay here." He

could feel her glare burning the back of his head as he hurried inside.

His eyes took a moment to adjust to the dim interior, but the room seemed well appointed with sleek, expensive furnishings in black and gold, like the lobby of a grand hotel. This was no peaceful place at the moment, however. Men shouted, doors slammed, and one of the pricey chairs crashed when Calvin tackled someone, adding to the noise of the chaos.

A face poked from behind a door. Vincent. Martin lunged, missing Vincent by an inch. Yelling for assistance, Martin chased him down a hall lit by bare bulbs dangling on cords from the ceiling. Vincent dashed through a door but couldn't shut it entirely before Martin caught up, ramming his wounded shoulder into the gap so Vincent couldn't close it. His old wound screamed in agony, but Martin ignored the pain and shoved the door open, pushing Vincent backward into the room.

There was Tim, curled in a ball in the corner.

Martin ran to him, helping him stand. "It's over now."

"Oh no you don't!" Calvin's voice shouted. Martin looked over his shoulder at Calvin, gripping Vincent. "You're under arrest, sonny. Kidnapping and running an illegal drinking establishment."

"I don't run this place!"

"Then tell us who does, and that particular charge might get dropped—"

Martin didn't wait to hear more. His prayers had been answered, and the speakeasy was being raided. God would take care of the rest. Either Vincent would talk and expose Bernard, or the location of the speakeasy itself would implicate his sister's ne'er-do-well fiancé. His only concern now was Tim. Arm around the boy's thin shoulders, he led him out into the sunlight, to June.

"Thank the Lord. But look at you, poor boy." She tugged a pink-edged handkerchief from her sleeve and pressed it against the cut over his eye.

Wincing, Tim looked down. "I'm sorry, Dr. Howard. Vincent had a knife and made me come back here. Even though I told him I wouldn't say nothing about where this was or that it was him who—who did this—"

He broke off, too choked up to continue.

Martin laid a hand atop Tim's head. "Vincent won't hurt you again. Or your mother. He's going to jail."

After a few swallows, Tim regained his composure. "Is Mr. Galbraith going too?"

His gaze met June's. Tim had just confirmed that Bernard was up to his neck in this place. "I expect so, yes."

"I wanted to tell ya about him, on account of your sister, but I didn't think he or this place was that bad. You know? Not until I saw Mr. Galbraith holler at Myra last night. I didn't know they were keepin' time until then, honest. But I didn't like him yelling and smacking her, so I told Vincent I quit. I swore I wouldn't tell where this place is, but he beat me up anyway. And when I went to find you at the carousel, he dragged me back here to keep me quiet."

"It's over now." Martin wrapped an arm around the boy's shoulders. "You're safe."

"How'd you find me?"

"June." He smiled at her. "She had the idea of linking the speakeasy's location to Bernard's business, and she was the one who found the door too."

Tim glanced up. "Thanks, ma'am."

Her head shook. "I did nothing extraordinary, Tim."

"I disagree," Martin said. "You came to help and knocked on the door to rescue him. That seems rather extraordinary to me."

"Nonsense. I didn't do anything a decent person wouldn't do." June checked under the handkerchief, but the cut was still bleeding, so she resumed pressure. "Now, Tim, it's your turn with the handkerchief. Hold it here until Dr. Howard gets you to the physician."

Once Tim's hand held the hanky, she stepped back. Martin met her gaze. "I'll drive you back to the carousel first. Or take you home, whichever you prefer."

But June took another step away. "Don't concern yourself with me. You have enough to handle right now."

Not just Tim. Evelyn too. She was right, and so thoughtful to consider how much others needed him. But that didn't mean he couldn't drive her back. "I'm happy to drive you."

"I think you should fetch Tim's mother promptly. Take her with you to the doctor."

Of course. At least he could see June later. Couldn't he? He'd hoped to invite her to spend time together, but who knew how long things with Tim would take. He glanced back at Tim, the police, Vincent in handcuffs. He could step away for a moment. Touching June's elbow, he led her a few more steps away. "I don't know how long I'll be with Tim, but I'd like to talk to you. Monday, may I eat lunch with you by the lily pond?"

She met his gaze. Took a breath. "Mr. Willard saw us on the carousel Thursday night."

Her boss?

At once he remembered an earlier conversation they'd had, nearly two weeks ago. Something about a code of conduct between the office staff and the scientists. He let out a long breath. "Forgive me, I forgot there's a rule about us talking, but you didn't receive a reprimand, did you?"

"The rule isn't about talking, exactly. It's about fraternizing. I wasn't clearer with you before, because I—well, I was embarrassed. The word intimated something that didn't exist. A relationship. In any case," she hurried on, "I had permission to plan Evelyn's wedding, but beyond that?" She shrugged. "I knew it was wrong, but I did it anyway. That is why I could go home early yesterday. Mr. Willard fired me."

Fired. His blood boiled again, darkening his vision. "This is my fault. I all but forced you to ride the carousel. I'll speak to him—"

"Forced, my eye. I climbed atop that pig in my own power. The truth is, I chose to break the rule, and it's appropriate for me to pay the consequence. Don't be upset, truly. This is a good thing, because I needed to be reminded of my responsibilities."

Maybe it was his pulse pounding loudly in his ears, but this made no sense. "I don't understand."

Her hands fluttered. "I was twenty when my parents died, absorbed with my friends. But suddenly I had a sixteen-year-old boy to clothe and feed, and my parents didn't leave much of an inheritance. Rent, food, bills took my entire paycheck. Anything extra was given to Kelly so he could have as normal a high school experience as possible. There was nothing left over for me. On a few occasions, I felt resentful, wanting things. Jealous of others who could be frivolous, and I did things for myself. A ticket to the ballet, things like that."

"That sounds good, though, June. You surely needed an evening to enjoy yourself."

"Yet on each of those instances, there was a consequence—a

struggle, an argument, a tighter budget that cost Kelly something he needed or wanted. It taught me it was better, easier to never take things for myself. This time, the consequence is a job I enjoyed. Needed. So I'll heed the reminder and focus on work and nothing else. Not until Kelly's out of college and law school and on his feet, at least."

"You're saying you cannot do a single thing beyond work because of Kelly. For the next few years." That sounded ridiculous. "But there's nothing wrong with doing things for yourself, June."

"There is if it means Kelly goes without."

"Kelly is an adult now. Older than you were when you gave up everything for him—"

"I had no choice."

"But you deserve—need—balance. Ride the carousel if you want. It's clearly something you enjoyed, but you hadn't ridden it in years."

"How long had it been since *you* rode the carousel, hmm?" June's eyes flashed beneath her spectacles. "Because you sacrificed for your sister. You should understand my motivation."

"I haven't sacrificed anything."

"Haven't you?" She looked down. "Focusing on another's happiness above your own—that's what I did for Kelly. But I am aware I'm not responsible for Kelly's happiness. Can you say the same with Evelyn? You've said more than once it's your duty."

That was different. He was honoring his father's dying wish.

Her smile was sad. "I shall miss you, Martin. Miss our talks, however *prohibited* they might have been."

He couldn't find a shred of humor at her small joke, a clear attempt to lighten the moment. Miss him? Truly, now that she was free of Willard and *could* fraternize with him, she was making

428

it clear that she wanted nothing to do with him.

Just like that, his heart cracked. He'd taken a risk allowing himself to fall for her—he knew that. But she, who'd seemed to care for him, whose heart was sweet and pure, didn't want him.

Perhaps he was just unlovable.

No, that wasn't true. Evelyn and Beulah loved him. But everyone else, from his parents to June? He wasn't enough for any of them.

At once he felt older than the fossils in the museum. An ossified shell of the man he could have been.

There was no use yearning to be that man anymore. Hearts were not like starfish, able to regenerate parts that had been lost or injured. This sort of love was not in his future.

But God could use the part of Martin's heart that still worked, and Tim was waiting, handkerchief pressed to his eye. He turned away from June's retreat and beckoned the boy. "Let's get your mother, eh? And maybe later, when you're all stitched up, I'll let you steer the car."

Chapter 8

The remainder of the weekend passed slowly for June. Had Bernard been arrested? Was Tim healing up? What happened to Myra?

She might never know this side of heaven, and she'd just have to entrust it all to God's care. Meanwhile, she had a job to find. After informing Gladys she'd been fired, June spent Monday searching for work, returning that evening to a curious message from her landlady. The museum had telephoned, requesting she come by Tuesday. June hardly slept for wondering about it.

Tuesday morning as the sun's first rays glowed through the red gingham kitchen curtains, June set the coffee to percolate. The thought of drinking the acidic brew made her nervous stomach turn, but Kelly would appreciate the coffee. Even though she was too anxious to eat, she cracked eggs into a bowl and whisked them.

Kelly's whistling preceded him into the kitchen.

She poured the eggs into a hot skillet. "You're happy this morning."

"I'm going to see Evie later. Just to talk. Later on, who knows? But for now, I'm here for her as a friend while she puts Bernard in the past."

"You're a good friend, Kelly."

"I try. You know, she told me why she accepted his proposal. He came on strong, and believe it or not, she grew up thinking only her family loved her. No one else ever could."

"I never would have thought that of her. Her parents doted on her, from what I heard."

Kelly poured cream in a mug for his coffee "Put her at the center of the universe. I don't think her brother got as much attention."

"I don't think so either." How would that make a person feel, knowing they weren't as favored as a sibling? Unnoticed? Unwanted? June frowned. Had she exacerbated any of those feelings in him, walking away as she had?

But she'd had to protect herself and her responsibilities. She'd had no choice.

Nevertheless, her heart ached.

Kelly cut two thick slices of bread. "You look nice this morning."

She'd worn her favorite ensemble, a lace-trimmed cream dress she usually saved for church, paired with her favorite green sweater. June needed the confidence of looking her best today. "Thanks. If only I knew what the museum wants from me today. Maybe it's something short, like giving me my final paycheck."

"They could save the awkwardness and mail it though."

"They're saving a stamp then." She stirred the eggs. "Or they want me to show them where I left things so they can train my replacement."

"Unless they're offering you your job back." Kelly took two plates from the scuffed hutch in the corner and topped each with a slice of bread. "Would you take it?"

"Sure." She needed the work and she liked the museum.

"I've been thinking maybe you shouldn't go back. You're good at planning things like the wedding. Maybe a different type of job would be better suited to your skills."

She served up the eggs and placed the skillet in the sink. "Honestly, I'm not sure I can be that picky. I just hope whatever job I get turns out to be as fun as my job at the museum."

"What makes that job fun?" He peppered his eggs.

She didn't even have to think. "I learned things from the exhibits. And I liked seeing other people learn, especially children. I sure hope the board approves a summer program like Martin and I proposed last week."

After she sat and they said grace, Kelly forked his eggs. "You like students. Maybe you could be a teacher."

"That would require additional schooling. When you're finished with law school, I could consider it, I suppose."

Kelly set down his utensils. "That's what I've been thinking about, June. You've been bearing more than your share of burdens around here for a long time so I could study and have a good time now and again. Isn't it your turn to do what you want now?"

"Not quite." He had one more year of college. "I intend to see you through law school, unless you get a scholarship—"

"I'll get a scholarship, or I won't go."

"What nonsense is this?" June pushed away her plate of uneaten eggs. "I'm going to get you through law school. No arguments."

"Sorry, but an argument is what you're gonna get. One more year of college, living here with you, yes, but next year? I'm on my own. God will provide a scholarship or He won't, in which case He'll tell me what He wants me to do. Which means next year you're going to be on your own too. So you might as well be doing what you want to do."

"But Kelly, I can't let you—"

"What, grow up? It's time, Junie. You've helped me so much, so let me help you now. What is it you want?"

What did she want? If she were free to do anything? A ridiculous question, considering she couldn't possibly do anything she wished. Her skill set was limited.

No, that's not quite true. If working at the Natural History Museum had taught her anything, it was that the world was fascinating and huge, with countless subjects to explore. God had given his sons and daughters a curiosity about His creation and was probably quite glad when they enjoyed it as much as He did. The earth was full of wonder.

Work didn't have to be just about obligation. Sure, bills needed paying and mouths needed feeding. But God had given humanity the ability to serve Him through their work. Kelly's love for his studies and even being around the carousel shone in his eyes and gave him a purpose to function as the unique person God made him to be.

Nowhere else, though, had she seen someone so alive in his work as Martin. His love of the ocean and its animals reflected God's love for the watery world. Surely God shared Martin's delight in starfish and swordfish, water and whales.

Which meant surely God took delight in everything He'd

made, including her. And He had a purpose for her too. Serving Him, absolutely. That was everyone's purpose. Caring for Kelly, sure—that would never end. But maybe Kelly was right—and Martin too—and the time had come to learn how to love and care for him as an adult sibling. It was time to discover new ways to live out who God had made her to be.

It was just happening much earlier than she'd expected, leaving her unprepared.

As she forced down a bite of eggs, she saw how wrong she was about that. God *had* been preparing her, hadn't He? She'd been feeling a growing sense of—not dissatisfaction, exactly. More like an itch. Lately she'd wriggled, ever so slowly, toward wanting something beyond her typing job, like a butterfly starting to break open its chrysalis. She'd thoroughly enjoyed putting together ideas for a children's summer program.

And she'd fallen in love, despite her best attempts not to. God hadn't removed those butterflies from her stomach. She couldn't regret any of it, despite how much it hurt walking away from Martin at the speakeasy on Saturday. Perhaps God had used the situation to remind her to rely on Him. And she would, wherever He called her.

Wherever that was.

Any hints, God? How would You have me serve You now?

Instead of receiving answers, her mind raced. Another office or in a classroom? The possibilities were endless. And overwhelming. Meanwhile, Kelly watched her, waiting for her answer.

At last she shrugged. "I—don't know."

"Don't you?" He stood and kissed her brow. "Then I'm sorry, sis, because you lost yourself on my account."

"I didn't lose myself. I made a choice."

"And I'm making one now too. I will not allow you to sacrifice any more for me than you already have."

"Kelly."

"Junie." His tone was firm but gentle. "Just think about it, all right? A job that does more for you than pay the bills. Not everyone has that luxury, I know, but maybe we can both have it."

All right then. She had no idea what it looked like, but right now she'd give the matter over to God. She'd walk in hopeful expectation, knowing He'd provide in His own time.

After a quick, silent prayer, she stood and tousled Kelly's hair. "How'd you get so wise?"

"Listening to my big sister. Now we should pack lunches. Maybe you can see Gladys for lunch."

She'd hoped for the same thing, once her meeting at the museum was over and done with. And now that she'd prayed about it, she was no longer nervous about the meeting. What could Mr. Willard do to her? God would take care of her. He always had.

She had to trust He'd take care of her broken heart too and help her forget Martin Howard so she could move forward in His plan. It was time to turn the page.

"Martin, you're an idiot. Just talk to June." Evelyn playfully punched Martin's shoulder as they strolled down El Prado. It was intended to be a playful thump, sure, but his old war wound hadn't quite recovered from ramming down the speakeasy door three days ago.

Martin rubbed the ache in his arm. "She doesn't want to see me."

"It's about time you had woman troubles."

"I do not have woman troubles."

"Yes you do. I'm a woman, and I give you trouble. And June gives you trouble too, because you care about her."

"Fine then." But when had Martin gone from being a mild-mannered marine zoologist to a door-busting fellow with woman troubles? Aunt Beulah was right. His life had changed considerably of late.

Evelyn sighed and took his arm as they walked. She'd come to meet him for lunch, and now they were taking advantage of the warm sunshine, making a loop past the carousel and back toward the museum. "You don't need to worry about me. I see where I went wrong with Bernard. I just wanted someone to love me who didn't have to, you know."

"I know. But I don't have to love you. You're just special."

"That's not true, Martin. Of the two of us, you're the one who cares about people. And critters. The world. I haven't been good about that, but I'm going to try. I decided I'm going to help Aunt Beulah with that church luncheon."

"Really? That's wonderful."

"And I'm going to volunteer more. Kelly says it's always more of a blessing to help than it is to be helped."

"Kelly says, eh?"

She pinked. "We're friends. But maybe later, more. He has a year of college to finish, you know. And I want him to succeed."

"That's mature of you, Evelyn."

"Well, sometimes it takes a smack on the head like your fiancé having a secret woman and a speakeasy for a gal to see the light. So maybe I ought to smack your head now so you'll talk to June." She lifted her hand in mock threat. "She's crazy about you."

"If she was crazy about me, then she wouldn't have said we

can't be friends before walking away from me."

"It's got to have been hard for her, losing her parents and being responsible for Kelly. You had Aunt Beulah, but she didn't have anyone."

He hadn't thought of that. "She must have been lonely."

"And scared, with only Kelly left."

June must have had dreams in her youth. She'd mentioned buying a ballet ticket. Maybe there had been a path she wanted or a gentlemen she admired, but she'd given up everything to raise Kelly, despite how much it must have hurt. He stared at his shoes as they walked toward the lily pond. "I shouldn't have been so hard on her."

"Well, go apologize for being such a hardhead. She's right there."

"Where?" But all he had to do was look up. On a bench by the lily pond, two women sat side by side, faces hidden by cloche hats, but he knew the posture of the one on the left. The tilt of her head. The cross of her ankles. The green sweater that so perfectly matched the lily pads in the pond.

"June." Sitting beside Gladys. Eating lunch.

Evelyn jiggled his arm. Hard. "What are you waiting for?"

Words. He didn't have any, but he went anyway. He at least owed June an apology, and he thanked God for the chance.

"June?"

The masculine call caused June's head to turn so fast she went dizzy. Or maybe she was woozy because Martin was six feet away from her, hat in hand. And oh, that dark curl of his had flopped onto his forehead.

"Hello, Martin." She sounded breathless.

God, how long have I prayed for You to remove these butterflies? If You don't wish to, please help me to better cope with them. I sound like a moony idiot.

"I'm glad to see you." Martin's worried gaze scanned hers. "How are you?"

Gladys stood, patting June's shoulder. "I'm going to say hi to your sister, Dr. Howard. Why don't you take my seat?"

He did without saying a word to Gladys. His attention was on June, and she felt it to her core.

Say something. "Evelyn looks well."

"She is. Tim too. And Calvin says there's plenty of evidence to get a jury to convict Bernard and Vincent."

"That's good."

"I talked to Mr. Willard. About your job."

"That was kind but unnecessary. I'm sure he told you he wouldn't rehire me, but it's fine. I have a new job."

"Already? Wonderful." He genuinely looked pleased. Poor man must have felt guilty about her losing work here.

"Dr. Abbott requested that I come in today. I didn't know why, but he offered me a new position at the museum. Administrator of Youth Events. The summer program is mine. I start tomorrow."

"Congratulations, June. I couldn't be happier for you." His smile was wide, but she caught the tinge of sadness in his eyes. "I hope you'll grant me one more moment of your time though, to apologize."

"Whatever for? I'm the one who should apologize to you. Saying those things at the speakeasy."

"You were right about everything, including how I judged your choice to sacrifice for your brother. And about how I've treated

438

Evelyn too. She's an adult, and I need to allow her to be one."

"Speaking of young adults, Kelly informed me he would refuse my help for law school. He'll go on scholarship or not at all. Which left me in a conundrum."

"How so?"

"Because if I wasn't focused on Kelly, I didn't know what to do. I had no answers, but this morning I decided to trust that God would provide. And look how quickly He did, in a way that shows me something about myself and what I am gifted to do. This is the perfect fit. Educating children. Planning events for them. Learning about the world as I go. I count myself blessed indeed."

"You're the perfect person for the position. And this time I'll stay out of your way. You won't get into trouble for talking to me."

"Mr. Willard isn't my supervisor anymore. I'm allowed to fraternize with whomever I wish. Gladys. Or. . .anyone. You. I want us to be friends."

June folded her trembling hands. If Martin had been cast aside by his parents, he may well have a wound from it. She hated that she may have poked at it, and her next words required bravery beyond her ability. Praying, she took a breath.

"The truth is, Martin, you're dear to me. A true friend, one who helped me see things in myself that weren't right. One who is like no other friend I've ever had before, and that is why I walked away from you at the speakeasy. My fondness for you threatened my stupid resolve to be solitary and all-sufficient to myself. You're easy to. . .to love, you see. So knowing that, you may not wish to be friends with me anymore. Regardless, I hope you can forgive me."

He looked at his hands. Then at her. "I forgive you anything. And I will always be your friend, June."

"Thank you." She'd hoped for more, now that she'd told him how she felt about him.

But then he reached for her hand. His calloused fingers twined with hers, sending shivers over her skin. "What if I wish for something different? To be more than friends with you. Because I find you easy to love too."

"Yes." She couldn't say it fast enough. "I would like that."

"I don't want anything to distract you from your work though. I know you and Kelly are relying on this job, and I don't want to make things difficult for you. How can I help?"

It was hard to concentrate, the way his thumb drew lazy circles over the back of her hand. "Well, someone recently told me I need balance in my life. Perhaps you can help me with that."

His lips twitched. "Perhaps we could start with lunch here tomorrow?"

"I would like that."

His gaze fixed on her lips. "And maybe, if you wish, we could go to the moving pictures on Saturday. If you like."

"I would." Her heart felt like an expanding balloon.

"I want to kiss you, but you deserve better than a public kiss by a lily pond."

Oh! "I don't think there are, ahem, too many people about to notice."

He glanced around, grinning. His sister and Gladys had wandered off. "I suppose that's true."

And then he took her chin, tipped up her face, and smiling, lowered his lips to hers. It was brief perhaps, but her toes curled nonetheless.

Martin wasn't unaffected either, judging by his lopsided grin and firm grip on her hands. "Ah, June. I always hoped for you, and here you are."

She'd always hoped for him too but never thought she'd have this. And she never expected it would feel this perfect, but when she shifted beside him on the bench and curled under his arm, her head fit into the curve of his shoulder just right.

Epilogue

June 1923

The carousel had never looked lovelier. The animals, from the frogs to the dragon, shone from a thorough cleaning and polishing. White and green ribbons tied about the necks or tails of the carousel animals fluttered in the sea-tinged afternoon breeze. The carousel was empty of riders, ready for a spin by the wedding party and their guests.

"Ready, Mrs. Howard?" Martin grinned down at his June.

"Mrs. Howard. How I like the sound of that." She thrilled as Martin took her by the waist and lifted her into the saddle of one of the two jumping horses. The look he gave her when he finished spoke of promises and love. How blessed she was that the Lord had given her such a fine husband.

In a double wedding with their siblings, no less!

They hadn't married at the carousel but in church. Then, in a caravan of touring cars, everyone had come to Balboa Park to ride the carousel before a luncheon at the Howards' house. Everyone clambered aboard the carousel, from Kelly and his new bride, Evie, perched on the zebras, to their pastor and Aunt Beulah, who settled in one of the chariots.

Martin climbed atop the jumping horse beside June's and looked into the center of the carousel, where two workers waited for everyone to be seated. "Tim, are we ready?"

"Almost, Dr. Howard." After a year of taking tickets, Tim had been granted permission to help run the carousel on this special occasion. His mother, who now climbed on one of the jumping cats, had become a dear friend in the past year, and June and Martin were delighted to invite them both to the wedding today.

Gladys's shriek drew their attention. June's maid of honor was being assisted atop one of the roosters by Martin's best man, Calvin, who'd done something to startle her—flirtatiously, by the way she lightly slapped his shoulder as he climbed aboard the second rooster.

"Seems like they're getting along well," Martin noted.

Indeed. "I'm happy for them."

"And for us." Martin took her hand—the one with the shiny new wedding band on it.

June had never been happier than at this moment. Everyone she cared about was here and smiling. She loved her job. Kelly had graduated college, received a full scholarship to attend law school, and had been hired to help in a law office. He and Evie wouldn't have a lot of money to spare for a while, but they would be comfortable in a modest cottage in Logan Heights near Martin's house, where June would join him and Aunt Beulah, who'd just announced she'd be off traveling most of the time.

The bell rang, warning everyone the carousel was about to

start. The festive music began, and slowly June's horse began to move. Up and down, faster and faster, until they were at full speed. Martin kissed her hand, and then they were laughing, thrilling in the experience.

Their lives together would be something like this carousel perhaps. Up times and down. But all she had to do was look at Martin and take his hand and be reminded of how blessed they were to journey together. God had gotten them here and wouldn't abandon them along the way.

It would be a wonderful ride.

Acknowledgments

Thanks to Bill Brown, manager of the Balboa Park carousel, and the Friends of Balboa Park for their gracious assistance with my research questions. Any errors in the story, however, are mine, including a few areas where I took creative license: the timing of the carousel's move to Balboa Park from Tent City, and the invention of an office structure at the Natural History Museum. In 1922 the director was indeed Dr. Clinton Abbott, but the marine zoologist working with the museum was Dr. Howard R. Hill. To honor him, I borrowed his first name for Martin's surname.

Balboa Park still features many museums and attractions. You can ride the carousel, although it's now located near the world-renowned San Diego Zoo. And in 1933 the Natural History Museum moved to its current location in the park. Things may not look the same as they did in 1922, but Balboa Park is one of my favorite places. I'm so glad for the chance to set a story there.

Thanks to Karl, Hannah, Matthew, Mom, and Dad for riding the carousel with me last summer. Many thanks also to Debra E. Marvin for her critiques and encouragement. And always, thanks to the readers who make it possible for me to write, and to the Lord for His faithfulness, provision, and grace.

Susanne Dietze began writing love stories in high school, casting her friends in the starring roles. Today she is the award-winning author of a dozen new and upcoming historical romances who has seen her work on the ECPA and *Publishers Weekly* bestseller lists for inspirational fiction. Married to a pastor and the mom of two, Susanne lives in California and enjoys fancy-schmancy tea parties, the beach, and curling up on the couch with a costume drama and a plate of nachos. You can visit her online at www.susannedietze.com and subscribe to her newsletters at http://eepurl.com/bieza5.

JOIN US ONLINE!

Christian Fiction for Women

Christian Fiction for Women is your online home for the latest in Christian fiction.

Check us out online for:

- Giveaways
- Recipes
- Info about Upcoming Releases
- Book Trailers
- News and More!

Find Christian Fiction for Women at Your Favorite Social Media Site:

 Search "Christian Fiction for Women"

 @fictionforwomen